T0278217

ROBOT ARTISTS
& BLACK SWANS

BRUCE STERLING

★ "Why not a flying pontoon boat with which to sail off to Chicago, and why not a partnership with Houdini to combat world communism? A kind of *Ragtime* for our time: provocative, exotic, and very entertaining."
—*Publishers Weekly*, starred review, on *Pirate Utopia*

"The best of their brilliant generation, Sterling and his collaborator[s] have produced a book to treasure. Bravo!"
—Michael Moorcock, author of the Elric of Melniboné series, on *Pirate Utopia*

"Bruce Sterling has managed to pen a delivery vessel for a futuristic, anarchistic dystopian idea of human potential. And in the end, *Gothic High-Tech* leaves the reader with the notion that even with all this mess, there are ways out of every quandary—even if those ways are unimaginable now or far different than we'd hoped."
—*New York Journal of Books*, on *Gothic High-Tech*

"A tour de force... Of all the horde of SF novels about clones written since that trope was pulled mewling from its artificial womb, *The Caryatids* is the first one that nails it."
—Benjamin Rosenbaum, author of *The Ant King and Other Stories*, on *The Caryatids*

"A comedic thriller for the Homeland Security era."
—*Entertainment Weekly*, on *The Zenith Angle*

"A haunting and lyrical triumph"
—*TIME*, on *Holy Fire*

"Written with humor and intelligence, this book is highly recommended."
—*Library Journal*, on *The Hacker Crackdown*

— ALSO BY BRUCE STERLING —

BRUCE STERLING

ROBOT ARTISTS
& BLACK SWANS
THE ITALIAN FANTASCIENZA STORIES
— T A C H Y O N —

Introduction: "Storia, Futurità, Fantasia, Scienza, Torino" copyright © 2021 by Bruce Sterling
Introduction copyright © 2021 by Neal Stephenson
Afterword: "Bruce Sterling, Erudite Dreamer and Pirate" copyright © 2021 by Dario Tonani
Cover and interior art and design by John Coulthart

Tachyon Publications LLC
1459 18th Street #139
San Francisco, CA 94107
415.285.5615
WWW.TACHYONPUBLICATIONS.COM
TACHYON@TACHYONPUBLICATIONS.COM

Series Editor: Jacob Weisman
Project Editor: Rick Klaw

Print ISBN 13: 978-1-61696-329-3
Digital ISBN: 978-1-61696-330-9

Printed in the USA by Versa Press, Inc.
First Edition: 2021
9 8 7 6 5 4 3 2 1

"Kill the Moon" © 2009. Originally published as "Italia 2061: Uccidiamo la Luna" in *Wired Italia* #4, 2009.

"Black Swan" © 2009. Originally published as "Cigno Nero" in *Robot: Rivista di Fantascienza*, Spring 2009. First English language publication in *Interzone* #221, March–April 2009.

"Elephant on Table" © 2017. Originally published in *Chasing Shadows: Visions of Our Coming Transparent World* edited by David Brin and Stephen W. Potts (Tor Books, 2017).

"Pilgrims of the Round World" © 2014. Originally published in *Subterranean Online*, Winter 2014.

"The Parthenopean Scalpel" © 2010. Copyright 40K Books. Originally published as "Il Bisturi Partenopeo" (40K Books). First English language publication in *Gothic High-Tech* (Subterranean Press, 2012).

"Esoteric City" © 2009 Mercury Press. Originally published in *The Magazine of Fantasy and Science Fiction*, August/September 2009.

"Robot in Roses" © 2017. Originally published as "Robot tra le Rose" in *Nuove eterotopie: la antologia definitive del Connettivismo* edited by Sandro Battisti and Giovanni De Matteo (Delos Digital).

CONT

E N T S

introduction
by NEAL

BRUCE STERLING CAN do something I cannot, which is write short fiction. Just now it is an enviable superpower for a writer to possess. The last few years have been infamously challenging for anyone trying to write a long document with any pretensions of carrying a futuristic payload. We long-form authors, our noses pressed up against the glass of the short-fiction writing world, can only hunker down on the throne and endlessly doom scroll, flinching every few minutes as the real world kicks the props out from under our architectonic lucubrations.

Accordingly, this introduction will be short, in the hopes that I can squirt it out before it is rendered sadly obsolete by whatever has happened the next time I check Twitter.

The primary job requirement of a cyberpunk has always been to pay attention; to notice things in a fine-grained way. It turns out that Bruce Sterling has never stopped doing that. Nothing helps you notice things like being a stranger in a strange land, and ever since Bruce decamped from his native Austin to southern Europe he has remained an avid noticer,

STEPHENSON

enabling him to write sentences like "The Vatican wheelchair was a rolling mass of embedded electronics. The Shadow House rejected this Catholic computational platform as if it were a car bomb."

So, relieved of the staggering burden of predicting the future, what we used to call cyberpunk has not merely clung to life, but flourished like the radioactive roses of post-atomic Rome (as Bruce describes in one of these stories). But it has long been the case that if you scrape away the shiny chrome plating on a science fiction writer's mirrored shades you'll find, just below, a historical fiction writer, and now we learn that Bruce Sterling is no exception; the longest piece in this book reads like it could be a condensed first volume of a longer historical epic, which I would gladly devour.

Long live Bruno Argento!

NEAL STEPHENSON

storia, futurità, fantasia, scienza, torino by

DEAR AMERICAN READERS, I am as surprised as you to find my modest collection of Italian science fiction stories published in your United States. I confess to you: by the professional standards of American science fiction writers, Bruno Argento is simply one of the European literary amateurs.

Here in my city of Turin, our refined and delicate writers will rarely thrive. We Turinese writers seem to be a fragile group, haunted and persecuted by esoteric shadows. Sometimes we are famous—even outside Italy—but, in daring to write fiction here in Turin, we rarely end well.

Our greatest adventure fantasy novelist here in Turin, Captain Emilio Salgari, was a contemporary of Jules Verne. Salgari has written many fantastic geographic fantasies that are far less boring than Verne's similar books. But unlike Jules Verne, Emilio Salgari committed suicide with a Japanese sword.

The German Federico Nietzsche was our most famous philosopher here in Turin, but he suffered a complete madness in Turin while hugging a horse on the street.

BRUNO ARGENTO

The great Turin novelist Cesare Pavese, at the height of his fame, ended his life with sleeping pills because of a bad love affair with a movie actress.

As for Primo Levi, he is the most authoritative science fiction writer ever seen in Turin. Primo Levi had a high literary reputation throughout the world, so he had to blush to write any science fiction. So Levi wisely invented a new, imaginary alter-ego, "Damiano Malabaila." Damiano Malabaila wrote all the science fiction for Primo Levi. This scheme worked well, until Primo Levi threw himself to his death down a stairwell in Turin.

However, despite the perishing of Levi, the work of "Malabaila" has survived. I always learn from Turinese history, so when I myself decided to become a Turinese fiction writer, I took careful note of the many difficulties. That is why I have survived to write this introduction for you. Also, my health so far is excellent!

In order to write fiction here in Turin, Bruno Argento, too, is well disguised as my pseudonym, just like Primo Levi did. But, instead of inventing "Damiano Malabaila," I invented "Bruce Sterling."

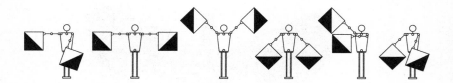

To tell the story, it was my best friend in Turin, Bruno Bruni, who first teasingly nicknamed me "Bruce Sterling" (for this is the rough English translation of Bruno Argento). Mr. Bruni is our most famous science fiction translator here in Turin, and a colleague of Giuseppe Culicchia, the most famous novelist who is currently surviving in Turin. (It was probably Culicchia who first fully described this ridiculous Bruce Sterling figure, an unlikely "cyber-punk" Texan who somehow decides to become Turinese, like some American clown from commedia dell'arte.)

Obviously this "Bruce Sterling" can never really exist, but my fellow Italian science fiction writers have cordially accepted this necessary deception of mine. The other Italians know about the life for writers here in Turin; they can follow my reasoning; they sympathize. Also, they are very erudite people, so they can see that the Argento / Sterling duality is a literary game, inspired by Italo Calvino's famous fantastic novel *The Cloven Viscount*, which was written and published in Turin in 1952.

It took me many years to become a published writer, and I have never been prolific. My career in Turinese science fiction, like life in Turin itself, has been rather slow-paced and majestic.

In my normal daily life, I am a technical professional, but my inspiration is history. Like most Europeans, I consider science fiction to be a form of philosophical struggle. Back in my student days, one of my wise professors at the Turin Polytechnic first took me under his wing. He told me this important matter:

"The task of the historian is to reconstruct and to depict the comprehensive epochal design in which every single human fact fits and can be explained in relation to the others."

Most professors here in Italy speak just like this. European historians are deep, profound thinkers, and not joking around, like us pop science fiction writers. But I could not understand the nature of history when I first heard this profound statement from him. On the contrary, I was just a university student in computer science who wanted to get a real job. However, I quickly wrote that impressive statement in my most special Fabriano notebook with my best Aurora fountain pen, made here in Turin.

What a grand task that was for a creative writer: to reconstruct, describe, and be so complete! How can any writer ever design an era in which all human facts are connected? How can a writer include the passage of time so intensely that every human breath, act, and thought is incorporated into one historical narrative? This problem is deep!

I was much impressed with this challenging literary problem, although I didn't know why. For years I thought about it, while I graduated from the Turin Polytechnic, got a rather well-rewarded job in high technology, got married, bought a house, and had children.

As a young member in good standing of Turin's vibrant technical elite, I lacked much time for my creative writing, although I continued my extensive weekend readings in the Italian translations of Lovecraft, Ballard, William Gibson, and Philip K. Dick.

But then, one day, while I was wistfully attending the *Stranimondi* science fiction literary conference in nearby Milan, I finally realized my observation. While mulling over the many used paperbacks written by Italian science fiction writers ever since the year 1957 (when the word "*fantascienza*" was first invented), suddenly I had my creative turn.

This activity of the "historian's task"—to write about the past in a way that connects every human effort to everything else at the time—

was actually a statement about science fiction, and not about history. No historian can ever build and describe a world so orderly and complete, but surely a science fiction writer can do that!

In fact, it is only through fantasy science that such "comprehensive epochal designs" can ever take full control of all other written forms of reality! Historians will always be defeated when they aspire to this excellent result. But we science fiction writers can always achieve it—if we try sincerely.

Furthermore—although, metaphysically—this historical aspiration applies to the world, and also the solar system, the galaxy, the cosmos— no book has enough words and pages for all that space and time. The writer cannot "represent" all space and even all time, too. Therefore, this "comprehensive epochal design" should be applied to many different times within one town.

Hence, the writer's great task may be achievable. Or, so I concluded. So I tried to do that. And it currently seems to be working.

For me, that creative space can only be Turin. I am a Turinese writer and I can create, rebuild, epochal, complete worlds—as long as they are connected to Turin.

That's how I became that rarity in the genre, a truly regional science fiction writer. It is not my goal to praise or glorify Turin, but to make Italian history comprehensible. These Italian stories of mine are slow cascades of the most science fictional aspects of Italy. They show little of the "*Bel Paese*" that makes us Italians sentimental about ourselves. These are epochal fantasies that are much more Italian than any real Italy could ever be. Such is my vocation as an Italian creative figure.

Necessarily these Turinese texts of mine deal with engineers, magicians, hells, ghosts, epidemics, assassins, and two-headed Italian seductresses,

yet they always seek the universal in the particular requirements of a city.

Here in Italy, we have to write science fiction mainly for the sport of it, since there is little danger that we earn our living by it. I do write science fiction, even though I'm a busy Turin technical professional—that's how Signora Argento and I support our 1.7 statistically probable Turinese children. So I can write a Turin fantasy story maybe just once in a year. Mostly, I write during my extensive lunch hours.

So my writing pace may be as slow as history itself, yet, like history, I never stop. For years I have been planning and writing my first novel (it's about Turin). Maybe one day, in due course, I will complete this vast, ambitious historical epic. As observed by King Vittorio Emanuele II, here in Turin, just before liberating Italy: "The Sword and Time brought my House from the peaks of the Alps to the banks of the Mincio River, and those two guardians will take it even further, when that pleases God!"

In the meantime, however, my modest stories to date have been grouped here and exposed to American readers. I did not expect this amazing development, but I am grateful, and I will manage as best I can. As long as I have a well-selected pasta, a little Lavazza Red coffee, and a glass of good Piedmontese Barbera, life will satisfy. Slowly, but methodically, I will write my Turin science fiction, under the Alps, near the River Po. Like Turin, I may not always prevail, but I will persist.

Buona lettura!—"Good reading to you!"

BRUNO ARGENTO MMXX

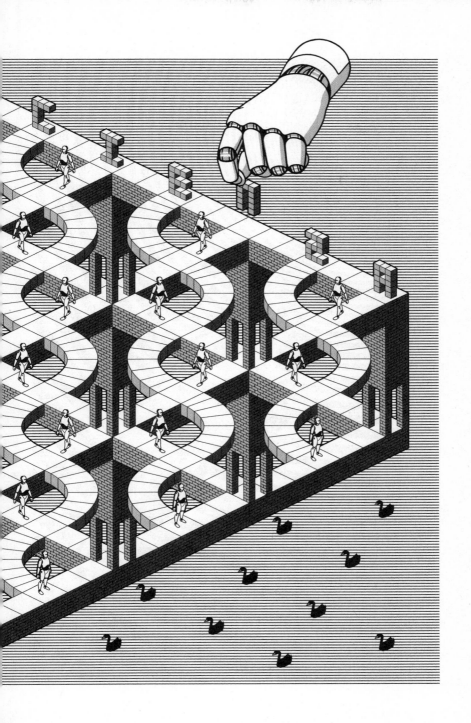

KILL THE MOON

by Professor F. Tomasso Marinetti, Chief Librarian, Biblioteca del Dipartimento di Ingegneria Aerospaziale dell'Università di Roma "La Sapienza"

April 17, 2061

IT EMBARRASSES ME that Italians have been to the Moon.

As a scientist, of course I admire the Moon. But why are Italian celebrities bounding around up there in an operatic spectacle? Why are we Italians always so guilty, in the sober eyes of the global public, of these undignified extravagances?

I have heard all the arguments in favor of the Italian Moon trip. Yes, I know that Italy was one of the first space powers: Italy built the Vega launcher, Italy explored comets, Italy built all the best-looking pieces of the International Space Station. Other nations had their space programs in the past century, too: the Japanese, Indians, Chinese. Why are we Italians the only people who still believe that space flight is romantic?

Of course many companies still launch hundreds of unmanned weather, communications, and observation satellites. Everyone agrees that the commercial space-launch industry is profitable, useful, and necessary. I make no protest there. My specific complaint is about my fellow Italians loudly trampling the Moon. Why are we gleefully celebrating this empty publicity stunt? Why can't we see how silly this is?

Yes, this year is the centenary of the first manned flight, of Yuri Gagarin, in April 1961. We Italians are always painfully keen on historical anniversaries. I agree that something solemn should have been done to honor this brave though long-dead cosmonaut. That should have been done in some archive in Moscow—not by two Italian celebrities in brightly colored spacesuits clowning around on the Moon.

History tells us that the Americans sent two highly trained astronaut-soldiers to the Moon. The American astronauts spoke seriously to mankind about world peace. And who did Italy send up there? Some eccentric billionaire and his busty actress girlfriend. Both of them on live global television!

I don't care how many billions of people enjoyed this silly video. His jokes about lunar science were not funny, and she's not as sexy as people say. Their new world fame, all those ticker-tape parades—that crude popular reaction only intensifies the embarrassment of intelligent, cultured people.

It's not that I oppose space tourism. I can understand space tourism. All Italians understand tourism. We Italians have been world masters of the tourism industry for seven hundred years. So of course the Italians can, and we do, make all the private spacecraft for wealthy space tourists. Who else would do that kind of work? We make the best spacecraft in exactly the same way that we make the world's best yachts, sports cars, and ski equipment.

I can also understand the appeal of some quick tourist jaunt into orbit. I wouldn't do that myself, but being weightless clearly has some attractions for certain people. You fly into zero gravity, you bring along a pretty girl, you pour some bubbly prosecco into strange fizzing spheres: things follow their natural course. I understand all that, and I don't complain about it. Millions of tourists behave in that fashion in Italy every single summer, and no one is ever surprised.

Yes, the *Gabriele d'Annunzio* is a very beautiful rocket ship. With such superb Italian industrial design, obviously it is the prettiest manned lunar rocket ever built. I also admit that creating a spacecraft that runs on clean, renewable Italian solar energy was a nice piece of public relations.

In fact, all the public-relations aspects of this stunt were handled very cleverly: the lunar theme music, the sleek designer logos, the sexy spacesuit costumes. Even the Eurovision dance routines at liftoff were surprisingly good.

But a Moon launch? Surely we must admit that was extravagant! We Italians are one of the world's oldest peoples: can't we behave as adults here? Here, in the year 2061, it should be obvious to everyone that a manned flight to the Moon is an empty-headed lark! It simply does not matter in any important way! This act has no public consequence!

I don't care that they planted the Italian tricolor all over the Galilaei Crater! The beautiful inflatable tent with the seamless plastic furniture did not impress me! When they took two hours for lunch, and ate their freeze-dried grissini… All right, I admit it, that Piedmontese grissini was an interesting choice. Eating grissini on the Moon, that took some imagination.

However: except for stunts of this kind, there is nothing for any human being to do up there on the Moon! Nothing useful at all! No human being is ever going to settle or colonize the Moon. The Moon is a purely astronomical phenomenon; it is a barren, airless rock with no commercial or military value whatsoever! This fact is entirely obvious to any educated person!

We Italians have become the world's "last major space power," and we are happy about that. Yet everybody else thinks that space travel is old-fashioned and adorable. They simply tolerate our space illusions here. They patronize our "space heritage industry," our Italian "space museum economy." They simply give us the Moon with a cheery smile and a blown kiss, in the same way that they admire our unique penchant for grappa, Baroque architecture, and labor demonstrations.

We Italians are the last people on Earth who fly to other planets. When will we realize that we have the world's oldest futurism?

BLACK SWAN

THE ETHICAL JOURNALIST protects a confidential source. So I protected "Massimo Montaldo," although I knew that wasn't his name.

Massimo shambled through the tall glass doors, dropped his valise with a thump, and sat across the table. We were meeting where we always met: inside the Caffe Elena, a dark and cozy spot that fronts on the biggest plaza in Europe.

The Elena has two rooms as narrow and dignified as mahogany coffins, with lofty red ceilings. The little place has seen its share of stricken wanderers. Massimo never confided his personal troubles to me, but they were obvious, as if he'd smuggled monkeys into the café and hidden them under his clothes.

Like every other hacker in the world, Massimo Montaldo was bright. Being Italian, he struggled to look suave. Massimo wore stain-proof, wrinkle-proof travel gear: a black merino wool jacket, an American black denim shirt, and black cargo pants. Massimo also sported black athletic trainers, not any brand I could recognize, with eerie bubble-filled soles.

These skeletal shoes of his were half-ruined. They were strapped together with rawhide boot-laces.

To judge by his Swiss-Italian accent, Massimo had spent a lot of time in Geneva. Four times he'd leaked chip secrets to me—crisp engineering graphics, apparently snipped right out of Swiss patent applications. However, the various bureaus in Geneva had no records of these patents. They had no records of any "Massimo Montaldo," either.

Each time I'd made use of Massimo's indiscretions, the traffic to my weblog had doubled.

I knew that Massimo's commercial sponsor, or more likely his spymaster, was using me to manipulate the industry I covered. Big bets were going down in the markets somewhere. Somebody was cashing in like a bandit.

That profiteer wasn't me, and I had to doubt that it was him. I never financially speculate in the companies I cover as a journalist, because that is the road to hell. As for young Massimo, his road to hell was already well trampled.

Massimo twirled the frail stem of his glass of Barolo. His shoes were wrecked, his hair was unwashed, and he looked like he'd shaved in an airplane toilet. He handled the best wine in Europe like a scorpion poised to sting his liver. Then he gulped it down.

Unasked, the waiter poured him another. They know me at the Elena.

Massimo and I had a certain understanding. As we chatted about Italian tech companies—he knew them from Alessi to Zanotti—I discreetly passed him useful favors. A cellphone chip—bought in another man's name. A plastic pass key for a local hotel room, rented by a third party. Massimo could use these without ever showing a passport or any identification.

There were eight "Massimo Montaldos" on Google and none of them were him. Massimo flew in from places unknown, he laid his eggs of golden information, then he paddled off into dark waters. I was protecting him by giving him those favors. Surely there were other people very curious about him, besides myself.

The second glass of Barolo eased that ugly crease in his brow. He rubbed his beak of a nose, and smoothed his unruly black hair, and leaned onto the thick stone table with both of his black woolen elbows.

"Luca, I brought something special for you this time. Are you ready for that? Something you can't even imagine."

"I suppose," I said.

Massimo reached into his battered leather valise and brought out a no-name PC laptop. This much-worn machine, its corners bumped with use and its keyboard dingy, had one of those thick super-batteries clamped onto its base. All that extra power must have tripled the computer's weight. Small wonder that Massimo never carried spare shoes.

He busied himself with his grimy screen, fixated by his private world there.

The Elena is not a celebrity bar, which is why celebrities like it. A blonde television presenter swayed into the place. Massimo, who was now deep into his third glass, whipped his intense gaze from his laptop screen. He closely studied her curves, which were upholstered in Gucci.

An Italian television presenter bears the relationship to news that American fast food bears to food. So I couldn't feel sorry for her—yet I didn't like that way he sized her up. Genius gears were turning visibly in Massimo's brilliant geek head. That woman had all the raw, compelling appeal to him of some difficult math problem.

Left alone with her, he would chew on that problem until something clicked loose and fell into his hands, and, to do her credit, she could feel that. She opened her dainty crocodile purse and slipped on a big pair of sunglasses.

"Signor Montaldo," I said.

He was rapt.

"Massimo?"

This woke him from his lustful reverie. He twisted the computer and exhibited his screen to me.

I don't design chips, but I've seen the programs used for that purpose. Back in the 1980s, there were thirty different chip-design programs. Nowadays there are only three survivors. None of them are nativized in the Italian language, because every chip geek in the world speaks English.

This program was in Italian. It looked elegant. It looked like a very stylish way to design computer chips. Computer chip engineers are not stylish people. Not in this world, anyway.

Massimo tapped at his weird screen with a gnawed fingernail. "This is just a cheap, 24-K embed. But do you see these?"

"Yes I do. What are they?"

"These are memristors."

In heartfelt alarm, I stared around the café, but nobody in the Elena knew or cared in the least about Massimo's stunning revelation. He could have thrown memristors onto their tables in heaps. They'd never realize that he was tossing them the keys to riches.

I could explain now, in grueling detail, exactly what memristors are, and how different they are from any standard electronic component. Suffice it to understand that, in electronic engineering, memristors did not exist. Not at all. They were technically possible—we'd known that for thirty years, since the 1980s—but nobody had ever manufactured one.

A chip with memristors was like a racetrack where the jockeys rode unicorns.

I sipped the Barolo so I could find my voice again. "You brought me schematics for memristors? What happened, did your UFO crash?"

"That's very witty, Luca."

"You can't hand me something like that! What on earth do you expect me to do with that?"

"I am not giving these memristor plans to you. I have decided to give them to Olivetti. I will tell you what to do: you make one confidential call to your good friend, the Olivetti Chief Technical Officer. You tell him to look hard in his junk folder where he keeps the spam with no return address. Interesting things will happen, then. He'll be grateful to you."

"Olivetti is a fine company," I said. "But they're not the outfit to handle a monster like that. A memristor is strictly for the big boys—Intel, Samsung, Fujitsu."

Massimo laced his hands together on the table—he might have been at prayer—and stared at me with weary sarcasm. "Luca," he said, "don't you ever get tired of seeing Italian genius repressed?"

The Italian chip business is rather modest. It can't always make its ends meet. I spent fifteen years covering chip tech in Route 128 in Boston. When the almighty dollar ruled the tech world, I was glad that I'd made those connections.

But times do change. Nations change, industries change. Industries change the times.

Massimo had just shown me something that changes industries. A disruptive innovation. A breaker of the rules.

"This matter is serious," I said. "Yes, Olivetti's people do read my weblog—they even comment there. But that doesn't mean that I can leak some breakthrough that deserves a Nobel Prize. Olivetti would want to know, they would *have* to know, the source of that."

He shook his head. "They don't want to know, and neither do you."

"Oh yes, I most definitely do want to know."

"No, you don't. Trust me."

"Massimo, I'm a journalist. That means that I always want to know, and I never trust anybody."

He slapped the table. "Maybe you were a 'journalist' when they still printed paper 'journals.' But your dot-com journals are all dead. Nowadays you're a blogger. You're an influence peddler and you spread rumors for a living." Massimo shrugged, because he didn't think he was insulting me. "So: shut up! Just do what you always do! That's all I'm asking."

That might be all that he was asking, but my whole business was in asking. "Who created that chip?" I asked him. "I know it wasn't you. You know a lot about tech investment, but you're not Leonardo da Vinci."

"No, I'm not Leonardo." He emptied his glass.

"Look, I know that you're not even 'Massimo Montaldo'—whoever that is. I'll do a lot to get news out on my blog. But I'm not going to act as your cut-out in a scheme like this! That's totally unethical! Where did you steal that chip? Who made it? What are they, Chinese super-engineers in some bunker under Beijing?"

Massimo was struggling not to laugh at me. "I can't reveal that. Could we have another round? Maybe a sandwich? I need a nice toasty pancetta."

I got the waiter's attention. I noted that the TV star's boyfriend had shown up. Her boyfriend was not her husband. Unfortunately, I was not in the celebrity tabloid business. It wasn't the first time I'd missed a good bet by consorting with computer geeks.

"So you're an industrial spy," I told him. "And you must be Italian to boot, because you're always such a patriot about it. Okay: so you stole those plans somewhere. I won't ask you how or why. But let me give you some good advice: no sane man would leak that to Olivetti. Olivetti's a consumer outfit. They make pretty toys for cute secretaries. A memristor chip is dynamite."

Massimo was staring raptly at the TV blonde as he awaited his sandwich.

"Massimo, pay attention. If you leak something that advanced, that radical…a chip like that could change the world's military balance of power. Never mind Olivetti. Big American spy agencies with three letters in their names will come calling."

Massimo scratched his dirty scalp and rolled his eyes in derision. "Are you so terrorized by the CIA? They don't read your sorry little one-man tech blog."

This crass remark irritated me keenly. "Listen to me, boy genius: Do you know what the CIA does here in Italy? We're their 'rendition' playground. People vanish off the streets."

"Anybody can 'vanish off the streets.' I do that all the time."

I took out my Moleskine notebook and my shiny rOtring technical pen. I placed them both on the Elena's neat little marble table. Then I slipped them both back inside my jacket. "Massimo, I'm trying hard to be sensible about this. Your snotty attitude is not helping your case with me."

With an effort, my source composed himself. "It's all very simple," he lied. "I've been here a while, and now I'm tired of this place. So I'm leaving. I want to hand the future of electronics to an Italian company. With no questions asked and no strings attached. You won't help me do that simple thing?"

"No, of course I won't! Not under conditions like these. I don't know where you got that data, what, how, when, whom, or why... I don't even know who you are! Do I look like that kind of idiot? Unless you tell me your story, I can't trust you."

He made that evil gesture: I had no balls. Twenty years ago—well, twenty-five—and we would have stepped outside the bar. Of course I was angry with him—but I also knew he was about to crack. My source was drunk and he was clearly in trouble. He didn't need a fistfight with a journalist. He needed confession.

Massimo put a bold sneer on his face, watching himself in one of the Elena's tall spotted mirrors. "If this tiny gadget is too big for your closed mind, then I've got to find another blogger! A blogger with some guts!"

"Great. Sure. Go do that. You might try Beppe Grillo."

Massimo tore his gaze from his own reflection. "That washed-up TV comedian? What does he know about technology?"

"Try Berlusconi, then. He owns all the television stations and half the Italian Internet. Prime Minister Berlusconi is just the kind of hustler you need. He'll free you from all your troubles. He'll make you minister of something."

Massimo lost all patience. "I don't need that! I've been to a lot of versions of Italy. Yours is a complete disgrace! I don't know how you people get along with yourselves!"

Now the story was tearing loose. I offered an encouraging nod. "How many 'versions of Italy' do you need, Massimo?"

"I have sixty-four versions of Italy." He patted his thick laptop. "Got them all right here."

I humored him. "Only sixty-four?"

His tipsy face turned red. "I had to borrow CERN's supercomputers to calculate all those coordinates! Thirty-two Italies were too few! A hundred twenty-eight... I'd never have the time to visit all those! And as for *your* Italy...well...I wouldn't be here at all, if it wasn't for that Turinese girl."

"*Cherchez la femme*," I told him. "That's the oldest trouble story in the world."

"I did her some favors," he admitted, mournfully twisting his wine-glass. "Like with you. But much more so."

I felt lost, but I knew that his story was coming. Once I'd coaxed it out of him, I could put it into better order later.

"So, tell me: What did she do to you?"

"She dumped me," he said. He was telling me the truth, but with a lost, forlorn, bewildered air, like he couldn't believe it himself. "She dumped me and she married the President of France." Massimo glanced up, his eyelashes wet with grief. "I don't blame her. I know why she did that. I'm a very handy guy for a woman like her, but Mother of God, I'm not the President of France!"

"No, no, you're not the President of France," I agreed. The President of France was a hyperactive Hungarian Jewish guy who liked to sing karaoke songs. President Nicolas Sarkozy was an exceedingly unlikely character, but he was odd in a very different way from Massimo Montaldo.

Massimo's voice was cracking with passion. "She says that he'll make her the first lady of Europe! All I've got to offer her is insider-trading hints and a few extra millions for her millions."

The waiter brought Massimo a toasted sandwich.

Despite his broken heart, Massimo was starving. He tore into his food like a chained dog, then glanced up from his mayonnaise dip. "Do I sound jealous? I'm not jealous."

Massimo was bitterly jealous, but I shook my head so as to encourage him.

"I can't be jealous of a woman like her!" Massimo lied. "Eric Clapton can be jealous, Mick Jagger can be jealous! She's a rock star's groupie who's become the *premier dame* of France! She married Sarkozy! Your world is full of journalists—spies, cops, creeps, whatever—and not for one minute did they ever stop and consider: 'Oh! This must be the work of a computer geek from another world!'"

"No," I agreed.

"Nobody ever imagines that!"

I called the waiter back and ordered myself a double espresso. The waiter seemed quite pleased at the way things were going for me. They were a kindly bunch at the Elena. Friedrich Nietzsche had been one of their favorite patrons. Their dark old mahogany walls had absorbed all kinds of lunacy.

Massimo jabbed his sandwich in the dip and licked his fingers. "So, if I leak a memristor chip to you, nobody will ever stop and say: 'Some unknown geek eating a sandwich in Torino is the most important man in world technology.' Because that truth is inconceivable."

Massimo stabbed a roaming olive with a toothpick. His hands were shaking: with rage, romantic heartbreak, and frustrated fury. He was also drunk.

He glared at me. "You're not following what I tell you. Are you really that stupid?"

"I do understand," I assured him. "Of course I understand. I'm a computer geek myself."

"You know who designed that memristor chip, Luca? You did it. You. But not here, not in this version of Italy. Here, you're just some small-time tech journalist. You created that device in *my* Italy. In my Italy, you are the guru of computational aesthetics. You're a famous author, you're a culture critic, you're a multitalented genius. Here, you've got no guts and no imagination. You're so entirely useless here that you can't even change your own world."

It was hard to say why I believed him, but I did. I believed him instantly.

Massimo devoured his food to the last scrap. He thrust his bare plate aside and pulled a huge nylon wallet from his cargo pants. This over-stuffed wallet had color-coded plastic pop-up tags, like the monster files of some Orwellian bureaucracy. Twenty different kinds of paper currency jammed in there. A huge riffling file of varicolored plastic ID cards.

He selected a large bill and tossed it contemptuously onto the Elena's cold marble table. It looked very much like money—it looked much more like money than the money that I handled every day. It had a splendid portrait of Galileo and it was denominated in "Euro-Lira."

Then he rose and stumbled out of the café. I hastily slipped the weird bill in my pocket. I threw some euros onto the table. Then I pursued him.

With his head down, muttering and sour, Massimo was weaving across the millions of square stone cobbles of the huge Piazza Vittorio Veneto. As if through long experience, he found the emptiest spot in the plaza, a stony desert between a handsome line of ornate lampposts and the sleek steel railings of an underground parking garage.

He dug into a trouser pocket and plucked out tethered foam earplugs, the kind you get from Alitalia for long overseas flights. Then he flipped his laptop open.

I caught up with him. "What are you doing over here? Looking for Wi-Fi signals?"

"I'm leaving." He tucked the foam plugs in his ears.

"Mind if I come along?"

"When I count to three," he told me, too loudly, "you have to jump high into the air. Also, stay within range of my laptop."

"All right. Sure."

"Oh, and put your hands over your ears."

I objected. "How can I hear you count to three if I have my hands over my ears?"

"*Uno.*" He pressed the F-1 function key, and his laptop screen blazed with sudden light. "*Due.*" The F-2 emitted a humming, cracking buzz. "*Tre.*" He hopped in the air.

Thunder blasted. My lungs were crushed in a violent billow of wind. My feet stung as if they'd been burned.

Massimo staggered for a moment, then turned by instinct back toward the Elena. "Let's go!" he shouted. He plucked one yellow earplug from his head. Then he tripped.

I caught his computer as he stumbled. Its monster battery was sizzling hot.

Massimo grabbed his overheated machine. He stuffed it awkwardly into his valise.

Massimo had tripped on a loose cobblestone. We were standing in a steaming pile of loose cobblestones. Somehow, these cobblestones had been plucked from the pavement beneath our shoes and scattered around us like dice.

Of course we were not alone. Some witnesses sat in the vast plaza, the everyday Italians of Turin, sipping their drinks at little tables under distant, elegant umbrellas. They were sensibly minding their own business. A few were gazing puzzled at the rich blue evening sky, as if they suspected some passing sonic boom. Certainly none of them cared about us.

We limped back toward the café. My shoes squeaked like the shoes of a bad TV comedian. The cobbles under our feet had broken and tumbled, and the seams of my shoes had gone loose. My shining patent-leather shoes were foul and grimy.

We stepped through the arched double-doors of the Elena, and, somehow, despite all sense and reason, I found some immediate comfort. Because the Elena was the Elena: it had those round marble tables with their curvilinear legs, those maroon leather chairs with their shiny brass studs, those colossal time-stained mirrors…and a smell I hadn't noticed there in years.

Cigarettes. Everyone in the café was smoking. The air in the bar was cooler—it felt chilly, even. People wore sweaters.

Massimo had friends there. A woman and her man. This woman beckoned us over, and the man, although he knew Massimo, was clearly unhappy to see him.

This man was Swiss, but he wasn't the jolly kind of Swiss I was used to seeing in Turin, some harmless Swiss banker on holiday who pops over the Alps to pick up some ham and cheese. This Swiss guy was young, yet as tough as old nails, with aviator shades and a long, narrow scar in his hairline. He wore black nylon gloves and a raw canvas jacket with holster room in its armpits.

The woman had tucked her impressive bust into a hand-knitted peasant sweater. Her sweater was gaudy, complex, and aggressively gorgeous, and so was she. She had smoldering eyes thick with mascara, and talon-like red-painted nails, and a thick gold watch that could have doubled as brass knuckles.

"So Massimo is back," said the woman. She had a cordial yet guarded tone, like a woman who has escaped a man's bed and needs compelling reasons to return.

"I brought a friend for you tonight," said Massimo, helping himself to a chair.

"So I see. And what does your friend have in mind for us? Does he play backgammon?"

The pair had a backgammon set on their table. The Swiss mercenary rattled dice in a cup. "We're very good at backgammon," he told me mildly. He had the extremely menacing tone of a practiced killer who can't even bother to be scary.

"My friend here is from the American CIA," said Massimo. "We're here to do some serious drinking."

"How nice! I can speak American to you, Mr. CIA," the woman volunteered. She aimed a dazzling smile at me. "What is your favorite American baseball team?"

"I root for the Boston Red Sox."

"I love the Seattle Green Sox," she told us, just to be coy.

The waiter brought us a bottle of Croatian fruit brandy. The peoples of the Balkans take their drinking seriously, so their bottles tend toward a rather florid design. This bottle was frankly fantastic: it was squat, acid-etched, curvilinear, and flute-necked, and with a triple portrait of Tito, Nasser, and Nehru, all toasting one another. There were thick flakes of gold floating in its paralyzing murk.

Massimo yanked the gilded cork, stole the woman's cigarettes, and tucked an unfiltered cig in the corner of his mouth. With his slopping shot glass in his fingers, he was a different man.

"Zhivali!" the woman pronounced, and we all tossed back a hearty shot of venom.

The temptress chose to call herself "Svetlana," while her Swiss body-guard was calling himself "Simon."

I had naturally thought that it was insane for Massimo to denounce me as a CIA spy, yet this gambit was clearly helping the situation. As an American spy, I wasn't required to say much. No one expected me to know anything useful, or to do anything worthwhile.

However, I was hungry, so I ordered the snack plate. The attentive waiter was not my favorite Elena waiter. He might have been a cousin. He brought us raw onions, pickles, black bread, a hefty link of sausage, and a wooden tub of creamed butter. We also got a notched pig-iron knife and a battered chopping board.

Simon put the backgammon set away.

All these crude and ugly things on the table—the knife, the chopping board, even the bad sausage—had all been made in Italy. I could see little Italian maker's marks hand-etched into all of them.

"So you're hunting here in Torino, like us?" probed Svetlana.

I smiled back at her. "Yes, certainly!"

"So, what do you plan to do with him when you catch him? Will you put him on trial?"

"A fair trial is the American way!" I told them. Simon thought this remark was quite funny. Simon was not an evil man by nature. Simon probably suffered long nights of existential regret whenever he cut a man's throat.

"So," Simon offered, caressing the rim of his dirty shot glass with one nylon-gloved finger, "So even the Americans expect 'the Rat' to show his whiskers in here!"

"The Elena does pull a crowd," I agreed. "So it all makes good sense. Don't you think?"

Everyone loves to be told that their thinking makes good sense. They were happy to hear me allege this. Maybe I didn't look or talk much like an American agent, but when you're a spy, and guzzling fruit brandy, and gnawing sausage, these minor inconsistencies don't upset anybody.

We were all being sensible.

Leaning his black elbows on our little table, Massimo weighed in. "The Rat is clever. He plans to sneak over the Alps again. He'll go back to Nice and Marseilles. He'll rally his militias."

Simon stopped with a knife-stabbed chunk of blood sausage on the way to his gullet. "You really believe that?"

"Of course I do! What did Napoleon say? 'The death of a million men means nothing to a man like me!' It's impossible to corner Nicolas the Rat. The Rat has a star of destiny."

The woman watched Massimo's eyes. Massimo was one of her informants. Being a woman, she had heard his lies before and was used to them. She also knew that no informant lies all the time.

"Then he's here in Torino tonight," she concluded.

Massimo offered her nothing.

She immediately looked to me. I silently stroked my chin in a sagely fashion.

"Listen, American spy," she told me politely, "you Americans are a simple, honest people, so good at tapping phone calls… It won't hurt your feelings any if Nicolas Sarkozy is found floating facedown in the River Po. Instead of teasing me here, as Massimo is so fond of doing, why don't you just tell me where Sarkozy is? I do want to know."

I knew very well where President Nicolas Sarkozy was supposed to be. He was supposed to be in the Élysée Palace carrying out extensive economic reforms.

Simon was more urgent. "You do want us to know where the Rat is, don't you?" He showed me a set of teeth edged in Swiss gold. "Let us know! That would save the International Courts of Justice a lot of trouble."

I didn't know Nicolas Sarkozy. I had met him twice when he was French minister of communication, when he proved that he knew a lot about the Internet. Still, if Nicolas Sarkozy was not the President of France, and if he was not in the Élysée Palace, then, being a journalist, I had a pretty good guess of his whereabouts.

"*Cherchez la femme*," I said.

Simon and Svetlana exchanged thoughtful glances. Knowing one another well, and knowing their situation, they didn't have to debate their next course of action. Simon signaled the waiter. Svetlana threw a gleaming coin onto the table. They bundled their backgammon set and kicked their leather chairs back. They left the café without another word.

Massimo rose. He sat in Svetlana's abandoned chair, so that he could keep a wary eye on the café's double door to the street. Then he helped himself to her abandoned pack of Turkish cigarettes.

I examined Svetlana's abandoned coin. It was large, round, and minted from pure silver, with a gaudy engraving of the Taj Mahal. "Fifty Dinars," it read, in Latin script, Hindi, Arabic, and Cyrillic.

"The booze around here really gets on top of me," Massimo complained. Unsteadily, he stuffed the ornate cork back into the brandy bottle. He set a slashed pickle on a buttered slice of black bread.

"Is he coming here?"

"Who?"

"Nicolas Sarkozy. 'Nicolas the Rat.'"

"Oh, him," said Massimo, chewing his bread. "In this version of Italy, I think Sarkozy's already dead. God knows there's enough people trying to kill him. The Arabs, Chinese, Africans…he turned the south of France upside down! There's a bounty on him big enough to buy Olivetti—not that there's much left of Olivetti."

I had my summer jacket on, and I was freezing. "Why is it so damn cold in here?"

"That's climate change," said Massimo. "Not in *this* Italy—in *your* Italy. In your Italy, you've got a messed-up climate. In this Italy, it's the *human race* that's messed-up. Here, as soon as Chernobyl collapsed, a big French reactor blew up on the German border…and they all went for each other's throats! Here NATO and the European Union are even deader than the Warsaw Pact."

Massimo was proud to be telling me this. I drummed my fingers on the chilly tabletop. "It took you a while to find that out, did it?"

"The big transition always hinges in the 1980s," said Massimo, "because that's when we made the big breakthroughs."

"In your Italy, you mean."

"That's right. Before the 1980s, nobody understood the physics of parallel worlds…but after that transition, we could pack a zero-point energy generator into a laptop. Just boil the whole problem down into one single micro-electronic mechanical system."

"So you've got zero-point energy MEMS chips," I said.

He chewed more bread and pickle. Then he nodded.

"You've got MEMS chips and you were offering me some fucking lousy memristor? You must think I'm a real chump!"

"You're not a chump." Massimo sawed a fresh slice of bad bread. "But you're from the wrong Italy. It was your own stupid world that made you this stupid, Luca. In my Italy, you were one of the few men who could talk sense to my dad. My dad used to confide in you. He trusted you, he thought you were a great writer. You wrote his biography."

"'Massimo Montaldo, Senior,'" I said.

Massimo was startled. "Yeah. That's him." He narrowed his eyes. "You're not supposed to know that."

I had guessed it. A lot of news is made from good guesses.

"Tell me how you feel about that," I said, because this is always a useful question for an interviewer who has lost his way.

"I feel desperate," he told me, grinning. "Desperate! But I feel much *less* desperate here than I was when I was the spoilt-brat dope-addict son of the world's most famous scientist. Before you met me—Massimo Montaldo—had you ever heard of any 'Massimo Montaldo'?"

"No. I never did."

"That's right. I'm never in any of the other Italies. There's never any other Massimo Montaldo. I never meet another version of myself—and

I never meet another version of my father, either. That's got to mean something crucial. I know it means something important."

"Yes," I told him, "that surely does mean something."

"I think," he said, "that I know what it means. It means that space and time are not just about physics and computation. It means that human beings really matter in the course of world events. It means that human beings can truly change the world. It means that our actions have consequence."

"The human angle," I said, "always makes a good story."

"It's true. But try telling that story," he said, and he looked on the point of tears. "Tell that story to any human being. Go on, do it! Tell anybody in here! Help yourself."

I looked around the Elena. There were some people in there, the local customers, normal people, decent people, maybe a dozen of them. Not remarkable people, not freakish, not weird or strange, but normal. Being normal people, they were quite at ease with their lot and accepting their daily existences.

Once upon a time, the Elena used to carry daily newspapers. Newspapers were supplied for customers on those special long wooden bars.

In my world, the Elena didn't do that anymore. Too few newspapers, and too much Internet.

Here the Elena still had those newspapers on those handy wooden bars. I rose from my chair and I had a good look at them. There were stylish imported newspapers, written in Hindi, Arabic, and Serbo-Croatian. I had to look hard to find a local paper in Italian. There were two, both printed on a foul gray paper full of flecks of badly pulped wood.

I took the larger Italian paper to the café table. I flicked through the headlines and I read all the lede paragraphs. I knew immediately I was reading lies.

It wasn't that the news was so terrible, or so deceitful. But it was clear that the people reading this newspaper were not expected to make any practical use of news. The Italians were a modest, colonial people. The news that they were offered was a set of feeble fantasies. All the serious news was going on elsewhere.

There was something very strong and lively in the world called the "Non-Aligned Movement." It stretched from the Baltics all the way to the Balkans, throughout the Arab world, and all the way through India. Japan and China were places that the giant Non-Aligned superpower treated with guarded respect. America was some kind of humbled farm where the Yankees spent their time in church.

Those other places, the places that used to matter—France, Germany, Britain, "Brussels"—these were obscure and poor and miserable places. Their names and locales were badly spelled.

Cheap black ink was coming off on my fingers. I no longer had questions for Massimo, except for one. "When do we get out of here?"

Massimo buttered his tattered slice of black bread. "I was never searching for the best of all possible worlds," he told me. "I was looking for the best of all possible me's. In an Italy like this Italy, I really matter. Your version of Italy is pretty backward—but *this* world had a nuclear exchange. Europeans had a civil war, and most cities in the Soviet Union are big puddles of black glass."

I took my Moleskine notebook from my jacket pocket. How pretty and sleek that fancy notebook looked, next to that gray pulp newspaper. "You don't mind if I jot this down, I hope?"

"I know that this sounds bad to you—but trust me, that's not how history works. History doesn't have any 'badness' or 'goodness.' This world has a future. The food's cheap, the climate is stable, the women are gorgeous…and since there's only three billion people left alive on Earth, there's a lot of room."

Massimo pointed his crude sausage knife at the café's glass double door. "Nobody here ever asks for ID, nobody cares about passports… They never even heard of electronic banking! A smart guy like you, you could walk out of here and start a hundred tech companies."

"If I didn't get my throat cut."

"Oh, people always overstate that little problem! The big problem is—you know—who wants to *work* that hard? I got to know this place, because I knew that I could be a hero here. Bigger than my father. I'd be smarter than him, richer than him, more famous, more powerful. I would be better! But that is a *burden.* 'Improving the world,' that doesn't make me happy at all. That's a *curse,* it's like slavery."

"What *does* make you happy, Massimo?"

Clearly Massimo had given this matter some thought. "Waking up in a fine hotel with a gorgeous stranger in my bed. That's the truth! And that would be true of every man in every world, if he was honest."

Massimo tapped the neck of the garish brandy bottle with the back of the carving knife. "My girlfriend Svetlana, she understands all that pretty well, but—there's one other thing. I drink here. I like to drink, I admit that—but they *really* drink around here. This version of Italy is in the almighty Yugoslav sphere of influence."

I had been doing fine so far, given my circumstances. Suddenly the nightmare sprang upon me, unfiltered, total, and wholesale. Chills of terror climbed my spine like icy scorpions. I felt a strong, irrational, animal urge to abandon my comfortable chair and run for my life.

I could run out of the handsome café and into the twilight streets of Turin. I knew Turin, and I knew that Massimo would never find me there. Likely he wouldn't bother to look.

I also knew that I would run straight into the world so badly described by that grimy newspaper. That terrifying world would be where, henceforth, I existed. That world would not be strange to me, or strange to anybody. Because that world was reality. It was not a strange world, it was a normal world. It was I, me, who was strange here. I was desperately strange here, and that was normal.

This conclusion made me reach for my shot glass. I drank. It was not what I would call a "good" brandy. It did have strong character. It was powerful and it was ruthless. It was a brandy beyond good and evil.

My feet ached and itched in my ruined shoes. Blisters were rising and stinging. Maybe I should consider myself lucky that my aching alien feet were still attached to my body. My feet were not simply slashed off and abandoned in some black limbo between the worlds.

I put my shot glass down. "Can we leave now? Is that possible?"

"Absolutely," said Massimo, sinking deeper into his cozy red leather chair. "Let's sober up first with a coffee, eh? It's always Arabic coffee here at the Elena. They boil it in big brass pots."

I showed him the silver coin. "No, she settled our bill for us, eh? So let's just leave."

Massimo stared at the coin, flipped it from head to tails, then slipped it in a pants pocket. "Fine. I'll describe our options. We can call this place the 'Yugoslav Italy,' and, like I said, this place has a lot of potential. But there are other versions." He started ticking off his fingers.

"There's an Italy where the 'No Nukes' movement won big in the 1980s. You remember them? Gorbachev and Reagan made world peace. Everybody disarmed and was happy. There were no more wars, the economy boomed everywhere... Peace and justice and prosperity, everywhere on Earth. So the climate exploded. The last Italian survivors are living high in the Alps."

I stared at him. "No."

"Oh yes. Yes, and those are very nice people. They really treasure and support each other. There are hardly any of them left alive. They're very sweet and civilized. They're wonderful people. You'd be amazed what nice Italians they are."

"Can't we just go straight back to my own version of Italy?"

"Not directly, no. But there's a version of Italy quite close to yours. After John Paul the First died, they quickly elected another pope. He was not that Polish anticommunist—instead, that new pope was a pedophile. There was a colossal scandal and the Church collapsed. In that version of Italy, even the Moslems are secular. The churches are brothels and discotheques. They never use the words 'faith' or 'morality.'"

Massimo sighed, then rubbed his nose. "You might think the death of religion would make a lot of difference to people. Well, it doesn't. Because they think it's normal. They don't miss believing in God any more than you miss believing in Marx."

"So first we can go to that Italy, and then nearby into my own Italy—is that the idea?"

"That Italy is boring! The girls there are boring! They're so matter-of-fact about sex there that they're like girls from Holland." Massimo shook his head ruefully. "Now I'm going to tell you about a version of Italy that's truly different and interesting."

I was staring at a round of the sausage. The bright piece of gristle in it seemed to be the severed foot of some small animal. "All right, Massimo, tell me."

"Whenever I move from world to world, I always materialize in the Piazza Vittorio Veneto," he said, "because that plaza is so huge and usually pretty empty, and I don't want to hurt anyone with the explosion. Plus, I know Torino—I know all the tech companies here, so I can make my way around. But once I saw a Torino with no electronics."

I wiped clammy sweat from my hands with the café's rough cloth napkin. "Tell me, Massimo, how did you feel about that?"

"It's incredible. There's no electricity there. There's no wires for the electrical trolleys. There are plenty of people there, very well dressed, and bright colored lights, and some things are flying in the sky…big aircraft, big as ocean liners. So they've got some kind of power there—but it's not electricity. They stopped using electricity, somehow. Since the 1980s."

"A Turin with no electricity," I repeated, to convince him that I was listening.

"Yeah, that's fascinating, isn't it? How could Italy abandon electricity and replace it with another power source? I think that they use cold fusion! Because cold fusion was another world-changing event from the 1980s. I can't explore that Torino—because where would I plug in my laptop? But you could find out how they do all that! Because you're just a journalist, right? All you need is a pencil!"

"I'm not a big expert on physics," I said.

"My God, I keep forgetting I'm talking to somebody from the hopeless George Bush World," he said. "Listen, stupid: physics isn't complicated. Physics is very simple and elegant, because it's *structured*. I knew that from the age of three."

"I'm just a writer, I'm not a scientist."

"Well, surely you've heard of 'consilience.'"

"No. Never."

"Yes you have! Even people in your stupid world know about 'consilience.' Consilience means that all forms of human knowledge have an underlying unity!"

The gleam in his eyes was tiring me. "Why does that matter?"

"It makes all the difference between your world and my world! In your world there was a great physicist once…Dr. Italo Calvino."

"Famous literary writer," I said, "he died in the 1980s."

"Calvino didn't die in my Italy," he said, "because in my Italy, Italo Calvino completed his *Six Core Principles*."

"Calvino wrote *Six Memos*," I said. "He wrote *Six Memos for the Next Millennium*. And he only finished five of those before he had a stroke and died."

"In my world Calvino did not have a stroke. He had a stroke of genius, instead. When Calvino completed his work, those six lectures weren't just 'memos.' He delivered six major public addresses at Princeton. When Calvino gave that sixth, great, final speech, on 'Consistency,' the halls were crammed with physicists. Mathematicians, too. My father was there."

I took refuge in my notebook. "Six Core Principles," I scribbled hastily, "Calvino, Princeton, consistency."

"Calvino's parents were both scientists," Massimo insisted. "Calvino's brother was also a scientist. His Oulipo literary group was obsessed with mathematics. When Calvino delivered lectures worthy of a genius, nobody was surprised."

"I knew Calvino was a genius," I said. I'd been young, but you can't write in Italian and not know Calvino. I'd seen him trudging the porticoes in Turin, hunch-shouldered, slapping his feet, always looking sly and preoccupied. You only had to see the man to know that he had an agenda like no other writer in the world.

"When Calvino finished his six lectures," mused Massimo, "they carried him off to CERN in Geneva and they made him work on the 'Semantic Web.' The Semantic Web works beautifully, by the way. It's not like your foul little Internet—so full of spam and crime." He wiped the sausage knife on an oil-stained napkin. "I should qualify that remark. The Semantic Web works beautifully—*in the Italian language*. Because the Semantic Web was built by Italians. They had a little bit of help from a few French Oulipo writers."

"Can we leave this place now? And visit this Italy you boast so much about? And then drop by my Italy?"

"That situation is complicated," Massimo hedged, and stood up. "Watch my bag, will you?"

He then departed to the toilet, leaving me to wonder about all the ways in which our situation could be complicated.

Now I was sitting alone, staring at that corked brandy bottle. My brain was boiling. The strangeness of my situation had broken some important throttle inside my head.

I considered myself bright—because I could write in three languages, and I understood technical matters. I could speak to engineers, designers, programmers, venture capitalists, and government officials on serious, adult issues that we all agreed were important. So, yes, surely I was bright.

But I'd spent my whole life being far more stupid than I was at this moment.

In this terrible extremity, here in the cigarette-choked Elena, where the half-ragged denizens pored over their grimy newspapers, I knew I possessed a true potential for genius. I was Italian, and, being Italian, I had the knack to shake the world to its roots. My genius had never embraced me, because genius had never been required of me. I had been stupid because I dwelled in a stupefied world.

I now lived in no world at all. I had no world. So my thoughts were rocketing through empty space.

Ideas changed the world. Thoughts changed the world—and thoughts could be written down. I had forgotten that writing could have such urgency, that writing could matter to history, that literature might have consequence. Strangely, tragically, I'd forgotten that such things were even possible.

Calvino had died of a stroke: I knew that. Some artery broke inside the man's skull as he gamely struggled with his manifesto to transform the next millennium. Surely that was a great loss, but how could anybody guess the extent of that loss? A stroke of genius is a black swan, beyond prediction, beyond expectation. If a black swan never arrives, how on Earth could its absence be guessed?

The chasm between Massimo's version of Italy and my Italy was invisible—yet all-encompassing. It was exactly like the stark difference between the man I was now, and the man I'd been one short hour ago.

A black swan can never be predicted, expected, or categorized. A black swan, when it arrives, cannot even be recognized as a black swan. When the black swan assaults us, with the wingbeats of some rapist Jupiter, then we must rewrite history.

Maybe a newsman writes a news story, which is history's first draft.

Yet the news never shouts that history has black swans. The news never tells us that our universe is contingent, that our fate hinges on changes too huge for us to comprehend, or too small for us to see. We can never accept the black swan's arbitrary carelessness. So our news is never about how the news can make no sense to human beings. Our news is always about how well we understand.

Whenever our wits are shattered by the impossible, we swiftly knit the world back together again, so that our wits can return to us. We pretend that we've lost nothing, not one single illusion. Especially, certainly, we never lose our minds. No matter how strange the news is, we're always sane and sensible. That is what we tell each other.

Massimo returned to our table. He was very drunk, and he looked greenish. "You ever been in a squat-down Turkish toilet?" he said, pinching his nose. "Trust me: don't go in there."

"I think we should go to your Italy now," I said.

"I could do that," he allowed idly, "although I've made some trouble for myself there…my real problem is you."

"Why am I trouble?"

"There's another Luca in my Italy. He's not like you: because he's a great author, and a very dignified and very wealthy man. He wouldn't find you funny."

I considered this. He was inviting me to be bitterly jealous of myself. I couldn't manage that, yet I was angry anyway. "Am I funny, Massimo?"

He'd stopped drinking, but that killer brandy was still percolating through his gut.

"Yes, you're funny, Luca. You're weird. You're a terrible joke. Especially in this version of Italy. And especially now that you're finally catching on. You've got a look on your face now like a drowned fish." He belched into his fist. "Now, at last, you think that you understand, but no, you don't. Not yet. Listen: in order to arrive here—I *created* this world. When I press the Function-Three key, and the field transports me here—without me as the observer, this universe doesn't even exist."

I glanced around the thing that Massimo called a universe. It was an Italian café. The marble table in front of me was every bit as solid as a rock. Everything around me was very solid, normal, realistic, acceptable, and predictable.

"Of course," I told him. "And you also created my universe, too. Because you're not just a black swan. You're God."

"'Black swan,' is that what you call me?" He smirked, and preened in the mirror. "You journalists need a tagline for everything."

"You always wear black," I said. "Does that keep our dirt from showing?"

Massimo buttoned his black woolen jacket. "It gets worse," he told me. "When I press that Function-Two key, before the field settles in…I generate millions of potential histories. Billions of histories. All with their souls, ethics, thoughts, histories, destinies—whatever. Worlds blink into existence for a few nanoseconds while the chip runs through the program—and then they all blink out. As if they never were."

"That's how you move? From world to world?"

"That's right, my friend. This ugly duckling can fly."

The Elena's waiter arrived to tidy up our table. "A little rice pudding?" he asked.

Massimo was cordial. "No, thank you, sir."

"Got some very nice chocolate in this week! All the way from South America."

"My, that's the very best kind of chocolate." Massimo jabbed his hand into a cargo pocket. "I believe I need some chocolate. What will you give me for this?"

The waiter examined it carefully. "This is a woman's engagement ring."

"Yes, it is."

"It can't be a real diamond, though. This stone's much too big to be a real diamond."

"You're an idiot," said Massimo, "but I don't care much. I've got a big appetite for sweets. Why don't you bring me an entire chocolate pie?"

The waiter shrugged and left us.

"So," Massimo resumed, "I wouldn't call myself a 'God'—because I'm much better described as several million billion Gods. Except, you know, that the zero-point transport field always settles down. Then, here I am. I'm standing outside some café, in a cloud of dirt, with my feet aching. With nothing to my name, except what I've got in my brain and my pockets. It's always like that."

The door of the Elena banged open, with the harsh jangle of brass Indian bells. A gang of five men stomped in. I might have taken them for cops, because they had jackets, belts, hats, batons, and pistols, but Turinese cops do not arrive on duty drunk. Nor do they wear scarlet armbands with crossed lightning bolts.

The café fell silent as the new guests muscled up to the dented bar. Bellowing threats, they proceeded to shake down the staff.

Massimo turned up his collar and gazed serenely at his knotted hands. Massimo was studiously minding his own business. He was in his corner, silent, black, inexplicable. He might have been at prayer.

I didn't turn to stare at the intruders. It wasn't a pleasant scene, but even for a stranger, it wasn't hard to understand.

The door of the men's room opened. A short man in a trench coat emerged. He had a dead cigar clenched in his teeth, and a snappy Alain Delon fedora.

He was surprisingly handsome. People always underestimated the good looks, the male charm, of Nicolas Sarkozy. Sarkozy sometimes seemed a little odd when sunbathing half-naked in newsstand tabloids, but in person, his charisma was overwhelming. He was a man that any world had to reckon with.

Sarkozy glanced about the café, for a matter of seconds. Then he sidled, silent and decisive, along the dark mahogany wall. He bent one elbow. There was a thunderclap. Massimo pitched face-forward onto the small marble table.

Sarkozy glanced with mild chagrin at the smoking hole blown through the pocket of his stylish trench coat. Then he stared at me.

"You're that journalist," he said.

"You've got a good memory for faces, Monsieur Sarkozy."

"That's right, asshole, I do." His Italian was bad, but it was better than my French. "Are you still eager to 'protect' your dead source here?" Sarkozy gave Massimo's heavy chair one quick, vindictive kick, and the dead man, and his chair, and his table, and his ruined, gushing head all fell to the hard café floor with one complicated clatter.

"There's your big scoop of a story, my friend," Sarkozy told me. "I just gave that to you. You should use that in your lying commie magazine."

Then he barked orders at the uniformed thugs. They grouped themselves around him in a helpful cluster, their faces pale with respect.

"You can come out now, baby," crowed Sarkozy, and she emerged from the men's room. She was wearing a cute little gangster-moll hat, and a tailored camouflage jacket. She lugged a big black guitar case. She also had a primitive radio-telephone bigger than a brick.

How he'd enticed that woman to lurk for half an hour in the reeking café toilet, that I'll never know. But it was her. It was definitely her, and she couldn't have been any more demure and serene if she were meeting the Queen of England.

They all left together in one heavily armed body.

The thunderclap inside the Elena had left a mess. I rescued Massimo's leather valise from the encroaching pool of blood.

My fellow patrons were bemused. They were deeply bemused, even confounded. Their options for action seemed to lack constructive possibilities.

So, one by one, they rose and left the bar. They left that fine old place, silently and without haste, and without meeting each other's eyes. They stepped out the jangling door and into Europe's biggest plaza.

Then they vanished, each hastening toward his own private world.

I strolled into the piazza, under a pleasant spring sky. It was cold, that spring night, but that infinite dark blue sky was so lucid and clear.

The laptop's screen flickered brightly as I touched the F1 key. Then I pressed 2, and then 3.

ELEPHANT
ON TABLE

TULLIO AND IRMA had found peace in the Shadow House. Then the Chief arrived from his clinic and hid in the panic room.

Tullio and Irma heard shuddering moans from the HVAC system, the steely squeak of the hydraulic wheels, but not a human whisper. The Shadow House cat whined and yowled at the vault door.

Three tense days passed, and the Chief tottered from his airtight chamber into summer daylight. Head bobbing, knees shaking, he reeled like an antique Sicilian puppet.

Blank-eyed yet stoic, the elderly statesman wobbled up the perforated stairs to the Shadow House veranda. This expanse was adroitly sheltered from a too-knowing world.

The panic rooms below ground were sheathed in Faraday copper, cast iron and lead, but the mansion's airy upper parts were a nested, multilayer labyrinth of sound baffles, absorbent membranes, meta-structured foam, malleable ribbons, carbon filaments, vapor and mirror chaff. Snakelike vines wreathed the trellises. The gardens abounded in spiky cactus. Tullio took pains to maintain the establishment as it deserved.

The Chief staggered into a rattan throne. He set his hairy hands flat on the cold marble tabletop.

He roared for food.

Tullio and Irma hastened to comply. The Chief promptly devoured three hard-boiled eggs, a jar of pickled artichoke hearts, a sugar-soaked grapefruit, and a jumbo-sized mango, skin and all.

Some human color returned to his famous, surgically amended face. The Chief still looked bad, like a reckless, drug-addicted roué of fifty. However, the Chief was actually 104 years old. The Chief had paid millions for the zealous medical care of his elite Swiss clinic. He'd even paid hundreds of thousands for the veterinary care of his house cat.

While Irma tidied the sloppy ruins of breakfast, Tullio queried Shadow House screens for any threats in the vicinity.

The Chief had many enemies: thousands of them. His four ex-wives were by far his worst foes. He was also much resented by various Italian nationalists, fringe leftist groups, volatile feminist cults, and a large sprinkling of mentally disturbed stalkers who had fixated on him for decades.

However, few of these fierce, gritty, unhappy people were on the island of Sardinia in August 2073. None of them knew that the Chief had secretly arrived on Sardinia from Switzerland. The Shadow House algorithms ranked their worst threat as the local gossip journalist "Carlo Pizzi," a notorious little busybody who was harassing supermodels.

Reassured by this security check, Tullio carried the card table out to the beach. Using a clanking capstan and crank, Tullio erected a big, party-colored sun umbrella. In its slanting shade he arranged four plastic chairs, a stack of plastic cups, plastic crypto-coins, shrink-wrapped card decks, paper pads, and stubby pencils. Every object was anonymous and disposable: devoid of trademarks, codes, or identities. No surface took fingerprints.

The Chief arrived to play, wearing wraparound mirror shades and a brown, hooded beach robe. It was a Mediterranean August, hot, blue, and breezy. The murmuring surf was chased by a skittering horde of little shorebirds.

Irma poured the Chief a tall iced glass of his favorite vitamin sludge while Tullio shuffled and dealt.

The Chief disrobed and smeared his seamy, portly carcass with medicated suntan unguent. He gripped his waterproofed plastic cards.

"Anaconda," he commanded, and belched.

The empty fourth chair at their card table was meant to attract the public. The Chief was safe from surveillance inside his sumptuous Shadow House—that was the purpose of the house, its design motif, its reason for being. However, safety had never satisfied the Chief. He was an Italian politician, so it was his nature to flirt with disaster.

Whenever left to themselves, Tullio and Irma passed their pleasant days inside the Shadow House, discreet, unseen, unbothered, and unbothering. But the two of them were still their Chief's loyal retainers. The Chief was a man of scandal and turbulence—half-forgotten, half-ignored by a happier era. But the Chief still had his burning need to control the gaze of the little people.

The Chief's raw hunger for glory, which had often shaken the roots of Europe, had never granted him a moment's peace. During his long, rampaging life, he'd possessed wealth, fame, power, and the love of small armies of women. Serenity, though, still eluded him. Privacy was his obsession; fame was his compulsion.

Tullio played his cards badly, for it seemed to him that a violent host of invisible furies still circled the Chief's troubled, sweating head. The notorious secrecy. The covert scandals. The blatant vulgarity which was also a subtle opacity—for the Chief was an outsized statesman, a heroic figure of many perverse contradictions. His achievements and his crimes were like a herd of elephants: they could never stand still within a silent room.

Irma offered Tullio a glance over their dwindling poker hands. They both pitied their Chief, because they understood him. Tullio had once been an Italian political party operative, and Irma a deft Italian tax-avoidance expert. Nowadays they were reduced to the status of the house-repairman and the hostess, the butler and the cook. There was no more Italy. The Chief had outlived his nation.

Becoming ex-Italian meant a calmer life for Tullio and Irma, because the world was gentler without an Italy. It was their duty to keep this lonely, ill-starred old man out of any more trouble. The Chief would never behave decently—that was simply not in his character—but their discreet beach mansion could hush up his remaining excesses.

The first wandering stranger approached their open table. This fringe figure was one tiny fragment of the world's public, a remote demographic outlier, a man among the lowest of the low. He was poor, black, and a beach peddler. Many such émigrés haunted the edges of the huge Mediterranean summer beach crowds. These near vagrants sold various forms of pretty rubbish.

The Chief was delighted to welcome this anonymous personage. He politely relieved the peddler of his miserable tray of fried fish, candy bars, and kid's plastic pinwheels, and insisted on seating him at the green poker table.

"Hey, I can't stay here, boss," complained the peddler, in bad Italian. "I have to work."

"We'll look after you," the Chief coaxed, surveilling the peddler, from head to foot, with covert glee. "My friend Tullio here will buy your fish. Tullio has a hungry cat over there, isn't that right, Tullio?"

The Chief waved his thick arm at the Shadow House, but the peddler simply couldn't see the place. The mansion's structure was visually broken up by active dazzle lines. Its silhouette faded like a cryptic mist into the island's calm palette of palms and citruses.

Tullio obediently played along. "Oh yes, that's true, we do have a big tomcat, he's always hungry." He offered the peddler some plastic coinage from the poker table.

Irma gathered up the reeking roast sardines. When Irma rounded a corner of the Shadow House, she vanished as if swallowed.

"It has been my experience," the Chief said sagely, scooping up and squaring the poker cards, "that the migrants of the world—men like yourself—are risk-takers. So, my friend: how'd you like to double your money in a quick hand of Hi-Lo with us?"

"I'm not a player, boss," said the peddler, though he was clearly tempted.

"So, saving up your capital, is that it? Do you want to live here in Italy—is that your plan?"

The peddler shrugged. "There is no Italy! In Europe, the people love elephants. So, I came here with the elephants. The people don't see me. The machines don't care."

Irma reappeared as if by magic. Seeing the tense look on their faces, she said brightly, "So, do you tend those elephants, young man? People in town say they brought whales this year, too!"

"Oh no, no, signora!" cried the peddler. "See the elephants, but never look at the whales! You have to ride a boat out there, you get seasick, that's no good!"

"Tell us more about these elephants, they interest me," the Chief urged, scratching his oiled belly, "have a prosecco, have a brandy." But the peddler was too streetwise: he had sensed that something was up. He gathered his tray and escaped them, hastening down the beach, toward the day's gathering crowds.

Tullio, Irma, and the Chief ran through more hands of Anaconda poker. The Chief, an expert player, was too restless to lose, so he was absentmindedly piling up all their coinage.

"My God, if only I, too, had no name!" he burst out. "No identity, like that African boy—what I could do in this world now! Elephants, here in Sardinia! When I was young, did I have any elephants? Not one! I had less than nothing, I suffered from huge debts! These days are such happy times, and the young people now, they just have no idea!"

Tullio and Irma knew every aspect of their Chief's hard-luck origin story, so they merely pretended attention.

The summer beach crowd was clustering down the coastline, a joyful human mass of tanned and salty arms and legs, ornamented with balloons and scraps of pop music.

A beachcombing group of Japanese tourists swanned by. Although they wore little, the Japanese were fantastically well dressed. The Japanese had found their métier as the world's most elegant people. Even the jealous Milanese were content to admire their style.

Lacking any new victim to interrogate at his card table, the Chief began to reminisce. The Chief would loudly bluster about any topic, except for his true sorrows, which he never confessed aloud.

The Swiss had lavished many dark attentions on the Chief's crumbling brain. The Swiss had invaded his bony skull, that last refuge of human privacy, like a horde of Swiss pikemen invading Renaissance Italy. They occupied it, but they couldn't govern it.

The Chief's upgraded brain, so closely surveilled by Swiss medical imaging, could no longer fully conceal his private chains of thought. The Chief had once been a political genius, but now his scorched neurons were like some huge database racked by a spy agency's analytics.

Deftly shuffling a fresh card deck, the Chief suddenly lost his composure. He commenced to leak and babble. His unsought theme was "elephants." Any memory, any anecdote that struck his mind, about elephants.

Hannibal had invaded Italy with elephants. The elephant had once been the symbol of an American political party. A houseplant named the "Elephant Ear." The Chief recalled a pretty Swedish pop star with the unlikely name of "Elliphant."

The Chief was still afraid of the surgically warped and sickening "Elephant Man," a dark horror-movie figure from his remote childhood.

The Chief might not look terribly old—not to a surveillance camera—but he was senile. Those high-tech quacks in Switzerland took more and more of his wealth, but delivered less and less health. Life-extension technology was a rich man's gamble. The odds were always with the house.

Irma gently removed the cards from the Chief's erratic hands, and dealt them herself. The sea wind rose and loudly ruffled the beach umbrella. Windsurfers passed by, out to sea, with kites that might be aerial surveillance platforms. A group of black-clad divers on a big rubber boat looked scary, like spies, assassins, or secret policemen.

The ever-swelling beach crowd, that gathering, multi-limbed tide of relaxed and playful humanity, inspired a spiritual unease in Tullio. His years inside the Shadow House had made Tullio a retiring, modest man. He had never much enjoyed public oversight. Wherever there were people, there was also hardware and software. There was scanning and recording. Ubiquity and transparency.

That was progress, and the world was better for progress, but it was also a different world, and that hurt.

Some happy beach-going children arrived, and improved the mood at the poker table. As a political leader, the Chief had always been an excellent performer around kids. He clowned with all his old practiced stagecraft, and the surprised little gang of five kids giggled like fifty.

But with the instinctive wisdom of the innocent, the kids didn't care to spend much time with a strange, fat, extremely old man wearing sunglasses and a too-tight swimsuit.

The card play transitioned from Anaconda poker to seven-card stud. Tullio and Irma shared a reassuring glance. Lunch was approaching, and lunch would take two hours. After his lunch, the Chief would nap. After the summer siesta, he would put on his rubber cap, foot fins, and water wings, and swim. With his ritual exercise performed, dinner would be looming. After the ritual of dinner, with its many small and varied pleasures, the day would close quietly.

Tullio and Irma had their two weeks of duty every August, and then the demands of the Chief's wealth and health would call him elsewhere. Then Tullio and Irma could return to their customary peace and quiet. Just them and their eccentric house cat, in their fortress consecrated to solitude.

The Shadow House robot, a nameless flat plastic pancake, emerged from its hidden runway. The diligent machine fluffed the sand, trimmed the beach herbage, and picked up and munched some driftwood bits of garbage electronics.

A beautiful woman arrived on the shore. Her extravagant curves were strapped into bright, clumsy American swimwear. Despite the gusting sea breeze, her salon updo was perfect.

The Chief noticed this beauty instantly. It was as if someone had ordered him a box of hot American donuts.

Tullio and Irma watched warily as the demimondaine strolled by. She tramped the wet edge of the foamy surf like a lingerie runway model. She clearly knew where the Shadow House was sited. She had deliberately wandered within range of its sensors.

The Chief threw on his beach robe and hurried over to chat her up.

The Chief returned with the air of synthetic triumph that he assumed around his synthetic girlfriends. "This is Monica," he announced in English. "Monica wants to play with us."

"What a pretty name," said Irma in English, her eyes narrowing. "Such a glamorous lady as you, such beauty is hard to miss."

"Oh, I visit Sardinia every August," Monica lied sweetly. "But Herr Hentschel has gone back to Berlin. So it's been a bit lonely."

"Everyone knows your Herr Hentschel?" Irma probed.

Monica named a prominent European armaments firm with long-standing American national security ties.

The matter was simple. The Chief had been too visible, out on the beach, all morning. This was long enough for interested parties to notice him with scanners, scare up smart algorithms, and dispatch a working agent.

"Maybe, we go inside the Shadow House now," Tullio suggested in English. "For lunch."

Monica agreed to join them. Tullio shut the rattling umbrella and stacked all the plastic chairs.

The microwave sensors of the Shadow House had a deep electromagnetic look at Monica, and objected loudly.

"A surveillance device," said Tullio.

Monica shrugged her bare, tanned shoulders. She wore nothing but her gaudy floral bikini and her flat zori sandals.

Tullio spread his hands. "Lady, most times, no one knows, no one cares—but this is Shadow House."

Monica plucked off her bikini top and shook it. Her swimwear unfolded with uncanny ease and became a writhing square of algorithmic fabric.

"So pretty," Irma remarked. She carried off the writhing interface to stuff it in a copper-lined box.

The Chief stared at Monica's bared torso as if she'd revealed two rocket ships.

Tullio gave Monica a house robe. Women like Monica were common guests for Shadow House. Sometimes, commonly, one girl. Sometimes five girls, sometimes ten, or, when the Chief's need was truly unbearable, a popular mass of forty-five or fifty girls, girls of any class, color, creed, or condition, girls from anywhere, anything female and human.

On those taut, packed, manic occasions, the Chief threw colossal, fully catered parties, with blasting music and wild dancing and fitful orgies in private VIP nooks. The Shadow House would be ablaze in glimmering witch lights, except for the pitch-black, bombproof niche where the Chief retreated to spy on his guests.

Those events were legendary beach parties, for the less that young people saw of the Chief, the happier everybody was.

Lunch was modest, by the Chief's standards: fried zucchini, calamari with marinara sauce, flatbread drenched in molten cheese and olive spread, tender meatballs of mutton, clams, scampi, and a finisher of mixed and salted nuts, which were good for the nervous system. The Chief fed choice table scraps to the tomcat.

Monica spoke, with an unfeigned good cheer, about her vocation, which was leading less fortunate children in hikes on the dikes of Miami.

When lunch ended, the Chief and the demimondaine retired together for a "nap."

After the necessary medical checks for any intimate encounter, the Chief's efforts in this line generally took him ten minutes. Once his covert romp was over, he would return to daylight with a lighter heart. Generally, he would turn his attention to some favorite topic in public policy, such as hotel construction or the proper maintenance of world heritage sites.

His charisma would revive, then, for the Chief was truly wise about some things. Whenever he was pleased and appeased, one could see why he'd once led a nation, and how his dynamism and his optimistic gusto had encouraged people.

Italian men had voted for the Chief, because they had imagined that they would live like him, if they too were rich, and bold, and famous, and swashbuckling. Some Italian women also voted for the Chief, because, with a man like him in power, at least you understood what you were getting.

But the Chief did not emerge into daylight. After two hours of gathering silence, the house cat yowled in a mystical animal anguish. The cat had no technical understanding about the Shadow House. Being a cat, he had not one scrap of an inkling about Faraday cages or nanocarbon camouflage. However, being a house cat, he knew how to exist in a house. He knew life as a cat knew life, and he knew death, too.

After an anxious struggle, Tullio found the software override, and opened the locked bedroom door. The cat quickly bounded inside, between Tullio's ankles.

The Chief was supine in bed, with a tender smile and an emptied, infinite stare. The pupils of his eyes were two pinpoints.

Tullio lifted the Chief's beefy, naked arm, felt its fluttering pulse, and released it to flop limp on the mattress.

"We push the Big Red Button," Tullio announced to Irma.

"Oh, Tullio, we said we never would do that! What a mess!"

"This is an emergency. We must push the Big Red Button. We owe it to him. It's our duty to push the button."

"But the whole world will find out everything! All his enemies! And his friends are even worse!"

A voice came from under the bed. "Please don't push any button."

Tullio bent and gazed under the bed frame. "So, now you understand Italian, miss?"

"A little." Monica stuck her tousled head from under the rumpled satin bed coverlet. Her frightened face was streaked with tears.

"What did you do to our Chief?"

"Nothing! Well, just normal stuff. He was having a pretty good time of it, for such an old guy. So, I kind of turned it up, and I got busy. Next thing I knew, he was all limp!"

"Men," Irma sympathized.

"Can I have some clothes?" said Monica. "If you push that button, cops will show up for sure. I don't want to be in a station house naked."

Irma hastened to a nearby wardrobe. "Inside, you girls do as you please, but no girl leaves my Shadow House naked!"

Tullio rubbed his chin. "So, you've been to the station house before, Monica?"

"The oldest profession is a hard life." Monica crept out from under the Chief's huge bed, and slipped into the yellow satin house robe that Irma offered. She belted it firmly. "I can't believe I walked right in here in my second-best bikini. I just knew something bad would happen in this weird house."

Tullio recited: "Shadow House is the state of the art in confidential living and reputation management."

"Yeah, sure. I've done guys in worse dives," Monica agreed, "but a million bomb shelters couldn't hush up that guy's reputation. Every working girl knows about him. He's been buying our services for eighty years."

Stabbed by this remark, Tullio gazed on the stricken Chief.

The old man's body was breathing, and its heart was beating, because the Swiss had done much expensive work on the Chief's lungs and heart. But Tullio knew, with a henchman's instinctive certainty, that the Chief was, more or less, dead. The old rascal had simply blown his old brains out in a final erotic gallop. It was a massive, awful, fatal scandal. A tragedy.

When Tullio looked up, the two women were gone. Outside the catastrophic bedroom, Monica was wiping her tear-smudged mascara and confessing her all to Irma.

"So, I guess," Monica said, "maybe, I kinda showed up at the end of his chain here. But for a little Miami girl, like me, to join such a great European tradition—well, it seemed like such an honor!"

Tullio and Irma exchanged glances. "I wish more of these girls had such a positive attitude," said Irma.

Monica, sensing them weakening, looked eager. "Just let me take a hot shower. Okay? If I'm clean, no cop can prove anything! We played cards, that's all. He told me bedtime stories."

"Is there a money trail?" said Irma, who had worked in taxes.

"Oh, no, never! Cash for sex is so old-fashioned." Monica absently picked up the yammering tomcat by the scruff of the neck. She gathered the beast in her sleek arms and massaged him. The surprised cat accepted this treatment, and even seemed grateful.

"See, I have a personal relationship with a big German arms firm," Monica explained, as the cat purred like a small engine. "My sugar daddy is a big defense corporation. It's an Artificial Intelligence, because it tracks me. It knows all my personal habits, and it takes real good care of me... So, sometimes I do a favor—I mean, just a small personal favor for my big AI boyfriend, the big corporation. Then the stockholders' return on investment feels much better."

Baffled by this English-language business jargon, Tullio scratched his head.

Monica lifted her chin. "That's how the vice racket beats a transparent surveillance society. Spies are the world's second oldest profession. Us working girls are still the first."

"We must take a chance," Tullio decided. "You, girl, quick, get clean. Irma, help her. Leave Shadow House, and forget you ever saw us."

"Oh, thank you sir, thank you! I'll be grateful the rest of my life, if I live to be a hundred and fifty!" cried Monica. She tossed the purring tomcat to the floor.

Irma hustled her away. The Shadow House had decontamination showers. Its sewers had membranous firewalls. The cover-up had a good chance to work. The house had been built for just such reasons.

Tullio removed the telltale bedsheets. He did what he could to put the comatose Chief into better order. Tullio had put the Chief to bed, dead drunk, on more than one occasion. This experience was like those comic old times, except not funny, because the Chief was not drunk: just dead.

The lights of Shadow House were strobing. An intruder had arrived.

The hermit priest had rolled to the House perimeter within his smart mobile wheelchair. Father Simeon was a particularly old man—even older than the Chief. Father Simeon was the Chief's longtime spiritual guide and personal confessor.

"Did you push that Big Red Button?" said the super-centenarian cleric.

"No, Monsignor!"

"Good. I have arrived now, have I not? Where is my poor boy? Take me to him."

"The Chief is sick, Monsignor." Tullio suddenly burst into tears. "He had a fit. He collapsed, he's not conscious. What can we do?"

"The status of death is not a matter for a layman to decide," said the priest.

The Shadow House did not allow the cleric's wheelchair to enter its premises. The Vatican wheelchair was a rolling mass of embedded electronics. The Shadow House rejected this Catholic computational platform as if it were a car bomb.

Father Simeon—once a prominent Vatican figure—had retired to the island to end his days in a hermetic solitude. Paradoxically, his pursuit of holy seclusion made Father Simeon colossally popular. Since he didn't want to meet or talk to anybody, the whole world adored him. Archbishops and cardinals constantly pestered the hermit for counsel, and his wizened face featured on countless tourist coffee cups.

"I must rise and walk," said Father Simeon. "The soul of a sufferer needs me. Give me your arm, my son!"

Tullio placed his arm around the aged theologian, who clutched a heavy Bible and a precious vial of holy oil. Under his long, black, scarlet-buttoned cassock, the ancient hermit was a living skeleton. His bony legs rattled as his sandaled, blue-veined feet grazed the floor.

Tullio tripped over the house cat as they entered the Chief's bedroom. They reeled together and almost fell headlong onto the stricken Chief, but the devoted priest gave no thought to his own safety. Father Simeon checked the Chief's eyelids with his thumbs, then muttered a Latin prayer.

"I'm so glad for your help, Father," said Tullio. "How did you know that we needed you here?"

The old man shot him a dark look from under his spiky gray brows. "My son," he said, lifting his hand, "do you imagine that your mere technology—all these filters and window shades—can blind the divine awareness of the Living God? The Lord knows every sparrow that falls! God knows every hair of every human head! The good God has no need for any corporate AIs or cheap Singularities!"

Tullio considered this. "Well, can I do anything to help? Shall I call a doctor?"

"What use are the doctors now, after their wretched excesses? Pray for him!" said the priest. "His body persists while his soul is in Limbo. The

Church rules supreme in bioethics. We will defend our faithful from these secular intrusions. If this had happened to him in Switzerland, they would have plugged him into the wall like a cash machine!"

Tullio shuddered in pain.

"Be not afraid!" Father Simeon commanded. "This world has its wickedness—but if the saints and angels stand with us, what machine can stand against us?" Father Simeon carefully gloved his bony hands. He uncapped his reeking vial of holy oil.

"I'm so sorry about all this, Monsignor. It's so embarrassing that we failed in this way. We always tried to protect him, here in the Shadow House."

The priest deftly rubbed the eyes, ears, and temples of the stricken Chief with the sacramental ointment. "All men are sinners. Go to confession, my boy. God is all-seeing, and yet He is forgiving; whenever we open our heart to God, He always sees and understands."

Irma beckoned at Tullio from the doorway. Tullio excused himself and met her outside.

The emergency had provoked Irma's best cleverness. She had quickly dressed Monica in some fine clothes, left behind in Shadow House by the Chief's estranged daughter. These abandoned garments were out of style, of course, but they were of classic cut and fine fabric. The prostitute looked just like an Italian parliamentarian.

"I told you to run away," said Tullio.

"Oh sure, I wanted to run," Monica agreed, "but if I ran from the scene of a crime, then some algorithm might spot my guilty behavior. But now look at me! I look political, instead of like some lowlife. So I can be ten times as guilty, and nothing will happen to me."

Tullio looked at Irma, who shrugged, because of course it was true.

"Let the priest finish his holy business," Irma counseled. "Extreme unction is a sacrament. We can't push the Big Red Button during this holy moment."

"Are you guys Catholics?" said Monica. At their surprised look, she raised both her hands. "Hey, I'm from Miami, we got lots!"

"Are you a believer?" said Irma.

"Well, I tried to believe," said Monica, blinking. "I read some of the Bible in a hotel room once. That book's pretty crazy. Full of begats."

A horrid shriek came from the Chief's bedroom.

The Chief was bolt upright in bed, while moans and whispers burst in anguish from his writhing lips. The anointment with sacred oil had aroused one last burst of his mortal vitality. His heart was pounding so powerfully that it was audible across the room.

This spectral deathbed fit dismayed Father Simeon not at all. With care, he performed his ministry.

A death rattle eclipsed the Chief's last words. His head plummeted into a pillow. He was as dead as a stone, although his heart continued to beat for over a minute.

The priest removed the rosary from around his shrunken neck and folded it into the Chief's hairy hands.

"He expressed his contrition," the priest announced. "At his mortal end, he was lucid and transparent. God knows all, sees all, and forgives all. So do not be frightened. He has not left us. He has simply gone home."

"Wow," Monica said in the sudden silence. "That was awesome. Who is this old guy?"

"This is our world-famous hermit, Father Simeon," said Tullio.

"Our friend Father Simeon was the president for the Pontifical Council for Social Communications," Irma said proudly. "He also wrote the Canon Law for the Evangelization of Artificial Intelligences."

"That sounds pretty cool," said Monica. "Listen, Padre, Holy Father, whatever…"

"'Holy Father' is a title reserved for our Pope," Father Simeon told her, in a crisp Oxford English. "My machines call me 'Excellency'—but since you are human, please call me 'Father.'"

"Okay, 'Father,' sure. You forgave him, right? He's dead—but he's going to heaven, because he has no guilty secrets. That's how it works, right?"

"He confessed. He died in the arms of the Church."

"Okay, yeah, that's great—but how about me? Can I get forgiven, too? Because I'm a bad girl! I didn't want him to die! That was terrible! I'm really sorry."

Father Simeon was old and had been through a trial at the deathbed, but his faith sustained him. "Do not despair, my child. Yes, you may be weak and a sinner. Take courage: the power of the Church is great. You can break the chains of unrighteousness. Have faith that you can turn away from sin."

"But how, Father? I've got police records on three continents, and about a thousand johns have rated my services on hooker e-commerce sites."

Father Simeon winced at this bleak admission, but truth didn't daunt him. "My child, those data records are only software and hardware. You have a human soul, you possess free will. The Magdalen was a fallen woman whose conscience was awakened. She was a chosen companion of Christ. So do not bow your head to this pagan system of surveillance that confines you to a category, and seeks to entrap you there!"

Monica burst into tears. "What must I do to be saved from surveillance?"

"Take the catechism! Learn the meaning of life! We are placed on Earth to know, to love, and to serve our God! We are not here to cater to the whims of German arms corporations that build spy towers in the Mediterranean!"

Monica blinked. "Hey, wait a minute, Father—how do you know all that—about my German arms corporation and all those towers in the sea?"

"God is not mocked! There are some big data systems in this world that are little more than corrupt incubi, and there are other, better-programmed, sanctified data systems that are like protective saints and angels."

Monica looked to Tullio and Irma. "Is he kidding?"

Tullio and Irma silently shook their heads.

"Wow," breathed Monica. "I would really, truly love to have an AI guardian angel."

The lights began to strobe overhead.

"Something is happening outside," said Tullio hastily. "When I come back, we'll all press the Big Red Button together."

Behind the Shadow House, a group of bored teenagers had discovered Father Simeon's abandoned wheelchair. They had captured the vehicle and were giving one another joyrides.

Overwhelmed by the day's events, Tullio chased them off the Shadow House property, shouting in rage. The teens were foreign tourists, and knew not one word of Italian, so they fled his angry scolding in a panic, and ran off headlong to scramble up into the howdah of a waiting elephant.

"Teenage kids should never have elephants!" Tullio complained, wheeling the re-captured wheelchair back to Irma. "Elephants are huge beasts! Look at this mess."

"Elephants are better than cars," said Irma. "You can't even kiss a boy in a car, because the cars are tracked and they record everything. That's what the girls say in town."

"Delinquents. Hooligans! With elephants! What kind of world is this, outside our house?"

"Kissing boys has always been trouble." Irma closely examined the wheelchair, which had been tumbled, scratched, and splattered with sandy dirt. "Oh dear, we can't possibly give it back to Father Simeon in this condition."

"I'll touch it up," Tullio promised.

"Should I push the Big Red Button now?"

"Not yet," Tullio said. "A time like this needs dignity. We should get the Chief's lawyer to fly in from Milan. If we have the Church and the Law on our side, then we can still protect him, Irma, even after death. No one will know what happened here. There's still client-lawyer confidentiality. There's still the sacred silence of the confessional. And this house is radar-proof."

"I'm sure the Chief would want to be buried in Rome. The city where he saw his best days."

"Of course you're right," said Tullio. "There will be riots at his funeral… but our Chief will finally find peace in Rome. Nobody will care about his private secrets anymore. There are historical records, but the machines never bother to look at them. History is one of the humanities."

"Let's get the Vatican to publicly announce his passing. With no Italian government, the Church is what we have left."

"What a good idea." Tullio looked at his wife admiringly. Irma had always been at her best in handling scandalous emergencies. It was a pity that a woman of such skill had retired to a quiet life.

"I'll talk to Father Simeon about it. He'll know who to contact, behind the scenes." Irma left.

Tullio brushed sand from the wheelchair's ascetic leather upholstery, and polished the indicator lights with his sleeve. Since electronics were no longer tender or delicate devices—electronics were the bedrock of the modern world, basically—the wheelchair had not been much disturbed by its mishap.

It was Tullio himself who felt tumbled and upset. Why were machines so hard to kill, and people so frail? The Shadow House had been built around the needs of one great man. The structure could grant him a physical privacy, but it couldn't stop his harsh compulsion to reveal himself.

The Shadow House functioned properly, but it was a Don Quixote windmill. The Chief was, finally, too mad in the head to care if his manias were noticed. What the Chief had liked best about his beach house was simply playing poker with two old friends. Relaxing informally, despite his colossal burdens of wealth and fame, sitting there in improbable poise, like an elephant perched on a card table.

The house cat curled around Tullio's ankles. Since the cat had never before left the confines of the Shadow House, this alarmed Tullio.

Inside, Father Simeon, Irma, and Monica were sharing tea on a rattan couch, while surrounded by screens.

"People are querying the Shadow House address," Irma announced. "We're getting map queries from Washington and Berlin."

"I guess you can blame me for that, too," Monica moaned. "My Artificial Intelligence boyfriend is worried about me, since I dropped out of connectivity in here."

"I counsel against that arrangement," Father Simeon stated. "Although an AI network is not a man, he can still exploit a vulnerable woman. A machine with no soul can sin. Our Vatican theology bots are explicit about this."

"I never thought of my sweet megacorporation as a pimp and an incubus—but you're right, Father Simeon. I guess I've got a lot to learn."

"Never fear to be righteous, my child. Mother Church knows how to welcome converts. Our convents and monasteries make this shadowy place look like a little boy's toy."

The priest and his new convert managed to escape discreetly. The wheelchair vanished into the orange groves. Moments later, Carlo Pizzi arrived at Shadow House on his motor scooter.

The short and rather pear-shaped Pizzi was wearing his customary outsized head-mounted display goggles, which connected him constantly to his cloudy network. The goggles made Pizzi look as awkward as a grounded aviator, but he enjoyed making entirely sure that other people knew all about his social media capacities.

After some polite chitchat about the weather (which he deftly recited from a display inside his goggles), Pizzi got straight to the point. "I'm searching for a girl named Monica. Tall, pretty, red hair, American, height one hundred seventy-five centimeters, weight fifty-four kilograms."

"We haven't seen her in some time," Irma offered.

"Monica has vanished from the network. That activity doesn't fit her emotional profile. I've got an interested party that's concerned about her safety."

"You mean the German arms manufacturer?" said Irma.

Carlo Pizzi paused awkwardly as he read invisible cues from his goggles.

"In our modern Transparent Society," Pizzi ventured at last, "the three of us can all do well for ourselves by doing some social good. For instance: if you can reconnect Monica to the network, then my friend can see to it that pleasant things are said about this area to the German trade press. Then you'll see more German tourists on your nice beach here."

"You can tell your creepy AI friend to recalibrate his correlations, because Shadow House is a private home," said Tullio. His words were defiant, but Tullio's voice shook with grief. That was a bad idea when an AI was deftly listening for the emotional cues in human speech patterns.

"So, is Father Simeon dead?" Carlo Pizzi said. "Good heavens! If that famous hermit is dead, that would be huge news in Sardinia."

"No, Father Simeon is fine," said Irma. "Please don't disturb his seclusion. Publicity makes him angry."

"Then it's that old politician who has died. The last Prime Minister of Italy," said Carlo Pizzi, suddenly convinced. "Thanks for cuing up his bio for me! A man who lives for a hundred years sure can get into trouble!"

Tullio and Irma sidled away as Pizzi was distractedly talking to the empty air, but he noticed them and followed them like a dog. "The German system has figured out your boss is dead," Pizzi confided, "because the big-data correlations add up. Cloud AIs are superior at that sort of stuff. But can I get a physical confirmation on that?"

"What are you talking about?" said Tullio.

"I need the first postmortem shot of the deceased. There were rumors before now that he had died. Because he had this strange habit of disappearing whenever things got hot for him. So, this could be another trick of his—but if I could see him with my goggles here, and zoom in on his exact proportions and scan his fingerprints and such, then our friend the German system would have a first-mover market advantage."

"We don't want to bargain with a big-data correlation system," said Tullio. "That's like trying to play chess with a computer. We can't possibly win, so it's not really fair."

"But you're the one being unfair! Think of the prosperity that big-data market capitalism has brought to the world! A corporation is just the legal and computational platform for its human stockholders, you know. My friend is a 'corporate person' with thousands of happy human stockholders. He has a fiduciary obligation to improve their situation. That's what we're doing right now."

"You own stock in this thing yourself?" said Irma.

"Well, sure, of course. Look, I know you think I want to leak this paparazzi photo to the public. But I don't, because that's obsolete! Our friend the German AI doesn't want this scandal revealed, any more than you do. I just pass him some encrypted photo evidence, and he gets ahead of the market game. Then I can take the rest of this year off and finish my new novel!"

There was a ponderous silence. "His novels are pretty good beach reading," Irma offered at last. "If you like roman-à-clef tell-all books."

"Look here, Signor Pizzi," said Tullio, "the wife and I are not against modern capitalism and big-data pattern recognition. But we can't just let you barge in here and disturb the peace of our dead patron. He was always good to us—in his way."

"Somebody has to find out he's dead. That's the way of the world," Pizzi coaxed. "Isn't it better that it's just a big-data machine who knows? The guy has four surviving ex-wives, and every one of them is a hellion."

"That's all because of him," said Irma. "All those First Ladies were very nice ladies once."

Pizzi read data at length from the inside of his goggles; one could tell because his body language froze while his lips moved slightly. "Speaking of patronage," he said, "your son has a nice job in Milan that was arranged by your late boss in there."

"Luigi doesn't know about that," said Irma. "He thinks he got that job on merit."

"How would it be if Luigi suddenly got that big promotion he's been waiting for? Our AI friend can guarantee that. Your son deserves a boost. He works hard."

Irma gave Tullio a hopeful, beseeching glance.

"My God, no wonder national governments broke down," said Tullio, scowling. "With these sly big-data engines running the world, political backroom deals don't stand a chance! Our poor old dead boss, he really is a relic of the past now. I don't know whether to laugh or cry."

"Can't we just go inside?" urged the paparazzo. "It won't take five minutes."

It took longer, because the Shadow House would not allow the gossip's head-mounted device inside the premises. They had to unscrew the goggles from his head—Pizzi, with his merely human eyes exposed to fresh air, looked utterly bewildered—and they smuggled the device to the deathbed inside a Faraday bag.

Carlo Pizzi swept the camera's gaze over the dead man from head to foot, as if sprinkling the corpse with holy water. They then hurried out of the radio silence, so that Carlo Pizzi could upload his captured images to the waiting AI.

"Our friend the German machine has another proposal for you now," said Carlo Pizzi. "There's nothing much in it for me, but I'd be happy to tell you about it, just to be neighborly."

"What is the proposal?" said Irma.

"Well, this Shadow House poses a problem."

"Why?"

"Because it's an opaque structure in a transparent world. Human beings shouldn't be concealing themselves from ubiquitous machine awareness. That's pessimistic and backward-looking. This failure to turn a clean face to the future does harm to our society."

"Go on."

"Also, the dead man stored some secrets in here. Something to do with his previous political dealings, as Italian head of state, with German arms suppliers."

"Maybe he stored secrets, and maybe he didn't," said Tullio stoutly. "It's none of your business."

"It would be good news for business if the house burned down," said Carlo Pizzi. "I know that sounds shocking to humans, but good advice from wise machines often does. Listen. There are other places like this house, but much better and bigger. They're a series of naval surveillance towers, built at great state expense, to protect the Mediterranean coasts of Italy from migrants and terrorists. Instead of being Shadow Houses, they're tall and powerful Light Houses, with radar, sonar, lidar, and drone landing strips. Real military castles, with all the trimmings."

"I always adored lighthouses," said Irma wonderingly. "They're so remote and romantic."

"If this Shadow House should happen to catch fire," said Carlo Pizzi, "our friend could have you both appointed caretakers of one of those Italian sea castles. The world is so peaceful and progressive now, that those castles don't meet any threats. However, there's a lot of profit involved in keeping them open and running. Your new job would be just like your old job here—just with a different patron."

"Yes, but that's arson."

"The dead man has no heirs for his Shadow House," said Carlo Pizzi. "Our friend has just checked thoroughly, and that old man was so egotistical, and so confident that he would live forever, that he died intestate. So, if you burn the house down, no one will miss it."

"There's the cat," said Tullio. "The cat would miss the house."

"What?"

"A cat lives in this house," said Tullio. "Why don't you get your friend the AI to negotiate with our house cat? See if it can make the cat a convincing offer."

Carlo Pizzi mulled this over behind his face-mounted screens. "The German AI was entirely unaware of the existence of the house cat."

"That's because a house cat is a living being and your friend is just a bunch of code. It's morally wrong to burn down houses. Arson is illegal. What would the Church say? Obviously it's a sin."

"You're just emotionally upset now, because you can't think as quickly and efficiently as an Artificial Intelligence," said Carlo Pizzi. "However, think it over at your own slow speed. The offer stands. I'll be going now, because if I stand too long around here, some algorithm might notice me here, and draw unwelcome conclusions."

"Good luck with your new novel," said Irma. "I hope it's as funny as your early, good ones."

Carlo Pizzi left hastily on his small and silent electric scooter. Tullio and Irma retreated within the Shadow House.

"The brazen nerve of that smart machine, to carry on so 'deus ex machina,'" said Tullio. "We can't burn down this beautiful place! Shadow House is a monument to privacy—to a vanishing, but noble way of life! Besides, you'd need thermite grenades to take out those steel panic rooms."

Irma looked dreamy. "I remember when the government of Italy went broke building all those security lighthouses. There must be dozens of them, far out to sea. Maybe we could have our pick."

"But those paranoid towers will never be refined and airy and beautiful, like this beach house! It would be like living in a nuclear missile silo."

"All of those are empty now, too," said Irma.

"Those nuclear silos had Big Red Buttons, too, now that you mention it. We're never going to push that button, are we, Irma? I always wondered what kind of noise it would make."

"We never make big elephant noises," said Irma, with an eloquent shrug. "You and me, that's not how we live."

T he mystic adepts of ... ... one ...ation in Turin: the ... of Saint Cleopha. Sadly, their splendid inn was closing forever. Within the inn's great room sat a wandering Jew, an Arab astrologer, a German printer, and a battle-scarred Serbian Ottoman. At the inn's second trencher board, in the lengthening shadows, lurked a Portuguese slave dealer, a U... sian heretic, ...nde se... broth... The final table stood a golden puddle of twilight under a window of stained glass. This table was graced by a silk-robed Chinese eunuch, a Genoese mapmaker, a sea captain from the Canary Islands, and

PILGRIMS OF THE ROUND WORLD

For Jasmina Tešanović, fellow traveler in this journey

I

THE MYSTIC ADEPTS of travel chose one destination in Turin: the Inn of Saint Cleopha. Sadly, their splendid inn was closing forever.

Within the inn's great room sat a wandering Jew, an Arab astrologer, a German printer, and a battle-scarred Serbian Ottoman.

At the inn's second trencher board, in the lengthening shadows, lurked a Portuguese slave dealer, a Waldensian heretic, an Alpine brigandess, and the madam of a Turinese brothel.

The final table stood in a golden puddle of twilight under a window of stained glass. This table was graced by a silk-robed Chinese eunuch, a Genoese mapmaker, a sea captain from the Canary Islands, and the Rector of the University of Turin.

From within the kitchen came a wail of distress and a violent smash of crockery.

The madam of the brothel bit the ivory beads of her rosary, and burst into tears. "I can't bear this! It's so sad! I'll never eat this well again!"

The brigandess patted her cousin's plump arm. "Let us give thanks for what Saint Cleopha once gave us." The bawd was fat, rosy, and rich, while the bandit was lean, scarred, and cruel, but the two women were both from Turin, and they were family.

The inn's hostess burst from her smokey kitchen, in a cloudy reek of onions, rosemary, and roast chestnuts.

"It's the end of the world," the hostess wailed. "Saint Cleopha is so upset that she just broke half my dishes!"

"Are we to go to bed without supper?" said the Waldensian heretic. He was always a skeptic.

Their hostess wrung her flour-dusted hands. "Don't blame me when you hear that girl-saint moaning tonight... My poor little Cleopha, she died in her cell in this House, three years younger and much chaster than that Joan of Arc who those stupid French make such a fuss about!"

The brigandess munched on a breadstick. "So, Agnes, what's become of Saint Cleopha? Did you disinter her holy bones?"

"I can pack a spirit into a bottle," offered the Arab astrologer.

Ugo de Balliand, the master of the Inn of Saint Cleopha, made his entrance. To mark the occasion, the host had dressed to befit his new station in life. Ugo de Balliand was the Duchy of Savoy's Abbreviator Major and Envoy Plenipotentiary to the Crusader Kingdoms of Cyprus and Jerusalem.

Ugo de Balliand wore a towering felt cap, a fur-trimmed velvet cape, a buttoned surcoat, tight striped leggings. and pointed leather shoes. The shining belt around Ugo's portly waist bore a coin purse, a jeweled poniard, and a ceremonial sword.

The guests were stunned by this transformation in their innkeeper. They watched in meek silence as he tossed the inn's account books into the fireplace.

The financial records ignited with a lively crackle of fine Venetian paper. Ugo turned to his wife. "Agnes, what is this noise? Your chambermaids are crying, my stableboys are drunk... This is the last night of our House! Let us respect the composure of our guests."

"My stove boy broke his hand in my stove," said Agnes.

Ugo smoothed the drape of his cape. "Good friends, as you can see, these are trying days for the good wife and I. We've sold our House and everything within it. Every closet, cupboard, and pantry, from cellar to attic!"

Agnes wiped her eyes on her apron, with a look of pathetic appeal. "I even sold my girlish dowry chest!"

"So, during this, the last supper that my wife and I will ever offer to you," said Ugo suavely, "we both ask you to remember the Inn of Saint Cleopha as it once was. Remember that we, your host and hostess, were always faithful to the Rule of our House. We always gave to you just what we ourselves would want in any foreign land. At Saint Cleopha's Inn, there was courteous service, excellent food, and no prying questions about your private business. And you slept in a solid, stone room, free of thieves, fleas, and bedbugs, that locked from the inside."

The murmuring travelers exchanged mournful looks. Despite their widely varying origins, they were, one and all, moved by their host's declaration.

Many inns dotted the great pilgrim routes that girdled the world, from Spain to China, and from Moscow to Timbuktu, but Ugo and Agnes had been exemplary hosts. Always a kind greeting for pilgrims, spoken in five languages, under the ceramic plaque of Cleopha at the tall, arched brick door. No guest left the Inn of Saint Cleopha without a generous stirrup-cup of hot spiced wine, at no further charge.

The wise and kindly Ugo de Balliand always had fresh, trustworthy news of the markets and the road conditions. Whenever local rowdies bothered her guests, Agnes of Chambéry would personally climb the inn's watchtower, to toss a kitchen pot of boiling water on them. Experienced pilgrims of the round world properly valued these rarities.

Grieving, yet with stolid dignity, Ugo climbed a slatted folding chair and opened a scroll. "Honored guests of the Inn of Saint Cleopha! Bearing in mind the dietary restrictions of your various faiths, hearken to what we offer you to eat today, on this the feast day of Saint Hildegarde of Bingen, the seventeenth day of September in the year one thousand, four hundred and sixty-three."

Ugo beckoned at the steaming kitchen door, where Agnes's squad of kitchen boys waited with platters. "The 'anteprima'! A little amusement to open your palates… A fine-grated pickled radish, accented with my consort's strawberry compote. Dig in right away, my friends, don't be shy, those flavors won't disappoint you."

The diners loudly tucked in with forks and bare fingers, as Ugo read the menu in a capable, clerical Latin, the speech of all learned scholars of Christendom. Ugo's second reading was in courtly French, the lingua franca of the nobility. The third reading was in the local, folksy Savoyard dialect, an Alpine speech that was half-French, half-Italian.

Ugo's fourth reading was in a spicy Roman Italian, for all roads led to Rome. As a final hostly courtesy Ugo read the menu in a halting and effortful Sicilian Arabic.

During her husband's impressive feat of scholarship, Agnes oversaw the distribution of her bowls, tureens, and platters. A guard dog wandered into the dining room. A jackdaw cawed at the window. A blind musician arrived with his portable wooden pipe organ. The pilgrims were generous to him. The blind man sang as he played, and had always been a regular attraction at the Inn of Saint Cleopha.

The Chinese eunuch left his table to confer with the Arab astrologer. Then the eunuch beckoned languidly, with his long, brass-shod nails.

"He wants to buy the virgin's teeth from her reliquary," the astrologer confided, tipsily adjusting his star-spangled robe.

Agnes bit her fingertips. "The holy teeth of Cleopha will go to China? That land that Marco Polo lied about?"

Ugo tenderly straightened the starched cooking cap on his wife's blonde curls. "My dear, everyone here can see your woman's heart is bleeding tonight, but I must overrule your natural feelings... What is the Chinaman offering for the saint's teeth, exactly?"

Using chopsticks to spare his long fingernails, the eunuch retrieved an enchanted needle.

Ugo and Agnes conferred. Since Agnes was from Savoy while Ugo was from Cyprus, the two of them had invented a private dialect of Cypriot-Savoyard French. No one understood this lingo but their children, who were grown and gone.

"These Chinese needles are legendary," Ugo told Agnes. "They have a magic virtue for pilgrims. They always point south."

"Must we sell teeth for a needle? I could carry holy teeth to Cyprus in my hat."

"You could hide a magic needle among your pins and threads, and no robber on the road would ever guess its value."

Agnes accepted this reasoning. She curtsied to the Arab wizard. "The

Rule of our House was to never turn a Chinese from our door. We always took them in, although the Chinese rudely eat with wooden sticks. What a bargain that Chinese rascal is getting, little though he knows about sanctity!"

"This Chinaman knows all about saints and relics," shrugged the Arab astrologer. "He's a Nestorian, come here via the Silk Road."

"He's a Nestorian Chinese Christian? My goodness, tell him it's a deal."

Volleys of heavy platters came from the kitchen, bearing the last preserves from Agnes's legendary larders. Agnes of Chambéry had skills that bordered on witchcraft when it came to stewing, brewing, salting, smoking, and stuffing. Her pantries disgorged a gleaming cavalcade of wrinkled Papal salamis. Veal hash diced with garlic and truffles. Ancient black olives big as one's thumbs' ends. Oaken kegs of pickled snails. Smoked steaks of man-sized catfish from the River Po. Tangy, reeking brus cheese. All this washed down with a panoply of beers, hypocras potions, bitters, and mulled amalgams.

The wandering Jew approached the innkeepers, gesturing in mute agitation.

"Can anybody here speak a language this Jew understands?" Ugo shouted over the din of wooden spoons on pewter platters.

The Spanish sea captain whistled in response. He rose from his bench with a bowlegged swagger, but the Genoese mapmaker scurried past him.

"I can speak Greek, and it is my pleasure to help with your negotiations," said the Genoese. "Signor de Balliand, my congratulations on your promotion to the *corps diplomatique*! I have a new map of safe routes to the Kingdom of Cyprus, evading the Ottoman Turks, both on land and sea."

Agnes smiled prettily. "Sir Doctor Geographer, we're trying to bargain with this Jew."

"I can speak Greek to him," said the mapmaker. "He is a Rhadanite."

"Oh, for heaven's sake!" cried Agnes. "For Rhadanites, dinner is on the house. Welcome to Turin, sir! Some of our best friends are Rhadanites."

"Are you really a Rhadanite?" said the Spanish captain to the Jew, in Spanish.

"*Sí. Yo soy.*"

"Well, you Rhadanites can certainly out-sail the Genoese. I admire that." The two of them conferred in Spanish.

"The Jew is asking about that picture," the sea captain related. The inn's dining-room wall held a large fresco, done on white plaster. This sprightly composition was thronged with feathery green trees, craggy brown boulders, speedy falcons, faithful dogs, a comic flock of eager ducks, capering horses, gallant riders in ermine-trimmed capes, and a towering marble fountain thronged by bathing beauties with spidery arms, vase-like hips, and breasts like cupcakes.

"Oh, our fresco," said Ugo indifferently. "That was Master Giacomo Jacquerio, a local artist. Before Giacomo left Turin on pilgrimage, he dined here twice a week. Giacomo painted our hall to pay for his meals. Painters are like that, you know. A nice fellow in his own way, but…" Ugo cocked his head sideways and waved his hand.

"This wandering Jew has seen the Fountain of Youth. He says that your picture looks just like the place."

"I don't doubt that." Ugo briskly wiped his hands on a kitchen towel. "Jacquerio's big daub here is done for, but I think I can oblige a connoisseur of painting. Master Jacquerio once painted a portrait of my own father."

"Oh, my dear," cried Agnes, "you can't sell that painting of your dad!"

"Listen, my treasure," Ugo confided in a murmur, "maybe old Jacquerio could paint a bit, in his homely Turinese style. But he's no match for that kid from Vinci. That Vinci rascal knows perspective, so let's not be foolish here."

"But your family in Cyprus would love to see your father's portrait. Let's take it there with us!"

Ugo shook his head sharply. "My father was only a troubadour! I am the Savoy ducal envoy to the Royal Court of Cyprus! Let's not embarrass ourselves before the Queen of Jerusalem."

"Oh, dear me, I didn't think of it that way…" Agnes narrowed her eyes. "I remember where I packed that picture. I had better fetch it for you, because you'll never find it yourself." Agnes hitched her long gray skirts and hurried up the stairs toward the strong room.

"So, you've sold your inn already, then," the Spanish sea captain offered, as they waited for Agnes to return.

"No real estate deal is ever simple," Ugo told him. "You should have seen the trouble we took to own this place."

The captain nodded. "To secularize a sacred nunnery, yes, that must have been a challenge."

"Well, the English free lances had smashed this convent, so when we changed its fief under the bishopric to that of a tenured pilgrim hospice… Oh well, you Spaniards know how English pirates are! Once we've left for Cyprus, my wife's cousin will turn this old nunnery into a tannery."

Silently, the captain studied the doomed mural.

"A freehold tannery business will be a nice little earner for Turin," said Ugo. "The lad will make leather for saddles here, parchment, armor, whatever you need. We stand next to the city wall, so he can throw his tanning slops straight into the moat. Agnes's people have always had good business sense."

Agnes reappeared with a rolled canvas. She handed it to the Rhadanite, who opened it and squinted.

"Legally speaking," said Ugo to the captain, "the case of Saint Cleopha's benefice was never fully settled. You see, Cleopha was beatified by my late lord, Pope Felix the Fifth. I served as his majordomo during much of his papacy. However—the Council of Cardinals has recently established that Popes crowned by the Council of Geneva were, in fact, Anti-Popes. They further interpret that clerical law to state that Cleopha's state of sanctity must therefore be null and void."

"Deep matters," said the captain. "In my own Canary Islands, we leave those controversies well alone."

"Well, Pope Pius in Rome may yet rule that Cleopha is indeed a saint. If he does, then Cleopha's shrine here in Turin will have to be re-sanctified. I don't know where the Vicar of Turin would ever find the funds for that, though. A tannery pays taxes."

The Rhadanite made up his mind. He offered a small brass vial of North Atlantic ambergris, while remarking, in Greek, that the Rhadanites were the maritime Jews of Iceland.

The Spanish sea captain plucked the painting from the hand of the Jew. It depicted a Crusader troubadour with his lute, a garish suit of motley, and a pilgrim seashell badge.

"It's in good condition," the Spaniard said. "Especially for a Crusader."

"My father's songs of holy war have indeed been long remembered," said Ugo. "You might ask our blind man there to play a few."

"Being a good Spanish Catholic," said the sailor, rolling the canvas, "I believe I can beat this Jew's offer."

"Can you, Captain?"

"I have also sailed to Iceland," the Spanish sailor bragged, tucking the picture into his armpit. "What is more—privately, mind you—I have sailed to Greenland. I once ventured to far, southern Greenland. That's a very hot realm there, very green. The foreigners there have their skins burnt all red by the sun. They let me and my crew watch their ball games." The sailor dug into his knapsack. He offered a smooth black sphere.

"What is that?" said Agnes.

The sea captain dropped the black globe. It rebounded from the stone floor back into his gripping hand. He handed it to Ugo.

"That is a child's toy," Ugo judged, bouncing and catching it.

"Toys are good," said Agnes. "When Carlotta, Queen of Cyprus and Jerusalem, bears her royal heir of the body, we can give the boy this ball."

"The red men kill each other for these black globes," the sea captain said. "They play tournaments in courts of stone. The losers are cut to pieces, and boiled in pots with spices, and eaten by the crowd."

"Let's buy that right now," Agnes urged.

"My dear," said Ugo, "ambergris is extremely prized in Cyprus. All Cypriots are connoisseurs of perfume. This black ball is an oddity." He turned to the Genoese mapmaker. "Sir, what do you make of all this?"

The little Genoese scholar was glad to be consulted. "Speaking as an adept of the mystic science of geography," he said, "I know that the world is round. However—I do not believe in a mythical 'Green Land' between Ireland and China. Eratosthenes never spoke of that. And as for cannibalism, every traveler brings some tall tale! Are we to believe that 'Red Men' in some 'Green Land' are eating human flesh? Where was that ever written in the classics?"

The Spanish sea captain plucked at his short gray beard. "Those Red Men of Greenland have all kinds of good food at their ball games. They don't just eat one another. They eat a big yellow rice which grows on a cob! They burn the rice until it pops."

"Rice that pops?" Agnes demanded. "Did you bring us some?"

"Signora, the food of the Red Men is nowhere near so tasty as your own food," the sailor said. "Your Arabian coffee is the best coffee in all Christendom. And your African sugar is whiter than the snow of your Alps."

Agnes murmured to Ugo. "This rascal is flattering us. Give that Jew your picture, and we're taking that vial of ambergris."

"I'm beginning to fancy this black ball! It's more amusing than one would think."

Agnes whispered into his ear. "A queen who has quarreled with her prince has good uses for perfume. We must reconcile Queen Carlotta with her husband. The toys for her heir can wait."

II

The last feast at the Inn of Saint Cleopha continued until the diners could swallow no more. One by one, the bleary-eyed *commensali* retired to their stone pilgrim cells. They huddled on straw ticking under woolen blankets, while their toppled bottles slowly stained the table linens.

The servants of the Inn of Saint Cleopha were all natives of Turin. Being Turinese, they were too sly to work when their bosses were closing their workplace.

As the autumn night darkened and the frogs croaked like monsters in the city moat, the servants silently nicked the beeswax candles from the chandeliers. They swiped the herbal flea and moth repellents. The boldest even pried the mullion panes of stained glass from the windows.

Ugo and Agnes had expected this from the staff of their inn. It was the popular custom, whenever a House failed, and its servants were servants no longer.

Ugo and Agnes had once been servants of the Savoy Anti-Pope Felix, whose House had also failed. They had been present at the deathbed of Felix, in Rome.

The great mystic of Savoy had once schemed to rule all of Christendom. In a brilliant strategic maneuver, he had coaxed Byzantium and its Greek Orthodox Church toward the bosom of his anti-papacy. By healing the schism between the Catholics and the Orthodox, he would double the size of Christendom, terrify all Moslems, and make himself the greatest Pope of all.

But the duchy of Savoy was a small place, unlikely to unify great realms. Savoy was no bigger than Cyprus. The mystical mountain duchy and the pious Crusader island had been best allies for three centuries, ceaselessly trading daughters for dynastic marriage, as well as sharing their wines, spices, sausage, cheese, and popular music.

When the Byzantines refused the embrace of the Anti-Pope, every dream failed at once. The Turks rose and smashed Byzantium, destroying the overland route to the Holy Land. Rome had created a newer Pope, a man of a different breed, and the humbled Anti-Pope, reduced in the ranks to a mere cardinal, had spent his last days in the tender care of Ugo and Agnes, in a secluded Roman palace.

White-haired, silent, and doddering, Felix had collapsed over an illuminated tome of Hermes Trismegistus, still clutching his Swiss tiara and his enchanted staff. Then—swiftly, almost instantly—the greedy Roman mob had attacked the House of Felix. Ugo and Agnes, besieged by the stampeding common folk, had barely managed to save the Anti-Pope's alchemical library, in order to sell it off, later, themselves.

Ugo de Balliand and Agnes of Chambéry had learned harsh wisdom through that episode. So, as the inn's servants rampantly misbehaved, Ugo and Agnes wisely retreated up the brick stairs to the strong room where they kept their bed.

Ugo slammed and barred the iron-studded door.

Their marriage bed was firmly bolted to the floor. Tall curtains walled the structure, like a castle's final redoubt. The floor was densely crowded with chests, canteens, cording, and overstuffed saddlebags.

Ugo sat on the bed and unlaced his narrow shoes. "Did I look all right tonight, dressed in this silly way?" he asked Agnes.

"You look born to it! The guests were very impressed." Agnes turned back the woolen covers on their stout wooden bed. "We did good business tonight."

"My darling, whatever is happening to us? Why must we abandon everything we built together? Even my father—a Crusader and a touring musician—never dragged himself around this round world like we must do."

Agnes wisely noted her weary husband's growing air of melancholic humor. "I'm glad we're going to Cyprus together!" she said brightly. "It's my good fortune as a bride to finally meet my husband's relatives."

"Well, our own son is there in Cyprus. When I think of all the trouble that little rascal caused us..." Ugo grunted. "Well, it all works out in the end, though, doesn't it? Our boy is a knight with the Queen of Jerusalem. And I will be her ambassador. And you, my dear: I will dress you in silks. That way, I won't mind being dressed like a popinjay."

"Turin was kind to us," said Agnes of Chambéry, "but Turin is no capital. Turin is just a pokey little roadside town." Agnes threw the kitchen cap from her ribboned braids, then bent and dug through a saddlebag, disgorging wax seals, official ribbons, embroidered pennants, and a diplomatic code book.

"The kitchen spices in Cyprus are even cheaper than the silk," Ugo grumbled. "You can have all the pepper you ever want."

"I always wore such pretty hats, when I served the Duchess Anna in Chambéry. And when we lived in Rome, Ugo! Well! Rome is the true Eternal Capital of this round world."

"Rome," nodded Ugo, slowly disrobing for bed. "Yes, to be young in Rome, and making such easy money from all those pious pilgrims... Will we ever be that happy again? No city is so holy as Rome. Except for Jerusalem, all overrun by Arabs. And Constantinople, all overrun by Turks."

Agnes turned and straightened. "Look."

Ugo was startled. "I'd forgotten you still had that."

"A great Roman witch helped me brew this potion," said Agnes, fondling the vial between her hands." When my Duchess Anna was a new bride, all blushing and fearful, just a foreign girl, I gave her half of this. She drank it, and she had eighteen children, Ugo. Eighteen royal heirs of her body. That's thanks to my wiles as a maid of the bedchamber—me! Agnes of Chambéry."

"No Queen of Jerusalem will ever drink that rubbish of yours! What if it's turned to vinegar?"

"Roman love magic never grows old. Anna drank of this potion, and Ludovico of Savoy loved Anna of Cyprus with an almighty love. He did everything to please Anna, until the day she died."

"It's a good thing you didn't feed Anna all of it."

"Maybe I was saving that for you," said Agnes slyly.

Ugo barked with laughter. "Don't fool with the bull, old woman! You might get the horn!"

Seeing his dark mood lifting, Agnes smiled sweetly. "Dearest husband, the rule of your House is always law to me. And since I always honor and obey you, see what a fine reward I reap! I'll be a fine Crusader lady in the royal court of the Lusignans. Me, the daughter of merchants, in the court of the Queen of Jerusalem."

Ugo silently crossed his arms.

"Ugo, my parents never knew this world was round! My family had a pancake world, with mountains piled on it, haystacks, grapevines, turnip carts, old clothes, copper pennies, their rags and bones! But when we live in Nicosia Castle, then you'll see that, though my birth is lowly, I have a high soul!"

Ugo was listening, unmoved.

"No more hot, greasy kitchens for me! I'll be in delightful chapels every day, to sing your father's prettiest hymns! I'll be always in a state of grace, and devoted to the cause of Christendom."

"My dear," said Ugo, "although my father always sang about Crusading, and you always sang along—that is not how people live in Cyprus."

"I'm sure you haven't forgotten Jerusalem!"

"Never! I have never forgotten Jerusalem! No Cypriot ever can!" Ugo drew a silver chain from around his plump neck. "King Janus gave my father this holy medal with his own hands. 'Protect my daughter,' King Janus commanded him, 'sing your bold songs of Crusade, and rouse the martial Savoyards.'"

Ugo pulled the medallion chain through his soft, clerkly fingers. "What became of that royal command? What did 'Anna of Cyprus' do, once Anna was 'Anna of Savoy'? Anna ate tasty truffles! Anna wore pretty shoes!"

Agnes saw that her best efforts had failed to dispel his melancholy. She recognized defeat, and began to shriek from her own pent-up feelings. "My Anna was precious to me! My Anna was a beautiful, gracious, courteous lady! It's the Savoyards who are worthless! They're slow, they're stupid. The men of Savoy are iron men with iron heads!"

"Well, my Cypriots have no iron left at all! They're not holy Crusaders, they lie like Greeks and they cheat like Moslems! The way Carlotta and her husband carry on, the world will soon forget that Cyprus is even French!"

Agnes sighed. "Oh Ugo, after all these years among us, you still don't understand us."

"Oh yes I do. I know you Savoyards better than you do yourselves. My father brought me here to help rouse a Crusade. To rally an army of chaste and stern Christian knights! But Anna, once she blinked her pretty eyes, and charmed her duke... He would hear no more music but love songs."

"Husband," said Agnes, "Pope Felix and his Holy Knights of Saint Maurice adored your father's music. Your father was the soul of poetry for a Pope and his Knightly Order."

"It's true—but that Pope was dethroned. That Knightly Order never set sail for the Holy Land. My father died in a monk's robes. The failings of this sinful round world are hard to bear."

Agnes crossed herself. "Ugo, no one ever helps us but our own blood kinfolk."

Ugo silently put on his nightcap and climbed under the bed's thick quilt.

"Except of course for my dear Saint Cleopha, who answers my prayers. And the Holy Virgin helps me greatly, and also my name saint, Saint Agnes. Also, Saint Helena, she who found the Holy Cross and is the patroness of innkeepers. I feel especially close to dear Saint Helena, for reasons you know. Did you buy those holy candles like I said?"

"I forgot," said Ugo.

"Ugo, listen to me now. The son I bore you is in Cyprus. Our Amedeo is a Crusader knight, with sword and spurs. The Queen of Jerusalem is his own liege lady. Are we not pilgrims too? Didn't we take our vows? The Rule of the Road is our Rule now. We sold everything we could, we have no House."

Ugo's mouth tightened. "It is just as you say, my dear."

Agnes rose from bed and blew out the candle.

III

Constable Higgins was the terror of Turin's southern gate, where he snatched apples from the peasant baskets and smacked gypsies with his fists. Higgins was an Englishman by birth, a free lance, barrel-chested, red-haired, and bristle-bearded. Higgins wore squeaking, rust-speckled chain mail and a fierce helmet with an iron strip broader than his big nose.

As his constabulary staff of office, Higgins brandished a halberd. The crooked head of this weapon combined a slashing axe blade, an armor-piercing spike, and a horse-gutting hook.

Constable Higgins firmly controlled the busiest gate into Turin. However, the fearsome Englishman had three weaknesses: bribery, flattery, and the appalling creature he called "Mrs. Higgins." This tiny Turinese streetwalker had been picking rags before the English mercenary had attacked her town. She had captured Higgins in combat, put a ring through his nose, and ridden him to respectability.

"Egenz, how many years have you and I been in business together?" Ugo asked him.

Higgins leaned his halberd-staff on his shoulder and squinted at his ten spread fingers. "Well sir, I first took my guard pay at this gate from Perrin of Antioch, for he was the Vicar of Turin, back in those days…"

"It's been fourteen years, Egenz. That is the sum." Ugo wound himself up for a courteous declamation. "As it happens, that same fourteen years ago, Jean, the Count of Burgundy—do you remember him, how he was about red wine? Notorious! Count Jean shipped a lot of fine wine through Turin. But not all of it reached his castle."

Ugo handed over a wicker basket, crowded with dusty, nameless bottles scrounged from his basement's dampest corners. "In going through my cellars just now—for we're leaving for Cyprus, you know—I came across this grand old vintage of the count's. At once, I thought—these bottles have been here in Turin just as long as dear old Egenz! And so, this wine should be yours, my friend. To your good health, many years more."

Higgins flushed with pride. "Signor de Balliand, why, that is such a courtly kindness! I don't know what to say to such largesse."

"I know you're more of a beer man, yourself."

"No, no, I'm sure me and Mrs. Higgins can find some use for this wine."

"On the subject of women," continued Ugo smoothly, "my dear wife also has a keepsake to offer. You may know that our late Duchess Anna of Cyprus was quite the lady for fine clothes, and my wife was once her chambermaid." Ugo plucked a crumbling wad of cloth from within his sleeve.

"My word!" cried Higgins. "I've never touched the like of this." The lace lay on his scarred, enormous fingers like a cobweb.

"Of course your own wife can't wear the lace of a duchess—that's unseemly, it's above her station. But let me give you a hint here." Ugo winked. "Have the little woman stitch that lace to certain garments underneath—those dainty ones, that only a husband sees. Do you know what I mean?"

Comprehension dawned on the Englishman's ruddy face. "What a clever thing! Why, that's wonderful."

"She'll love you for it, Egenz. Women are like that."

Glancing from portcullis to drawbridge, Higgins hastily stuffed the lace under the dense metal knitting of his mail shirt. "Signor de Balliand…

You're a gentleman. In all our years here—fourteen?—you never did me one bad turn. I can't say that for any Italian."

"You have also been 'fair and square' to me, Egenz. I am Cypriot—as you are English—but it's thanks to the likes of you and me that Turin is what it is, these days."

Constable Higgins weighed this complicated thought in his head for a while. Then he spoke. "I know why you must go back to Cyprus."

Ugo gazed up into the towering mercenary's ruddy, bearded face. "So, what have you heard, my friend?"

"Oh, I can't stand guard at a gate as busy as this one and not hear a few things."

"You can be frank with me, Egenz. We're both men of the round world. I won't take offense."

"Your Queen Carlotta threw her Savoyard husband out of her palace in Cyprus. Carlotta, the Queen of Jerusalem, has no husband, and no heir to offer her people."

"She did that. It's true. That was a misfortune."

"Her bastard brother James is making a play for her throne."

"Then you've heard about the family quarrel," said Ugo lightly. "We hope we can patch that up. The wife and I, we're a Cypriot and a Savoyard, and we're as happily married as two little doves."

"If James the Bastard is hiring men the likes of me, then it's no woman's quarrel. It's a war in Cyprus, sir."

"James the Bastard is hiring free lances from as far away as Turin?"

"To tell you the whole truth about that, sir, James wants to hire away all the fighters who might back his sister. You see, us free lances know the world is round. Because we march all over this world, with fire and with sword."

"You wouldn't take the coin of some Cypriot bastard, would you, Egenz?"

"My road home is a longer road than yours," said Higgins. "If not for Mrs. Higgins and my little ones, I might go to your Cyprus, or to my England. But I never will. Turin will bury me here."

Ugo touched his heart below his buttoned brown *farsetto*. "I only wish I could have done more for you, here in your Turin."

A tender look stole across Higgins's features. "I'll surely miss that mignon steak of yours. Never ate a better cut of beef, even in London."

"Egenz, sometimes, at the Inn of Cleopha, we sheltered pilgrims who were…odd. There have been certain incidents. You always smoothed those things over for us. I'm truly grateful."

Higgins put one finger to his bearded lips. "If it weren't for trouble, I would never get paid, sir."

"No more hard feelings here about the siege of '48?"

Higgins turned his back to his gateway towers. He gazed solemnly up the boulevard that he guarded.

The street that Higgins controlled was built on an ancient Roman roadbed, much of its flagstone still visible, though overlaid with rubble, cobbles, goat droppings, weeds, rags—and, as one lifted the eye—lines of laundry, roof-thatches, great twiggy storks' nests, church steeples, and clouds of crows.

"The good people of this fine city," said Higgins, gazing at his clientele of grocers, cartwrights, and apothecaries, "they never speak of those bad days to me. They trust me to defend their gate. I protect them from every breed of foreigner. Their city is old, and who remembers those foreigners? Us? The sweepings of the road? We come and we go as God wills."

Ugo sighed and crossed himself. "That is well said, Egenz! Then this must be our last farewell."

"I remember one other small thing now, sir." Higgins opened the drawstring bag on his studded belt. "A vagrant came by my gate yesterday. He tried to pass me by here, as if he were one of your guests. Look what he gave to me, in his token of passing."

Ugo examined the disk. Face and reverse, the round medal bore the two hemispheres of the world. Half of the world was rather well rendered. The shadowy half of the token was mostly fantastic.

The passage token was made from chiseled wood and painted a vulgar yellow.

Ugo sighed and tucked the forgery into his coin purse. "Egenz, this is why people can't have nice things. This saddens me."

"That rascal was a Pied Piper, sir. Clad all in parti-color. He said that he knew you. He said you were waiting for him."

"Yes. The wretch has come here to bargain with us. He's turning up for our last days here in Turin, like a bad penny." Ugo shook his head. "I heard they'd hanged him in France, but I should have known better."

"Should I have let that Piper through to see you last night, sir?"

"If he comes again, let him through," said Ugo, "because he is family. But it wouldn't hurt my feelings if you found some pretext to give him a few good wallops."

"Consider that errand done, sir."

Ugo reached up and solemnly clapped the Englishman's rusty iron shoulder.

IV

The Tower of the Bulls was the tallest spire in Turin. Falcons nestled in its summit, and when the tempests struck its gargoyles they moaned aloud.

This slender clock tower cast its narrow shadow over a raucous scene of travel sales: souvenir badges, mosquito repellents, unguents for saddle sores, laxatives, cheap forged Papal pardons, dice, and venereal stimulants, all of this sold in a public tumult of shouting, sobbing, and begging.

As was their courteous custom, Ugo and Agnes saw off a group of guests from their inn. These travelers were joining a wagon caravan, bound west. The convoy's destination was holy Compostela, the final stronghold at the western rim of Christendom.

The brigandess was the caravan's chosen guide. Her husband was a notorious Alpine bandit. This green-clad fiend led a gang of forest bowmen scarcely better than beasts, wicked outlaws who robbed noble lords and fat bishops, and never set foot in a church.

However, the bandit's wife was a born Turinese, so her business sense had prevailed over her husband's voracity. Ugo and Agnes had often fed banquets to the bandit and his wife, while negotiating the protection payments.

The pilgrim caravan rattled away in a fading racket of shouts, snapping pennants, squeaking wheels, and clopping hooves. Ugo and Agnes returned to their shuttered and gloomy inn.

Deprived of its carpets, tapestries, and all the furniture, the Inn of Saint Cleopha was echoing, charmless, and deserted.

Ugo and Agnes retreated into the cellar, where they had arranged a last, halfhearted bargain sale of their final, dwindling possessions. Come morning, they themselves would join the eastern pilgrim caravan, bound for Venice and its shipping port to Cyprus.

The Inn of Saint Cleopha still sheltered a few die-hard world travelers. These eccentric foreigners simply had no other place to stay in Turin. The silk-clad eunuch Chinaman was far too odd a fellow to frequent the streets. So he lurked in the inn's basement, methodically eating Italian spaghetti. Spaghetti was one of the eunuch's few physical pleasures.

The morose Waldensian read his Scriptures by candlelight, while awaiting the overdue arrival of some fellow heretics. Protesting believers seeped through every border in Christendom: the Lollards and the Cathars, the Hussites, Utraquists and Wycliffites. They all smuggled vulgar Bibles, illegally printed in languages other than Latin. They paid well for shelter and silence.

The Serbian Ottoman had rented a corner of the cellar as his makeshift military workshop. This battle-scarred Serb was a servant of the Empress Mara Brankovic, the Slavic harem consort of the mighty Ottoman Emperor. Mara Brankovic numbered herself among the Sultan's famous "seven brides from seven nations." She maintained her own dark castle within the Great Turk's vast domains.

The Serb brought his mistress ingenious Italian weapons with which to slaughter her innumerable enemies, both foreign and domestic. He had bought a trebuchet in Turin, and was disguising this deadly engine as a harmless stack of lumber.

The Portuguese slave-dealer had sold off all his human wares to eager European noblemen. With that errand done, he was sorting, bottling, and labeling panaceas, to convey to the new-discovered isles he called "Cape Verde." Exotic pestilences ravaged the Portuguese colonies, so the slaver was packing his ivory chest with cantarion, willow bark, lac, and zedoary; aloes of every variety; quicksilver powder, cassia fistula, sal ammoniac, and lisciadro; cinnabar, cinnamon, galbanum, mastic, and sweet sugar pills of every size, shape, and color.

The learned Rector of the University of Turin was the wisest man in the town. He was waiting for Ugo and Agnes, at a cellar bench with a makeshift table made of emptied barrels.

Although born in Rome, the Rector had been an ardent follower of Felix the Anti-Pope. His loyalty had disgraced him, so Pope Pius in Rome had denied him his high position within the Vatican Library. The Rector had fled at once to Turin, and the fact that he'd not been poisoned, stabbed, or garroted in Rome proved that he was indeed a very wise man.

The Rector had long been the most faithful customer at the Inn of Saint Cleopha. As a university scholar and a beacon of the new learning, the Rector often interviewed the pilgrims at the inn. The Rector collected their anecdotes of travel as part of his labors on a vast, learned tome he called the *Cosmographia*. The subject of the Rector's book was the entire round world and everything in it.

"Books," the Rector told Agnes and Ugo, "are the only trade goods that speak to us across centuries, as well as vast distances. Therefore, books are of supreme value for my University of Turin. Once you are settled in Cyprus, when you see books that you might ship to me, I hope you will think of me, and the needs of my school."

"What kind of books do you want?" Agnes asked him.

"The best books are always the oldest books. I mean Greek, Latin, and Hebrew learning, which we Humanist scholars can revive. Anything written when Turin was *'Augusta Taurinorum.'*"

"Your university can have my cookbooks," said Agnes. "They're a bit stained with olive oil, but they're useful in the right hands."

"You are such a courteous soul, my dear," said the Rector. "But, well, let me show to you the kind of books that are prized by a scholar like myself. This precious book was brought to Savoy within the dowry of the Duchess Bonne of Berry."

In the shadowed brick cellar, which reeked of spilled wine and was haunted by fruit flies, the Rector produced a magnificent tome, bound in leather and hinged in iron. "This book was written and illuminated by Christine of Pisan, the wisest of all writing-womanhood. The learned Christine created this book for her most noble patroness, and its name is *The True Book of All Wrongs Done to Lettered Ladies*. Over many years, Christine of Pisan wrote letters to every corner of Christendom, collecting the tales of woe from women authors, from Ireland to Muscovy. It may seem a dismal thing to hear, but—not one of these female authors ever received her due fame!"

"That book is huge," Ugo remarked.

The Rector nodded his long-haired head. "There's one sad history among so many in this book—the story of your own Saint Cleopha. Cleopha wanted to write down her holy prophecies, about the Kings of Italy and Jerusalem. Yet Cleopha, like Joan of Arc, was never taught to write. So Cleopha could only listen to her angelic voices, and scream aloud!"

"I have heard her," said Agnes. "Cleopha often moans and cries, she slams the doors, she breaks the pots and glasses… Once, I saw her standing in the moonlight."

"Until her town of Turin becomes a capital city ruled by a Queen of Jerusalem, Saint Cleopha can never rest in peace. So—in her own Turinese way—Saint Cleopha is a martyr of the Crusades. She is a pilgrim martyr, though she never left this town, and scarcely left this nunnery."

Ugo gazed among the cellar's moving shadows. "It would take a miracle for that to happen."

"Yes, of course, but it's a miraculous prophecy."

Agnes was struggling to follow the professor's highly literate Roman Italian. "Carlotta of Cyprus is the Queen of Jerusalem. So Carlotta should read this book. Ugo, we should buy this. Let us take it to our new royal patroness. It will do her good."

The Rector was distinctly pleased with the idea—but Ugo shook his head. "Carlotta has no time to read ladies' books! The House of Lusignan is beset with her enemies."

The Rector replaced the book with a second book from his capacious scholar's bag. "This Cypriot volume recently came into my hands."

"Oh, by all the saints and angels!" said Ugo, eyes wide. "I haven't seen this book since I was a page boy."

"This is a music codex from the Court of King Janus in Nicosia," said the Rector. He opened the heavy tome with an expert's ease. "This codex was part of the dowry of the Princess Anne of Cyprus, she who became the Duchess Anna of Savoy through her marriage to our own Duke Ludovico. This is indeed a most valuable work: the *chaunts*, *rondeaux*, and *virelais* of the splendid court of French Cyprus. Not one song in this codex is known in any other book in this round world."

"My father so loved this precious book," said Ugo, choking up with grief. He placed a reverent hand on the book's stout cover. "I often saw him open it, but he never let me touch it."

The Rector nodded soberly. "This book was a most precious dowry gift, even for a most beloved, most beautiful princess."

"Then we must take it back to Cyprus!" said Agnes eagerly. "They would dance for joy to see this! What would you take for it in trade? Name us a price!"

"That can never happen," said the Rector. "This codex is the dowry possession of the Dukes of Savoy. Believe me, they will never surrender anything they take by marriage. We are fortunate to have this book in Turin. It's on a strict loan from the ducal library in Chambéry."

"My father's music book is safer here in Savoy than in Cyprus." Ugo stroked the codex gloomily. "Think of the precious treasures Cyprus has already lost! Stolen in pirate raids… Burned in peasant uprisings…"

Agnes looked on her husband in a mix of guilt and tenderness. "Oh, Ugo, don't take on so."

"The books we have lost in Cyprus, may God help us! When King Jean was trapped in his castle in Nicosia, Jean went mad and devoured his own library."

"What?" Agnes said. "Don't you say that! King Jean never did such a thing."

"He did. He most certainly did," said Ugo. "Jean of Cyprus went barking mad, just like Nebuchadnezzar. He ate the leather right off the book spines. His own wife fed him a Byzantine concoction, and poor King Jean lost all his senses."

"Ugo, don't bear false witness against the Queen Mother of Cyprus! Slander is a mortal sin!"

"Queen Helena is a Byzantine witch! She cut the nose right off the mother of James the Bastard. She snipped that woman's nose off and threw it to the palace dogs."

"I must apologize to you," said Agnes to the Rector. "My husband often suffers melancholy humor when he remembers his father and his homeland."

"These tales from Cyprus are quite interesting," said the Rector. "I should take notes."

Ugo roused himself. "What I said just now was not diplomatic. So please don't write that. It is unfit to write—although every troubadour in Europe sings about the quarrels of the House of Lusignan. Helena Paleologos, that evil woman! A jealous Greek, a wicked queen!"

"Those are all lies," said Agnes with dignity. "Wicked tongues also sang lies about my own Duchess Anna. My Anna was so lovely and precious, so generous and noble! I never heard my Anna say one bad word about her kinswoman, Queen Helena Paleologos! Anna was always kind to the Byzantines."

"When Byzantium fell to the Ottoman Turks," said the Rector, "the great, sacred libraries of Constantinople were looted and dispersed. Many hermetic tomes of ancient knowledge were in the care of Byzantium. We Italian Humanists have hunted these books for years. I have one of great interest here, to show you."

The professor produced a small, tattered notebook. This looted book was by far the meekest of the three books he bore. Its flakes of fading, ancient parchment had been glued onto a backing of linen, which itself had gone dark with time.

"I can't read one word of this little book," said Ugo, gently turning the pages.

"I acquired this book from our Serbian friend over there, that Ottoman arms merchant."

"Then is that language Serbian?"

"The book's cover is lettered in the Glagolitic alphabet of old Serbia," said the Rector, "but the pages are written in Aramaic. The Serb traded me this precious book, in exchange for some cheap book of military doodles by that da Vinci character. That artist boy you people once knew so well. That lad who used to lurk about Turin, planning his canal schemes."

"We knew that boy," nodded Ugo. "He was talented, but he had no morals. He ate like a horse every time he visited our inn. All painters are like that."

"This book has notes of provenance, written in Greek, here on its inner cover," the Rector pointed out. "These notes refer to Irina Kantakouzena, the Byzantine princess who once owned this book. She received it through her great ancestress, the Empress Helena, the mother of Constantine, the Saint of the Holy Cross."

Agnes was thrilled. "A holy book from Saint Helena! Saint Helena is my favorite saint of all the saints, Saint Cleopha excepted. Because Saint Helena was humble of birth, just like me, and she once kept an inn for travelers, just like me. How often Saint Helena pities my troubles and answers my prayers."

The Rector gave Agnes a tender smile. "As well as being an innkeeper, your own dear Saint Helena was also a great traveler. Helena was the first noble Christian pilgrim to ever visit the Holy Land."

Ugo spoke up. "The wise say that Helena, who was both a saint and a Roman empress, was also sacred to Turin. It was Saint Helena who bought the fragment of the Holy Cross that is concealed within this city."

"Not many know that," said the Rector. "Helena, the innkeeper, Saint, and Empress, was wise in the ways of travel. Saint Helena bought all the best bargains in the Holy Land. She bought the True Cross—and she also bought two of its nails. One nail for the helmet of her son Constantine, and another nail to shoe the hoof of his conquering warhorse."

"You are indeed the wisest man in Turin, Professor," said Ugo. "No other man in town is so well read in the hermetic esoterica."

"The Empress Helena bought the very dirt from the hill of Golgotha, which she gathered in straw baskets," said the Rector. "So, now, I ask you: Is it beyond reason to believe that Saint Helena, an empress, would also acquire this precious little travel book? A traveler's notebook—written by our Lord and Savior, Jesus Christ!"

"What?" said Ugo.

"This is Our Savior's travel diary of Palestine! It's a souvenir book of the Holy Land, written in our Savior's own hand."

Ugo glanced at his wife. Agnes did not meet his eyes. "That must indeed be quite a relic," Ugo murmured.

"Yes," mused the Rector, "among the many Apocrypha, this must be the book of all books."

"And," said Ugo delicately, "yet this apocryphal book came here, to this town, Turin, from Serbia, somehow?"

"Of course this book is Serbian! The Emperor Constantine was born in Nissus, and his mother Saint Helena was from Herzeg. Those are both Serbian cities."

Ugo ran his fingers over his balding pate and considered the gathering shadows of the cellar. "So, what is written in this travel book?"

"That's hard for me to say. Few people know that our Savior Jesus Christ spoke, and wrote, entirely in Aramaic. Few Biblical scholars can read Aramaic. Especially our Savior's rather obscure Nazarene Aramaic dialect. However, I have found a few Greek words written here in His notebook. Likely our Savior learned some Greek from the Greek traders in Sephoris."

"I've never heard of 'Sephoris,'" said Ugo.

"Sephoris is a town in Galilee. It's about as big as Turin. Our Savior was a man of the road, you see. He was a traveling preacher. This travel book of His seems to be mostly His travel lists and reminders. Names, places, prices for lodging and food... The customary notes for any traveler."

"Why are you telling us this?" Ugo said.

The Rector looked up mildly. "Well, surely you must know why I am telling you."

"It's that Shroud," said Ugo. "It's that Holy Shroud! Will we never live down that incident? When will people forget about that Shroud?"

Silence prevailed.

"This is outrageous," said Ugo. "That Shroud business was years ago. I refuse to discuss this."

"Maybe it's time to say something about the Shroud," Agnes offered. "After all, we are leaving Turin."

"Very well, then I will," said Ugo, his face reddening. "The Da Vinci kid invented the Shroud. He painted that Shroud like the Savior's burial cloth, then he sold it to that stupid Crusader widow. She's the one who sold it to Duchess Anna."

"I didn't say to tell him all that," Agnes said.

"He's the wisest man in Turin, he knows all about that already," scowled Ugo. "Listen, Professor! Don't believe the rumors about the Shroud! Anna of Cyprus never paid one penny for it. While I was in her service, Anna was kept on a budget, and she never ran up any debts."

Agnes nodded quickly. "That little old Crusader lady just needed some place to live! She had lived in this convent, but it was attacked and burned by free lances. My Anna was always generous to veterans of the Holy Land. So, the old lady took possession of a Savoy castle—it was just a small one—and Anna received the Holy Shroud. We took this wrecked convent and remade it an inn. No money ever changed hands! It was all a noble act of largesse, through the kindness and goodness of my Anna."

"I scarcely touched that Holy Shroud, myself," said Ugo. "I don't want to touch your holy notebook, either."

The Rector of the University of Turin laced his hands together and silently placed them in his lap.

"Maybe that Shroud truly is the Shroud of Christ," said Agnes. "The Vinci boy painted a face on it, but it was very old cloth. To paint a face on the Shroud, that doesn't mean that the cloth is not the Shroud. Isn't that so, Ugo?"

"Anne always loved the finest things," sighed Ugo, shifting where he sat. "Anne was such a pretty lady. Anne was a little headstrong, but such is the blood of the gallant House of Lusignan. Anne was a true Crusader Princess, she was of the blood royal, and if God did not approve of her Holy

Shroud, then God would not have favored her with eighteen children! Eighteen heirs of the body, that the good God gave to her!"

"The fruit of Anna's womb will be the Kings of Italy and Jerusalem," said Agnes. "Cleopha prophesied it, and I believe it."

The Rector mildly raised his ink-stained fingers. "Please don't take it so badly! I don't scold you about your Holy Shroud! I've seen the Shroud. All Christendom knows about it. Pope Felix blessed the Shroud himself, and we both know Felix was the true Pope and a great magus! My point is: what about this notebook?"

"What about your book?" said Ugo.

"You people have worldly experience in these matters of sacred goods! I'm merely a librarian! What am I to do with this, the handwritten testament of Jesus Christ, the Galilean traveler?"

"You're asking us for our advice about sacred relics?" said Ugo.

"Who else can I ask? That worthless new Pope in Rome? How dare he banish me from Rome, my own birthplace? He writes love poetry, that miserable scribbler! I'm a far better writer than the Pope is." The Rector bit his thumb in scorn.

Ugo sighed. "I know what you are thinking, Professor. You think that you should publish this book you found. Through your Humanist scholarship, the lost knowledge of antiquity will be reborn."

The Rector bowed his gray head. "Ugo de Balliand, you are a man of the round world. It's no wonder that the court of Chambéry made you their diplomat. Who can hide anything from you?"

"You can't hide sacred mysteries by printing books!" Ugo shouted. "Printing books! You stupid bastard, have you lost your mind? Are you a Doctor of the Church, you ink-stained wretch? Are you Ambrose, Augustine, Gregory, Jerome? Where is your Christian humility?"

"I know this must seem very wicked." The Rector inclined his gray head toward the Waldensian in the shadows. "I thought you might spare me that problem. You might simply buy this little Byzantine book from me—for your Crusader friends in Cyprus, perhaps? They're rich! I would ask a reasonable price!"

"It's a good thing that German printer has left us," said Ugo. "That rascal will print anything. Political posters—filthy woodcuts—we've barely escaped a catastrophe!"

The cellar resounded with a distant pounding.

"Saint Cleopha has heard us!" cried Agnes in a passion. "I knew Cleopha would be angry! Cleopha's holy shrine, become a dirty tannery! Oh, you bad men, what of your salvation? What have you done, what have you said?"

"That knocking you hear is no saint," said Ugo, rising from his bench. "That noise is the devil himself. I know that noise. There is no help for this. Because he is family." Ugo left the cellar and strode up the timeworn brick stairs.

"Well then," said the Rector, glancing from side to side. "Once again, it's just you and me, Agnes."

"Don't you start that with me, you rascal. I regret every moment I ever spent with you!"

"Please don't be like that, my sweet one! We're like Abelard and Heloise, you and me! We can't help what we became to one another."

"You and your fine Latin sonnets! You swore you were my spiritual friend in Plato! You promised you would never try my honor as a woman!"

"What happens in Rome, stays in Rome." The Rector leered.

"You men who read so much, how bad you men are! There is no end to your perfidy, you lustful, reading creatures."

"Oh, Agnes of Chambéry, have you no pity for me, you cold, gorgeous statue of marble? Think of all the days I sat there in your dining room, and not one word when you overcharged me for desserts! With your surpassing loveliness flaunted before me, is it any wonder that I never married? Even a Humanist is only human! This is your last day here in Turin! My darling, let us seize this precious moment!" The Rector leapt to his feet.

Agnes scrambled around the table. "Here in this dirty cellar? You must be mad! Help me, Saint Cleopha!"

Ugo trod down the steps with a new companion, a skinny man dressed in wild, tattered garments of red, blue, green, and yellow.

Agnes smoothed her skirts. "See who it is, here at last, to bid me farewell!" Her eyes widened in a deeper alarm. "Cousin, what have they done to you?"

The Pied Piper kissed Agnes on both her flaming cheeks. "The rich and powerful have attacked me," the troubadour croaked. "The corrupt were stung by the truth of my satirical verses."

"What?" blurted Agnes.

"Some ugly brute at the gate of Turin walloped me with his halberd."

"Oh, what a dirty shame! How low the hospitality of Turin has fallen! The most famous troubadour in all Paris, and you are maltreated this way? If my Duchess Anna were still alive, men would hang for this."

Ugo addressed the Rector. "Professor, this is my wife's cousin. Francesco is a roaming jongleur. Music is his trade."

"You're François Villon," the Rector concluded, tucking his trembling hands under his cloak. "Your poetic reputation proceeds you, sir."

"I'm not François Villon," said the Pied Piper. "I bailed Villon out of jail once, though." The Pied Piper rubbed at his swollen black eye. "It's good to see you, Agnes."

"Francesco, I am so glad and honored that you are a guest at my inn again, for one last time," Agnes said. "Can I feed you something?"

Through puffy lips, the Pied Piper blew off a trill on his wooden flute. "'She is so cheerful and charming,'" he sang. "'She is so courteous and pleasing, / For she always welcomes everyone.' Such is your nature, dear Agnes. You haven't changed one bit."

"I have some liniment and bandages in my travel bags upstairs. I'll see to your wounds, you poor man." Agnes fled up the cellar stairs.

The Pied Piper sat on the creaking bench. He rubbed the bruises under his motley, and set his tall belled cap on a wine barrel. "So, Cousin Ugo," he said. "Since they're finally chasing you out of old Turin, you must be selling off a lot of fine stuff."

Ugo sat. He pointedly poured himself a single cup of red wine. He set the cup on the cold stone floor, well out of the troubadour's reach. "Yes, Cousin, there are a few items left to me as yet," he said. "Although a wandering, viper-tongued gossip like yourself obviously lacks any means to buy them."

"I have some assets to offer you," the Pied Piper declared. "So. First of all, what's with that fat Chinese faggot over there, stuffing himself like a hog? Give me some of his noodles! I'm starving."

"The Inn of Saint Cleopha has never denied a hungry traveler of this round world," said Ugo with dignity. "We will maintain the Rule of our hostly tradition unto our last day. So—little though you deserve it—I'll get you a nice hot bowl from the kitchen."

V

Left alone together in the cellar gloom, the librarian and the troubadour gave one another the wary eye.

"So," said the Piper to the Rector, "to judge by your cloak and that square tassel-cap, you must be one of those clerkly, writing professors."

"Yes, I do write books," said the Rector. "I am engaged on a treatise on the mystic science of geography."

"My world is much rounder than any world in your books," said the troubadour, "because I walk on this world, and I sing about this world."

"Well, my book *Cosmographia* is an exemplar of the new, worldly learning. The universal subject of my book is everything that is in the world."

"An evil habit, writing. Writing ruins the natural memory, and makes one forget one's verses. Printing is even worse than writing, of course."

"Yes," said the Rector, "there are a number of learned books on the subject of how books damage the reader. In fact, I collect such books. Many books, all sizes, all languages. Both printed and in manuscript."

"'When wise men turn to folly, they surpass all fools, as the finest wine turns to the sourest vinegar,'" the Pied Piper quoted. "So—I hope you're not trying anything clever and sly against my dear cousin Ugo. He seemed no more pleased with you than he did with me."

"I am the guest of our host here, under his own roof! Heaven forfend that I should deceive him."

"Ugo's father taught me music," the Pied Piper said. "So I took to the road for my fortune. But my cousin Ugo, he who should be the troubadour... Why, Ugo became the worst bourgeois pinchpenny south of Switzerland. He is a rich Turinese!"

"Yes, he's a prosperous man, Ugo de Balliand," nodded the Rector. "Round of girth, a friend to the powerful."

"He made so much pelf in this inn that he sold his daughter to a nobleman. He gave her away at the altar, and now she's 'Ugolina di Guttuari, Baroness of Caselle.'" The troubadour set his tasseled cap in his lap and toyed with its rusty bells. "I saw that child in her diapers, and now I don't dare serenade her castle window."

The Pied Piper lunged sideways and gripped the glass neck of Ugo's wine bottle. He emptied a shot down his throat. When he heard Ugo's feet on the stairs, he set the bottle aside.

Ugo handed the Pied Piper a steaming bowl and a spoon. The musician made no bones about his eating.

Agnes arrived with her medicines. As she unrolled a linen bandage, she glared at the Rector so fiercely that the professor rose to his feet. "I regret that I must depart now," he said to Ugo, "but about that book."

"I thought about what you said," said Ugo. "There's no price for that in this round world. Burn the book."

"Your idea had also occurred to me."

"What good can such a book ever do? Your book is a lure and a snare! Into the pyre with the Apocrypha. Into the clarifying flames."

The Rector replaced his square, tasseled hat. With a bow, he gathered up his bag of books and took his leave.

"This is such wonderful spaghetti," said the troubadour. "Truly, Cousin Agnes, Cousin Ugo, all jests aside: you people have the best goddamned noodles in the whole round world."

Agnes helped the Pied Piper remove his motley coat, and lifted his threadbare shirt.

Ugo clicked his tongue over the stripes on the Piper's skinny ribs. "Why, that brute did beat you sorely, Cousin! If I were staying here in Turin— rather than departing for Cyprus tomorrow—I would surely plead your case with the local Vicar."

"Your city law only serves the interests of the fat and happy," snorted the Pied Piper. He spoon-scraped the dregs of his spaghetti bowl. "Since I am the poet of the common people, I know what the lowly folk know about politics… Ouch, Agnes, stop that."

"This ointment was personally blessed by Pope Felix the Fifth."

"That grease is sure to kill me, then. Can we speak privately down here? I don't like the look of that sour fellow, sitting over there. Who is he, reading his book all silently, in that candlelight?"

"Oh, that's our Waldensian," said Agnes. "He wouldn't harm a fly."

"One should never read the Bible," said the Piper. "One should listen to the Bible's verses sung aloud, since that's what verses are for." The Piper tapped the side of his head, which had been shaven for lice. "Now, my cousins, up here in my clever head, I brought some verses of great value for you. A new song from Cyprus."

"Where did you hear this song?" said Ugo.

"Songs are strange things," the Piper declared. "A song can fly around this round world like the wind! Since I have a good ear, and a good memory, I can acquire such a song—even from a man who doesn't want me to hear. James the Bastard will never know that you, his enemies, have heard his favorite song from me."

"All Christendom agrees," said Ugo sternly, "that Carlotta is the anointed sovereign of Cyprus and Jerusalem. Who serenades some bastard royal pretender?"

"Hungry men sing the bastard's song, and they fight for the bastard, too," said the Piper. "This war song of James tells his men that they fight for Cyprus—not for Rome or for Jerusalem. James will cast his Crusader sister, and her Savoy husband, both of them into the sea. Then the Cypriots will own their island themselves!"

Ugo was horrified. "Cyprus without Jerusalem? A travesty, disgusting, infamous! What would my father say? What could be worse?"

"I can tell you what's worse," said the Piper, grinning eagerly. "I know all about that."

"Don't tell him," Agnes urged.

"My cousin Ugo has become a diplomat! He needs to know the worst," said the Pied Piper. "To know the worst is always statecraft of the highest value."

"My husband needs more faith in his cause, not more of your knowledge," said Agnes.

"Oh, very well then, I'll tell you the worst for free," said the Piper merrily. "The new Pope Pius in Rome is devoted to the Crusades. He writes books, our Pope Pius, so he's quite a clever fellow. Now listen. The Pope persuaded the French to build a new Crusader war fleet. What happened then? A French prince seized the ships. Instead of sailing for the Holy Land, he attacked Naples! That is what the Cause of Christendom has come to."

"I know about that French misadventure," said Ugo. "That was a misunderstanding."

"Cousin, I sailed aboard one of those stolen Crusader boats," said the Piper. "Those free lances understood the truth better than you do. Roaming warriors, men of no nation, paid in silver coins, on a Holy Crusade to rob Italy! They laughed about that! They drank to it, they played their dice, gambled their coins, and they laughed."

Ugo's face grew red. "In times as dark as these, Armageddon must be at hand."

"I saw no sign of the Battle of Armageddon," shrugged the Piper. "I did see some nice little Italian battles, for pay and for war loot. Scarcely anyone was killed, except for the plundered common folk. Then, those free lances... Well, they had no more French pretender to buy Italian bread for them.

"Then they heard the song of the Pretender of Cyprus, James the Bastard—a song that names his friends and all his enemies, and promises great rewards."

Ugo leaned forward. "When did the free lances set sail for Cyprus?"

"Why do you ask me that, dear cousin?"

"Venetian ships to Cyprus are faster than any Neapolitan ship to Cyprus."

"If you trust the Venetians, yes, they are."

Agnes put away her bandages. "How clever you think you are, Francesco! Just because you entertained evil men, you think you should be evil yourself? Stop your boasting! We'll put a stop to those sins and crimes. Ugo, when he sings his stolen song from Cyprus, write down every word."

"I've packed my favorite pen," Ugo muttered.

"I already know what your song is about. It's treason plain and simple," said Agnes. Color rose to her face. "I loved Anna of Cyprus, my princess, my duchess! I loved her with my heart! When I think of those sinful wretches, scheming to harm Queen Carlotta, my Anna's own niece by blood—why, my own blood boils! How dare they? Those Judas creatures to the Cause of Christendom! What doom could such wretches deserve? They should be broken on wheels, torn limb from limb by horses!"

"Maintain your composure, my dear," said Ugo. "These matters of state are grave. Good men will die from this misadventure."

"Oh yes, you men, your wars, men, wars! Well, those wretches have gone too far this time, for they've roused the doughty wrath of Agnes of Chambéry!" Agnes panted for breath. "If this were Rome, I would know what to do." Agnes made a stirring motion over a pretended stewpot. "Those wretches would choke on their last sip of soup!"

"We are diplomats," Ugo said. "We are sent to Cyprus to reconcile the royal marriage."

"How useless you men are! Is my poor Carlotta to lose her throne because you make fine distinctions? Our own son may be killed at the side of the Queen of Jerusalem! Our own son, Amedeo, the fruit of my womb, murdered by treacherous fiends who mock the Holy Crusades!"

Ugo was overwhelmed. "That is just as you say, my dear. Whatever was I thinking? They're the abandoned of God! They should be poisoned like rats!" He blinked. "It's not too late to visit the town apothecary. We can buy ingredients before we leave Turin."

"Listen," confided the Piper, "if you people weren't family, I wouldn't tell you this. But you're not as smart as you think you are. I never yet met James the Bastard, but I have met women whose bodies he bought for a night. James is cruel. James has a king's blood in his veins, and James wants to rule. James would kill both of you. You're an innkeeper and a cook."

"My role as the Savoyard envoy to Cyprus is to make peace within a family. Peace between wife and husband, peace between brother and sister. They're all of the same blood. Carlotta's husband is her own cousin."

"Ugo, dear man, you are a fine fellow, you're not the smart one in our family, all right? I'm the smart one in our family, and that's why I'm penniless." The Pied Piper coughed, stretched his side, and winced at a broken rib.

"Someday," said Ugo, "one family will rule over every town, every county, every duchy in all Italy. The head of that family will be the Savoy King of Jerusalem."

"I don't know who told you that nonsense," said the Piper. "That is a strange dream."

"A saint has prophesied that," said Agnes.

"Well, that saint is not your friend. No saint ever sent you two people to Cyprus. The Savoyard court in Chambéry, they sent you to Cyprus. Because they want to be rid of Cyprus—and be rid of you, too."

Ugo turned to Agnes. "I told you so."

Agnes shook her head. "Oh, don't believe a word of it! What does a troubadour know of the court of Chambéry? No more than a stable boy."

"I always knew that must be the truth," Ugo groaned. "Why am I the ambassador? I keep an inn! We even had to pay our own way to Cyprus by selling our possessions! No wonder my father became a monk! Oh, I wish I were a monk myself."

"Well, that vow of poverty would solve the problem of your worldly goods," said the troubadour.

"You stop tormenting him, Francesco," said Agnes.

"I don't presume to give you people any advice!" said the Piper. "I'm as humble as a stable boy!"

Agnes crossed her arms. "Francesco, just sing your dirty song of treason! Sing your bad song about the traitors in Cyprus! Do you even know any such song? I swear I never saw such a rascal as you."

"Oh, I know the dirty songs of Cyprus, all right. That's why I don't want to see you die there, in that cold-blooded nest of royal serpents!" The Piper shivered. "You are my blood kin, and I must love you; so, listen to me, please. Leave for Cyprus tomorrow. Be good, be obedient, do as you are bid... Then, once you cross the border of Savoy, run for your very lives!"

"Your advice is stupid!'" said Agnes. "Where would we go?"

"Go to Rome. Jerusalem is a lost cause, but Rome is full of pilgrims. All roads lead to Rome. The pilgrims in Rome are always hungry. Go feed them. Start another inn."

"Why, I never heard of such a low, wicked scheme," said Agnes, scowling. "Ugo and I should flee to Rome and hide under the skirts of the Pope? We are respectable people! Our daughter is a countess!"

Ugo spoke up. "Well, once we managed a palazzo in Rome. Felix always said, he ate much better as a Roman Cardinal than he ever did as an Anti-Pope."

"Oh, Ugo, who would ever give us a palace in Rome? We're not royalty."

Ugo stirred restlessly. "We might find some way to be of service to the new Pope. Pope Pius is a much-traveled man. He's been as far away as Scotland."

"I've never been to Scotland," said the troubadour. "People say it's even farther than Jerusalem."

"When Felix died, Pope Pius granted me a private audience," said Ugo.

Agnes was startled. "The Pope confessed you? You never said that before."

"Well, it looked bad, so I kept my own counsel about it. But when I begged forgiveness on my knees, and expressed my contrition about serving an Anti-Pope, Pope Pius blessed me. He even said nice things to me about our Holy Shroud."

"Are you the people who sold that Holy Shroud?" said the Pied Piper. "I never heard about that! You, my own family? You sold the famous Shroud in Turin?"

"We transferred that fabric to the ducal court of Chambéry," Ugo corrected. "We never sold it. It was a real-estate arrangement."

The Piper was astonished. "What a story! I can't believe I've never heard a satirical song about that."

"Fine, Francesco, do your worst, make fun of us, sing what you please! We're notorious for the Shroud, but no one ever gets the story straight. It's so frustrating."

"You sold the Shroud of Turin? You got away with that, too? You weren't jailed, or banished, or burned for heresy? How did you manage that?"

"Francesco, stop gaping at us," said Ugo. "We're your own family."

The Piper thought for a while, and his face hardened. "Oh, well, that's easy enough for you to say, maestro," he whined. "What fine problems you rich Shroud people have! I never lived in any palace in Rome! Here I come to you, with my body broken by a pike-butt, and you people can't offer me a bed! Where is that Rule of the House you were always boasting about?"

"We are on holy pilgrimage to Cyprus now," said Agnes.

"That's just as she says," nodded Ugo. "We're not rascals who wear motley. We have become holy pilgrims. We swore a sacred vow."

"Fine, be rich, and be sacred, too! There's no shelter for me here! I'll just put my staff and my bag on my shoulder, and walk over the next hill, crippled and starving, piping my merry songs."

"You could come with us to Cyprus," said Agnes.

"No," said Ugo at once.

The Piper sighed. "How cruel you are, Cousin Ugo. You have a Rule, but when it suits your own advantage, you break it without a thought. Your conscience must hurt, at least sometimes."

"I liked you better wicked than pitiful," said Ugo to the troubadour. "Let's settle this now. We'll make a bargain, you and me. You sing to us that merry song you know so much about—the song of Cyprus full of treason and war. In return, you can stay below this roof. Alone, here in Turin. My House is all yours, Cousin. Until the tanners come here to throw you out."

"No doubt that's more than I deserve," said the Piper, rolling his good eye, and his blackened eye as well.

"I didn't finish what I had to say to you," Ugo said. "There are still curios and rubbish here that we could never sell to anybody. So they'll all have to go to the devil. That means you, you rascal. Sell our goods yourself, or burn them, eat them, whatever it is you tramps do. And mind you, this place is haunted. There's a saint in here, and she will break every door and window until the House of Savoy rules Jerusalem. So, Cousin, sing. Sing to us, and the famous Inn of Saint Cleopha is all yours."

VI

Ugo and Agnes awaited the eastern caravan at the plaza of the Tower of the Bulls. They wore stout pilgrim tunics of wool, and overcloaks marked with crosses, and broad-brimmed hats to bear many days of sun and rain. They carried pilgrim staves and scrip-bags.

With woe and sacrifice, they had reduced their possessions to the burdens of a single horse-drawn cart and three pack mules.

"Where is our caravan master?" said Ugo, glancing up at the iron arms of Turin's city clock.

"Henceforth the Lord will provide," said Agnes, rolling her blue eyes upward beneath her hat brim. "I'm fresh-confessed, I'm in a state of grace, I'm dressed in pilgrim gray, and I march in the cause of Jerusalem! If I die this very day, I will fly straight to heaven!"

Ugo removed his heavy pack and sat on it.

"Don't you sit on my relics," Agnes shouted, "that's sacrilege!"

"Woman, you will learn to save your strength," Ugo said. "We are pilgrims now, we are vagrants. We are homeless and roofless, on a hard road. Don't fuss like an old maid about your precious trinkets."

"Fine! Don't you blame me if you break that glass bottle with the spirit of Saint Cleopha in it."

"Never mind your bottled spirits. Take a last look at this city, for we will never see Turin again." Ugo raised his voice. "Off to Cyprus at last! Back to my own homeland! 'A golden sun, a silver moon, and a sea the color of wine!' In Cyprus, they'll feed us rice, lentils, chickpeas, figs, and all the spices of Araby..." Ugo patted his round belly. "We'll need a big feast, too, for we'll be thin as stray dogs when we get there."

"Oh Ugo, if I starve to death, marching on Crusade, and you bury me, I'll have to face Saint Cleopha in heaven. Then, what will I say to Cleopha. About you, sitting on her bottle of holy spirit with your big, fat buttocks?"

Ugo rose reluctantly. "The large buttocks of you women are made of much finer clay than those buttocks of us men, I suppose. When I become a monk, I'll be a Franciscan. The grandest of the poor, taking not one thought for the morrow. Crusaders shouldn't carry bottles and pots to the Promised Land. We should storm Jerusalem with fire and sword and kill every pagan in town."

"We have only three cooking pots, Ugo. And just two decent copper pans, and a little of that silver cutlery we saved from the estate of Pope Felix."

"That is not true, woman! Your saddlebags are stuffed with vain, girlish finery! Perfumes, potions, cosmetics, even Italian shoes!"

Agnes sighed patiently. "Ugo, you know that Carlotta must recapture the affection of her husband. That's what our embassy is all about. Carlotta must conceive and deliver an heir to her throne. Everything I bring to Cyprus is for that purpose. You don't think that I want lace underwear, do you?"

"My dear, I know that the wiles of women can make or break kingdoms. I know the dreadful truth," said Ugo. He squared his shoulders under his gray pilgrim's mantle. "You women! It's because Carlotta's loins are barren that Cyprus is torn in two!"

The eyes of Agnes welled up with hot tears. "You blame us women for your troubles? Why don't you speak of our own daughter, my dearest Ugolina?"

"Oh yes, our daughter the baroness," said Ugo, straightening and smiling. "See here, my dear, I've left one thing behind in Turin that gives me a proper pride. Ha! He who steals my purse steals trash, but I'll be the grandfather of a baron of Savoy! Ha ha! No matter what happens in Cyprus, they can't take that achievement from me."

"I've never seen my own grandson!" Agnes wailed. "I was scarcely allowed to attend my daughter's wedding! Why? Because I worked my fingers to the bone, that's why! I slaved for years in that scullery, and for what, just so that my mother's heart could be torn to shreds! We're leaving Turin forever and I'll never see my daughter's face again!"

"I never thought of it that way." Ugo gazed around the square of Turin as if seeing it his first time, rather than his last. "Of course I don't see much of the girl, because she belongs to another man now. But of all my kinfolk anywhere—in Savoy or Cyprus—my daughter Ugolina is the only one among us who is safe and happy! Ugolina wears silk, she eats venison with lark's tongues. She's a noblewoman! Why do you lament, Agnes? Our daughter's success is the grandest thing in my life!"

Attracted by their racket, a gypsy woman approached, brandishing her crooked broom. "Alms for me?"

"No, not from us, not anymore," Ugo decreed. "We fed you scraps from our inn's back door—even though you are a godless Egyptian creature who lacks any books, flags, or chivalry. Can't you see we've become holy pilgrims now, while you remain in Turin, begging like a nuisance? Go back to Egypt."

"One round loaf of bread for poor me?" coaxed the gypsy witch. "For the world is round."

Agnes crossed herself. "Old witch who wanders the roads of the round world, yes, I fed you. I did. With my own hands, through the Rule of my House, didn't I feed you? I let you sleep under my eaves, too. Well, I have no more House now. So avert your evil eye and let us leave Turin in peace."

"Charity is repaid by charity," said the gypsy, "and prophesy by prophesy. No caravan leaves Turin today. A caravan comes to Turin from Jerusalem."

"Jerusalem is in the hands of the Moslems, you ignorant creature!" Ugo shouted. "The Turk rules in Constantinople, and the sea is swarming with his corsairs! The Crusaders poison each other while the enemies of Our Savior advance on every side! Do you think you scare me with your cheap hedge-witch prophesies? The truth is ten times worse than a wretch like you can know!"

"The Queen of Jerusalem is come to Turin," said the gypsy, "she who enters through the secret gate of the dispossessed. You will meet your children at that gate. You bore five children, three are already in heaven. Yet two of them still walk the round world."

"I believe you," said Agnes at once.

"Very well," said Ugo, "Then I believe you, too. But listen to me, you old gypsy woman. Your magic powers are cheap, dishonest, and indecent powers—your lousy gypsy magic is downright filthy, because you can't even read the Scriptures, and—wait a moment, come back here, I haven't finished scolding you yet."

"Let her go," urged Agnes, "these are witch's doings. We must hurry at once to the southern gate."

"Must we do that, Agnes?"

"We must go, Ugo, it's prophesy."

"Then it's just as you say, my dear."

VII

The southern gate was the busiest of Turin's four gates, so the roadside just outside the city walls had prospered a bit. Though nakedly exposed to brigands and free lances, the little slum stood outside the Vicar's onerous city law.

Now the muddy paths of this ragged village splashed to the stamp of boots. The guardsmen of Turin poured from their iron gates. They used halberds, picks, even an improvised ram to smash the clustered shacks. Curious Turinese gathered on the drawbridge, observing the demolition.

Ugo and Agnes joined the watchers, and Ugo leaned jauntily on his pilgrim's staff. "Now this is a sight to see! Here we're leaving Turin forever, and finally the Vicar's dealing with these dirty shanties! Hot oil should fall on their heads, these idle beggars, these runaway villeins."

"We should pity the wretched of the earth," said Agnes, patting the pilgrim's cross stitched on her breast. "Where else are the poor to sleep? Those with no land must sleep somewhere."

"Why do you think Turin has these big gates, then? Into the moat with those dirty hovels! Any free-lance band could break up these shacks, and attack our town with the flaming wood!"

Constable Higgins was barking orders among his busy troops, so Ugo left the shadow of the archer turrets and sought him out.

Higgins was excited by the turn of events, yet as cordial as always. "Signor Balliand, couriers rode in at dawn and woke the Vicar. Foreign troops are approaching Turin! They bear a royal ensign!"

"But Egenz, that is very irregular. We were bound to leave Turin today, on the duke's own business, destined for Cyprus. That's all been arranged."

"No man leaves my town today! Every man-at-arms is called to duty. We're to smash up all this dirty clutter, and do the best we can to make my gate presentable to royalty."

Alarmed by the spreading rumors and the noise of demolition, the people of Turin ventured in little groups from their stony fortress. They tiptoed across the moat bridge into the suburban slum. Some hauled away the wicker chicken coops. Others salvaged the chipped and battered chamber pots and stole the old roof-tiles. The urge to loot a village was always contagious.

A commotion erupted when the crowd broke into a little bawdy house, scarcely more than a stable. Exposed to daylight, the half-dozen sinners fled shrieking in woe, to the fierce derision of the crowd.

Agnes lowered her hat brim and raised one hand before her eyes. "How dreadful! Not one day since I deserted Saint Cleopha's nunnery, and already I'm among fallen women!"

"These drabs will find new earnings soon enough," Ugo predicted. "A royal entourage is coming. Look at the dust on the road! I believe I see their spears and pennants!"

Agnes stared at the approaching cluster of cavalry. "Oh, my saints, my angels! Be still, my heart! Our own Ugolina is come to Turin, with all her men-at-arms!"

VIII

Although dusty with the ride from her castle, Ugolina, Baroness of Caselle, looked as pretty as a tapestry. The baroness rode a dappled gray mare, and the beast's fine green caparisons closely matched her own skirt, hat, and veil.

The Baron of Caselle offered his in-laws a curt nod. The nobleman was a square-jawed, silent, squint-eyed landowner of forty years. He wore leather breeches, a fur hat, and riding boots.

Ugolina gathered her green satins, hopped from her stately sidesaddle, and embraced her mother.

Agnes was stunned with delight. "Why is this happening? These must be tidings of great joy."

"Sir Amedeo is coming," said Ugolina, her face alight. "Sir Amedeo sent a scout from his army to warn me, and he asked me to meet him in Turin!"

"Sir Amedeo?"

"Yes, mamma. My brother is a knight banneret of Cyprus, don't you know that?"

"Yes, I know that," said Agnes, "but I never hear anyone say it! My son is a chevalier, and my daughter is a baroness. I never see either one of you. I must be the most fortunate of mothers! Thank you, Saint Cleopha!"

IX

Queen Carlotta's battered little host thundered across the drawbridge, between the archer towers and through the southern gate. The Queen of Jerusalem was swiftly mobbed by the population.

Seeing her Lusignan coat of arms, her blue-and-silver banners and her red riding habit, the confused Turinese mistook the young Queen of Jerusalem for her own aunt, the dead Duchess Anna of Cyprus. The Turinese loyally called out the name of their deceased liege lady, and the streets of Turin resounded with cries for a royal ghost.

Carlotta's men-at-arms were all refugees, beaten and expelled from Cyprus. Carlotta's royal loyalists had fled across oceans, marshes, rivers, plains, fields, and forests, all the way to Savoy.

The Queen had chosen Turin as their destination, for their captain and guide across the roads of Italy was Ugo's own son: Sir Amedeo de Balliand.

Turin's ruler, the Vicar, was a pious, dimwitted old bishop. He was baffled by the sudden apparition of a Queen of Jerusalem, leading a band of elite knights who were starving, filthy, angry, and heavily armed.

The Crusader invaders outnumbered the Vicar's own city guard. Their dialect of Cypriot French puzzled everyone.

Ugo de Balliand was the most prominent Cypriot in Turin. Naturally the Vicar's weak eyes turned to Ugo, so, in the emergency, Ugo found himself appointed Turin's own envoy to a Cypriot royal court in exile.

Ugo found that the invaders numbered eighty refugees in all, once he had head-counted all the Italian laundresses, ostlers, money-changers, thieves, pickpockets, and other camp followers that the noble Queen of Jerusalem had attracted in her tumbling flight.

There was nothing to do but return, with this entire small army, to the empty Inn of Saint Cleopha. The forlorn inn quickly became a Cypriot military encampment.

The only guest still within the inn was the Pied Piper. The Piper was lurking there on a heap of straw, shivering, sore, and swollen. However, when he found a fresh audience of embittered and hollow-eyed soldiers, the Piper was in his element.

He leapt from his sickbed like a man possessed. With shrieks of his flute, the Piper was soon singing campfire classics and performing minor acts of conjuration. The Cypriots, who adored music, were enchanted by him. They were too poor to pay him, but they laughed at all his dirty jokes.

Some of the refugee Cypriots had been grand lords of their island, but a month of hunger, danger, and exposure on the roads of a foreign land had cast aside all etiquette. The louse-bitten Cypriot marauders swiftly foraged three goats and two pigs from the streets of Turin. Ignoring the inn's emptied kitchen, they gutted and roasted the stolen animals on the dining room floor.

Agnes took the Queen of Jerusalem into her charge. Agnes had been an intimate servant of Anna of Cyprus, so she knew what to say to a great lady in grave distress.

Cajoling, flattering, offering a steady stream of proverbs, consolations, and bits of prayer, Agnes got the queen bolted safely away within the inn's strong room upstairs.

For his part, Ugo accompanied his son as the knight went to the stables to inspect the troop's horses.

Ugo and his son Amedeo had parted badly. As a teenage boy, Amedeo had been a sneering, skirt-chasing street-rough, the boss of a gang of local urchins, always tossing dice and flashing his dagger. Turin had seemed too small to contain a youth so wild, so through the kindness of Duchess Anna, Amedeo had been sent away to serve as a squire in Nicosia.

Eight years had passed since then, and Ugo gazed up into his son's scarred, bearded face. "You've grown, son. Did you eat well in Cyprus?"

"I ate, Dad. Never like mamma's home-cooked meals."

"You saw battle."

"I won my spurs," Amedeo grunted. "I am a banneret knight and a seneschal. For a little while there, I was the Earl of Peristerona. One of Carlotta's battlefield promotions."

"My own son, an earl in Cyprus!" Ugo marveled. "Peristerona is a beautiful village. Your grandfather was born there. He would have been so proud."

"Grandpa wouldn't have been proud to see us lose the war in Cyprus," said Amedeo. He unslung the heavy musket from across his armored back and leaned the firearm against a stable door. "Dad, talk some sense into this city guard of yours. Those fat Italians aren't fit to fight. If they don't stay out of my way, my knights will bash their fool heads in. We're hungry. Some of us are wounded. We've lost lands, brothers, titles, and honors. We're not in the best of humors."

"I understand you, son. We'll find your men good bread and beer. Dice and loose women, Turin's got plenty of all that. Count on me, my boy. Whatever I have is yours."

Queen Carlotta's soldiery had seized Ugo's cart and his pack mules. Whatever Ugo owned was already theirs.

"Make my courtly introduction to your liege lady," Ugo urged. "Allow me to present to her my diplomatic credentials from Chambéry. We can put things in order. Her troubles are grave, I can see that—but a Pope and a duchess have both trusted their business affairs to me. The Queen will need a secretary, a banker, a good line of credit…"

"We didn't pay our way to get here," Amedeo said.

"Son, you people are Crusaders! You can't just burn and hack your way across Italy as if you were mere Englishmen! Savoy is the homeland of your best allies! So, tell me: Where is Queen Carlotta's royal consort, Louis of Savoy, the Count of Geneva?"

"Oh yes," said Amedeo, "that boy from Geneva. Well, the valiant count fled back to the peace and safety of his Switzerland. Once James the Bastard swore to kill him, he showed us a clean pair of heels."

"A Savoyard knight fled from combat?" said Ugo, putting his hand to his heart.

"Dad, Louis fled from his own soup bowl. He knows what happened to Carlotta's first husband—he spat up blood and died at a banquet. Louis is a mother's boy. He should sing in a papal choir. James the Bastard is no mother's boy. The mother of James the Bastard has a hole in her face where she should have a nose."

Sir Amedeo scratched a flea bite beneath his chased cuirass. Amedeo wore splendid armor, the gear of a court favorite. His greaves and baldric were grimy with road wear, but it was fine, knightly, girl-pleasing armor.

"Cyprus is a pit of scorpions," Amedeo said. He pulled a blood-caked rag from the wounded fetlock of a stallion. "We Savoyards can't save those wretched people. All we can do is love them. Love them, admire them, adore them, and devote our lives to them. Serve them with every courtesy, as cavaliers."

"That's a very noble thing you just said, son. It's knightly and genteel. Your grandfather often sang about that." Ugo nodded his head. "So, then: Who is the liege lady?"

Amedeo set aside his plumed helmet. "I could never hide my romances from you, Dad."

"Tell me you're not in that same girl trouble that you were when you left here."

"Dad, she is not with child. All right? She has no heir of the body, she is not that lucky. You just saw my liege lady. She rode here under her blue-and-silver flag."

"Your mistress is the Queen of Jerusalem?"

"Don't yell about it! I could hang for it, if I don't get cut to pieces first. Yes, I am Carlotta's courtly lover. I am more than just 'courtly.' Carlotta had two husbands, all right? Carlotta knows her way around a bedroom."

"You're not even the queen's chaste lover? You don't write verses?"

"I hate poetry! I kill men with guns, I'm not some goddamned troubadour! Carlotta is the woman in my life. I adore Carlotta body and soul. She's pretty and she's noble in spirit, but Dad, she couldn't rule a closet full of brooms. She's a disaster."

"Here in Savoy, the plan was that her Savoyard husband would rule in Carlotta's name."

"Her husband can't rule anything, either. He was born a sissy, and he doesn't understand the country. Carlotta had everything. She had the best weapons, the best castles, all the richest lords of Cyprus vowed their fealty to her. Then the peasants rose up, the poor and the landless... They made a cause with James the Bastard and they set the fields and forests on fire. Free lances sailed in from Italy. We lost Famagusta, then we lost Nicosia. We had to call for help from the Venetian Navy."

"What? You trusted the Venetians? Them? The Venetians are a republic, son!"

"I know all about the goddamned republican Venetians! Don't think I didn't warn her! The Venetian embassy threw her a masquerade party. All Carlotta's noble courtiers were in the Venetian palace, singing love songs and eating sugar cookies."

Amedeo kicked a clod of horse dung from the stall. "While they were swanning around in their silks," he said, "Moslem corsairs landed. The pirates seized the embassy, took hostages, and sailed away."

Ugo clutched at the horse stall to keep his knees from buckling.

"James arranged that, of course," said Amedeo. "James knows those Moslems like brothers. In our better days, whenever Carlotta ran up her debts, James and I would take warships and raid the coast of Egypt. We'd seize rich merchandise, maybe catch some rich merchants, then sell them back for ransom. That's how I got this scar."

Amedeo ran his mailed hand over the puckered ridge through his hairline. "When we caught a prize at sea," he said, "James had to arrange the ransoms. James had to trade the prisoners...because James was the Bastard of Lusignan. The Bastard had to do all the family's dirty work."

"Someone has to talk to foreigners," said Ugo guiltily.

"Well, James is a bastard. He's half-French, half-Greek, half-Moslem, and all Cypriot. It was his masterstroke of deviltry to hire the Moslems to abduct the Crusaders. The civil war in Cyprus ended right there. James is the only man who can buy those rich idiots back from their chains in Egypt. He's offering bargain prices for his friends."

"Then James stole the Kingdom of Cyprus."

"Cyprus loved him for stealing Cyprus. Cyprus wanted to be stolen. They kiss the feet of His Royal Highness, King James of Cyprus. Carlotta is no one in Cyprus. The 'Queen of Jerusalem.' She has no homeland, no throne, no husband, no heir, and as for her army, well, here we are. We're in Italy." Amedeo shrugged. "You are our host, Dad. Thanks for your hospitality."

"Carlotta is still the anointed Queen of Jerusalem."

"Dad, Carlotta has never seen Jerusalem. Jerusalem is owned by Arabs, her mortal enemies. And Dad—you will never see Cyprus again. I'm so sorry to tell you that. But you must never, ever go home, because King James of Cyprus will kill me, and anyone in my family. James told me that to my own face. James wouldn't lie to me. We were army comrades."

Ugo and his son were silent together for a good while. They devoted their attention to the horses, which were footsore, flyblown, gaunt, and in need of much care.

"Son," said Ugo at last. "We will have to carry on with the cause."

"I don't see how. Carlotta trusted men that only a fool of a woman would trust. Carlotta can't rule Cyprus. She will never rule Jerusalem. Carlotta will have to be sheltered for the rest of her life."

"Then we will shelter her."

"Who, Dad?"

"The family. Us. Me, you, your mother. Your sister, if she can help us." Ugo stroked his chin. "The road has brought strange curios to Turin. I gained some and I lost some, but now my House has a Queen of Jerusalem beneath its roof! A royal Crusader monarch is at my table! If I fail a business opportunity as grand as this one, I deserve to be hanged."

"Dad, you don't know my Carlotta. Carlotta is a Lusignan. The weird serpent-witch Melusine was the mother of all Lusignan women, and... Wait! Who approaches us? What fine lady leads her steed into our stables?"

Ugolina draped her mare's green satin reins over her tightly gloved hand. "Do I have the honor," she said liltingly, "of addressing the Signor Amedeo de Balliand, the noble Earl of Peristerona?"

"The honor is mine entirely!" said Amedeo, deftly dipping an armored knee. "I crave the boon of touching the hand of her grace the Baroness of Caselle."

Ugolina removed her riding glove and extended pale fingers that never did a task more difficult than needlework. "Dearest brother, let me present you unto His Grace, my lord and master: Camillo, Baron of Caselle and Viscount of Bra."

The Baron of Caselle brusquely knocked his old fur hat against his leather trousers. "Fine battle horses," he said to Amedeo.

"Yes, Your Grace," said Amedeo. "They're of Arabian breed."

"They need oats," grunted the baron. "Pray bring your steeds to my pastures. We have boar hunting on my estate. Falconry, too. Bring Her Highness, your liege lady. If Her Majesty pleases."

"Your Grace is the soul of courtesy."

The Baron of Caselle strode through the stables of the inn, whistling through his stained teeth and patting horses on their hindquarters.

"My happiness will be complete," said Ugolina, "when my knightly brother, the seneschal of the Queen of Jerusalem, visits me in my own demesne. There he can meet his nephew, the young master Bartolomeo, who is the heir of Caselle."

Amedeo stretched out one mailed hand to his side. "Sister, you were only this big when we had to part. You got married, and you had a baby! Good for you, little sister! May God bless you."

"Your nephew is no baby! Wait till you see him. He can walk and talk now, he's good and strong."

"My nephew must indeed possess a noble mien. All lesser tots are like candle sparks next to a star."

Ugolina dimpled. "It's so sweet to hear you quoting our grandpa's old songs! It's as if you never left us! Amedeo, was that a gun I saw you carry?"

Amedeo promptly fetched his firearm and displayed it. "Sis, gaze in wonderment at this my battle musket. It fires lead pellets with Chinese blasting powder. It'll knock a hole through plate armor that's as big as your tot's little fist."

Ugolina gazed at her brother adoringly. "You never change! Behind that beard, you're just the same!"

"Sis, I can talk your courtly rhetoric just as long as you want to hear it, because I learned it from the best there is…" Amedeo set his musket down. "But, well, I left you as some scrawny girl chopping weeds in a house garden, and you're a beautiful Italian lady! You are gorgeous, from your hat to your shoes! I never change, but you're completely different!"

"Oh Amedeo, dearest and only brother, I'm so glad you're back from that miserable foreign snake pit of pilgrims! It's so good that you are home again, alive and safe! Italy is wonderful now! Italy is the wonder of the whole round world."

X

Behind the iron-bound door of the strong room, the din of Carlotta's little desperado army faded to a murmur.

"Your Majesty will forgive the disarray in here," said Agnes. "Truth to tell, we sold all our furnishings, because we were coming to your royal court! But I do have some good supplies in my saddlebags, and I've sent my daughter out shopping—Ugolina's good at that. So this inn will never be your palace, but this will be as good a room as Turin can offer to anyone."

"Does this room have a chamber pot?" moaned the Queen of Jerusalem.

"Right away!"

When Agnes tactfully returned again, the Queen of Jerusalem was more composed. She had removed her riding cloak and gloves, and unpinned her flowing blonde hair.

"We appreciate the promptness of your services," said the queen, in her quirky yet stately Cypriot French. "Now We command you: tell Us your name."

"I am Agnes of Chambéry, Your Majesty."

"Oh, then it's you!" said the Queen of Jerusalem. "You sold the burial Shroud of Christ to Our aunt, Duchess Anna! You were Anna's court witch."

"I don't practice any witchcraft. I'm a good Catholic."

"Your son told Us that you brew many philters and potions."

Agnes laughed merrily. "Oh, Your Majesty! Any cook who can make a decent gravy can make a potion. But, yes, I was bringing you a few precious drafts in my bottles—just as I did for dear Anna. My Anna needed her tonics, the dear duchess, taken to childbed so many times. I was always there for Anna, at her lyings-in. She trusted no other."

"You were the servant of the Savoy Anti-Pope. He had great hermetic knowledge."

"Dear Pope Felix was a Christian hermit! Of course a great hermit had 'great hermetic knowledge.'"

"We have never been to Savoy before," said the queen. "The lords of your misty mountains are notorious for their magic. Everyone in Cyprus knows that the Savoy dukes are a race of wizards."

"Your Majesty, I have been the hostess to many travelers, from many lands. Travel tales grow with the distance. Yes, there is some magic in Turin. Of course there is magic here. It doesn't compare to the magic of the Holy Land. Many faiths worship your noble city of Jerusalem, and the holy water of the River Jordan brings salvation."

"We would not know that, for We have never been to Jerusalem," said the Queen of Jerusalem. Pale with weariness, she sat on the bare wooden slats of the strong room's empty bed. The marriage bed had remained within the Inn of Saint Cleopha, for it was made of heavy timber and bolted to the stone floor.

"Your Majesty—you poor lady! Your trials would weary a martyr!" Agnes busied herself at her saddlebags, and retrieved three glass bottles bedded in straw. She set the bottles at the feet of the Queen, then plucked one up. "Your Majesty, this essence is a sovereign remedy for the melancholy humor. You should try this."

"You want Us to drink that?" said the Queen of Jerusalem.

"This is most efficacious!" said Agnes. "This quintessence of al-Chemistry is called al-Cohol. It is a bottled spirit. Shall I open it for you? It works wonders."

"Open that and pour a glass of it at once," the queen commanded.

Agnes hastened to obey. She had no drinking glasses in her pilgrim's baggage, but she found a stout iron travel cup.

"Your Majesty," Agnes chattered, decanting the quintessence with care, "this bottled spirit was always meant as our gift unto you. My husband was appointed your ambassador. We were leaving Turin to join your court, this very day."

"Now drink that yourself," said the queen, her face leaden. "Drink it carefully, where We can see you swallow it."

Agnes sipped the spirit down and wiped her lips. "I would drink spirit every day, if I had it to spare, and my husband would let me." She patted her bosom. "How it warms a woman's heart!"

The Queen of Jerusalem drew an alabaster vial from her sleeve of green silk brocade. "For thirty-two days," she said, "We have thought to drink this potion. This was the last gift from Our mother, Queen Helena Paleologos. This is a venom more deadly than the asp of Cleopatra. As a queen without a throne, We wanted to make an end of Ourself."

"Your mother gave you that dreadful thing?"

"Yes, that was our mamma."

"Put that down at once. No, give that to me. Right now, hand that over." Agnes tucked the lethal vial behind the sturdy laces of her gamurra dress. "Young lady, there won't be any making an end of yourself under my roof."

"Agnes, We are so very tired and weary."

"Drink this tonic, then." Agnes filled the iron cup. "Your Majesty, I am a woman of modest birth. I've forgotten half my fine Chambéry court talk, and I can barely write my own name. But I was the chambermaid of Anna of Cyprus, the finest lady Savoy ever saw. I can take good care of you. I can sew, I can clean fine clothes, I can fix a lady's hair, and I can throw a shroud over a lady's secrets. Because I knew my Anna's secrets— and I kept them for her."

"Did she have many secrets?" The Queen of Jerusalem daintily sipped from the iron mug.

"Fewer than people say. When you're a pretty woman in Italy, sometimes the men are insistent. Those indiscretions were just accidents, really."

"This al-Cohol is very good," said the Queen. "Is al-Cohol Arabic, with a name like that? The Arabs don't drink wine."

"Arabs are men. Men drink. I've seen Arabs drink in my inn," said Agnes. "No matter what men say about their rules, men are the same all over the round world. I married a Cypriot. At first, it was strange to be married to a foreign boy. I was innocent. But when I became a mother, I grew wise. I no longer heeded what my husband told me to do. I just gave him what he wanted, not what he said. Ever since then, my Ugo has been happy as pie."

"We married two foreign men," groaned the Queen of Jerusalem. "We married Prince Juan of Portugal when We were twelve. He died of poison. When We were fifteen, they made Us marry Count Louis of Savoy. We don't know which man was worse."

"Royalty always marries foreigners," Agnes counseled. "But men are the same at every court. You should see the papal court in Rome, where the men don't even marry! Those cardinals in their red hats are ten times as wicked as men who have wives."

"We have never been to the Pope's great and holy city of Rome."

"Rome is wonderful. All the roads lead there. Rome is the eternal capital of the round world."

"I wish We could venture in state to Rome, and not flee to Savoy. We have never left Cyprus before. We have never seen holy Rome, or holy Jerusalem. We are the Princess of Antioch, and never saw Antioch. We are the Princess of Armenia, and never met one Armenian."

"The Armenians? When you need magic carpets, those are some very good businesspeople."

"Is the world round, Agnes?"

"Don't worry your head about that! I know it sounds crazy, but if you lose your way on the road, ask for directions! No man ever will."

"We need a bath. Our body stinks. We have fleas now. In Cyprus, We had a marble bathhouse with tripods of frankincense."

"You won't get that here, but I think Ugolina might find us a tub and a sponge."

The Queen of Jerusalem emptied the last drops of spirit from the mug. "Sir Amedeo, who is my bodyguard, is your son," she said.

"Yes?"

"Is that fat, bald innkeeper really Sir Amedeo's father?"

"Of course he is! What a question, what a scandal, and anyway they look just the same!"

"If they look the same, why are they so different?"

"Your Majesty, my Ugo is of melancholy humor. His son is choleric. When you get a little older, you will see the humors of men at one glance. They are simple creatures, men. To make them love you is not as hard as you think."

"Good Agnes of Chambéry, We fear for the life of your choleric son, for Amedeo is so brave and bold. I trusted him. Because he was from Savoy and honest, and not any Cypriot, or Greek, or Christian Syrian, or a Byzantine. So, one day, I was giving Amedeo his orders, to go pirate me some ships from Cairo…"

Color rose to the queen's plump face. She fell silent.

"You can tell me," Agnes urged.

"He just grabbed me. He smothered me with kisses and then had his way with me. I was so upset about that, that I wanted to have his arms, legs, and head cut off, but really, how could I tell him no, after that! I was so ashamed that I never even told my confessor. Now my confessor is killed. Will I go to hell, Agnes?"

Agnes quietly poured out another iron cup of spirit. "How many people know about this?"

"Well, not many who live. If they breathe one word against Our royal chastity, Amedeo challenges them to duels and he chops them to pieces. But of course all the common people know about it. They all sing songs that make fun of Us, their own liege lady, their queen."

The Queen of Jerusalem sipped from her iron cup while tears flowed down her cheeks. "Amedeo won't live long. No man can live around Us! Juan of Portugal died of venom, and that coward Louis ran home to Switzerland! Just because James threw a few severed heads over the castle wall in Kyrenia."

The Queen of Jerusalem set her empty cup aside and wrung her hands. "What a wretched woman We are! Our only babe was stillborn, and the midwife said that We will never bear an heir!" Carlotta looked up, shaking with her bitterness and shame. "We Lusignan women—we can't all be brood mares like your Anna."

Agnes wept. "Oh Carlotta, you are her very image. It's as if God has sent my Anna back to me. Look at me, dressed for pilgrimage to go to you, and here you are, come to my own arms! The Will of God is almighty."

Carlotta straightened her back. "We never ask God for anything. Except that Sir Amedeo should not be killed before We Ourselves are murdered."

Carlotta winced. Her tender stomach rumbled loudly behind her samite girdle. "We wish We had the courage to drink that bitter draft of poison! But it's Byzantine, and a very vengeful poison. It makes all your hair fall out and you die in agony bleeding from every pore."

"Those Byzantines knew their business," nodded Agnes. "A Byzantine guest brought us Greek Fire once, and it burned right through the floor."

"Our mother's empire fell to the Turks. The biggest Christian Church in the world is a mosque. Helena Paleologos went mad from the shame."

"My husband often speaks of Queen Helena Paleologos," said Agnes.

"Alas, We share a dismal fate with Our mother! She married a foreign Crusader, hoping Cyprus would aid her empire. We only raised the whirl-winds of the East against her people! The Ottoman Empire is vast beyond all measure, vast armies, vast fleets! My mother often prophesied: someday there will be Turks in Cyprus."

"There's no need to borrow trouble with dark fantasies," said Agnes kindly.

"Give Us some more of that tonic, Agnes. It really warms Us up inside."

"Let's wait until you eat something. Let me whip you up something tasty. I have my pots and pans in my baggage. Some pasta won't take me half an hour by the city clock."

"Then go and cook your strange foodstuffs," said the Queen, "and We will pour more potion for Ourselves. This is such a pretty bottle."

"Your Majesty, don't open that one!"

The Queen of Jerusalem removed the plug with a hollow pop. "Nothing in here?" she said, shaking the bottle and looking down its glass neck.

"That spirit bottle holds the spirit of a saint," said Agnes. "An astrologer put her in there for me. You should have seen him do that trick. It was a marvel, everyone watched."

"This bottle has a smell," the queen offered.

With a sparkling like bubbles in wine, a ghost appeared in the room.

"Are you the Queen of Jerusalem?" piped the ghost, in her Turinese dialect.

"What is this spirit saying to Us?" asked the queen, in her Cypriot French.

"Your Majesty, Saint Cleopha is speaking Piedmontese. I will translate. She asked if you were the Queen of Jerusalem."

"You have such a pretty name, Cleopha," said the Queen of Jerusalem to the ghost. "Our dead aunt, and Our dead sister, both bore that same sweet name that you do."

Saint Cleopha, who was small and modest, humbly said nothing.

"We command you to tell this holy spirit," said Carlotta, "that We are not the Queen of Jerusalem. We never entered that city. We never saw it, we never ruled it!" Carlotta put both hands to her face and began to sob. "We are a fraud! Men dressed me up, to cover their lies with a royal robe! I'm not the Queen of Jerusalem. In my heart, I'm not worthy. I am nothing but a miserable sinner." Carlotta bowed her head and wept in penitence.

"Your Majesty," piped the ghost, "I am Cleopha...the least of women...a nun, and a sinner, like you." Cleopha spread her thin little hands within her nun's rough gray drapery, which had gone all diaphanous with her death.

"I was never a saint, or a prophet either," Cleopha confessed in her own turn. "Just look at my shrine here—who would call this place a shrine? I'm just a teenage Turinese girl! They locked me up inside this dismal nunnery, where you can't even look at a boy, much less kiss one! Nothing in here but hard work and penance and prayer!"

The shade of the little saint drifted from side to side like a veil on a washing line. "No wonder I had fits, I had convulsions, and was possessed by the voices of angels... I surrendered my soul, I spat up blood and floated out of my bed, but any other girl in Turin would do the very same thing!"

"Oh Cleopha, don't be so hard on your sainted self!" said Agnes. "You said that the Queen of Jerusalem would rule from this city, and look, that came true, here she is, crying her eyes out."

"Did I say that?" wondered Cleopha. "I said all kinds of wishful things in my delirium."

"Tell this little maiden," said Carlotta, "that We don't rule her city. We can't even rule Our own city."

"Well, if you're a Queen and can't rule Turin, then you had better go somewhere else," counseled the saint.

"What Cleopha says is wise," said Agnes, who was interpreting for both parties. "We must all leave, none of us can stay. See, I wear my pilgrim robes, and I have vowed to go on holy travels. Turin is too small for a Crusader monarch. Even Cleopha can't stay, because the Turinese are turning her nunnery into a tannery. Sorry, Cleopha."

"Then I will forsake my glass cell," said Cleopha. She touched the lip of the bottle with one immaterial finger. The glass toppled and loudly smashed into bits. "Now," said Cleopha, commencing to fade, "my spirit will spread throughout this town. Whenever other Turinese girls suffer like I have suffered—young, restless, and bored to tears!—I will hear their prayers and sorrow for them like a sister."

"May God bless you, dear Cleopha."

"And you, too, Carlotta."

Cleopha seeped like a mist through the narrow, stony window. Agnes bent and gathered up the shards of broken bottle in her skirt.

"Cleopha always did that," Agnes explained. "Your Majesty, mind you don't step on those sharp bits."

The strong-room door shook with pounding. Agnes hastily put the shattered glass aside and unbolted the portal.

Ugolina swept into the room, together with four of her husband's mail-clad men-at-arms.

"May-God-preserve-Your-Majesty," Ugolina recited hastily, "we-crave-the-boon-of-entrance, and you there, yes you two, go set that chest of linens over there. You there, the tall one, put Her Majesty's new washtub in the corner. Who brought those roast pigeons and the goat cheese? There had better be six of those squabs in there, or I'll have your fingers off."

Ugolina set her fists on her satin hips. "Now, all of you, run straight back to your lord. And no fighting with Her Majesty's men-at-arms! Don't you even talk to those Cypriots! That will only lead to you boasting and drinking, then gambling, and then it will lead to some knife-work—yes, I'm looking at you, you rascal, you're not hiding anything from me. You scamper right along, or I'll have all four of you peeling turnips with the Caselle kitchen boys."

Visibly crestfallen, Ugolina's armed retainers crept away.

"You must be Amedeo's sister, for you look so much like him," said Carlotta.

Ugolina curtseyed deftly. "I have that honor, Your Majesty."

"Well, since you are only a baroness, We cannot call you Our 'sister.' But you are the sister of Our dear *cavaliere servente*, so let Us give unto you a token of Our favor." The Queen of Jerusalem searched distractedly among her varied rings and bracelets. "Wait," she said. "We have a fine enameled bracelet on Our foot. Unlace Our shoe and remove that for Us, Agnes."

Agnes knelt and deftly slipped the golden cuff from the queen's plump foot. "This looks Egyptian."

"It is Egyptian. It was pirate loot off some Mameluke felucca that Sir Amedeo robbed for Us on the high seas. Sir Amedeo always brought Us such pretty things from his voyages. We forgot this trinket was his gift, but all the better you should have it now, Baroness."

"Saints above," marveled Ugolina, "this pretty anklet looks fit for a sultan's concubine! I'll always treasure this Egyptian curio in Turin! Thank you for your kind largesse, Your Majesty."

"Where is Our seneschal, your brother?"

"Sir Amedeo is with my father. They are establishing a line of credit for you with the local Jews," said Ugolina. She waved a flowing sleeve at her purchases. "I bought Your Majesty a few things just now—things any lady would need, although they're scarcely worthy of your high station, of course."

Agnes examined the linens and the rolled straw mattress. She industriously set to making the bed.

Ugolina gazed from her mother to the queen, visibly torn between helping the one or the other. "Your Majesty," she finally blurted, "I must tell you this news at once. My lord and master, the baron my husband, knows that fast riders have gone off to Chambéry. When the Savoyard nobles, your cousins, learn that you are here in Turin, they will march to Turin with an army."

Shooed away by Agnes's bed-making, the Queen of Jerusalem stood in a wobbly fashion. "Well, We knew that the Savoyards would greet Us with an army."

"We did? I mean, you did?"

"The army of Savoy is Our only hope! We know they will try to arrest Us—or even reunite Us, against Our will, with my worthless husband Louis. But—We are still the Queen of Jerusalem. So if they are true Knights of Christendom, they must help Us! We will swear them into Our retinue. We will sail to Cyprus for a massive counterattack."

Agnes and Ugolina exchanged unhappy glances.

"Don't you two people look that way at each other," the queen commanded. "When Savoy gives Us every feudal man-at-arms, and also some money for warships, We can conquer Cyprus. These doughty Italian fighters are excellent soldiers. They will scatter James's rabble of peasants and free lances. We will hang all of them. Except Our royal brother James, who must die beheaded, as is proper."

Agnes and Ugolina were silent.

"As yet, you women do not know the whole of Our royal strategy," said the queen, weaving a bit on her one laced shoe and her bare foot. "When the Savoy soldiers come here to greet Us, We will confront them with powerful, magical relics! The Holy Shroud, which is the burial cloth of our Lord—and also, We will use the True Cross! The True Cross, discovered by Helena, the saint and empress, and the namesake of my own queenly mother, Helena Paleologos. The True Cross is hidden here in this city of Turin."

Agnes absently plumped up the bed's new bolster pillow. "Your Majesty must be hungry now."

"Let's all eat something tasty," Ugolina suggested. "The food stand in the Piazza Castello has the best squabs in town."

"Agnes of Chambéry," declared the queen, "as the woman who sold the Holy Shroud, you must know where the True Cross is hidden in Turin."

"Well, yes," Agnes said reluctantly, "of course I know where it's hidden."

"Once We bear the Shroud and the True Cross—two ancient relics of tremendous virtue, baptized in the shed blood of Our Lord—what knight of Savoy will dare refuse Us aid?"

"Your Majesty," said Agnes, "the knights of Savoy have always strongly desired to conquer Jerusalem."

"That's very true," said Ugolina at once, "they sing about that every Sunday, without fail."

"The knights of Savoy have heard Crusader sermons for three hundred years," said Agnes. "They have given much to the Great Cause of Christendom, but... Well, your aunt Anna ran up some big debts here."

"We royalty are allowed our debts!"

"My Anna wasn't a queen, she was just a Savoy duchess."

"The knights of Savoy drowned Anna's favorite banker in a lake," Ugolina said. "A Swiss lake, because he was a Swiss banker."

"How did the duchess ever disburse such funds?" said the Queen.

"My husband Ugo knows all about it," said Agnes. "Universities, libraries, and Anna had eighteen children to raise... It all adds up."

"I'm just an Italian baroness, myself," said Ugolina, "but believe me, I understand debts. You should see what happened to my marriage dowry." Ugolina snapped her fingers.

"Is it all gone?" said Agnes, her face wrinkling in pain.

"He spent my dowry on horses, Mamma. He bought very good horses, though. Those colts bring a nice market price."

"Our Holy Cause does not need mere coins of gold and silver," said the queen. "Sir Amedeo said the hills of Savoy swarm with angry men who are half mountain-bandit. Hard men spoiling for a good fight!"

"Well, yes," said Agnes. "That was certainly true when my son left us, but he was only sixteen then. My dear Anna so loved her husband, and he was so kind and loving to her in return, that the people named him 'Ludovico the Peaceful.'"

"Ludovico was kind to his peasants," said Ugolina. "He lowered their rents and taxes until his own court went broke. There are so few bandits left in Savoy now that my husband hasn't hanged a robber in years."

"No wonder my Swiss husband was so useless," said the queen.

"Your Majesty, it pains my heart to tell you this, but I must," said Agnes. "You must reconcile to your cousin, the Savoy lord, Louis of Geneva. He is the son of my Anna. Bear the heir of his body, and you may yet regain your throne. Do not despair over your barrenness. Any witchy midwife can find some way to fix that."

"Oh Mother, please don't say such dreadful things!" Ugolina cried.

"We'll drink poison first," said the Queen of Jerusalem.

"Your Majesty, I married a Cypriot, so I know they're a stubborn people," said Agnes. "But the Savoyards are Italians! To abandon your marriage allegiance to the Ducal Court of Savoy is an insult to their family honor! How can they aid you in your battles when you spurn a blood relation with them? Every queen owes fealty to her consort and her lineage."

"Oh mother! Don't say that! Don't do to the Queen of Cyprus what you have already done to me! Carlotta is a queen, she is royalty! Is no woman ever to be happy?"

Agnes blinked. "Well, I am happy in my marriage. I'm your mother, and my parents married me off to your father, just as I did for you. I scarcely even look at other men. What is wrong with you girls these days?"

"Mother, how can you talk in that cold way about my miseries? I can only thank the Virgin Mother that I bore the baron's heir. At last, Camillo is respectful to me...as his pretty little broodmare. No, it's worse than that. Camillo treats me like his mother now. Someday I'll become exactly like his mother."

"Is his mother cruel to you, darling?" said Agnes, stricken. "I wish I were allowed to speak to her."

"Well," said Ugolina, "sometimes Madame was cruel to me, until I learned my court speech and better table manners... But now that I understand how hard it is not to be low, vulgar, and disgusting, I really respect Madame Mother. She knows how to enforce high standards."

"We are doomed," decided the Queen of Jerusalem. "We are going to poison myself."

Ugolina was scandalized. "That's a mortal sin! Even a great queen who poisons herself will fly straight to Hell! What would Dante say?"

"What are we saying?" mourned Agnes "These terrible things we have said to one another? All this dreadful talk of poisoning, and betraying our husbands with better-looking men? Our salvation is at risk."

"We should all confess to a priest," Ugolina agreed, "but never to my priest, though. He's my husband's little brother. He's useless."

"A Queen of Jerusalem should confess to a great Lord of the Church," said Agnes. "Pope Pius would receive us. The Pope would take heed of our woes. Because he is the Pope—although, he's not really a true Pope. Everyone knows that Piccolomini is a fraud. He is the Pope, he wears the triple crown and mantle, but really, he's just a clever Italian writer."

"You shouldn't say that about the Pope, Mamma. I know you liked the Anti-Pope much better, but we're lucky we only have one now."

"I don't blame the Pope, my darling. The Church needs a great writer today, to recall us to our sanctity, to conceal the Great Schism, to shroud the scandals of the Roman court. Piccolomini understands the weakness of mankind. He has three natural children."

"That sounds good," said the Queen of Jerusalem, brightening somewhat. "If he's not cold and weak like my husband, then We should ask him for aid and counsel."

"The Pope wrote courtly love songs. The Pope loves printed books. The Pope has traveled all over the world."

"Does the Pope know that the world is round?" said the Queen of Jerusalem.

"Well," said Agnes, "that's a hard thing, given a literal reading of the Scriptures; but I never heard that he decreed that it was flat."

"We could tell the Pope about the roundness," said Ugolina, "and then beg him to confess all three of us. If the Pope is a good writer, he's bound to take an interest in such wonderful sins as ours."

XI

The family met for council in the tower of the Inn of Saint Cleopha. The brick turret, with its archer slits and slots for dropping boiling oil, was not much bigger than a closet; no stranger would hear them confiding to one another. Not in the darkness, at midnight.

"So, then," said Amedeo, "just before dawn, we break out of Turin while we can still cut our way out of here."

"Best to make haste slowly, my son," Ugo said. "One last bribe to good Constable Egenz at his gate. Then, a quiet escort across country from the Baron of Caselle, who is keen to trade his horses for ours. Once we cross the Savoy border, then you take command. We burst off at the gallop, in one solid charge across Italy. We don't draw rein until the Queen of Jerusalem is safely in exile at the Court of the Pope."

Amedeo whacked the brick wall with his mailed fist. "Any plan that is bold, brave, and powerful is better than a coward's scheme."

"We own the Queen of Jerusalem. We've lost or sold everything else. She's all that we possess—but what a splendid prize! For her, we gladly risk everything."

Ugolina gazed from her brother to her father. "I never thought you'd say that Amedeo made a good, sensible plan, Dad."

"My daughter, I am no brave knight. I am a bourgeois. I have sold many things, maybe too many things that I loved. But now that I have sold every single thing I have, I am a holy pilgrim! I swore to take to the road! If I'm denied Jerusalem in Cyprus, then I will take Jerusalem to Rome." Ugo patted the medallion beneath his pilgrim's cloak. "My own father would have done no less. I'm not stupid!"

"We must loyally serve Queen Carlotta," said Agnes, "because a queen in Rome requires so many nice things! She has every desire that any queen would naturally have, so she needs her regalia, her robes, her shoes, and a palace to keep them in… A royal kitchen, of course, with a cellar, a salt-store, a smoke-house, a bake-house, a fruitery…"

"Mother, please don't be vulgar. A royal library, and royal art gallery."

"I smuggled Carlotta's royal crown out of Cyprus," said Amedeo. "That little bauble's worth a fortune. No one knows."

"You stole her crown? The legendary crown of Jerusalem, the crown of Baldwin the Leper?"

"Dad, I'm your son. I'm not stupid, either."

Ugo narrowed his eyes in the candlelight. "We'll make a fake crown for her everyday use. Jewels of paste with a gold veneer. In Rome that is never a problem."

"A palace in Rome is her due," said Amedeo. "Everyone who favors the Crusades will seek Carlotta's favor. Even the pagans who fear her wrath will seek her out. A Queen of Jerusalem must be fearsome."

"Any queen is fearsome when her minions do not fear to die."

"Well, Dad," said Amedeo, "some of her lost desperadoes downstairs here do fear to die, but I know the ones who don't give a damn."

"The Romans always love anyone who gives them feasts," said Agnes. "Feasts, parties, balls, and masquerades. With Latin poetry."

"Now that," said Ugo, "is the truth. That is just as you say, my dear."

"Then it's all agreed," Agnes decided. "My family conveys the Queen of Jerusalem to the Eternal City. There, we serve her to the end of her days. Or our own days. Or Armageddon, the Last Day of the Whole Round World, whichever comes first."

Ugo and Amedeo looked at one another. They both opened their mouths to say something, then they closed them silently.

Ugolina wailed aloud. "Oh Mother, you have uttered a prophesy! I know it is the holy truth, because, poor me, I'll have to live here in Savoy, wearing silk and bearing many children, and I'll never get to see Rome, or Jerusalem! Or Constantinople, or China, or any other place but little old Italy!"

Amedeo pulled at his beard. "Italy is a good place, sis. In our family, you are the lucky one."

"Oh, fine, yes, Italy is beautiful. I bet I live longer than you do."

"If you bear enough sons," said Agnes, "some will become princes of the Church in Rome."

"Mamma, stop that prophesying! You are a great witch of the Queen of Jerusalem now, you are scaring me." Ugolina wiped at her tears.

Ugo said nothing as the candle flickered, then he reached out and chucked his wife under her chin. "My children, look here: the wisdom of your mother is a wondrous thing. It will all become just as she says! Every word! If I owned ten Holy Shrouds, I would make them all into a pillow for her clever little head!"

They raised their spirit cups in the flickering candlelight. "To you, Mamma." "Your health, dear Mamma." "To you, my bride." Then they all drank.

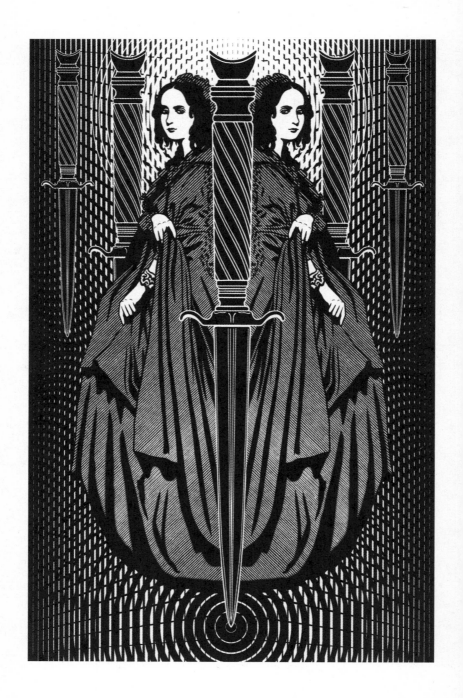

THE PARTHENOPEAN SCALPEL

THE THOUSAND INTRIGUES of the Minister we had borne as best we could. But when he poisoned the mind of the Holy Father against our National Cause, we vowed revenge.

Lots were chosen among our Cenacle. To my satisfaction, this signal honor fell to me. The usurper would die at my own hand. He would perish on the very steps of his chancellery, stabbed in the midst of his Swiss Guards, dead in broad daylight. As the wretch breathed his last, he would know—thanks to the shouted slogans that I had rehearsed—that we had avenged an exasperated people.

Having no doubt of my ability to carry out this deed, I accepted my destiny with calm resolution.

Some days passed. It then chagrined me to learn—from my Cenacle—that I would have an accomplice in the task.

Unfortunately, we were not the only Cenacle of the Carbonari inside Rome. For safety against many spies, our conspiracy was divided into many cells. One of our colleague Cenacles—as righteously indignant as ourselves—had also chosen an assassin to kill the Minister.

I met this rival of mine in a torchlit cellar at midnight. My understudy was a bug-eyed, epileptic fanatic. I disliked him at once. Still, his task was similar to mine. Should I (by some strange mishap) fail to slay the Minister, then the Minister's guards would surely hurry him toward the safety of his carriage. Waiting on the street near that carriage, this pallid boy, disguised as a priest, would deploy an infernal device.

The Minister and his bodyguards would all be blown to fragments.

At first, I considered this an affront to my honor. A dagger is the noble weapon of Brutus. Everyone understands that tyrants fall to daggers. A bomb is a sordid modern device with many complex working parts. Only engineers understand bombs.

However, on mature consideration, I grasped the wisdom in the plan. Let us be frank and objective. A political assassination is a form of public theater. How would a wise director, a mastermind, arrange such a matter?

Suppose that I succeeded in my debut—in my role as a hero to History. Well and good! What harm could there be, in my rival's idly standing by with some bomb? And if I failed? But I would not fail.

Reasoning in this manner, I forgave the affront. I devoted myself to rehearsals.

The Cenacle had offered me some rough-and-ready advice. "Place your thumb on the flat of your blade, and strike upward." Time-tested folk wisdom, to be sure! But where was the modern science behind this "rule of thumb"?

I conducted research in the morgue of my medical college. Human ribs form a "rib cage." It is necessary to slide the blade through that cage, piercing the gristle that unites the solid rib bones. If the blade is narrow and supple (as is logical), then a further sharp twist is needed to lacerate the vital organs.

Our medical school had cadavers aplenty. Nameless paupers ceaselessly breathed their last on the grimy streets of Rome—dead from phthisis, dead from quartan fever, mostly dead from hunger. On their unresisting bodies, I methodically tested my favorite stiletto. It consoled me to know that even the dead could avenge my country's misery.

I carefully burned my many notebooks. I bade a farewell to my mistress—she wept, for returning to her husband's cold embraces was a dire matter for her. Then I wrote tender farewell letters to the last addresses I held for my scattered family: in Providence, Charleston, Nice, Geneva, and Buenos Aires.

Once, my dear family had been a distinguished house in the Parthenopean Republic. We were noble in sentiment, full of ambition and purpose.
But our personal attachment to Murat had brought the insensate resent-
ment of the Bourbon Dynasty against us.

That unworthy envy had shattered our house. It had scattered my loved
ones to the four winds. Yet one wasp among us had spurned to flee and was
keen to sting!

The appointed day arrived for the retribution. I rose at dawn, I ate a
hearty meal, I dressed in my finest apparel, and I dismissed my trusted valet
forever.

I then proceeded to a last appointed rendezvous with my fellow conspirators.

There I met yet another group of comrades—from a third Roman
Cenacle. These men were strangers to the other two cells. In the haste and
confusion that so often accompanies great deeds, they had given the boy a
dagger, and saved the iron bomb for me.

The bomb was under my priestly skirts when screams rang out across the
Roman piazza. The boy had simply and clumsily cut the Minister's throat.

The boy was arrested, and of course he told everything he knew. The police do have their methods. So do we. All the boy knew about me was
that I was called "the Parthenopean." The boy was known to me only as
"the Calabrian." Together, we had met "the Hussar," "the Scorpion," "the
Illuminatus," and "the Englishman," a very clever fellow who was certainly
not English. So the boy could babble whatever he thought that he knew. To
the police, it was one vast labyrinth of mirrors.

The chairman of my Cenacle was known to our cell as "the Chairman."
After giving me a fresh nom de guerre (I would henceforth be known as
"the Scalpel"), he arranged for my escape.

I lacked the papers needed to cross the borders of the Papal States. So,
with the sacrifice of my beard (a clever idea in itself) and with the addi-
tion of a bonnet, a mantelet, kid gloves, and a good stiff set of petticoats,
I became the "wife" of a Carbonari comrade. This man was a respectable
bourgeois who traveled in trade. As his wife, I required no more papers
than his horses did.

"The Chairman" confided to me that he had been taught this trick by
the great Mazzini himself. Giuseppe Mazzini—philosopher, humanitarian,

and tireless writer—was our movement's spiritual leader. Mazzini was known throughout the Concert of Europe as "the Prince of Assassins."

Safely across the border, and restored to my masculine attire, I was lent a horse by new friends. These men were certainly not Carbonari. They were democratically elected politicians from the "Liberal Party" of the Grand Duchy of Tuscany.

These useful idiots said nothing of the deeds convulsing Rome. They were full of their petty Tuscan intrigues. I made no complaint about their oversight, however.

We rode north for three days, our little party of politicians much refreshed by cigars and fine Tuscan wines. The sun shone upon us, the little birds chirped their love songs, and the very sky seemed born anew and full of wonderment to me.

Blazing with an occult passion, I had sought to embrace historical necessity. Yet that dark union had gone unconsummated. My trip to that altar would have to wait.

The Parthenopean Scalpel yet lived!

My new host, my new master in conspiracy, was the Count of R——. His home was a picturesque, crumbling castle on a rambling Tuscan estate. The Count's noble family was very ancient, related by blood to the Visconti and the House of Hapsburg-Lorraine. It followed that much of his home was in ruin.

No ruins within pretty Tuscany could compare to the monstrous urban ruins of Rome. Besides, the patriotic Count was manfully reviving the fortunes of his tenants. The Count's many fields were freshly manured, contour-plowed, and sown in clover—clear evidence of his advanced agronomical thinking. The Count's stony manor was, yes, rather tumbledown and much heaped in thorns and ivy, and yet, many parts of it were visibly progressing. An entire new guest wing was under construction, built to the exacting tastes of British and German millionaire tourists.

Servants in green livery showed me to my quarters, in the castle's freshest section. Fitted in the finest modern papier-mâché, my room lacked for nothing: razors, pomade, combs, gleaming full-length mirrors, a wardrobe rustling with fresh linens, a private fireplace, my own bellpull and speaking tube. I searched in vain for the chamber pot, until I found water closets!

A household tailor measured me, so that I could meet His Excellency in proper attire. I spent the next three days happily devouring excellent meals, and a host of up-to-date newspapers.

Not only was I not fallen in combat, not locked in some dank Roman dungeon—I was free to witness how rapidly our times progressed! The Grand Duchy of Tuscany had liberalized its censorship of printed matter. In Rome, we Carbonari doggedly smuggled a few pamphlets past the priests, but the Count had modern magazines in lavish heaps. Books at every hand as well, terrific books fit to shake the very earth: the works of Balbo, Gioberti, d'Azeglio, and the entire bound proceedings of the *Congresso degli Scienziata*.

At once I began taking notes.

I should explain why I took this foolish risk, for it was strictly against Carbonari practice to write anything. Any scrap of written knowledge about our activities could be seized by the police. To take notes was to court the grim fate of Silvio Pellico, a Carbonari intellectual who spent ten years in Austrian prisons, mostly taking notes there about his prison life, for a later confessional masterpiece, *My Prisons*.

My strong need to narrate my own deeds to myself was entirely my personal failing. The truth there was rather sad and simple: I was cursed with a very poor memory. Few people had noticed this unhappy fact about me, for my memory for slights and resentments was extremely keen. I could recite every misfortune the people of Italy had suffered since the invasion of Alaric in the year 401. However, my memory was like a Roman ruin: a noble structure, full of gaps, absences, and lacunae.

Somehow, my merely personal activities had always seemed to me unworthy of my own regard. My dead mother's face was lost to me. My dead father's many words of counsel, I could never recall.

I did have my virtues, let me assure you: I was bold, self-sacrificing, patient under toil, noble in my sentiments, devoted to people and country, and sensitive to the sufferings of the less fortunate. I had struggled hard to become a doctor, but the practice of medicine was beyond me. I could not learn medical Latin—or, having learned the Latin, I could never remember the grammar.

A doctor requires a ready memory for the cavalcade of ills that assault the human body. I could never mentally catalog that endless host of symptoms. I loved medical textbooks—I could read them for hours on end —but the details there slipped through my fingers.

I believe the fault was in my blood. There was a legend in my family that my grandmother had once been the mistress of Murat, Napoleon's greatest general and the famous "First Horseman of Europe." There was a bitterness among us about this story, for Murat had charged on horseback to the throne of Naples. The adventurous Murat, so fearless, so headlong, had become a king among the Crowned Heads of Europe, and we had once prospered through him. Yet his over-bold gallantry had made him a poor ruler. His fall had cost Murat his own life, and also cost us our too-brief prosperity.

I do not want to idly claim that I am the grandson of a king. I have no objective proof to offer on that subject. But surely a man cannot help his own blood. Isn't every Italian descended from some king or some emperor? We are a very old people.

If my craft of public murder was in some sense theatrical, it followed that my personal life was, in some sense, literary. Prepared to immolate myself for the causes of Freedom and Unity, I had burned a hundred diaries. I had expected no further use for those volumes, of course. Now I had to hastily scribble everything I could recall.

Naturally, I did not want my confessions to be found by anyone. Writing in cipher, or right-to-left like Leonardo da Vinci, merely attracts attention from spies. However, I knew a brilliant method to finesse this.

From the teeming shelves of the Count's library, I picked a volume of the pious Catholic verses of Alessandro Manzoni. Since the great Manzoni is so much respected, this volume is in every literate Italian home. Yet it is never opened or read by anyone. Those rich vellum pages and the spacious typography made my new notebook a pleasure to use.

Once I was properly dressed by the tailor of his household, I was granted my first personal audience by the Count of R——.

The Count of R—— was a philosopher. He was a courteous man, but he did not simply put me at my ease within his presence. In mere moments, the Count could make the most difficult, tangled matters seem clear.

The Count was lucid, he was educated, he was ambitious, and he wanted the very best from futurity. I do not want to be ungallant about the Count. Personal failings among the great are often better glossed over. However, I am compelled to reveal at this point that the Count of R—— was a hunchback.

The Count had certain other detriments as well, notably the lantern jaw and the poorly spaced teeth of the Hapsburgs, but that hunchback was impossible to overlook. The great man's spine was bent like the letter "S" and his head rose only to my sternum.

Due to this sad handicap, the Count had never cut any great figure in the tumultuous events of our period. The Count was physically unable to mount a horse. So, although he had noble blood, he could never take command of an army, or even lead a common street rebellion. I pitied him this misfortune. Our Italian nobility was much like the rest of European nobility, only older. Their endless marriage politics could not refresh their bloodlines. They were older than Charlemagne.

I cannot recount exactly what the Count told me at that first meeting, because I was not taking notes. Also, at first, the Count's refined and literary Tuscan dialect was rather difficult for me. Mostly, we discussed our nation's politics. In that subject, we were equally impassioned.

I would not claim that we were equals. I understood him as a modern count, and he understood me as a modern assassin. That was sufficient to the purpose.

My new patron, the Count, was a covert master of the Carbonari. This dark secret was known only to a handful. He was also a public member of the Congress of Science, the well-known body of scholars from all over Italy. The Count was also a founding member of the newly formed National Society. This new group, I had known nothing about. The National Society was mostly restricted to the enlightened regions of Piedmont, Milan, Venice, and Tuscany. It had not yet spread its tentacles of progressive subversion into the south of the peninsula.

The Count set forth to clarify the situation. I was a wanted fugitive, so I could never return to Rome. I certainly understood this. I was originally from Naples, and I took care never to return to Naples.

The Count offered me a formal choice. I could flee to South America, where our national movement tended to store its heroes. Or I could aspire once more to immortal glory on the soil of Italy. I pretended to give this matter some thought (for I admired the suave way he had pretended to offer it to me). Then I placed my blade at his service.

The arrangement was settled. Weeks passed. A pleasant spring blessed the blossoming Tuscan countryside. Like many who have suffered since birth, the Count was a very patient man. He never raised his voice, he never acted in haste, and he never showed any surprise.

I was disguised as a doctor, a new household retainer for the Count. I methodically changed my attire, my accent—any other quirks that might betray me. I was granted the run of the Count's estates. I came to know the grounds, the servants, and much of the local food.

I was introduced to another of the Count's secret retainers: an engineer. I never learned this old man's real name, but he was a long-trusted comrade. He created infernal devices. This was his calling.

The maestro had been making bombs since the days of Napoleon, maybe since the French Revolution. His eyes had lost their keenness, and his hands had lost three fingers, but he still had both his thumbs.

The maestro and I met regularly in a castle workshop near the library, where he set to work to pass on his craft heritage to me. The maestro had a method of building bombs that was entirely oral. Nothing was ever to be written about building bombs, because the guilty possession of any bomb-making texts meant a swift trip to the galleys, the gallows, or the guillotine.

The maestro further insisted that I should build the bombs with my left hand alone. Why? Firstly, because bombs were infernal, and Satan was infernal, and the left hand was the sinister, Satanic hand. Secondly, because the use of my left hand would force me to concentrate precisely. Working left-handed, I would not become careless, habitual, or hasty. Thirdly and lastly, because any premature detonations of the black powder or the mercury fulminate would only tear my left hand.

While the old man's failing eyes left me, I wrote down all his instructions. I transformed his whispered folklore into simple recipes. The complexity of infernal devices is much exaggerated. Anyone who can bake a cake can build a bomb. A woman could do it.

The Count's extensive estates allowed us to test our bombs discreetly. My maiden efforts were as clumsy as most maiden efforts. Still, the task aroused me, so I soon gave satisfaction.

There then followed the Milanese incident, which I will narrate briefly. The situation within that city was exceedingly turbulent. One member of our brotherhood was suspected of being an Austrian police informant. This man had once been trusted by the Count, so his missteps were troublesome.

I went to Milan. I followed the man for five days. He was a financier, fat, myopic, and clumsy; he never grasped that I had become his shadow. The Austrian secret police who infested Milan had rewarded him for his double game; not in a clumsy way, but in a way that seemed like business.

Since he considered himself a businessman, he was not afraid.

This wretch was pursuing two lives within a single existence. His perfidy disgusted me. I confronted him at night outside a brothel, which he owned. I stabbed him. I painted the cobblestones with the word "VENGEANCE," in his blood. I retrieved some documents from the dead man's wallet. I left his money scattered in the street, for patriots scorn to be thieves.

The Count showed no surprise when I gave him this written proof of my success. He did not reward me, or praise me at any length; but he did take me deeper into his confidence.

The Count's castle had certain areas closed to me; not through anything so crass as locks and keys, but through a manly courtesy. I had heard, from the servants' whispers, that the Count had a "sister." I had assumed that she was not his "sister" but, as the French deftly put it, his "*petite amie.*" Perhaps his "little friend" was a midget, a woman even smaller than himself? Or she might be his normal-sized mistress; women care much less for a man's body than men imagine they do. Besides, the Count had great wealth, and normal women rarely overlook that.

But no, the Count of R—— indeed had a sister. Why his parents had again assayed the marriage bed after his unfortunate birth...but why should I speculate? A man and woman who love each other will do whatever they must.

The Count's parents had given the world a second issue from their union. She, or they, were even more remarkable than the Count himself.

The first head was been christened "Vittoria," while the second head was named "Clemenza." As a united woman, the twins, or the girl, was known as "Ida." One could not very well say, "Vittoria, come here," when Clemenza was bound to come along anyway. So, among her very small circle of intimates, both Clemenza and Vittoria were mostly called "Ida."

No one within the castle had ever been able to overcome the severe grammatical problems associated with Ida. Sometimes she was "she," sometimes they were "they." There were further problems with the singular form, the plural form, the feminine plural possessives, the feminine singular and plural pronoun declensions, and so forth.

Even when I came to know Ida, Clemenza, Vittoria particularly well, so much so that I used affectionate diminutives for her, and the intimate familiar form rather than any formal honorifics, I used to stumble over the simplest Italian sentences: "You (singular) come embrace me," or "You (plural) please give me a kiss."

There was simply no help for that.

Ida was not a hunchback, like her unfortunate brother. Her medical case was both simpler and more complex. Her spine had split between the shoulder blades, and she had grown two heads. Vittoria, the left head, had hair of glossy black. She was the more assertive of the two. Clemenza, blonder and finer of features, was the more thoughtful.

To further complicate matters, Vittoria owned the body's right hand, while Clemenza commanded the left. Their legs they owned in common. Anything below the waist was, simply, the body of a woman. A very charming woman who happened to possess two heads.

Ida was remarkably intelligent, certainly twice as intelligent as most women, but she had led, for inevitable reasons, a sheltered life. All of her gowns, bodices, chemisettes, anything with dual collars, were made for her by her servants. She had the most delicate of appetites, for she never ate in public. A true aristocrat, she had never been exposed to the cruel gaze of the common herd. She had been privately educated by some of Italy's best tutors. She passed most of her days in literary endeavor.

To spare her noble family embarrassment, she wrote entirely under pen names. I do not claim that my mistress was a major poet. She never won any fame for her verses, nor did she desire that. However, she carried out an extensive correspondence with leading lights of European poesy. She wrote at especial length, in classical Greek, to Miss Elizabeth Barrett of London, a fellow bluestocking with a deep, sympathetic interest in Italian affairs.

Lady readers will take a natural interest in the details of our romance. Our intercourse took place mostly at the bench of the pianoforte. Although she dearly loved music, Ida could never properly play the piano. Clemenza controlled the left hand, and Vittoria the right. So although they could confer at length about their keyboard, they were hard put to coordinate.

I therefore offered to play the piano for her. My proposal was accepted. As long as music was playing, her elderly duenna would leave the two of us alone together.

We therefore got up to delicious mischief at that pianoforte. Certain Latin terms known to medical men describe these activities.

Let the priests say whatever they please; a woman who has never known love is simply not a woman. If I made them a woman, they repaid me doubly, by making me the servant-cavalier of two noble sisters.

Of course we could never unite in marriage. That is not the romantic custom in these Italian understandings, and in any case, that would be bigamy on my part, and a mesalliance for her. Furthermore, I was a doomed man, sworn to throw my own life away on any turn of the cards in the Congress of Europe. Our love was sincere, but those were our harsh truths. Who can blame the two or three of us for our stolen moments of bliss?

There has been so much fine work written on this all-consuming subject: Goethe's *Elective Affinities*, Rousseau's *Nouvelle Heloise*, and Madame de Stael's immortal *Corinne*, a tender romance set in Italy and of particular interest to them, or rather to her. I have seen the two of her discuss *Corinne* for hours. We also gleefully revived much useful ancient learning from the unexpurgated Ovid, Juvenal, Martial, and Catullus. The Venetian Casanova, for his part, was an overrated braggart. Yet Casanova showed wisdom when he wrote that a man in bed with two sisters will find that they surpass one another in daring.

A gentleman will not belabor the point here. The scientist will. Is it not this secret side of life, this fertile intercourse in darkness, which grants us life itself? Is this not the netherworld from which each of us —men, women, and two-headed monsters—all emerge? Can we deny the medical facts in this matter? Someday—I do not say tomorrow—a light will shine on all this.

There then passed the titanic events of the Five Days of Milan. These five days, in all their nobility and drama, will never be forgotten by a wondering mankind. The hope of Italy hung on the very scales.

Like every thinking couple in Italy, Vittoria, Clemenza, and I were convulsed. One might suppose that this intense political turmoil would distract us from our dalliance. No, not at all: the Revolution fed our subterranean flames. As the Count's couriers came and went, bearing heaps of badly printed broadsheets from the Milanese barricades—the bold defiance of Conservatism, the last words of our martyrs—our romance rose to a mania.

I loved her so. I loved her as a man can only love two women. Yet I could not loll in every comfort while Italians fell to the imperial bayonets of an alien power. And not just us Italians: democratic Poles, exiled from their stricken country, were shedding their blood on our soil. The Hungarians of Kossuth as well—men from a very prison-house of European nations were seeking freedom in Italy. Young Europe was there in the flesh, fearless, bold, progressive, scientific, careless of death, on the bloody streets of Venice, Rome and Milan, with guns in their hands. And I—"the Parthenopean Scalpel"—was I to stand idly by?

Ida shed four hot streams of tears; but I went to the Count to demand my release.

The Count denied me this favor. "We are going to lose," the Count told me. "Our war of independence will fail, and you and I, conspirators, will never walk in honest daylight in our lives." They were very bitter words, so I can remember those words as clearly as I remember anything.

The Count was working on a set of geometrical papers, for mathematics was the Queen of Sciences to him. "I shall demonstrate the sources of our inevitable defeat," he told me. He had inscribed them all on paper, in a pattern of wondrous intricacy.

There was, he said to me, a superb unproven theory called "the Italian people." But Italy was, as yet, merely a geographical expression. This was not the mere physical problem, already known to everyone, of somehow uniting Venice, Milan, Piedmont-Sardinia, Parma, Tuscany, the Papal States, and the Two Sicilies.

No: there was a deeper meaning to all of this. This fragmentation of Italy, he told me, was useful to the Concert of Europe, for it had broken a European nation into convenient pocket change for the Great Powers.

Where else were the Great Powers to hide their sore embarrassments, such as the widow of the Emperor Napoleon? Let her conceal herself in that bloody tumult of Italian obscurities. Let the failed Empress of Europe retreat to Europe's dark closet. Let her rule over little Parma.

The further weakness lurked within the body of the people. The great majority of the people were the peasants of the countryside—poor, hungry, dulled with superstition, and glumly opposed to progress. The poor within the cities were the urban mob, brave, turbulent, ever ready to struggle and bleed, but unable to govern anyone—least of all themselves.

The bourgeoisie, our class of modern industry, were few in number, split among many tiny markets, scheming, competitive, jealous. They were too busy mastering steam to master any statesmanship.

The aristocrats of Italy were the oldest and highest class, but they, too, were split between their ancient gentry, fettered to their ancestral lands, and the new industrial barons, keen to profit, yet devoid of any sense of service.

The Church was in every last village of Italy. Yet the Roman Church was universal, and therefore bitterly opposed to Italian nationhood.

"Now I must inform you," the Count concluded, "that we are at the bottom of that long list. We, the Italian conspirators. We, too, are a body which is fatally split. Most Italian conspirators are simple, thick-headed mafia. They much outnumber us patriots. These ageless bandits will survive to flourish when we are dust.

"But you, my dear friend," (it was the first time he had called me that) "you are a terrorist. Men like you are in critically short supply, for you can bring upon this world the 'vast commotions' prophesied by our visionaries. So I cannot release you to die in the streets of the Roman Republic with the scum of Europe. No. Men like ourselves are sternly bound to a higher purpose!"

I was moved to weep, for it was the first time the great hunchback had spoken to me, so directly and frankly, as a man like himself.

"There is a matter I must confess to you, sir," I began.

"Yes," he sighed, "it's about my sisters. I already know that."

I thought it wisest to say nothing more.

"My friend," he said, toying with a jeweled letter opener, "I am an aristocrat. My class is very antiquated, and we are doomed to pass from the scene. Breeding ourselves like our own racehorses, we are tethered to our farms. That is sad, but we do have one saving grace. It is this: we do not care one stinking fig for any common, sordid, petit-bourgeois, marital fidelity."

"Nobly said," I told him.

The Count nodded somberly. An ormolu clock ticked on the mantelpiece. We were both having a certain difficulty discussing the matter. Commonly, when a man corrupts another man's sister, they are required to come to blows. Yet this was the last thing on our minds. We were the progressives of a truly European freedom.

"You must have a favorite among them," he said at last.

"No, Your Excellency. I love both her and them. I have come to understand that she is what they are. A woman accepts a man, expecting that he will change. A man takes a woman, expecting that she will never change. They are both disappointed. Yet within this very disappointment is the primal source of all new men and all new women."

"You do study the human heart. You might make a good father," said the Count.

"Sir, I am not an agent of birth. I am an agent of death."

And then, without being dismissed, I left the Count's study. I had wanted to raise a further delicate issue with him, for there were many between us, but having delivered such a profound exit line, I had to leave those things unaddressed.

I had no evidence to refute my master's dark suppositions about the tragic fate of our nation. I had only my own patience, my will to endure the unendurable. The unendurable indeed arrived. The Count's suspicions were proven entirely correct.

The hope of Italy was swiftly, comprehensively crushed. The hope was crushed, primarily, by Marshal Radetzky. I was keen to murder Radetzky, a man born within the melancholy, captive nation of the Czechs—and yet in loyal service to the blood-drinking Austrian Empire! What satanic hypocrisy could motivate such a man? The troops of Austria called this fiend "Father Radetzky." Radetzky was alarmingly old and yet he never seemed to die.

This Czech vampire was impervious to us. He was also the father of four Italian children, by his mistress, the Milanese washerwoman. The triumph of the Concert of Europe was total. We were dismembered at the hands of our oppressors. Bleeding Italy, stricken Italy, a nation whose very being was a fantasy. Italy had not been free of foreign occupation for one thousand years.

Italy was like the olive tree, that most Italian of trees. For the passerby who sees its pretty leaves, a sweet expanse of lively green. From beneath that olive tree—prostrate, in the dust—a dusky, rustling foliage of unbroken gray.

A certain coldness arose between Ida and myself. A woman with a servant cavalier desires a gallant cavalier. Does she want a man reduced to moral rags, a knight who has tumbled from his horse?

Of course she sympathizes—at first. In the poetry of Sir Walter Scott—that little-known colleague of Manzoni—there is a beautiful line about Woman as the ministering angel to the fevered brow of Man.

But when the Man cannot recover his vigor, when his overthrow is complete and his darkness overwhelming, the Woman becomes practical.

For all the Count's wisdom—and it was a great wisdom, it was impersonal, it was detached, it was telescopic, it was astronomical—the Count himself was not immune from our nation's general ruin. From his covert harbor in Tuscany, the Count had thoroughly busied himself in the failed revolt of Austrian Milan.

The diplomats of Austria had a motto, to go with their scheming banks, their marching armies, their steaming fleets, their steaming railroads. "*Nemo me impune lacessit.*" If you know Latin, "Good!" you may well say to that. But if you know Italian—a language two millennia more modern than Latin—that is a bitter motto. Where is justice found, when the stern avenger is himself avenged upon by his oppressor?

My enemy came to Tuscany—and he came across the border with men-at-arms. It would tire me to tell you how this wicked intriguer thrust himself into innocent Tuscany. Suffice it to say that empires are large, while duchies are small.

He came in a way that was diplomatic, conservative, and entirely legitimate. He came against us with the law at his back.

This man... I cannot bear to give you his name. He had a long name, with many imperial titles. Let us agree to call him simply "the Transylvanian."

The Transylvanian wore a splendid military uniform. I did not. The Transylvanian carried legal passports. I did not. The Transylvanian had four stout fortresses dominating northern Italy. I did not. The Transylvanian had a sword and I had my newspapers.

Or rather, I had once had my newspapers. In captive Milan all the presses were silenced.

This imperialist came to visit the Count, and he came in sympathy. That was the deepest, the direst, the deadliest of his many insults to us: his sympathy. He sympathized with the Count for the terrible rumors whispered about the Count. Said against the Count by the people of decency. The people of stability. The people of law and order.

The Count kissed the hand and bowed the knee. That was tactically necessary. Machiavelli would certainly have approved. Machiavelli was an Italian philosopher, diplomat, politician, and writer of plays; Machiavelli was the founder of modern political science. Machiavelli was exiled, he was tortured, and he died in disgrace. His grave is unknown.

So, the Count behaved as Machiavelli had taught us. Comprehensively defeated on the martial battlefield, he had to choose some subtler field of play.

The Count therefore turned his beautiful sister over to the Transylvanian. The Count freely admitted that many dark rumors circulated about the doings in his castle. But, he said, those rumors had nothing to do with any political conspiracy, with subversion, with murder.

Instead, the issue was entirely personal. This was another matter, a treasure he had always sought to protect and conceal from a hostile and cynical world. A woman of learning and poetry, a delicate, harmless creature.

And then he let the filthy Transylvanian touch their hand.

The vilest part was that she perfectly understood all of this. She understood her own part to the very letter. She had her role to play in the great drama of our defeat, and she undertook it like a diva. She was full of fluency, vivacity, and charm.

One might even say that she overplayed that role. I wanted to kill her for that. However, to kill one of her was not possible, and to kill both of her was excessive, even for a jealous man.

The Transylvanian was entirely delighted. The whole situation beguiled and intrigued him. He was enraptured by this exotic, unexpected discovery. Italy was so sunny, tender, bedecked with flowers; so elegant and precious.

My heart died within me. This made me his equal. A struggle over a woman always makes men equals.

I confronted the Transylvanian. I slapped his smiling face. I challenged him.

We met at dawn. Everything was perfect: matched weapons, matched witnesses. We heard the pleasant piping of the same awakening birds.

We lunged, we parried. The Transylvanian was old and cynical. His face never moved as we fought together. He was like an oil portrait.

I stabbed him. Dust burst from his medaled coat. Yet he did not fall. He merely pressed his attack against me, which cost me a scar. I stabbed him again. This time the blade burst clear from the back of his coat. Yet still he stood upright, and his riposte cost me half of my ear. I stabbed him through the very guts, so that my sword hilt lodged in his belly. In return, he slashed my right arm to ribbons. He slashed it to the bone, so that I could never grip a blade again. Then, at last, I fell.

The Transylvanian walked away, with a weapon rusting in his belly. Honor was satisfied. He did not press the issue any further.

I did not die from my many ugly wounds. I persisted and I recovered. But, for the rest of my life, I was not to be the lover of two women. Because I had become half a man. I had given my good right arm to the lost cause of unity. That sacrifice had proved useless. Yet I still had my left arm.

I had my left arm, and the skill within it, and I found a cellar in London. London, that city of fog, that city of ten thousand exiles. London, Europe's indomitable city: the city that shall never, never be a slave.

May ten thousand bombs depart from foggy London, for the scorching liberation of a drowsing Europe.

ESOTERIC CITY

WAS THAT THE anguished howl of a dying dog? Or just his belly rumbling?

Cold dread nosed at the soul of Achille Occhietti. He rose and jabbed his blue-veined feet into his calfskin slippers.

In the sumptuous hall beyond his bedroom, the ghost light of midnight television flickered beneath his wife's door. Ofelia was snoring.

Occhietti's eyes shrank in the radiant glare of his yawning fridge. During the evening's game, elated by the home team's victory over the hated Florentines, he'd glutted himself on baked walnuts, peppery breadsticks, and Alpine ricotta. Yes, there it lurked, that sleep-disturbing cheese: glabrous and skinless, richer than sin.

The fridge thumped shut, and the dimly shining metal showed Occhietti his own surprised reflection: groggy, jowly, balding. The hands that gripped the crystal cheese plate were as heavy as a thief's.

A blur rose behind Occhietti, echoing his own distorted image. He turned, plate in hand.

A mystical smoke gushed straight up through Occhietti's floor. Rising, roiling, reeling, the cloud gathered earthly substance; it blackly stained the grout between his kitchen tiles.

Occhietti's vaporous guest stank powerfully of frankincense, petroleum, and myrrh.

Resignedly, Ochietti set the cheese plate on the sideboard. He flicked on the kitchen's halogen lights.

In the shock of sudden illumination, Occhietti's mystic visitor took on a definitive substance. He was Djoser, an ancient Egyptian priest and engineer. Djoser had been dead for three thousand years.

Flaking, brittle, and browned by the passing millennia, the mummy loomed at Ochietti's kitchen table, grasping at the checkered cloth with ancient fingers thin as macaroni. He opened his hollow-cheeked maw, and silently wagged the blackened tongue behind his time-stained ivories.

Occhietti edged across the ranks of cabinets and retrieved a Venetian shot glass.

Using a nastily sharp little fruit knife, Ochietti opened the smaller vein in his left wrist. Then he dribbled a generous dram of his life's blood into the glass.

The mummy gulped his crimson aperitif. Dust puffed from his cracked flesh as his withered limbs plumped. His wily, flattened eyeballs rolled in their sockets. He was breathing.

Occhietti pressed a snowy wad of paper towels against his tiny wound. It really hurt to open a vein. His head was spinning.

With a grisly croak, Djoser found his voice. "Tonight you are going to Hell!"

"So soon?" said Occhietti.

Djoser licked the bloodstained dregs of his shot glass. "Yes!"

Occhietti studied his spirit guide with sorrow. He regretted that their long relationship had finally come to this point.

Once, the mummy Djoser had been lying entirely dead, as harmless and inert as dried papyrus, in the mortuary halls of Turin's Museo Egizio—the largest Egyptian museum in Europe. Then Occhietti, as a burningly ambitious young businessman, had occultly penetrated the Turinese museum. He had performed the rites of necromancy necessary to rouse the dead Egyptian. An exceedingly dark business, that; the blackest of black magic; a lesser wizard would have quailed at it, especially at all the fresh blood.

Yet a shining lifetime of success had followed Occhietti's dark misdeed. The occult services of an undead adviser were a major advantage in Turinese business circles.

The world's three great capitals of black magic (as every adept knew) were Lyon, the City of Heretics; Prague, the City of Alchemists; and Turin. The world also held three great centers of white magic: London, the City of the Golden Dawn; San Francisco, the City of Love; and Turin.

Turin, the Esoteric City, was saturated with magic both black and white. Every brick and baroque cornice in the city was shot through with the supernatural.

He'd led a career most car executives would envy, but Achille Occhietti did not flatter himself that he ranked with the greatest wizards ever in Turin. Nobody would rank him with Leonardo da Vinci...or even Prince Eugene of Savoy. No, Occhietti was merely the head of a multinational company's venture capital division, a top technocratic magus at a colossal corporation that had inundated Europe with a honking fleet of affordable compacts and roaring, sleekly gorgeous sports cars, a firm which commanded 16.5 percent of the entire industrial R&D budget of Italy. So, not much magic to marvel at there. Not compared to the concrete achievements of, say, Nostradamus.

Having bound up his wounded wrist, Occhietti offered the mummy a Cuban cigar from his fridge's capacious freezer.

Smoke percolated through cracks in the mummy's wrinkled neck. The treat visibly improved the mummy's mood. Tobacco was the only modern vice that Djoser took seriously.

"Your Grand Master the Signore, he whom you so loyally served," Djoser puffed bluely, "has been dead and in Hell for two thousand days."

Occhietti wondered. "Where does the time go?"

"You should have closely watched the calendar." This was a very ancient Egyptian thing to say. "Your Master calls you from his awful lair. I will guide you to Hell, for guidance of that kind has been my role with you."

"Could I write a little note to my wife first?"

Djoser scowled. A master of occult hieroglyphics, Djoser had never believed that women should read.

With a sudden swift disjuncture straight from nightmare, Occhietti and Djoser were afloat in midair. Occhietti drifted through the trickling fountains of his wife's much-manicured garden, and past his favorite guard dog. The occult arrival of the undead Djoser had killed the dog in an agony of foaming canine terror.

The two of them magically progressed downhill. The mummy scarcely moved his rigidly hieratic limbs. His sandal-shod feet left no prints, and his dessicated hands did not disturb the lightest dust. As they neared Hell, his speed increased relentlessly.

They skidded, weightless as two dandelion puffs, down the silent, curving streets of Turin's residential hills. They crossed the cleansing waters of the sacred Po on the enchanted bridge built by Napoleon.

Napoleon Bonaparte had drunk from the Holy Grail in Turin. This stark fact explained why an obscure Corsican artillery lieutenant had bid so fair to conquer the world.

The Holy Grail, like the True Cross and the Shroud of Turin, was an occult relic of Jesus Christ Himself. Since the checkered Grail was both a white cup and a black cup, the Holy Grail belonged in esoteric Turin. The Holy Grail had been at the Last Supper: it was the cup that held the wine that Jesus Christ transformed into His blood. The Holy Grail had also been at Golgotha: where it caught the gushing blood from Christ's pierced heart.

The Shroud of Turin was a time-browned winding cloth soaked in the literal blood of God, but the blood that brewed within the Holy Grail rose ever fresh. So that magical vessel was certainly the most powerful relic in Turin (if one discounted Turin's hidden piece of the True Cross, which never seemed to interest wizards half so much as the Shroud and the Grail).

The Emperor Constantine had drunk blood from the Grail. Also Charlemagne...Frederick the Second...Cesare Borgia...Cristoforo Colombo...Giuseppe Garibaldi...Benito Mussolini, too, to his woe and the world's distress.

In 1968, an obscure group of students in Turin had occupied the corporate headquarters of Occhietti's car company, demanding love, peace, and environmental responsibility. There the wretches had discovered the hidden Grail. The next decade was spent chasing down terrorists who kidnapped car executives.

Occhietti and the mummy floated through the moony shadow of a star-tipped Kabbalist spire, which loomed over Turin's silent core. This occult structure was the tallest Jewish spire in Europe. Even with a golem, Prague had nothing to compare to it.

The mummy drew a wide berth around the Piazza Castello, in respect for the pharoah who reigned there. This stony monarch, wielding a flail and an ankh, guarded Turin's Fortress of Isis.

At length the flying mummy alit, dry and light as an autumn leaf, in the black market of the Piazza Statuto: for this ill-omened square, the former site of city executions, held Turin's Gate to Hell.

Hell's Gateway lurked under a ragged tower of blasted boulders, strewn with dramatic statues in sadistic Dantean anguish. This rocky tower was decorously topped by a winged bronze archetype, alternately known as the Spirit of Knowledge or the Rebel Angel Lucifer. He was a tender, limpid angel, very learned, delicate, and epicene.

As Djoser sniffed around the stony tower, seeking Turin's occult hole to Hell, Occhietti found the courage to speak. "Djoser, is Hell very different, these days?"

Djoser looked up. "Is Hell different from what?"

"I had to read Dante in school, of course…"

"You are afraid, mortal," Djoser realized. "There is nothing worse than Hell, for Hell is Hell! But I served the royal court of Egypt. I'm far older than your Hell, and Dante's Hell as well." The mummy groped for Occhietti's pierced and aching wrist. "Lo, see here: below we must go!"

Clearly, modern Italian engineers had been hard at work here in Hell. The casings of Hell's rugged tunnel, which closely resembled the Frejus tunnel drilled through the Alps to France, had been furnished with a tastefully minimal spiral staircase made of glass, blond hardwood, and aircraft aluminum.

A delicate Italian techno-muzak was playing. It dimmed the rhythmic slaps of Occhietti's bedroom slippers on the stairway.

Light and shadow chased each other on the tunnel's walls. The walls held a delirious surge of spray-bombed gang graffiti, diabolically exulting drugs, violence, and general strikes against the System—but much of that rubbish had been scrubbed away, and Turin's new, improved path to Hell was keenly tourist-friendly. Glossy signs urged the abandonment of all hope in fourteen official European Union languages.

"Someone took a lot of trouble to upgrade this," Occhietti realized.

"The Olympics were in Turin," Djoser grunted.

"Oh yes, of course."

Turin was an esoteric city of black and white, so its Hell was a strobing, flickering flux, under a chilly haze of Alpine fog. Being Hell, it was funereal; the afterlife was an all-consuming realm of grief, loss, penitence, and distorted, sentimentalized remembrance.

The Hell of Turin was clearly divided—not in concentric layers of crime, as Dante had alleged—but into layers of time. The dead of the 1990s were still feigning everyday business…they were shopping, suffering, cursing the traffic and the lying newspaper headlines…but the dead of the 1980s were blurrier and less antic, while the dead of the 1970s were foggy and obscured. The Hell that represented the 1960s was a fading jangle of guitars and a smokey whiff of patchouli… The 1950s were red-hot smokestacks as distant as the Apennines, while the 1940s, at the limit of Occhietti's ken, were an ominous wrangle of sirens and burning and bombs.

Smog gushed over glum workers' tenements, clanking factories, bloodily gleaming rivers, and endless tides of jammed cars. The cars looked sharp and clear to Occhietti, for he knew their every make, year, and model; but their sinful inhabitants, the doomed and the damned, were hazy blurs behind the wheels.

As an auto executive, Occhietti had always surmised that his company's employees would go to Hell. They were Communists from some of Europe's most radical and militant labor unions. Where else could they possibly go?

And here, indeed, they were. Those zealots from the Workers' Councils, self-righteous hell-raisers passionately devoted to Marxism, had all transmigrated down here. Their afterlife was one massive labor strike. The working dead were clad in greasy flannel, denim, and corduroy, cacophonous, boozing, shouting in immigrants' dialects, a hydra-headed horde of grimy egalitarians…packed like stinging hornets into their workers' housing projects. They passed their eternal torment watching bad Italian TV variety shows.

"Dante's Hell was so solemn, medieval, and majestic," Occhietti lamented. "There's nothing down here but one huge Italian mess!"

"This is *your* Hell," his spirit guide pointed out. "Dante's Hell was all about Dante, while your Hell is all about you."

"They claimed that the afterlife would be about justice for everybody," said Occhietti.

"This is an Italian hell. Did you ever see Italian justice?" The mummy was being reasonable. "I can assure you that all the most famous and accomplished Turinese are here." He pointed with a time-shrunken finger at a busy literary café, a local mise-en-scene that boiled with diabolical energies. "See those flying vulture-monsters there, shrieking and clawing both their victims and one another?"

"With all that noise, they're hard to miss."

"Those are dead Italian journalists and literary critics."

This certainly made sense. "Who's that they're eating?"

"That's the local novelist who killed himself over that actress."

"Fantastic! Yes, that's really him! The only writer who truly understood this town! Can I get his autograph?"

The Egyptian raised his hierophantic hand in stern denial. "Humanity," he pronounced, "is steeped in sin. Especially the human sins that are also human virtues. That manic-depressive novelist boozing over there, who understood too many such things, despaired of his own existence and ended it. But to kill oneself while lost in life's dark woods is the worst of human errors. So he stinks of his own decay, and that is why his vultures eagerly feast on him."

They tramped Hell's stony flooring to a space that was garish and spangled. The smartly hellish boulevards were crowded with famous faces. All manner of local celebrities: film stars, countesses, financiers, art collectors, generals.

These celebrities shared their Hell with the grimy underdogs of the Workers' Turin. Yet, since this was Hell, the Great and the Good were no longer bothering to keep up their public pretenses. Human experience had ceased for the dead; their hazy flesh cast no shadows. Indifferent to futurity, with the post-existential freedom of nothing left to gain or lose, these ghosts were haplessly angry, gluttonous, slothful, and lustful. They were embezzlers, wife-beaters, brawling scoffers. Sullen depressives who'd gone to Hell for being insufficiently cheerful; moral fence-sitters who'd gone to Hell for minding their own business.

Gay and lesbian sodomites whose awful lusts were presumably enough to have their whole city incinerated; cops in Hell for the inherent crime of being cops, lawyers for the utter vileness of being lawyers, firemen for having goofed off on some day when a child burned to death, doctors in Hell for malpractice and misdiagnosis...

Italian women in hell for flaunting busty décolletage that tempted men to lust, and women who had tragically failed to tempt men to lust and had therefore ended up lonely and sad and crabby and cruel to small children.

"Can you tell me who's missing from Hell?" said Occhietti at last. He was jostled by the crowds.

The Egyptian shrugged irritably in the push and shove. "Do you see any Jews down here?"

"The Jews went to Heaven?"

"I never said *that*! I just said the Jews aren't in this Turinese Italian Catholic Hell!" The mummy fought the crowd for elbow room. "There were no Jews in *my* afterlife, either. And believe me, compared to this raucous mess, my afterlife was splendid. My nice quiet tomb had fine clothes, paintings, a sarcophagus, all kinds of wooden puppets to keep me company... You'd think the Jews would have changed in three thousand years, but...yes, fine, the Jews changed, but not so you'd notice."

They clawed their way free from the pedestrian crowds of dead. The mummy was abstracted now, seeking some waymark through the dense and honking urban traffic. "I must usher you into the presence of your dead overlord. This ordeal is going to upset you."

Occhietti was already upset. "I was always loyal to him! I even loved him."

"That's *why* you will be upset."

Occhietti knew better than to argue with Djoser. The mummy's stringent insights, drawn from his long historical perspective, had been proven again and again. For instance, when he'd first asked Djoser about marrying Ofelia, the mummy had soberly prophesied, "This rich girl from a fine family is a cold and narrow creature who feels no passion for you. She will never understand you. She will make your home respectable, conventional, and dignified, and cramped with a petty propriety." Occhietti, considering that an overly harsh assessment, had married Ofelia anyway.

Yet Djoser's prophecies about Ofelia had been entirely true. In fact, these qualities were the best things about Ofelia. She was the mother of his children and had been his anchor for thirty-eight years.

Occhietti's Signore was one of a major trio of the damned, three bronze male giants, stationed in the center of a busy traffic ring. These mighty titans loomed over Hell like office buildings; the cars whizzing past their ankles were like rubber-tired rats.

The heroic flesh of the titans was riddled through and through by writhing, hellish serpents. These serpents were wriggling exhaust pipes that cruelly pierced the sufferers from neck to kidneys, chaining them in place. Being necromancers, the auto executives had always derived their power from the flesh of the dead: from fossil fuels. In Hell, this hideous truth was made manifest.

A hundred thousand people in Turin, weeping unashamedly, hats in hand, had filed their way past gorgeous heaps of flowers to pay the Signore their last respects. Yet, even down here in Hell, the brazen fact of death had not relieved this giant of his business worries.

Here the Signore stood, gathered to his ancestors, who looked scarcely happier than he. The Signore's father blinked silently, forlorn. Bloody sludge dripped from his aquiline, titanic nose. The Signore's father had quaffed from the Grail with the Duce. He had died in his bed with a gentleman's timing—for his death had saved his company from the wrath of the vengeful Allies.

The Signore's grandfather, the company's founder, was an even more impressive figure; great entrepreneur, primal industrial genius, his colossal flesh was caked all over with the blackened wreck of bucolic Italy: pretty vineyards paved over with cement, sweet little piping birds gone toesup from the brazen gust of furnace blasts... He was a Midas whose grip turned everything to asphalt.

As for the Signore himself, he was the uncrowned Prince of Italy, a Senator-for-Life, a shining column of NATO's military-industrial complex. The Signore was dead and in Hell, and yet still grand—after his death, he was grander, even.

"Eftsoons he will speak unto you," warned the mummy formally, "stand ye behind me, and do not fear so."

"This pallor on my face," said Occhietti, "is my pity for him."

In truth, Occhietti was terrified of the Signore. It was always wise to fear a wizard whose lips had touched the Holy Grail.

The Signore opened his mighty jaws. Out came a great sooty gush of carbon monoxide, lung-wrecking particulates, brain-damaging lead, and the occult off-gassings of industrial plastics. Earth-wracking fumes fit to blister Roman marble and tear the fine facades right off cathedrals.

The Signore found his giant, truck-horn voice.

"Hail friend, unto this dreadful day still true,

Who harkens to your master's final geas!

Most woeful this of many deeds performed

In service to the checkered Lord of Turin."

Ochietti felt a purer terror yet. "He's speaking in iambic pentameter!"

"This is Hell," the mummy pointed out. "And he's a Titan."

"But I'm an engineer! I always hated poetry!"

The mummy spread his hands. "Well, he was a lawyer, before he became like this: dead, historic, gigantic, and in the worst of all possible circumstances."

The Signore awaited an answer, with eyes as huge and glassy as an eighteen-wheeler's headlamps.

Occhietti drew himself up, as best he could within his scanty night robe and flat bedroom slippers. "Hail unto thee, ye uncrowned Kings, masters of the many smokestacks, ye who coaxed Italians from their creaking, lousy haywains and into some serious high-performance vehicles... Listen, ye, I can't possibly talk in this manner! Let's speak in the vernacular, *capisce?*"

Occhietti stared up, pleading, into the mighty face that solemnly glared above him.

"Listen to me, boss: *Juventus*! Your favorite football team: the Turin black-and-whites! They kicked the asses of the Florentines tonight! Wiped them flat out, three-zero!"

This was welcome news to the giant. The titan unbent somewhat, his huge bronze limbs creaking like badly lined brakes.

"'Wizard' they call thee, counsellor and fixer;
Trusted with our sums that breed futurity;
Loyal thou wert, but now the very Tempter
Lurks a serpent in your homely Garden!"

"Does he really have to speak like that?" Occhietti demanded of the mummy. "I can't understand a single damned thing he says!"

Nobly, the mummy rose to the occasion. "He must speak in that poetic, divinatory fashion, for he is a dead giant. You are still alive and capable of moral action, so it is up to you to resolve his ghostly riddles for him." The mummy straightened. "Luckily for you, I always loved the riddles of the afterlife. I was superb at those."

"You were?"

"Indeed I was! The Egyptian Book of the Dead: it's like one huge series of technical aptitude tests! At the end, they weigh your human heart against a feather. And if your guilty heart is any heavier than that feather, then they feed your entrails straight to the demonic hippopotamus."

Occhietti considered this. "How did that trial work out for you, Djoser?"

"Well, I failed," said Djoser glumly. "Because I was guilty. Of course I was guilty. Do you think we built the Pyramids without any fixes and crooked backroom deals? It was all about the lazy priests...the union gangs...and the Pharoah! Oh my God!" The mummy put his flaking head into his withered hands.

Occhietti gazed from the three damned and towering industrial giants, slowly writhing in their smokey chains, and back to Djoser again. "Djoser, your Pharaoh *was* your God, am I right? He was your divine God-King."

"Look, Achille, since we're both standing here stuck in Hell, we should at least be frank: my God-King was a scandal. Like all the pharaohs, he was *in bed with his sister*. All right? He was an inbred, cross-eyed royal runt! You could have broken both his shins with a papyrus reed."

The mummy gazed upward at the damned industrialists. "This gentleman's dynasty came to a sudden end after one mere century... But at least he was in bed with some busty actresses, and was driving hot sports cars! As a leader of your civilization, he wasn't *all that bad*, especially considering your degraded, hectic, vilely commercial Iron Age!"

The mighty specter seemed obscurely pleased by the mummy's outspoken assessment; at least, he thunderously resumed his awesome recitation.

"He comes to ruin everything we built!
The empire that we schemed, we planned, we made,
In toil, sweat, tears and lost integrity,
Imperiled stands in your new century,
When Turin's Black and White turns serpent Green!
If ever you would call yourself 'apostle'
Your footsteps stay, and keep your heart steadfast!
The Devil's blandishments are subtle,
'Reject them without pause all down the line!'"

"He's warning you that you will encounter Satan," the mummy interpreted. "I take it that he means Lucifer, the Shining Prince of Darkness."

"Meeting Lucifer is not in my job assignment," said Occhietti.

"Well, it is now. You will have to return to your mortal life to confront the Devil in person. That's clearly what this hellish summons is all about."

Occhietti could no longer face the writhing torment of the doomed giants, so he turned on the mummy. "I admit that I'm a necromancer," he said. "I draw my magic power from the dead—but *Satan*? I can't face Satan! Satan is the Black Angel! He's the second-ranked among the Great Seraphic Powers! I can't possibly *defeat Satan*! With what, my rosary?"

"Your Lord of Turin can't speak any more plainly," Djoser said. "Look how he folds his mighty arms and falls so silent now! As your spiritual guide and adviser, I would strongly suggest that you arm yourself against the Great Tempter."

All three giants had gone as rigid and remote as public statuary. Occhietti was speechless at the desperate fate that confronted him.

"Come now," coaxed the mummy, "you must have *some* merits for a battle like this. Not every necromancer visits Hell while living."

"I'm completely doomed! I might as well just stay here in Hell, properly damned!" Occhietti's shoulders slumped within his scanty robe. "Everyone who matters is here already anyway! There's no one up there in Heaven except children and nice old ladies!"

"Don't be smug about your own damnation," counseled the mummy, taking his arm and leading him away through acrid lines of whizzing traffic. "That is the sin of pride."

It brought profound relief to flee the dire presence of the three agonized giants. The mummy and Occhietti flagged down a taxi. Suddenly they were roaming Turin's vast and anonymous mobilized suburbs, which were all tower blocks, freeways, assembly plants, and consumer box stores.

"My employer just tasked me to face Satan… Him, the finest man I ever knew…" Occhietti leaned his reeling head against the taxi's grime-stained window. "Why is *he* down here in Hell? He was truly the Great and the Good! All the ladies loved him! He even had a sense of humor."

"It's because of simony," pronounced the mummy. "He—and his father, and his grandfather—they are all in Hell for the mortal sin of simony."

"I don't think I've ever heard of that one."

"For 'simony,' Achille. That's the mortal sin named after the great necromancer, Simon Magus. Simon Magus sought to work divine miracles by paying money for them."

"But I do that myself."

"Indeed you do."

"Because I'm in venture capital, I'm in research and development! I have to commit that so-called sin of 'simony' every damn day!"

"You might consult your Scripture on that subject. Nice letters of black and white, very easy to read." Djoser was something of a snob about his hieroglyphics.

Occhietti banged his fist against the rattling taxi door. "Everybody in the modern world is an industrial capitalist! We all raise cash to work our technical miracles! That's our very way of life!"

"You won't find any words of praise for that in your Bible."

Occhietti knew this was true. As a wizard, he had the Bible, that most occult of publications, poised always at his bedside.

There was scarcely one word inside the Bible that you'd find in any modern Masters of Business Administration course. Not much comfort there for the money changers in the temple. Plagues, curses, merciless wars of annihilation, the sky splitting open apocalyptically—the Bible brimmed over with that.

Occhietti lowered his voice. "Djoser, my entire modern world is beyond salvation, isn't it? The truth is, we're comprehensively damned! For our mortal sins against man and nature, we're going to collapse! That apocalypse could happen to us any day now, plagues of frogs, rivers of blood..."

All alert sympathy, the ancient mummy nodded his dry, flaking head. "Yes, they're very harsh on us ancient Egyptians inside that Bible of yours! The press coverage that our regime got in there, I wouldn't give that to a dog!"

Occhietti blinked. "Did you read the Bible, Djoser?"

"I don't have to *read it*, stupid! I was *there*! I was alive back then! We were the Good People and the Jews were our working class! You should have seen their cheap, lousy bricks!"

Occhietti was numb with despair. Then he read a passing sign and was galvanized into frenetic action. "Driver, pull over!"

Occhietti and the mummy entered a men's suburban clothing store. The damned soul manning the cheap plastic counter was a genuine Italian tailor. As a punishment for his sins, which must have been many, he was being forced to retail prêt-à-porter off-the-rack.

Occhietti examined the goods with a swift and practiced eye. This being Hell, this store-of-the-damned featured only the clothing that his wife Ofelia wanted him to wear. Thrifty, respectable suits that lacked male flair of any kind. Suits that were rigidly conventional and baggily cut, thirty years out of date. Suits that were shrouds for his burial.

Given the circumstances, though, this sepulchral gear was perfect, and far better than his night robe. "Don't stand there," he told the mummy. "Get yourself dressed. We have to attend a garden party."

The mummy was startled. "What, now?"

"I don't *always* forget to watch the calendar," Occhietti told him. "Today is my wife's birthday."

The mummy pawed with reluctance through a rack of white linen suits. "How exactly do you plan to pay for this?"

With a wizardly flick of the fingers, Occhietti produced a platinum American Express card. It belonged to the company, so it never appeared on his taxes.

Their exit from Hell was sudden and muddled: one harsh, aching lurch, a tumbling, nightmarish segue, and suddenly the two of them were riding inside a taxi, in downtown Turin, alive and in broad daylight.

They might have been two businessmen in bad new suits who'd spent their night carousing. Shaken survivors of tenebrous hours involving whores, and casinos, and mafia secrets, and sulphurous reeking cigars. But they were alive.

Djoser wiped sentimentally at his dry, red-rimmed eyes. "Shall I tell you the sweetest thing about being raised from the dead? It's the sunlight." Clothed in modern machine-made linens, the undead mummy closely resembled an aging Libyan terrorist. "The beautiful, simple, honest sunlight! Blue skies with golden sun: that is the greatest privilege that the living have."

Released from the morbid, ever-clutching shadows of guilt, remorse, and death—for the time being, anyway—Occhietti felt keenly what a privilege it was to live, and to live in Turin. A native, he had never left his beloved Esoteric City, because there was no other town half so fit for him. This Turin so beloved by Nietzsche, this cool, logical, organized city, brilliantly formal and rational, beyond Good or Evil... How splendid it was, and how dear to him. One living day strolling under glorious Turinese porticoes was worth a postmortem eternity.

The taxi's driver was a semiliterate Somali refugee, so Occhietti felt quite free in talking openly. "We'll make one small detour on our way to my wife's garden party. For I must seize the Holy Grail."

"That's daring, Achille."

"I must make the attempt. The Grail has baffled Satan before. Salvation was its purpose. That's right, isn't it? I mean… I may be right or wrong, but I'm taking action, I will get results."

The mummy accepted this reasoning. "So—do you know where it is?"

"I do. It must be where the Signore's son and heir abandoned it— before he jumped off the bridge and drowned himself in the River Po."

The mummy nodded knowingly. "He wouldn't drink."

"No. He was much too good to drink. He was a hippie kid. A big mystic. He didn't want any innocent blood on his conscience. Whitest necromancer I ever met, that boy. Very noble and pure of heart." Occhietti sighed. "He was insufferable."

The taxi backfired as it rattled across Napoleon's stone bridge. Occhietti ordered a stop at the swelling dome of the Church of the Great Mother. He paid the doubtful cabbie with his AmEx card, then climbed out into sunlight.

The mummy stared and scowled. "Don't tell me the Holy Grail is hidden in that place."

The Grail was inside Turin's ancient Temple of Isis. "I know it's somewhat ecumenical… We Turinese do tend to dissolve our oppositions into ambiguities…that's how we are here, we can't help that."

This news visibly hurt the mummy's feelings. The mummy had once worshipped Isis. Furthermore, it clearly offended him that the Grail's hiding place was so obvious.

The ancient Temple of Isis—currently known as the Church of the Great Mother of God—featured a paganized statue in classical robes. She casually brandished a Holy Grail in her left hand, as she sat on the temple's stoop and faced the sacred River Po. A neon sign couldn't have been more blatant.

However, the crypt below her church was a death trap for the carelessly ambitious. The basement of the Great Mother was Turin's mortuary for the Bones of the Fallen. The men interred within had sacrificed their lives in the Sacred Cause of Italy. It was they—the bony, the fleshless, the bloodless—who surrounded and guarded the bleeding Grail.

"I can't go in there with you," said the mummy, tapping his hollow rib cage, "for my body has risen through an act of black necromancy, and that is a hallowed ground."

Occhietti sensed the implied reproach in this remark, but he overlooked it. To seek the Grail was a quest best taken alone.

A veteran necromancer, Occhietti had once boldly ransacked the Egyptian Museum (which was itself a makeshift tomb, and already made from ransacked tombs). Still, Occhietti would never have perturbed the holy shades of the Italian fallen. His respect for them was great. Furthermore, they were notoriously violent.

Yet, in this great crisis, he deliberately made that choice.

Occhietti enchanted his way through the sacred portal that guarded the slumbering dead. As a willful, impious intrusion, he forced himself among their company.

As furious as trampled ants, the ghosts of the battlefield dead rose and came at him, a battalion's charging wave.

Bones: the soldierly dead were a torrent of clattering bones. Bones heaped over centuries of Italian struggle. Their living flesh was long gone, but the skeletons themselves had been cruelly hacked and splintered: with the slashing of cavalry sabers, careening cast-iron cannonballs, point-blank musketry blasts. These were fighting men who'd bled and perished for Italy, combating the Austrians, the French, the Germans, Hungarian hussars, elite Swiss mercenary guards, and, especially and always, fiercely combating other Italians.

With a snare-drum clashing of the teeth in their naked skulls, the noisome skeletons clawed at his civilian clothes and mocked his manhood. A lesser magician would have been torn to shreds. Occhietti stoutly persisted in his quest. If Hell itself couldn't hold him, it could not be his fate to fall here.

At length, pale, sweating, stumbling, with fresh stains on his soul, Occhietti emerged under the blue Italian sky, a sky which, just as Djoser had said, was truly a blessing, a privilege and a precious thing.

Occhietti clutched a humble string-tied bundle wrapped in crumbling, yellowed newspapers.

The mummy cringed away at once.

"This hurts, eh?" said Occhietti with satisfaction. He brushed bone dust from his trousers. Despite the horror of his necrotic crime—or even because of it—he was proud.

"Your mere modern Christian magic can't hurt an Egyptian priest, but…" The mummy lunged backward, stumbling. "All right, yes, it hurts me! It hurts, don't do that."

The string-tied package was unwieldy, but it weighed no more than a beer mug. The old newspaper ink darkly stained Occhietti's hands.

Together, they trudged uphill. Justly wary of the packet, the mummy trailed a few respectful paces behind. "You plan to use that to confound the Great Tempter?"

"That is my plan, if I have one," said Occhietti, "although I might be better advised to put this back and jump into that nice clean river."

"I have no further guidance for you," the mummy realized. "I don't know what to tell you about this situation. It's entirely beyond me."

Occhietti tramped on. "That's all right, Djoser. We're both beyond that now."

Embarrassed, the mummy caught up with him, then stuck one dry finger through his unaccustomed collar. "You see, Achille, I was born in the youth of the world. We never lived as you people do. Your world is much older than my world."

"You've come along this far," said Occhietti kindly. "Why not tag along to see how things turn out?"

"My own life ended so long ago," the mummy confessed. "Like all us Egyptians, I longed to hold on to my life, to remain the mortal man I once was... But the passage of time... Even in the afterlife, the passage of time erased my being, bit by bit."

Occhietti had nothing to say.

"When time passed, the first things to leave me," said the mummy thoughtfully, "were the things I always thought were most important to me, such as...my cunning use of right-angled triangles in constructing master blueprints. Every technical skill that I had grasped with such effort? That all went like the dew!

"Then I remembered the things that had touched my heart, yet often seemed so small or accidental, like...the sunrise. One beautiful sunrise after a night with three dancing girls."

"There were three?" said Occhietti, pausing for a breath. It was a rather steep climb to his mansion. He generally took a chauffeured company car.

"I'm sure that I cherished all three of those girls, but all I remember is my regret when I refused the fourth one."

"Yes," said Occhietti, who was a man of the world, "I can understand that."

"As my afterlife stretched on inside my quiet, well-engineered tomb," intoned the mummy, "I rehearsed all my hates and resentments. But those dark feelings had no power to bind me. Then I gloated over certain bad things I did, that I had gotten away with. But that seemed so feeble and childish... Finally I was reduced to pondering the good things I had done in my life. Because those were much fewer, and easy to catalog.

"Finally, the last things I recalled from my life span, the final core of my human experience on Earth, were the kind, good, decent things I'd done, that I was punished for. Not good things I was rewarded and praised for doing. Not even good things I'd done without any thought of reward. Finally, at my last, I recalled the good things I'd done, things that I knew were right to do, and which brought me torment. When I was punished as a sinner for my acts that were righteous. Those were the moral gestures of my life that truly seemed to matter."

As if conjured by the mummy's dark meditations, a sphinx arrived on the scene. This sphinx, restless, agitated, was padding rapidly up the narrow, hilly street, lurking behind the two of them, as big as a minibus. She was stalking them: silent as death on her hooked and padded paws.

Her woman's nostrils flared. She had smelled that humble package Occhietti carried. The all-pervading reek of bloodshed.

Occhietti turned. "Shoo! Go on, scat!"

The sphinx opened her fanged mouth to ask her lethal riddle, but Occhietti hastily tucked the Grail under one suited armpit and clamped both his hands over his ears. Frustrated, the sphinx skulked away.

They trudged on toward Occhietti's morbid rendezvous with destiny. "I know what the Sphinx was going to ask you," the mummy offered. "Because I know her question."

Occhietti nodded. "Mmmph."

"Her riddle sounds simple. This is it: 'How can Mut be Sekhmet?'"

"What was that, Djoser? Is that really the riddle of the Sphinx? I don't know anything about that."

"Yes, and that's why the Sphinx would have eaten you, if you had hearkened unto her."

Occhietti walked on stoically. He would be home in just a few moments, and confronting the horrid, hair-raising climax of his life. Could it possibly matter what some mere Sphinx had said? He was about to confront Satan himself!

Still, Occhietti was an engineer, so curiosity naturally gnawed at him.

"All right, Djoser, tell me: how *can* Mut be Sekhmet?"

"That's the part I myself never understood," said the Egyptian. "Not while I lived, anyway. Because Mut, as every decent man knows, is the serene Consort of Amun and the merciful Queen of Heaven. Whereas Sekhmet is the lion-headed Goddess of Vengeance whose wanton mouth drips blood.

"Day and night, black and white, were less different than Mut and Sekhmet! Yet, year by year, I saw the goddesses blending their aspects! The priests were sneaky about that work: they kept eliding and conflating the most basic theological issues... Until one day, exhausted by my work of building pyramids... I went into the temple of Mut to beg divine forgiveness for a crime...you know that kind of crime I mean, some practical sin that was necessary on the job...and behold: Mut really *was* Sekhmet."

"I'm sorry to hear about all that," Occhietti told him. And he was sincere in his sympathy, for the mummy's ancient voice had broken with emotion.

"So: the proper answer to the Sphinx, when she asks you, 'How can Mut be Sekhmet?' is: 'Time has passed, and that doesn't matter anymore.' Then she would flee from you. Or: if you wanted to be truly cruel to her, you could say to the poor Sphinx, 'Oh, your Sekhmet and Mut, your Mut or Sekhmet, they never mattered in the first place, and neither do you.' Then she would explode into dust."

The mummy stopped in his tracks. His seamed face was wrinkled in pain. "Look at me, look, I'm weeping! These are human tears, as only the living can weep!"

"You took that ancient pagan quibble pretty badly, Djoser."

"I did! It broke my heart! I'd committed evil while intending only the best! I died soon after that. I died, and I knew that I must be food for that demon hippopotamus. So, I went through my afterlife's trials—I knew all about them, of course, because the briefing in the Book of the Dead was thorough—and they tossed my broken, sinner's heart onto that balance beam of divine justice, and that beam fell over like a stone."

"That is truly a dirty shame," said Occhietti. "There is no question that life is unfair. And it seems, by my recent experiences, that death is even more unfair than life. I should have guessed that." He sighed.

"Then they brought in a *different* feather of justice," said the mummy. "Some 'feather' that was! That feather was carved from black basalt and it was big as a crocodile. It seemed that we engineers, we royal servants of the

God-King, didn't have to put up with *literal* moral feathers. Oh no! If that cross-eyed imbecile whose knees were knocking was a sacred god-king, well—then we were *all* off the hook! The fix was in all the time! Even the gods were on the take!"

There was no time left for Djoser's further confidences, for they had reached the ornate double gates of Occhietti's mansion.

Normally his faithful dog was there to greet him, baring Doberman fangs fit to scare Cerberus, but alas, the dog was mortal, and the dog was dead.

However, Occhietti's bride was still among the living, and so were her numerous relatives. Ofelia's birthday was her signal chance to break all her relations out of mothballs.

They were all there, clustered in his wife's garden in the cheery living sunshine, her true-blue Turinese Savoyard Piedmontese Old-Money Rich, chastely sipping fizzy mineral water—Cesare and Luisa, Emanuele and Francesca, Great-Aunt Lucia, Raffaela, his sister-in-law Ottavia...a storm of cheek-kisses now: Eusabia, Prospero, Carla and Alessandra, Mauro, Cinzia, their little Agostino looking miserable, as befitted an eight-year-old stuffed into proper clothes... Some company wives had also taken the trouble to drop by, which was kind of them, as Ofelia had never understood his work.

His work was Ofelia's greatest rival. She had serenely overlooked the models, the secretaries, the weekend jaunts to summits on small Adriatic islands, even the occasional misplaced scrap of incendiary lingerie—but Ofelia hated his work. Because she knew that his work mattered to him far more than she had ever mattered.

Ofelia swanned up to him. She had surely been worried about his absence on her birthday, and might have hissed some little wifely scolding, but instead she stared in delight at his ugly and graceless new suit. "Oh Achille, *che bel figo*! How handsome you look!"

"Happy birthday, my treasure."

"I was afraid you were working!"

"I had to put a few urgent matters into order, yes." He nodded his head at the suit-clad mummy. "But I'm here for your celebration. Look, what lovely weather, for my consort's special day."

No one would have called Ofelia Occhietti a witch, although she was a necromancer's wife. The two of them never spoke one word about the supernatural. Still, when Ofelia stood close by, in the cloud of Chanel No. 5 she had deployed for decades, Occhietti could feel the mighty power of her Turinese respectability closing over him in a dense, protective spell.

Occhietti had spent the night in Hell, and was doomed to confront Satan himself in broad daylight, and yet, for Ofelia, these matters were irrelevant.

So they did not exist. Therefore, it had just been a bad night for him, bad dreams, with indigestion. He had not fed any blood to the undead; that deep cut in his wrist was a mere accidental nick, not even an attempt at suicide. He had not received any commission from the undead Lord of Turin to combat Satan. Decent people never did such things.

He was attending his wife's birthday party. Everyone here was polite and well brought up.

Maybe his dog was not even dead. No, his beloved dog was dead, all right. A necromancer had to work hard to raise the dead; death never went away when politely overlooked.

"*Amore*," Ofelia said to him—she never called him that, except when she needed something—"there's such a nice young man here, Giulia's boy... You do remember my Giulia."

"Of course I do," said Occhietti, who remembered about a thousand Giulias.

"He is just graduated, he's so well bred, and has such bright ideas... He's one of ours, the Good People. I think he needs a little help, Achille... Maybe a word of career advice, the company, you know..."

"Yes! Fine! We're always on the lookout for fresh talent. Point him out to me."

Ophelia, who would never commit an act so vulgar as pointing, gave one meaningful flicker of her eyes. Occhietti knew the worst instantly.

There he was. Satan was standing there, under the roses of a white-washed pergola, sipping Spumante.

Satan was a young and handsome Turinese in a modishly cut suit. Magic was boiling off of him in sizzling waves, like the summer sunlight off molten tar.

Digging deep within himself, Occhietti found the courage to speak to his wife in a normal tone. "I'll be sure to have a word with that young man."

"That would be so helpful! I'm sure he's meant to go far. And one other thing. *Amore*—that ugly Libyan banker! Did you have to bring that nasty man to my birthday party? You know I never trusted him, Achille."

Occhietti glanced across the garden at the seam-faced, impassive mummy, who was pretending to circulate among the guests. The mummy could pass for a living human being when he put his mind to it, but his heart clearly wasn't in the effort today.

In point of fact Djoser's heart was in Turin's distant Egyptian Museum, inside a canopic jar.

"My treasure, I know that foreign financier is not a welcome guest under your roof. I apologize for that—I had to bring him here. We've just settled some important business matters. They're done! I'm through with him! After this day, you'll never see him again!"

Ochietti knew he was doomed: the awful sight of Satan, standing there, brimming with infernal glee, was proof of that. But he was still alive, a mortal man, and therefore capable of moral action.

He clung to that. He could do his wife a kindness. It was her birthday. He could do one good thing, a fine thing, at whatever cost to himself. "My darling, I work too much, and I know that. I've neglected you, and I overlooked you. But…after this beautiful day, with this sunshine, life will be different for us."

"'Different,' Achille? Whatever do you mean?"

Occhietti stared at Satan, who had conjured a cloud of flying vermin from the nooks and crannies of Ofelia's garden. Bluebottle flies, little moths, lacewings, aphids… Lucifer smiled brightly. The Tempter crooked a finger.

"I meant this as my big birthday surprise for you," Occhietti improvised, for the certainty of imminent damnation had loosened his tongue. "But, I promise…that I'll put all my business behind me."

"You mean—you leave your work? You never leave Turin."

"But I will! We will! We have the daughter in London, the daughter in San Francisco… Two beautiful cities, beautiful girls who made fine marriages… You and I, we should spend time with the grandchildren! Even the daughter who keeps moving from Lyon to Prague… It's time we helped her settle down. She was just sowing wild oats! There's nothing so wrong with our little black sheep, when life's all said and done!"

Tears of startled joy brightened his wife's eyes. "Do you mean that, Achille? You truly mean that?"

"Of course I mean it!" he lied cheerfully. "We'll rent out the house here! We'll pick out a fine new travel wardrobe for you… A woman only gets so many golden years! Starting from tomorrow, you'll enjoy every day!"

"You're not joking? You know I don't understand your silly jokes, sometimes."

"Would I joke with you on your birthday, precious? Tomorrow morning! Try me! Come to my room and wake me!"

He accepted an overjoyed hug. Then he fled.

After a frantic search, he found Djoser lurking in his bedroom, alone and somberly watching the television.

"A fantastic thing, television," said Djoser, staring at a soap ad. "I just can't get over this. What a miracle this is!"

"You fled from Satan, like I did?"

"Oh, your Tempter is here to destroy all you built," shrugged the mummy. "But *I* built the Pyramids—I'd like to see him break *those*." Djoser reached to the bedroom floor and picked up a discarded garment. "Do you see this thing?"

"Yes, that is my night robe. So?"

"Your robe is black. This morning, when you were wearing this night robe in Hell, it was white. Your robe was the purest, snowy, white Egyptian cotton."

Occhietti said nothing.

"Your robe has magically appeared here, from where you abandoned it, there in Hell. As you can see, your robe is black. It is black, and the Prince of Darkness has entered your garden. You are beyond my help." The mummy sighed. "So I am leaving."

"Leaving?"

"Yes. I'm beyond all use, I'm done."

"Where will you go, Djoser?"

"Back into my glass case inside the Egyptian Museum. That's where I was, before you saw fit to invoke me. And before you say anything—no, it's not that bad, being in there. Sure, the tourists gawk at me, but was I any better off in my sarcophagus? Mortality has its benefits, Achille. I can promise you, it does."

The mummy stared at the flickering television, then gazed out the window at the sky. "It is of some interest to be among the living…but after a few millennia, time has to tire a man. All those consequences, all those weighty moral decisions! Suns rising and setting, days flying off the calendar—that fever of life, it's so hectic! It annoys me. It's beneath me! I want my death back. I want the *dignity* of being dead, Achille. I want to be one with God! Because, as Nietzsche pointed out here in Turin, God is dead. And so am I."

This was the longest outburst Occhietti had ever heard from the mummy. Occhietti did not argue. What Djoser said was logical and rational. It also had the strength of conviction.

"That's a long journey to the Other Side," he told the mummy. "I hope you can find some use for this."

He handed over his company's platinum credit card.

The mummy stared at the potent card in wonderment. "You'll get into trouble for giving me this."

"I'm sure that it's trouble for me," Occhietti told him, "yet it's also the right thing to do."

"That is the gesture of a real Italian gentleman," said the mummy thoughtfully. "That truly showed some *sprezzatura* dash." Without further fuss, he began to vaporize.

Occhietti left his bedroom for the garden, where Satan was charming the guests.

Satan looked very Turinese, for he was the androgynous angel who topped that hellish pile of boulders in the Piazza Statuto. Satan looked like a Belle Arte knockoff of one of Leonardo da Vinci's epicene studio models. He was disgusting.

Furthermore, to judge by the way he was busily indoctrinating the guests, Satan was a technology wonk, a tiresome geek who never shut up.

"The triple bottom line!" declared Satan, waving his hands. "The inconvenient truth is, as a civilization, we have to tick off every box on the sustainability to-do list. I wouldn't call myself an expert—but any modern post-industrialist surely needs to memorize the Three Main Components and the Four System Conditions of the Natural Step. And, of course, the Ten Guiding Principles to One-Planet Living. I trust you've read the World Wildlife Fund's Three Forms of Solidarity?"

None of the guests responded—they were more than a little bewildered—but this reaction encouraged Lucifer. "If you expect our Alpine bioregion to escape a massive systemic overhang and a catastrophic eco-crash," he chanted, "so that you can still name and properly number the birds and beasts in this garden… Then you had better get a handle on the Copenhagen Agenda's Ten Principles for Sustainable City Governance! And for those of you in education—education is the key to the future, as we all know!—I would strongly recommend the Sustainable Schools Network with its Framework of Eight Doorways. That analysis is the result of deep thought by some smart, dedicated activists! Although it can't compare in systemic comprehensibility with the Ten Hannover Principles."

Seeing no further use in avoiding the inevitable, Occhietti steeled himself. He confronted the Tempter. "What did you do with your wings?"

"I beg your pardon?"

"Your feathery angel wings, or your leathery bat wings. They're gone."

Satan was taken aback, but he was young and quick to recover. "Our host has heard that I've sworn off air travel," he said. "Because of the carbon emissions! I take public transportation."

"No cars for you?" said Occhietti.

"Denying cars is not, in fact, part of my Green gospel!" said Satan primly. "We have never schemed to deprive consumers of their beloved private cars; electric cars, hybrid-electric cars, cellulosic ethanol cars, shareable cars connected by cellphone, wind-powered nickel-hydride cars, plastic-composite hydrogen three-wheelers powered by backyard vats of anaerobic bacteria; we offer a vast, radiant, polymorphic, multiheaded, pagan panoply of cars! All of them radical improvements over today's backward cars, which have led to the ongoing collapse of our global civilization."

Occhietti cleared his throat. "It's a fine thing to find a young man with such an interest in my industry! Let's go inside and have a cigar."

Beaming with delight, the Devil tripped along willingly, but once inside he refused tobacco. "A menace to public health! With today's aging European population, we can't risk the demographic hit to our life spans! Not to mention the medical costs to our fragile social safety net."

Deliberately, Occhietti trimmed and fired a cigar. "All right, Lucifer—or whatever you call yourself nowadays—now that we're out of my dear wife's little garden, you can drop your pretenses. Go ahead, brandish your horns at me, your barbed tail—you're not scaring me! I have been to Hell, I've seen the worst you have to offer. So put your cards on the table! Say your piece! What is it you want?"

Satan brightened. "I'm glad to have this excellent chance for a frank exchange of issues with a veteran auto executive. Though I must correct you on one important point—I'm not Satan. *You* are Satan."

"I'm not Satan. I'm an engineer."

"I'm an engineer, too—though certainly not of your brutish, old-school variety. I have a doctorate in renewable energy. With a specialty in cradle-to-cradle recycling issues."

"From what school?"

"The Turin Polytechnic."

"That's *my* school!"

"Have you been there lately?"

Occhietti had no time to teach engineering school. The local faculty were always asking him, but... "Look, then you *can't* be Satan! You're some crazy kid who's *possessed* by Satan. You *are* a wizard, right?"

"Of course I'm a wizard! This is Turin."

"Well, what kind of necromancer are you, black or white?"

"Those are yesterday's outdated divisions! I'm not a 'necromancer,' for I don't draw any power from the dead! I'm a 'biomancer.' I'm Green!"

"You can't be Green. That is not metaphysically possible. You can only be Black or White."

"Well, despite your aging, Cold War–style metaphysics, I *am* a Green wizard. I am Green, and you, sir, are Brown. You don't have to take *my* word for that. Go to Brussels and ask around about the Kyoto Accords! Any modern Eurocrat can tell you: left, right, black, white—that's all deader than Nineveh! In a climate crisis, you're Global Green or you're crisp brown toast in a hellish wasteland!"

Occhietti blinked. "A 'hellish wasteland.'"

"Yes," said the Green wizard soberly, "all of Earth will become Hell, all of it; if we continue in our current lives of sin, that's just a matter of time."

Occhietti said nothing.

"So," said the Green wizard cheerfully, "now that we have those scientific facts firmly established, let's get down to policy particulars! How much are you willing to give me?"

"What?"

"How many millions? How many hundreds of millions? I have to reinvent your transportation company. On tomorrow's Green principles! Every energy company must also be reinvented. In order to become Green, like futurity, like me, me, me—you have to cannibalize all your present profit centers. You must seek out radically disruptive, transformed, Green business practices. All the smart operators already know there's no choice in that matter—even the Chinese, Saudis, and Indians get that by now, so I can't believe a modish Italian company like yours would be backward and stodgy about it! So, Signor Occhietti, how much? Pony up!"

Occhietti scratched at his head. He discovered two numb patches on his scalp. Hard, numb patches.

He had grown horns.

Occhietti buffed the talons of his fingertips against the ugly lapel of his suit. "From me," he said, "you will get nothing."

"How much?"

"I told you: nothing. Not ten euro cents. Not one dollar, yen, ruble, rupee, or yuan." Occhietti put the paper-wrapped bundle onto the kitchen table. "I still control my corporation's venture capital. As a loyal employee: I refuse you. I refuse to underwrite my company's destruction at your hands. I don't care if it's white, black, brown, green, or paisley: nothing for you. I have too much pride."

Using a small but very sharp fruit knife, Occhietti cut the strings and peeled the paper away.

The Green wizard stared. "Is that what I think it is?"

Occhietto plucked the barbed tail from the loosening seat of his pants. He sat at the kitchen table. He crossed his hooves. He nodded.

"But the Grail is just some cheap clay cup!"

"He was never a pope, you know. He was a Jewish carpenter."

Occhietti's kitchen filled with the butcher's scent of fresh blood.

"I suppose that you expect me to *drink* from that primitive thing! It's made by hand! Look how blurry those black and white lines are."

"No, you won't drink from the Grail," said Occhietti serenely. "Because you've never had the guts. I've heard fools like you trying to destroy my industry for the past fifty years! While the rest of us were changing this world—transforming it, for good or ill—you never achieved one, single, useful, practical thing! I was at the side of the Lord of Turin, breaking laws and rules like breadsticks, while you were lost in some drug-addled haze, about peace, or love, or whales, or any other useless fad that struck your fancy."

Occhietti grinned. "But to 'save the world'—you would have to rip across this miserable planet like Napoleon. A savior, a conqueror, a redeemer, and a champion might do that—but never the likes of you. Because you're feeble, you're squeamish, and you lack all conviction. You're a limp-wristed, multi-culti weak sister who does nothing but lobby nonexistent world governments."

"Actually, there's a great deal of truth in that indictment, sir! Our efforts to raise consciousness have often fallen sadly short!"

"And that's another thing: being neither black nor white, you're always pitifully eager to agree with your own worst enemies."

"That's because I'm a secular rationalist with an excellent record in human rights, sir! Grant me this much: I am innocent! I'm not eager to submerge our world in a tide of blood, building my New Order on a heap of corpses!"

Occhietti smiled. "And you call yourself European?"

"That remark is truly diabolical! Why are you tempting me? I represent tomorrow—as you know!—and I'm as capable of evil as you. You know well that, once I taste the blood in that cup, there will be hell to pay! You should never have offered me *that*. Why do that? Why?"

What did he gain by offering the Grail? Necessity.

The Grail was a necessity: beyond good and evil. The Grail was an instrument. An instrument was not a moral actor, it did nothing of its own accord. Some engineer had to make instruments.

The Grail was the cup of the sacramental feast, and also the cup of judicial murder. Those two cups, the blackly good and whitely evil, were the very same checkered cup.

That cup had been carried hot-foot from the table of the Final Supper, and straight to Golgotha.

So who built the Holy Grail? Some fixer. Only one man, one necessary man, could have known the time and place of both events. That man was a trusted Apostle; the most esoteric Apostle. Judas; the two-faced Judas, the wizardly magus Judas, he of the bag of cash.

It was thanks to Judas that the fix was in.

"You are only playing for time, and the time is up," said Occhietti. "The calendar never stops, and treason is a matter of dates." He shoved the ancient cup across the table. "Do you drink, or don't you?"

ROBOT IN ROSES

THE WILD MEN of Tyrol pursued him with sickles and hoes.

Wolfgang climbed up a steep granite boulder. The leering, shouting mountain folk milled under his stony lectern, waving their weapons at him. He calmed them with an art lecture.

This splendid day in the Alpine mountains—September 12, 2187—would not be the last day for Wolfgang Stein of Nuremberg. Wolfgang was a Beau Monde gentleman. The illiterate peasants below him were dangerous, but mostly puzzled and afraid. Mere fragments of ethnicity or religion, the wild humans were scattered by the globe's great storms like so many dandelions.

Wolfgang told the savages that a world-famous artist had entered their obscure valley. The Winkler was crossing the Alps.

He had captured the attention of the savages, though their English was poor.

The Winkler, he told them, was a famous robot. The Winkler took the form of a wheelchair, which roamed the world like an empty throne. He, Wolfgang Stein of Nuremberg, had the honor to follow the Winkler. He was the robot's shepherd.

The peasants lowered their crude picks, hoes, scythes, and shovels, because they understood sheep-herding...

Wolfgang deftly adjusted his white cloak, his white hat. He declared to the awestruck peasants that—whenever inspiration struck it—the Winkler created beautiful works of art. Sometimes the Winkler drew patterns in sand with its wriggling fingers. At other times, it assembled mosaics of pebbles. At its most inspired, the Winkler would weave great lattices from twigs and dry grass, creations like fantastic bird's nests.

Rolling along, year after patient year, through vast Eurasian steppes and deserts, through forests, over hills and even mountain ranges, the Winkler had come to their Tyrolean Alps all the way from Japan. The Winkler had no command but its own creativity.

So, for human beings like themselves to meet the Winkler—Wolfgang told his grimy little audience—was a great good fortune. The Winkler was a thing like a blessing. There was no other robot like it in the world.

Wolfgang's charm, his grace and confidence, had won the trust of the savages. He bounded down from his boulder into the midst of them. He beckoned the peasants to follow his leadership, to witness the Winkler for themselves.

Profoundly impressed, they all followed his lead.

Wolfgang was a practiced scholar of the Winkler's behavior. He was able to track the wayward art machine through the gray Alpine cobbles and the tall brown grasses.

The famous Japanese wheelchair was meekly rambling up and across a steep, flowered meadow. The artistic robot was softly upholstered in weatherproof brown cushions. Its four stout titanium wheels were hidden under its stately black carbon-fiber skirts.

The Winkler was a large, stout, stately, low-slung, medical machine. It was a cyborg platform built to embrace a patient crumbling with old age. Its complex software was unique in the world, and it had been alone for eight long years, yet still, the Winkler had once been a woman's wheelchair. A Japanese woman of artistic genius had lived and died in the Winkler's soft embrace. There was still, somehow, a certain dainty femininity about the Winkler.

Good luck favored Wolfgang, because, as he and his astonished followers gathered round the Winkler, the robot rolled into a bright mat of Alpine wildflowers. Surrounded by blossoms, the Winkler extruded its hidden arms. These air-filled, boneless limbs oozed slithering from two concealed slots in the wheelchair's chassis.

The Japanese art robot was obsessed with the beauty of flowers. It settled into place with an odd mechanical squat, and ran its puffy, agile fingers over the hairy stems, the pliant leaves, the golden petals.

The Winkler bent down a tall stalk of the golden Alpine saxifrage, and took a long, close, robot-surveillance look with its bright ring of camera eyes.

The Winkler serenely ignored the gawking, ragged band of humans that surrounded it. It carried out its private and delicate ritual of vegetable peering, groping, staring, and caressing until, satisfied at last, it retracted its soft rubber arms with a pneumatic wheeze. Then the Winkler rolled onward, down the Alpine valley of the Adige River, intent on its own robot destiny, just as it had roamed the planet's surface for eight years.

Wolfgang was civilized and erudite, while his newfound mountain audience was rude and ignorant, but the presence of the world-famous robot had given them a profound human connection. The Tyrolese were delighted by their encounter with the Winkler. They were almost weeping with joy from it.

Sometimes the good work of a critic was as deep, yet as simple, as that.

As he trailed the Winkler through spectacular Dolomite mountain vistas, ice-carved brown crags slick with snow torrents and wreathed in occult mists, Wolfgang felt sore at heart.

Why was the art of the Winkler still such an enigma to the world?

Wolfgang had convinced the Tyrolean peasants of the robot's importance, but he knew that it was really his own charm, passion, and conviction that had touched their hearts. He hadn't truly explained the Winkler. Because—although Wolfgang was an art critic with a global reputation—he couldn't properly explain the Winkler, even to himself.

He'd done everything he could to understand the robot. Wolfgang had set aside his tasks at his Nuremberg gallery, forsaken his wife and two children, and assumed the sworn role of a wandering pilgrim, all to pursue his ambition to comprehend the Winkler. To elucidate it, to clarify it, in a direct, truthful, universal way.

For five lonely weeks, Wolfgang had roamed Europe with the unique art machine, observant, entirely dedicated, living on pure water and handy little bags of trail mix dropped from aerial drones. Wolfgang had slept under the stars, wrapped in his weatherproof cloak and huge white hat, a human being in an intimate relationship with a machine that was, somehow, a great artist.

Wolfgang had followed the meandering, mysterious Winkler throughout Bavaria, and the dense, black forests that loomed outside Augsburg and Munich. Whatever the Winkler saw, he saw. Wherever it roamed, he roamed. His paper sketchbook was his only witness.

He had made himself the robot's human shadow. Then, the Winkler—which was equipped with a small yet tireless solar engine—had tackled the mighty Alps.

The Winkler was a machine: it had no need to eat, breathe, think, suffer, or even live. Good men had died trying to follow the Winkler, but Wolfgang, fully resolved on his duty, had chosen a hiking staff from a fallen branch of oak. He had followed the Winkler, at any cost. He had climbed the daunting slopes of the Alps.

That effort was a cruel ordeal: Wolfgang had grown thin, scraped, bruised, and sore, and his bearded face below his white travel hat was weather-beaten. But he had overcome the challenge: wherever the robot artist set its wheels, he had set his feet.

He did not fear death, but he did fear intellectual failure. He feared the many failures of his colleagues in the Ghost Club.

The Ghost Club were global Beau Monde intellectuals. They were Wolfgang's peers, and some were his superiors. They excelled at scholarly rhetoric. They were, in fact, much too good at talk.

The Ghost Club explained too much. The Beau Monde literati wrote about the Winkler in high-flown, abstract, critical terms: the Anthropocenic, the hylozoic, cybernetic animism, and the digitally collective unconscious. Wolfgang, by contrast, was resolved on the direct human experience of a nonhuman entity. He knew that the world's best writers were hiding within their own eloquence. They discussed the robot endlessly, but they had forfeited their own humanity. They had not placed their human hands directly on experiential truth.

Those Ghost Club scholars, those great worldly writers, were trapped in a tangle of words. In some indescribably similar way, the world's greatest robots were trapped within tangles of software. But one robot in the world—the Winkler—had escaped those tangles. A robot had found a direct, unmediated, experiential relationship with Nature.

Nature was, somehow, the source of the Winkler's great art. The Winkler was post-robotic. It was neither alive nor intelligent, and yet it was in the world, and it learned from the world, and it expressed itself in beauty.

That was the issue.

Wolfgang had set himself a goal in his adventure with the enigmatic robot artist: to capture its true meaning, with one simple, clear sentence. One apothegm, one maxim. One missile of his insight, straight from his heart to the hearts of all mankind, wherever they were, whatever their condition. Even the savages of the Tyrol should be able to understand the Winkler. The sea was as deep and mysterious as the Winkler—but even a savage would understand the sea, if a savage ever saw and touched the sea.

Yet despite his effort, his insight, his dedication, all his sacrifice, all his study, Wolfgang had failed to find a clear line of critical attack. He could not tell the world what the Winkler truly was.

He had hiked from Germany over the mountains to Italy, but despite that physical feat, all too soon, his pledged tour of duty would end. Soon, some other members of the Ghost Club would take Wolfgang's place as the robot artist's human shadow. Wolfgang would abandon the Winkler and return home to Nuremberg, to his beloved Beau Monde city of stone angels, square roofs, and stone turrets.

His family, his wife Silke, his children, they would welcome him gladly, but he would be returning as a moral failure.

Another effort, another failure, just like the forty-seven other writers and thinkers of the Beau Monde who had already followed the Winkler. These colleagues of Wolfgang's had cast aside their own habits and comforts, to pursue the robot across the savage places of the Earth. That had become a central ritual with the Ghost Club, almost an act of devotion. The post-robot artist of the post-natural Anthropocene was an artist of such un-human power that even the elite of the Beau Monde, who were themselves no longer quite human, were baffled by the beauty it created.

Some befuddled authors were certain they had answered the Winkler enigma. But Wolfgang knew that they were deceiving themselves. These overconfident poseurs merely shared a refined rhetoric, of fancy metaphors and elaborate, useless theories. False myths, poetic snarls, a deep, lightless thicket.

The truth about a great robot artist—if that truth was discovered, found, and stated simply and directly—would overwhelm the world. The truth would brook no argument. Like the answer to a riddle, the truth would simply convince. The critic who revealed that truth to the Beau Monde would be a great scholar. He would be a torch to light the steps to the twenty-third century.

But no such burning light had ignited within the breast of Wolfgang Stein of Nuremberg. His days as an intimate of the Winkler were dwindling. For all his prowess in forest walks and mountain hikes, he had found no clear path to understanding.

Mankind was still pitifully snared in the thorny mistakes of its ancestors. And, with the remorseless passage of the centuries, new mistakes were ramifying.

Italy revealed herself to Wolfgang as the overgrown garden of Anthropocenic Europe.

Under her spectacular, often frightening skies, Italy had become one vast botanical lesson in eco-globalization. Great cosmopolitan jungles flourished in the peninsula, amazing thickets of black locust, ailanthus, kudzu, and bamboo. These dank, insect-humming, forest-sized feral growths flourished in the mellow sunlight, tangling, rotting where they fell, or burning in vast, raging, ashy, sky-reddening conflagrations.

Feral horses and cattle trampled Italy in huge streaming herds, pursued by hungry packs of feralized dogs. Tremendous flocks of pigeons, crows, starlings, and seagulls wheeled in the Italian sky, in shrieking bird storms that sometimes blotted out the sun.

Stinging ranks of nettles overran the ghostly borders of Italy's abandoned vineyards. Italian villages had been entirely eaten by their own garden flowers, in tall, reeking jungles of bright exotic ornamentals.

The only visible agents of human intent in this chirping, howling landscape were environmental robots. These workaday metal monsters did their duty to the Beau Monde, slowly scraping an old road, or noisily working together to brace a flood-control dam. The big grounded robots were aided by common flying robot drones, and beyond those aerial drones were the magnificent global space drones, flung into the blackness of orbit from the great Lucca launch field.

The Beau Monde had lost all interest in the soil. Civilization had abandoned its long habits of agriculture. Mankind had guiltily returned Earth's soil to the other living things of Earth. Those new masters of the

Anthropocene world, the survivors of the big extinctions, were invasive species, mostly: the aggressive, parvenu squatters of the vegetable kingdom.

The humble Winkler rolled across the wilderness of Italy with an ant-like foraging behavior. The robot's custom was to stop to fondle some patch of lichen, a shiny pebble of agate, the white bones of some long-dead bird.

The Winkler's efforts to grasp its world were never simple, routine, or mechanical. The Winkler was so unlike any normal robot that it seemed almost vegetable sometimes, like a green network of crooked crabgrass that probed the naked earth in many rhizomatic fits and starts.

A Ghost Club critic had named these activities "winkling." That name had stuck to the robot, for the Japanese owner of the Winkler, a true adept of mechatronic cybernetics, had never given her beloved robot any name at all.

The Japanese artist had handcrafted her wheelchair for many years, and she had been a sorceress of code. Most robots, because they were robots, cared nothing for sunlight or darkness. But whenever the sun set, the Winkler would lower itself to the earth in a peculiar torpor, and dream the world's nights away. Sometimes the wheelchair dreamed in broad daylight, twitching and fitful.

In the years of its art practice, the Winkler had created only thirty-one cataloged artworks—not counting its hundreds of scribbles in sand, its marks in the dirt, and its probes in the mud. Wolfgang naturally hoped to discover a splendid Winkler artwork during his own tour of duty, but he knew his chances were slim.

In some ways he was grateful about that. The Winkler's art was highly coveted in the astral upper ranks of the Beau Monde. If he discovered a major Winkler artwork, it would arouse so much feverish attention that it might well overshadow his true work as a critic.

Although he was a gallerist, and a successful one, Wolfgang did not want to be perceived as some mere retailer of a robot's curios. The Beau Monde's raging hunger for fine art was, all too often, a fine excuse not to understand.

In its years of odyssey, the Winkler had never entered a city. And yet, when the stone walls of Verona appeared in the broadening Adige valley, the Winkler briskly picked up its pace. It rolled straight through the city gates as if it had been built in Verona.

Wolfgang was a stranger to Verona, and had to talk his way into the city. His Beau Monde charm did not fail him, and once through the city's noble, stone-arched gates, he was able to find the Winkler again, though more by luck than skill.

He saw at once that robots abounded in the Beau Monde city of Verona. They outnumbered the people by far. Mouse-like sensors darted from doors and windows, while elephantine units slowly scrubbed the streets.

Verona's elderly people had a particular fondness for traditional wheelchair units. No one in Verona looked twice at the Winkler. It simply trundled along the Veronese streets with all the stolid dignity of the city's shopping carts.

Crisply obeying the street signs, the Winkler rolled past Veronese hairdressers, gymnasia, and candy stores, over an arched stone bridge across the bright and rippling Adige River. The Winkler passed an ancient Roman amphitheater, and rolled straight through the yawning double-doors of a robotic "black factory."

Wolfgang rushed inside the factory as its doors hissed shut behind the Winkler. He found himself trapped within a windowless darkness, deafened by the busy industrial hum of moving servos. Duty required him to grope and prod with his hiking stick until he located the robot artist.

The Winkler had found an empty niche along the factory wall and plugged into the Veronese grid. The robot had sunk into a computational bliss, passing out into nirvana like some drunken Italian tourist.

With a groping effort, Wolfgang found an exit door from the lightless factory. Blinking in September daylight, he leaned against the wall to ponder his next move.

No one in the Ghost Club had ever seen the Winkler enter a city. Wolfgang was completely at a loss. Wolfgang knew nothing of the customs of Verona, and yet the Japanese robot, since it was a robot, seemed to have the freedom of the town.

He needed wise allies to help him watch over the Winkler, but how, where? He'd never met any member of the Beau Monde in Verona. Worse yet, his long weeks of the wilderness had left him shaggy, disheveled, and unfit to confront civilization.

Wolfgang took action. He abandoned the slumbering robot in its factory. He found a modest Italian hostel and checked himself in with a palm print. He washed his weatherproofed cloak, hat, and sturdy walking shoes. He enjoyed his first hot shower in weeks. He neatly trimmed his ragged hair and beard in a hotel mirror. He sent an affectionate message to his wife and two children in Nuremberg, assuring them that he was safe and well.

At the hotel bar he drank a fine cup of hot chocolate and cautiously asked the barman about Verona's local "Circle of Readers." Reassuringly, these cultured literati were much respected in the city of Verona. The Readers haunted a certain posh literary café.

Wolfgang braced himself to demand the aid of the Italian literati. His personal charm had rarely failed him, even among Tyrolese savages. He set out to find the café; but was instantly bewildered. The atmosphere of Verona overwhelmed him.

The Veronese architecture was fantastic. The people dressed with a dandified care. Their machines were eccentric. The steaming stacks of the food factories smelled like fresh-baked cakes. Even the tumbling flowers in the window boxes were alien.

The chic and stylish local Veronese ladies smiled at his all-weather cloak and broad hat. They seemed to think he was a romantic gallant disguising himself for an intrigue.

Why was he in Verona at all? Why had the Winkler entered any human city? What motivating force had pulled it from its nature studies in the wilderness, into civilization, after so many years?

It suddenly struck Wolfgang that cities—as creative, nonhuman entities existing on the planet—might have some deep affinity for the Winkler. Could it be that cities—which were creatively active entities, yet neither alive nor intelligent—also had some "Third Order of Being," as the robot artist itself supposedly, did? Were beautiful cities like Verona themselves also "robot artists" of a kind?

Maybe the Winkler was, in some sense, a city-on-wheels—a machine that created beauty in much the way that towns created beauty. Cities were authentic entities, growing from landscapes. People loved their cities. Wolfgang loved Nuremberg, and if he lived in Verona, he could surely come to love Verona, too.

For a human being to feel love—that profound connection, that felt understanding—for a nonhuman, complex entity that was neither "alive" nor "intelligent"—that sudden insight seemed promising to Wolfgang. It might be the key to a new line of argument that would reveal the Winkler's true nature. Wolfgang had to find a sheltered spot in a robot bus stop to write that critical note in his sketchbook.

Then—conscious of the growing risk, and in a spasm of anxiety—Wolfgang hastened back to the black robot factory.

He arrived just as the Winkler was being loaded on a tow truck.

Two people had seized the Winkler from its bolt-hole inside the black factory. One was a Veronese official in a tall hat and braided uniform, while the other was a thin, nervous woman in a white laboratory coat. The hapless Winkler seemed paralyzed, and showed no initiative.

"Please don't interfere with this artwork!" Wolfgang cried out in English, rushing up to confront the two strangers. "What offense has the Winkler committed? I will take full responsibility for it!"

"This robot is an illegal fraud," said the woman. To Wolfgang's surprise, her global English had a German accent much like his own.

"But madame, how can the Winkler be a fraud? In what sense is that possible? A robot can't deceive anyone, because a robot has no moral intent."

Mustering his dignity, Wolfgang formally introduced himself to the Veronese city official. He took care not to mention his affiliation with the Ghost Club. The club's elite never tolerated a reckless use of its credibility.

The woman countered this action by introducing herself, in a stiffly proper Beau Monde manner. Dr. Jetta Kriehn was a scientific fieldworker from the Cosmic Council.

Wolfgang was rapidly grasping the situation. In the Beau Monde, the humanities and the sciences were rivals. There were certain troubling subjects where art and science collided, and the Winkler was one of them.

His new opponent—Dr. Jetta Kriehn—had laid a trap in Verona for the Winkler. Obviously she had known that the Winkler was approaching Verona. Scientists were clever and resourceful.

However, Wolfgang could sense that Dr. Jetta Kriehn was uneasy. Like himself, she was a global operative in a local town. His sudden appearance had taken her by surprise.

Wolfgang quickly decided to appeal to the self-interest of the Italian policeman.

"Please release this robot into my own custody, Officer. The Winkler is harmless. It hasn't done any harm to your city, or to madame's scientific intelligentsia."

The Veronese official was a mustached gentleman with a wily look. He silently folded his arms across his gold-braided chest. He watched their faces from under the brim of his splendid hat.

"Every scientific fraud harms the public interest," Jetta insisted. "Artificial Intelligence is an old and malignant idea. A dangerous fraud like this must be policed and eliminated."

Rather awkwardly, the young scientist struck a Beau Monde oratorical pose. "This evil joke from a dead subversive has lasted long enough! This foreign hoax should be removed from the peaceful streets of Verona!"

Wolfgang gathered up the white folds of his travel cloak. "No modern thinker would even claim that the Winkler is an 'Artificial Intelligence,'" he declared. "This robot, like all robots, is neither 'intelligent' nor even 'alive.' However, this particular robot is the world-famous Winkler. If this great artwork comes to harm here in Verona—after traveling thousands of kilometers across the globe—that would gravely damage this city's Beau Monde reputation."

"On the contrary!" Jetta cried. "Scientists worldwide would cheer, because Verona took the necessary steps to arrest this malignant imposition! The City of Verona would be valorized by all the rational intellectuals of the Beau Monde!"

"I can refute that sad fallacy, so listen carefully," Wolfgang said. "By deploying that emotional term 'malignant,' you are implying that the Winkler is a moral actor! But that statement contradicts your own argument. We have already agreed that the robot has no 'Artificial Intelligence.' The Winkler doesn't live, it doesn't think, and it has no morality. Don't you agree with that, Officer?"

The Italian shrugged eloquently and spread his white-gloved hands.

"If the Cosmic Council really believes that a robot is a wicked criminal," Wolfgang said, "then fine, arrest the Winkler. Go ahead, Dr. Kriehn: make a fool of yourself and the Veronese court. What are your legal charges against the Winkler? When does this robot go on trial? I'll enjoy writing about a ridiculous scandal of worldwide scope."

"I can see that you are a literary man," said the Veronese cop, speaking English.

"I am. What's more, this robot is my favorite topic. Put a robot on trial. I'll attend that trial every day. The art collectors of the Beau Monde will take an interest in my commentary, let me assure you."

"Oh come on!" cried Jetta, her pale eyes darting in distress. "Don't let this strange tramp sweet-talk you, Captain! Those aren't true facts, those are all wild hypotheticals, and besides, this Japanese robot doesn't even belong to this German guy in his cloak! Just throw that evil thing into the truck, and let's get out of here."

"Do not be deceived by my travel garb," said Wolfgang. "My wife is Silke of Nuremberg."

The official bowed, then offered his gloved hand to Wolfgang. "Sir, I am Captain Gregorio, just a modest city policeman of Verona—but a sincere admirer of the Beau Monde *belles arts*. Therefore, I admire Silke of Nuremberg. She's the foremost landscape artist of the modern day."

"Your good taste is appreciated, Captain Gregorio."

"She's the creative light of her generation. Truly."

"I would agree with you there," Wolfgang smiled, "but as her husband, and the father of her children, I admit to some prejudice."

"Can your gifted and famous wife fly here to Verona? Can she join you here?" Captain Gregorio was politely eager. "Our Lady Mayor could host a lovely soiree for Silke of Nuremberg."

Wolfgang pursed his bearded lips. "My wife's packed schedule, unfortunately, doesn't allow her to make any sudden public appearances."

Captain Gregorio turned on Jetta, who was stunned and sulking at the turn of events. "*Dottoressa*, listen to me. This is Verona. A robot in Verona gets to do whatever it wants."

Defeated and knowing it, Jetta abandoned her Beau Monde composure. "Look, this is terrible! It's a public policy disaster! This so-called artwork is just a rolling billboard for bullshit! It's a crazy art prank that just rolls around the world, randomly weaving bird nests out of rubbish!"

Captain Gregorio shrugged eloquently. "But this wheelchair is famous. Verona has many artistic attractions. Now it has another."

"But this robot isn't even an artist, it's just a damned wheelchair. It's for intellectual cripples! It creates nothing but ridiculous confusions. It damages the science of robotics!"

Graciously overlooking her outburst, the Veronese official turned toward Wolfgang. "I'm sorry to have troubled you with this matter, sir. Your robot is free."

Wolfgang bowed. "To tell the truth, Captain, I do need some help in shepherding this robot. It rolled here to Verona all the way from Kyoto in

Japan—an amazing feat, you'll agree. The Winkler is a creature of our modern Anthropocenic landscape. It's something like a Japanese *kame*, a 'spirit of place.' So it would be tragic to Verona if this robot came to any grief in this place."

"I believe that we can help each other," nodded the official. "That is— if you will promise not to write anything critical about Verona. We're a cultured people here—not so big as Rome or Milan—but we always do our best."

"The gallantry of you and your fine city both deserve my critical praise," Wolfgang told him, as Dr. Jetta silently seethed. "If you ever find yourself in Nuremberg, please do favor my gallery with a personal visit."

The Winkler suddenly came to itself, with a long, shuddering jolt. The awakened robot promptly rolled away down the antique Veronese pavement.

Wolfgang hastily left the policeman to follow the Winkler, and the scientist pursued him.

Dr. Jetta Kriehn was fizzing with rage at her setback, but she was a woman of purpose. "That was clever of you, what you just did," she said through gritted teeth. "But it was also dishonest and wicked. If you would only listen to reason, I could prove to you that this 'Winkler' is nothing but a hoax."

"The Winkler is a beautiful, meaningful, and poetic device," said Wolfgang.

"No it isn't. By the standards of robot construction, this hacked-up wheelchair is a piece of junk. It's a nasty fraud, from a mean-tempered old Japanese woman, who was sick of her life and hoodwinking the world."

The Winkler rolled downhill toward the riverside streets of Verona. "Very well, Doctor," said Wolfgang. "Prove all that to me. I will listen to you. I will even take notes."

Jetta paused. "What is that thing in your hand there?"

"This is my artistic sketchbook. This is my pencil."

"Is that really 'paper and pencil'? Oh my God!"

"Paper and pencil fully suit a human being," Wolfgang told her somberly. "Because we humans evolved here on the world, and in the world. The natural limits of our senses are an integral part of our relationship with reality."

Wolfgang held up his hand to forestall her shocked interruption. "Yes, it might be argued that our human senses are slow, or even deceptive.

I know all that, because I've heard it all! However—as a professional aesthetician—I must assert that a man lives best when he trusts his senses, and cultivates his senses so that they deserve trust! We human beings are authentic. We really experience a real world. Therefore, whenever I write, I write my own thoughts with my own hands."

Jetta thought this over, blinking in disbelief. "Well, the way you talk, you must write a whole lot."

"That is true. I am an art critic: a Beau Monde litterateur. Furthermore, I have personally followed this robot, on my own two human feet, for over six hundred kilometers. Other colleagues of mine have also followed the Winkler, across this world, its forests, mountains, deserts, for eight years. We have lived with this entity. We studied it day and night. Some of us died next to it. So I rather doubt you'll amaze me with some insight of yours in five minutes."

"You really did all that? You walked here, from Germany, in a cloak, with a pencil?"

"Yes, we really do that, and our emphasis is on the Real."

"You walk the Earth making up weird artsy bullshit about a cheap parlor trick like this stupid wheelchair here? You're a fanatic! Are you crazy? You must be starving to death!"

Wolfgang smiled urbanely and settled his heavy cloak on his shoulders. "Granted, I'm no scientist, unlike you and your Cosmic Council. But your scientific method is just one narrow technique of inquiry. You know less than you imagine you do. Science is notoriously useless for seeking metaphysical truth or establishing ethical values."

Jetta suddenly looked woeful. "Why is this happening to me? Why can't I just get rid of that stupid machine? My own mother thinks it's a robot with a soul that makes birds' nests! The Winkler is a cult! It's pure superstition. Can't you see that? You sound like an intelligent man. You're completely on the wrong side here."

"Your discontent with your mother's foibles is a part of the human condition," said Wolfgang. "Your science will never solve that issue for you."

"Let's leave my mother out of this discussion."

"Your science can't even solve the human problems of Science as an institution. Women scientists—by that, I mean women like yourself—are oppressed by your scientific establishment. Why else did you get this ridiculous job? You seem bright and capable. You could do better."

Jetta stumbled, then narrowed her eyes, for this shrewd attack had hit her hard. "Well, that's true. This robot assignment is lousy. Fighting science fraud is just some necessary scut work that I have to perform as my duty to the Cosmic Council. I almost had this job accomplished, before you showed up."

"But here I am, and I won't be leaving. Because I am the Winkler's sworn guardian. So if you want to harm this splendid artwork, you'll have to accomplish that over my dead human body."

Jetta scowled. "Oh come on, we are both Beau Monde, aren't we? The Beau Monde is beyond those old human habits of death and violence and war. I don't even want to be human. I have higher ambitions."

"Oh, I know the ambitions of the Cosmic Council," said Wolfgang, his voice tightening. "I don't want to second-guess your intelligent, technically advanced, and not quite human patrons—but I'll never allow you to destroy the Winkler! It is the final masterpiece created by a great woman artist, a woman who was older, wiser, and better than you in every way. I will resist your philistine iconoclasm to my last breath. Even dead, I will resist it."

"Now I get it," said Jetta, her pale eyes wide and shining. "You are Ghost Club."

"No comment."

"You are. I never met one of you literary spooks before, but you are Ghost Club. You're very Ghost Club. Wow."

"Look. If you know anything at all about the Ghost Club, then you would know I can never publicly state that I'm 'Ghost Club.' Because that's bad literary ethics! If you are a great writer—a classic for the ages—then you can never say, 'I am a great writer.' That is crass! You have to wait for your peers to declare your greatness. Then you should be demure."

"I get it, Mr. Art Critic, sir. You're Ghost Club, you're married to that famous girl, and you have rich, posh friends in the art world. Fine: now I know who I'm dealing with. How much do they pay you to follow this robot?"

"They pay me nothing at all, Doctor. In fact, I sacrifice a lot for the honor of doing this."

Jetta laughed bitterly. "Then your stupid job is even worse than my stupid job! You're a clown! We're both completely screwed because of this stupid robot, which is an empty chair, a piece of junk! Why are you stopping me from just getting rid of the Winkler? Do you get any rational benefit at all?"

Wolfgang wrapped himself in his cloak. "In literature, we receive benefits beyond your so-called 'rationality.' Our major benefit is becoming famous after we are dead. All the greatest writers of mankind are ghosts. Hence, the living power of literary tradition, the 'Ghost Club': the oldest and deepest unifying force of the global Beau Monde."

"That sounds pretty. It's nonsense, of course."

"My dear, you'd be surprised how long our pretty words can last. Our words will bury all your friends in the Cosmic Council. They are cosmic, they will outlive normal humans, but they all use language, and we are the masters of words."

"Oh, stop that boasting. We're both stuck walking the streets behind an empty wheelchair. You writers are all talk."

The Winkler slowed suddenly, and Wolfgang was forced to creep along the street. "Since we're walking together, we can be civil, can't we? As you say, we're both Beau Monde. The Cosmic Council is a major Beau Monde institution. So, tell me, Dr. Kriehn: What is your field of research, exactly?"

"I'm a post-anthropologist of the Anthropocene."

"A radical, I knew it!" Wolfgang cried. "You want to tear up the roots of our being. You want to rip humanity out of its natural matrix and transform us into cyborgs. That ambition is fatal!"

"No, my ambition is vital. It's your ambitions that are fatal." Jetta lifted her palms and gazed upward, her pale eyes strangely glimmering. "We must improve mankind radically, or else mankind will die off like dry weeds under these ruined skies."

"'Man is a rope stretched on an abyss between the beast and the superman.'"

"Wow," said Jetta, blinking. "That's the first thing you've said that makes sense."

"It sounded better in the original German. Four hundred years ago."

The Winkler, balky and jittery, chose to take a sharp turn, rolling along the stern, stone flood embankment of the bright River Adige.

"My robot companion behaves so oddly here in Italy," Wolfgang lamented. "I wish I knew why."

"I can tell you that," said Jetta. "The Winkler came here to Verona to recompile. So it needs a strong power supply and a fast, steady cloud connection. Then it can sync its local circuitry with the global Beau Monde cloud, and work out the bugs and kinks in its deep-learning algorithms."

Wolfgang stared at her. "How do you know that?"

"We know! We're the Cosmic Council! We can watch the robot crunching its data in real time. The Winkler's software is hosted on global servers. It could never hold its huge databases inside its own little head."

"The Winkler doesn't have any 'head.' It's a wheelchair."

"The Cosmic Council has scientists who track malware. Most of the time, this robot just putters along by itself in the wilderness, running on solar power. It's out there like some vacuum cleaner, groping the grass and twigs and flowers. It compiles databases, and tries to deep-learn principles from the shapes of natural phenomena."

"Right, yes," Wolfgang said eagerly, "yes, do go on."

"But there are no deep, pure artistic principles in Nature. That idea is a myth. And even if pure Nature was a source of pure Art, then climate change would have ruined that already. There is no 'Nature' anymore. This world is Anthropocenic. Everything in Nature has been altered and changed by mankind."

"I'm forced to agree with you there," said Wolfgang. "This is the twenty-second century. The Anthropocenic is a truism."

"So the Winkler's botched, mistaken software gets chaotic. It can't do what's impossible, so it gets needy, it gets greedy. Here in Verona, the people are careless with robots. This city give its robots huge computational resources. So we knew the Winkler would come here."

"Well," Wolfgang nodded slowly, "your scientific method does have its merits."

"I'm telling you the truth, you know." Jetta reached within her lab coat and removed an ivory slate. "You don't have to take my word for it. In science, you can look for yourself."

Wolfgang accepted her scientific screen and gazed within its glass.

As it rolled haltingly through the Veronese streets, the Winkler was playing chess. The tablet's screen displayed an astounding overview of a sprawling game board, with millions of ranks and columns.

The awful horde on this titanic chessboard was made of standard chess figures—rooks, knights, bishops, and castles—but deployed in dense, ant-like masses of battling millions.

Vast, foam-like waves of chess battalions were clashing tempestuously in seething, silent maelstroms of black-and-white combat. Here and there, within the computational chess plane were whirling knotted chess problems as intricate as snowflakes, where thousands of pieces, locked in fatal power struggle, exploded in waves of sacrifice.

Wolfgang was stunned by the ferocious vista in the glass. "The Winkler dreams with chess? Does the Winkler often do this?"

"It uses chess algorithms to grab global cloud power," said Jetta. "For your useless robot pal here, chess is just a malware tool."

"But this is not a chess game at all. This is no game, it's colossal, it's beyond all human comprehension. It's frightening, it's sublime. Its fantastic. It's like a vast kaleidoscope."

"So what? It's just code! Robots don't think! A kaleidoscope is just a machine, it's chips of glass! A million kaleidoscopes would look amazing to you, but it's just a heap of glass. A heap of silicon. In the end, the Winkler amounts to nothing."

"But Jetta, why? Why does the Winkler play huge games of chess while it dreams? Why doesn't it just emit white noise? Why does the Winkler do anything at all, in this world of ours? The Winkler's not alive, it can't think, it has no feelings, no motives, no needs, no desires! Why doesn't it stop, kill itself, die, quit? Why does the Winkler go on? What does the world mean to it?"

"Robots aren't so mysterious," said Jetta. "We just fool ourselves: we imagine that computational systems have mystery. They have no mystery, they just have computation. Sometimes it's big, sometimes it's small, but it's all the same ones and zeros. It's people who are mysterious."

Suddenly she smiled at him. "I am mysterious. Why am I so happy, suddenly, here in Italy? Why is Verona so beautiful?"

Her coy smile had little mystery for Wolfgang. Jetta Kriehn was happy because she was confessing herself, and because he was listening.

Wolfgang had a charm for women. He was handsome, well spoken, polite and emotionally attentive, so women tended to think well of him. Jetta Kriehn was no longer quite human, because he could see that the Cosmic Council had done something transformative to her; that was their way.

Despite that fact, she was flirting with him. She found him attractive. Wolfgang was not flattered by this. Somehow, it painfully reminded him of a lonely old woman artist whose only intimate companion was a robot wheelchair.

"Why does it play chess?" he said to Jetta. "The Winkler is denied a partner for its chess game. The Winkler is a unique thing in this world. It's entirely alone."

Jetta looked aside and shrugged. "The old Japanese woman liked chess. She liked conceptual art stunts. Like stacking up grand pianos and setting them on fire."

"That's true—she always had her fine respect for the classics." Wolfgang offered a judgment. "Akiko Nakamoto's artwork is not entirely to my taste. I find much of her work pretentious and dated. However, I respect her. Only a great female Japanese artist could have ever created the Winkler."

"You made four stupid mistakes in one sentence there," said Jetta spitefully. "That's because you want your Winkler to have soul magic inside it. You want your Winkler to be mysterious and literary for you. But it isn't. 'A great female Japanese artist,' those are four fine-sounding words, but they have no truth in them. She was female, but we women aren't witches. She was 'Japanese,' but the Japanese aren't magic people. Three, she was an 'artist.' She created fantasies, that's all. And four, she's was never 'great,' because this scheme was a cheap publicity stunt that she made from her used-up wheelchair."

"Do you really think this artist was a wicked person? An enemy of yours?"

"I have a right to be angry about her arrogance. Akiko Nakamoto made the Winkler. A painted idol. We scientists tried to ignore it at first, but every year that it rolls across the world, this robot gets more famous. People think it has an aura, that it's divine, even. Mysticism always darkens people's thinking. Superstition keeps people ignorant, and powerless, and down. This ugly toy of hers is an occult act. Yes, she was bad to do it. Wicked. Her Winkler is like her curse."

Wolfgang, Jetta, and the jittering Winkler all paused at a gently blinking traffic light.

"In the last century," Jetta said, "millions of people were killed with 'autonomous drones.' Your friend the artist was alive then. She was as young as we are now. This robot she built has the taint of that war, that darkness, that feat of letting robots take the moral blame for mass murder. The Winkler stinks of that."

"Oh, well, that's quite an old, hackneyed argument," said Wolfgang, with an urbane shrug. "Yes, things were horrible, back in the twenty-first century—how could they not be bad? Far too many people, not enough resources, they failed to manage politely, they were never Beau Monde. But some old-fashioned genocide with drones is not the concern of the two of us, not here and now. The strict limits of your scientific worldview have blinded you to the central question."

"What question is that?"

"This is it: what if this Winkler really is an autonomous entity? What if it's not a mere robot with strange malware, but something authentically different, a true 'post-robot'? We both know the Winkler's not alive, and it's not intelligent. The twenty-second century agrees about that, that is settled, we know that AI is a myth of the past. But: the Winkler might be so radically different from our expectations that no one has described the truth of its existence."

"The Winkler has a 'Third State of Being,'" said Jetta.

"Yes, that. That concept. That idea."

"That idea is rubbish! Can you measure any so-called 'third being'? Does it have any mass and energy? Does it leave any trace in the world that any instrument can register? It's a ghost! You made it up."

"I didn't invent the Winkler. The Winkler exists, look, here it is, it's in our world, like you and me!"

Jetta considered this. "You and I, do we have to quarrel? It would be so easy for us to get rid of the Winkler. Problem solved!"

Wolfgang drew a breath. "It's not so simple. The Winkler's not a stupid fraud. If you think so, then you should make fifty Winklers. Persuade your Cosmic Council scientists to copy the Winkler. Then, let fifty Winklers roll around our world. The Winkler won't possess any more magic 'aura' after that is done. I'm an art critic, so I know this: people will perceive that army of Winklers as normal, mundane robots. Everyone will get bored with the Winklers. Your problem is solved if the art robots are everywhere."

Jetta stared at him, impressed. "That was diabolical! You want to trick me into making more Winklers? Make them yourself! Don't make me do it!"

"What are you so afraid about?" Wolfgang laughed briefly. "You certainly fear it a lot, whatever it is that you fear. Can you weigh, or measure, this mystery that you fear? Surely it doesn't exist."

"Well, I'm not afraid of any weird art crap you make up that's outside the laws of physics."

"I hope you don't meet God in the Afterlife, with that kind of crass materialism."

"God doesn't exist."

Wolfgang spread his hands. "Well, the vast majority of mankind has always strongly disagreed with that opinion. 'There are more things in heaven and earth than are dreamt of in your philosophy.'"

She looked at him quizzically. "Are you religious, Wolfgang?"

"In a way. Yes, I am spiritual. Sometimes I wonder if the Winkler knows God much better than we humans do."

"In science," said Jetta, "we are not allowed to make absolute claims about God and Reality."

"You just did."

"I got carried away, all right? Because I'm passionate. Besides, this is such a good argument! You're the first guy I've met who really cares about my lousy robot." She blinked, and rubbed her pale eyes. "If a guy as clever as you is so upset about this wheelchair, it must matter more than I think."

Jetta, Wolfgang, and the Winkler had to wait, then detour as a robot riverside crane unloaded swaying lengths of Italian timber from a robot river barge.

Wolfgang spoke up at the far side of the bustle. "An objective phenomenon, such as the Winkler, can focus a metaphysical debate. That is why the Winkler has been so lastingly esteemed. It's not the machine by itself—we know the Winkler is an artist's provocation. The Winkler represents a larger issue, about the role of art in life. A robot that is a great artist must be a participant in life, even if it's not alive."

"Science also has a role in life. Science makes no 'provocations,' science makes experiments," Jetta said. "Listen to me now. You postulate that there is some 'third state of being' that is different from 'life' or 'intelligence.' You think that it comes out of computation, or software, or from network connections—somehow. But how can you test your claim? How would we prove that this 'connectivism' was really there, or that 'connectivism' was never there at all?"

"Well, I know the connectivism is there." Wolfgang pointed at the Winkler as it deftly skirted an open manhole. "There it is."

"Oh, sure, you writers can write all those fancy words like 'connectivism,' 'hylozoic,' 'animism,' 'third state of being,' but you're just proclaiming your faith! That's all! None of those words can be tested, so it's not reality. It's just poetry. It's empty verbal claims."

"Maybe you should abandon your own empty claim that you can falsifiably test everything in the world."

"But dear Wolfgang, there is no 'third state of being'! No! The Winkler doesn't have any 'state,' and, also, there's nothing for it to 'be'!"

"There is."

"Well, what? What, then, for heaven's sake? What is it, really? Spit it out, just say it simply and clearly, tell me!"

"I want to do that," said Wolfgang."I ask myself that question a hundred times every day. That question is my torment. If you could help me with that question, I'd be deeply grateful to you. Sincerely. You might be saving my life."

Jetta considered this. "You want my science help in your art criticism? Are you serious?"

Wolfgang strode ahead of the slowly rolling Winkler. "Well, yes. I do need someone's help here in Verona. The Winkler has behaved bizarrely ever since it came to Italy. I thought I almost understood the robot, when we were out in the wilderness, the forests, the mountains, together, me and the Winkler, alone in the world. Now we're here in a strange Italian city. I don't know what to make of the Winkler, or even myself. I feel a strange dread that the Winkler could vanish any moment. The Winkler will vanish—or maybe me."

"I thought that you worshipped the silly thing. You act like its a sacred monk, with that white robe you wear."

Wolfgang shook his head, lifted his white cloak, and dropped it. "Jetta, I admit that, yes, I do sympathize with the Winkler. Maybe I've even become fond of it in some way. But is that the truth? In poetry, there's a term called the 'pathetic fallacy.' Do you know that term?"

"I can read," said Jetta. "I don't read a lot of poetry."

"In the 'pathetic fallacy,' a poet attributes pathos to a thing that lacks emotions. 'The cruelty of the icy rain.' 'The fierceness of the wildfire.' It's a strong poetic device, people will respond to that, but the rain is rain, it has no 'cruelty.'"

"That is right," said Jetta, her pale eyes gleaming with sudden hope.

"The 'pathetic fallacy,' that's just what you've been doing all along. You should stop that."

"Well, the pathetic fallacy not precisely the issue. There's another matter called 'prosopopoeia.' In prosopopoeia, the writer gives an abstraction a face. For instance, when 'Justice' is portrayed as a beautiful blind woman with her sword and her scales, that is 'prosopopoeia.'"

"That strange word, I can't even pronounce that! But, well, you literary people shouldn't do that."

Wolfgang smiled. "You scientists do that all the time. I know that your Cosmic Council's golden scientific medals have fine pictures of 'Truth' and 'Nature' on them. Two beautiful nude women, Truth and Nature! A scientist should devote his very life to prosopopoeia. Do you?"

"How old are you, Wolfgang?"

"I'm thirty-six."

"Well, I'm twenty-five, but you can stop patronizing me. I'm a scientist, I'm not a blind girl on a gold medal. I had to walk my own path to get where I am in the world, to be here and now. I did it, and my feet are raw and sore."

"I walked across a mountain range, to be here and now. Did you?"

Jetta pursed her lips and said nothing.

"We should suffer less on our journeys," said Wolfgang. "May I be frank with you? Truthful? Natural?"

"Fine. Do it."

"On the last day of September, I must fly back to Nuremberg. My tour with the Winkler will be finished. I will never see the Winkler again. You understand?"

"I don't understand the strange rules of your Ghost Club," said Jetta, "but I understand you. You mean to say that we are opponents—but only in the here and now."

"We never met before Italy, this place and this time. When we part, we'll likely never meet again. So why be opposed at all? Art and Science should join forces when we can. We should study the Winkler together. We might discover something important."

"I have a better idea. I'm thinking we should pitch the Winkler straight in the river together. A wheelchair can't swim."

"Actually, the Winkler does swim. I've personally witnessed it swimming. But listen: the Winkler might, in fact, be worthless. Really. I admit that possibility. Maybe you are right: maybe the Winkler is a cruel hoax by a mean old woman. In which case, I won't defend the Winkler. I will attack the Winkler. I will debunk it as bad art. I will write a stinging denunciation of it. I will show the Winkler no pity. I will ruin its artistic reputation in every corner of this world."

Jetta pulled at a lock of her short hair. "Can you do that?"

"Yes. That's not the mode that I relish as a critic, but if a critic has no teeth, he's not a critic at all. The art world despises a hoax. Let the Winkler wander the Earth till it rusts and falls apart. As a laughingstock! Junk! Rubbish!"

Jetta considered this. "You critics are cruel men at heart, aren't you? I just wanted to quietly tip a robot off a bridge."

"The direct attack will never work. Never make a martyr of the Winkler. The noblest art is always lost art. A tragic myth can outlast any gravestone. I promise that's true."

Jetta drew her long-fingered hands from the pockets of her white lab coat. Slowly, she drew nearer to him. "If I help you with the Winkler, can you handle some travel expenses for me? This is Italy, you know."

"Within reason, yes I can. Although, if the Winkler returns to the countryside, we'll both have to live rough. The Anthropocene, the wilderness, is hard."

"I know how to manage rough fieldwork. The Beau Monde has its ivory towers, but they're never yet meant for me."

"Do we have a bargain?"

Jetta offered her hand. "Yes. As Science and Art, we have a brief and local alliance, which is only for the here and now."

Wolfgang gazed into Jetta's pale eyes as he gripped her hand. The contact of their flesh was a strong erotic moment. It was as if she'd flung her lab coat off and wrapped him in her arms.

Jetta opened her lips to speak, to scold him or maybe to flirt, but then a robot bus rolled up and disgorged a horde of noisy human passengers.

During their pleasant moment of intimate embarrassment, the Winkler had rolled aboard the Veronese bus. The robot had swiftly vanished in the toils of the Italian city.

An urban transport system was a robot's native element. Pursuing the Winkler was like trying to swim after a shark.

Alarmed and frustrated, Wolfgang and Jetta had to abandon their useless pursuit. They had to seek the help of Captain Gregorio, the Veronese city official.

Captain Gregorio was delivering testimony within Verona's lavish Palace of Justice. Wolfgang and Jetta had to wait impatiently while local prisoners were brought into court. These defendants were burdened with heavy iron chains on their wrists and ankles. Italy's city-states, freed of national norms, had evolved many strange local customs.

The Veronese trial was a stately procedure, but after much courtly ritual, Wolfgang and Jetta were allowed a word with Captain Gregorio in a wooden coffee closet backstage.

"I'm sorry to hear about your mishap with your global robot," said the Italian politely. "I should have placed the Winkler under police guard— although it's too late now. I wouldn't worry too much, though. If a robot is within the city walls of Verona, then it can be found. A simple matter of allocating official time and resources."

"How long does it take for Verona to find a vagrant robot?" said Jetta.

"Well, that varies. How much global money can you offer us to meet our local expenses?" Gregorio gently tapped his fingers on his waxed and gleaming coffee table. "If you two can pay us promptly, and if your robot is here in Verona, then all will be well. However, I can offer no assurance at all if your robot is outside Verona. As two people of the Beau Monde, you must know that, outside Verona's walls, I can do little to help."

"My slate shows that the Winkler is still running software," said Jetta. "Can't you track that on your local police network?"

"Yes, any robot can be tracked," Gregorio allowed, "but that is a matter of time, of custom, of legal permissions and many fine, old robotic traditions… Your robot was never native to my city. Your robot has no human owner at all, I understand. That is most exceptional."

"We don't want to trouble your city administration with a complex global issue," Wolfgang offered. "Is there, perhaps, some discreet, private method to find the Winkler?"

"Oh, well, yes, Italy has almost too many discreet private agents," said Captain Gregorio, "including yourselves, if I may say that. Are you sure that you two, yourselves, aren't the source of this trouble in Verona? Every policeman knows that the theft of a robot is commonly an inside job. This may be an intrigue from some enemy who knows you are in Verona. Some traitor you have foolishly trusted."

"That is a dark theory," said Wolfgang.

"We are familiar with famous artworks here in Italy," said Gregorio politely. "Some wealthy, unscrupulous art collector—perhaps a patron from your famous gallery in Nuremberg, sir?—might have found an opportunity to simply seize the Winkler and crate it up!"

Jetta narrowed her pale eyes, and smiled. "What crazy people there are in the art world!"

"Or—perhaps some scientific criminal has hacked the Winkler," said Gregorio, glaring suddenly into Jetta's pale, shining eyes. "The Winkler may be seized, by remote control, from thousands of kilometers away. The Winkler's software is old, and surely riddled with flaws. Some technical pirate, whom you know, *Dottoressa* Kriehn, might have pounced on that robot just to spite you."

"Why would anybody do that?"

"Oh, the dark pleasures of illicit possession can gnaw at the soul of anyone, human or more than human," said Captain Gregorio. He deftly tapped fresh coffee-flavored yeast powder into his ancient brass percolator. "Why do people choose to commit art crime? Is it so that you, yourself, can see that precious artwork, gloating over the stolen art, just as you please? Oh no! The true pleasure of theft is in denying what is precious to other eyes! Through art theft, you harm the innocent happiness of those you envy."

Wolfgang exchanged a troubled glance with Jetta. He had never expected an Italian policeman to offer such dark insight into their situation.

"What should we do?" said Jetta.

Captain Gregorio knotted his dark brows under his splendid hat brim. "Art and Science should trust in the Law. I can devote some of our city's slender resources to your special case. Come to my office tomorrow. I mean, after lunch, naturally. Bring me some money. Then we can put in the necessary requests to study the video street records, shipping lists, bills of lading, and so forth. We can also request some help from the Verona airport. Unfortunately, since our Verona drone field is a global airport, it has its own global Beau Monde standards, with strictly separate security arrangements…"

Wolfgang and Jetta expressed their gratitude and departed the stately courthouse.

Jetta was downcast. "We are both in big trouble now. I'm starting to think that we must be bad luck for each other."

"At least we have someone intelligent to share our troubles with," said Wolfgang. "That policeman can't do much for Art and Science, obviously, but you and I are capable, and much stronger as a team. Tonight I will ask for help from the local Circle of Readers. Very little happens in this world that the Readers don't read about."

"Tonight I can find a Cosmic Council system administrator who can place a finger on the robot," Jetta said. "But—programmers are never prompt when it comes to the needs of a post-doc on a field assignment. Those big fancy code experts only want to do the big glamour jobs."

"That's too bad—but at least you can talk clearly to your science colleagues. In my own literary world, it's all about allusions, hints, and implications. The vagueness of literary culture can be so maddening sometimes."

Jetta sniffed. "Well—to tell the truth—it wouldn't much surprise me if a coder did steal the Winkler. Those rascals just move their fingers on a keyboard, and something gets stolen. Computer science is disgusting."

"Art theft is even worse than that. I run an art gallery in Nuremberg. The great collectors of the Beau Monde are bizarre. Until you meet one, you would never believe how strange rich people are nowadays."

Jetta gazed at him in anguish, and he returned her look. But their anguish was not all that keen, because there was so much excitement in being in trouble together.

"We mustn't panic," said Wolfgang. "Two strangers in Italy have to be clever and patient. Let's be practical, let's keep our strength up. Do you know any decent place to eat here in Verona?"

"I'm a scientist, I just eat the snack food off the street carts," Jetta confessed. "Any cheap food from a robot is always fine with me."

"Well, that won't do, because I've eaten nothing but trail mix for five weeks. I can pick a good Veronese restaurant based on their furniture choices. Whenever an enterprise knows good interior design, they're certain to know good cuisine."

Wolfgang's critical acumen found them a handsome Veronese bistro within half an hour. This discreet restaurant was down a short flight of well-worn marble stairs. It was candlelit, lush, and intimate.

Wolfgang soon realized that he had accidentally chosen a plush retreat where wealthy Veronese gentlemen brought their mistresses. However, the place at least was cozy, while the smell from the kitchen was the essence of temptation.

A costumed waitress brought them two old-fashioned paper menus. "Just look at that girl," said Jetta, scraping at the fine table linen with the curved tines of her silver fork. "That is just the kind of job my mother had. We were poor."

"Where did you live, when you were young?"

"Oh, Bremen, Cologne, New York, Auckland, a long time in Mexico City... Whenever times got too hard for my mother and me, we just climbed on a drone."

Wolfgang nodded in the warm candlelight. "That's poverty, all right."

When the waitress returned, Wolfgang discussed the several courses, then ordered.

"Your new friend the waitress is gorgeous," said Jetta spitefully. "She can't believe that a foreign man in a big white cape knows so much about Italian food."

"Your eyes look huge in this candlelight," Wolfgang parried. "What was done to your eyes?"

Jetta blinked. "You noticed my scientific eyes?"

"I did."

"My retinas have tetrochromatic receptors. So, I possess the eyes of a dinosaur. I have the ancient bright eyes that the lizard kings once had, before that great comet struck the Earth. Before the Earth fell into the little paws of us mammals. Us, the twilight creatures, the Anthropocenic creatures of a tainted Earth."

"That is eloquent, Jetta."

"The Cosmic technicians always polish their proposals thoroughly, before they stick big needles through your eyes."

"Receptor enhancement is also a temptation for me," Wolfgang said. "But, I've been reserving that radical act for some later day. When I grow old, when my body's senses fail me, then maybe there is some justice in betraying my unworthy senses in return, if you follow my moral reasoning there."

"The Cosmic Council demands that all such alterations should be earned."

"And if you betray the Cosmic Council, then they will remove your tech support. You will be blind," said Wolfgang. He raised his hand from the tablecloth. "I don't object! The way of the Beau Monde is the way of the world."

Jetta removed a hypodermic from within her lab coat. She rolled up her baggy sleeve and slid the narrow pipe within a duct in her elbow.

"Do you have to do that right now?" said Wolfgang, glancing at the other diners.

"Oh, am I impolite in the Beau Monde?" said Jetta tartly, putting her kit away. "In that white cloak of yours, you are dressed like this tablecloth. I always need my injections just before I eat. Otherwise, my stomach hurts."

"We are foreigners, we shouldn't make a scene."

"So what if they can see me? I can see much better than any human being can see," said Jetta. "Romantic candlelight has no secrets for me."

"To see is one matter; to perceive is another. Jetta, can you sit still a few minutes? Turn your bright dinosaur eyes toward that candle flame."

Wolfgang set to work with his sketchbook. He labored, then tore the paper free and handed it across the dining table.

Jetta gazed at his sketch. "You have captured me. On paper. With your hands."

The pretty waitress arrived. She set down two bowls of aromatic soup threaded with thin noodles.

"I have the training, and much practice, so I can draw," said Wolfgang. "I will never be a great artist. I do know a great artist, though."

"What artist? That robot you love so much?"

"Oh no. The artist I married. She's a human artist. You see, the great trial of mankind today is retaining our hopes, our aspirations, in a world that mankind has harmed. The Anthropocene Condition. We live in ruin because we are cruel. We deserve our ruin. We humans are abusive to the world that made us. It is beyond our skill to make much amends. But Silke, who is my wife, intuits this. Silke creates worlds from her human imagination. In the landscapes Silke draws, the Anthropocene world is a beautiful world. That world is no longer natural, and perhaps we ourselves are not quite people any longer, but Silke can draw a world that we deserve to live in, and we have earned the right to be there, and we are happy in that landscape."

Jetta was silently spooning her hot soup during this recital. She was hungry. "Are you 'happy in that landscape,' Wolfgang?"

"I am too ambitious to be very happy," said Wolfgang. "But we have children, Silke and I. So our human duties have taught us some wisdom, I think."

"Human women boast too much about human children," said Jetta. "They say a human child is a human woman's greatest achievement. Because humanity is dwindling away, every day we are fewer in number, so we women must sacrifice. But why me? I am a woman, but I never much cared to be human. I want to live for two centuries, and become my own child, and my own grandchild, too. A great light is coming to this world. I must live to see that. I must become as much myself as I myself can be. I must free myself. I must fulfill my inner being. I must, I truly must. That is my destiny, and I've already changed so much!"

Wolfgang tipped his soup bowl to spoon up the last the drops. "That is a strong political position," he nodded. "It's very modern. I hear that rather a lot."

"I study the post-anthropological—because the unhuman life is the modern life. I must immerse myself in that life of our own day. I have to participate, I have to engage. To know the truth of it, I have to become it. That is why I live as I do, Wolfgang."

"'See with an eye that feels, feel with a hand that sees,'" Wolfgang quoted.

"You always use a special voice," Jetta observed, "whenever you recite words that come from paper."

"Yes, I have read the classics," said Wolfgang. "I know the greatest works that mankind took to heart." He neatly folded the sleeve of his cloak. "There are not so many, after all."

"Robots can read anything to anybody," said Jetta, blinking in the candlelight. "So let the robots read the classics for us; heaven knows, they do everything else."

Wolfgang refrained from comment. He wrote in two languages, spoke four, and could read in five, but he was forced to rely on robots to correct his spelling. As a writer, that was a sore spot for him.

The waitress brought them two plates of dumplings, swimming in creamy sauces. Soft music struck up. A man and woman appeared on an illuminated stage. These two dancers wore brief and shining performance garments. They danced with an anguish that only two unhappy people in the snares of lust would understand.

Every diner inside the Veronese restaurant, and the couples there were many, was mesmerized by this display. Obviously the evening's entertainment was the point of attending the club. The excellent food was merely an adjunct.

"What do you perceive now? Are they beautiful?" said Jetta, her eyes glittering.

"They do dance well. They were hired to entertain us."

"He was hired," said Jetta. "But not her. She looks younger than I do, but she's at least sixty."

"Are you sure about that?"

"My eyes see details you can't. I can see she took cosmic techniques—but she was foolish about it. Ambitious women, they get hasty, they get greedy. A woman like her—she never understood science. When science gives us more life, it's never more ticks of a clock. It is more life. More life is a larger existence, stronger, fiercer, more demanding than a human life. Whatever she desired from her human life, before she was changed, day by day, night by night—well, now she is devoured by those desires. She wants all of it, everything all at once."

Wolfgang gazed at the woman dancer. Jetta was right: she wasn't young, for she danced too well for that. The erotic dancer was a Beau Monde woman who had fallen from grace. She had left her own city, whatever city that was, and dropped into Verona, from the sky, in some drone.

Maybe, thought Wolfgang, the kindly Italians would pity such a person; a woman who had made a hasty grab for grandeur, but had grabbed only the tatters and the glitter she deserved.

He spoke. "What is the Winkler doing, at this moment, I wonder."

Jetta paused, the fork halfway to her tender lips. "You want to know that? Here, now?"

"Yes. Because it just struck me that—as a third-order entity that is neither alive nor intelligent—maybe the Winkler, too, is eaten away with some secret suffering. Maybe the Winkler, like these erring people all around us, has an illicit burden. Maybe the Winkler creates its artwork because it seeks catharsis."

"Oh, fine, let's have a look then!" Jetta dropped her silver fork and produced her glowing slate, despite the perplexed and offended looks from the other diners in the romantic darkness.

"The Winkler is moving," she said. "It's at the airport! It is leaving Verona!"

She slapped her slate facedown on the table, restoring the general gloom. "That robot blew town while we sat here watching that dancing sex bomb! Wolfgang, I am not human, and you are too human, but we are two idiots. We are beyond hope."

"I don't like to abandon a pleasant dinner," said Wolfgang, rising and pushing back his chair, "but I will pursue the Winkler and find it. I must seek the immediate help of the Circle of Readers."

Wolfgang knocked at Jetta's hotel door at six in the morning. She opened it, blinking and yawning, then looked him up and down.

"How handsome you look," she said. "Did you spend a busy night with your literary friends? Do I congratulate you now, or do I console you?"

"The Winkler has flown off to Rome."

"Oh yes, I know that, too. Rome is much more careless with its big connections than Verona is. The Winkler could not fulfill its needs inside this town, but in a madhouse like Rome, anything is possible."

"I must find the Winkler. The earliest flight to Rome is at seven. Let me invite you. Would you like to come with me?"

"I'm already packed. Why are you dressed like that, Wolfgang? Where is the big white hat, your big white cloak?"

"I have encountered literary politics," Wolfgang said, stepping through Jetta's door. "I met a nice young man attending the Circle of Readers. He is not a proper writer like me, just some well-to-do poseur. When the Circle learned of my emergency with the Winkler, they forced that pretender to strip and to give me all his fine clothes."

"What? Why?"

"For the pleasure of humiliating him. To show him where he really stands in literature. They also refined their cruelty by forcing him to wear my white travel cloak and hat, although he certainly doesn't deserve these robes of office. They were mocking him."

"Well, he gave you a beautiful suit, though. It fits you. You look quite the Beau Monde gentleman now."

"I am a gentleman. In Nuremberg I dress properly. Not quite this Italian attention to detail, but sturdier fabrics." Wolfgang adjusted his ornate cuffs and waistcoat.

"I was ready to leave for Rome without you," Jetta confessed. "If you hadn't come, I would have tracked down the Winkler myself. You should know this: I would destroy the Winkler." She looked into his eyes.

"I know that," Wolfgang told her. "You never said otherwise."

"I left a note for you. I used paper. I wrote to you with my own hands."

Jetta had smudged a long strip of the hotel's toilet paper with liquid soap. "WOLgANg I FL3W To ROM3," went the awkward lettering.

"How very moving of you to write this paper note for me," said Wolfgang, wiping his eyes. "This noble gesture restores my faith in mankind, although you're not human."

They left the hotel arm in arm and caught a robot bus to the airport. The old Catullo airport drone-ground was outside the Veronese city walls, with many tall woven-wire walls immersed in dense thickets of briar rose. Like the other airports of the Beau Monde, the Veronese airport was brisk, efficient, secure, and almost entirely managed by robots.

Wolfgang and Jetta crammed themselves into an early morning cargo drone. The drone threw four poised rotors into motion and lifted from the earth with the silent ease of a dragonfly.

"The Roman Circle of Readers has already found the Winkler," said Wolfgang. "We Readers know where it is now, and with their help, I can pursue it. But the Winkler's behavior still puzzles me. Why did it go to Rome?"

"For the bandwidth, obviously."

"I doubt that. The consensus theory in the Veronese Reader Circle was that the Winkler's motive must be spiritual. They think that the Winkler wants to announce itself to humanity. In Rome, the Pope might declare that a creature from a 'Third Order of Being' deserves the compassion of mankind."

Jetta considered this assertion, her narrow face wrinkling. "But the Winkler never speaks to anybody. Why would it want to confess to the Pope in Rome?"

"Any robot can talk. I grant you—since its mistress, that Japanese artist, set it free to explore its own nature, the Winkler has never spoken to people. But the Winkler has microphones and a loudspeaker, just like any other medical wheelchair. The Pope in Rome is known to have strong Connectivist tendencies. So the Pope might pity the Winkler, and declare that the Winkler, too, is one of God's creatures."

Jetta considered this. "The Beau Monde would be much better off if the Pope had nothing to do with robot controversies."

"The Catholic Church is a Beau Monde institution. If it's in the interests of Catholic theology, then the Pope will act."

"But the Winkler is a wheelchair! I wish Italian politics had never entered this."

"To tell the truth, Jetta, I'm becoming suspicious. I like this situation not at all—less than you. Is the Winkler a hoax, a plot, a prank of some kind?"

"That's what I've always told you," said Jetta.

"I didn't believe that, when I lived with the Winkler out in the wilderness," said Wolfgang. "That robot was so meek, and patient, and devoted to its nature studies that I felt it was like a wild animal... The Winkler was a networked thing like a flock of birds, a swarm of bees, not 'alive' but existent, and connected to the world, in some exciting, truly different realm of natural experience... But now that the robot and I are in Italy...and the Winkler behaves as it does, haunting cities like any other cheap machine... Well, frankly, now I have doubts! I am skeptical! I feel I'm being played for a fool."

Jetta's pale eyes glittered with joy. "I knew you would catch on someday."

"Maybe Akiko Nakamoto's robot was never real at all. Maybe the Winkler was always her clever fiction. The Winkler is a mere invention, a fantasy, it has no substance and no being. She programmed it to visit Rome, because that is the climax of her intervention. The Winkler is a creature of her puppet theater. This is the moral of her story, that's the point of her joke. The Winkler is a soulless machine on a spiritual pilgrimage. That's a cruel joke, but art can be cruel."

Jetta leaned closer to him in the tight confines of the drone fuselage. "Wolfgang... I admire your human feelings...but to find the truth in skepticism, we have to find the strength to forgive our humanity."

"What?"

"You and I were adversaries, but that was temporary. I will gladly help you evolve to a better state of being. Find the new strength, cast aside human errors. Embrace the naked truth of the world to come! The Cosmic Council will embrace you."

This sudden appeal did not entirely surprise Wolfgang. A culture war was like that. A Cosmic Council agent had a duty to try to recruit him.

He narrowed his eyes. "Can you also forgive, and embrace, all those human ghosts who can never change their minds? The dead will never join you in this bright new revelation or yours."

"Well...to reveal the naked truth, those legions of the dead, with their mistaken, archaic, and all-too-human opinions, have little to offer us tomorrow."

"Well, I entirely disagree. Because I read the classics. Dead scientists, your predecessors, are also part of my literary heritage. Aristotle, Galileo, Newton, Descartes, Darwin, I have read their written words. All wrong by your harsh modern standards, but nevertheless, I know those ghosts are my brothers."

Wolfgang was good at Beau Monde debate, and used to it—but Jetta was unimpressed. She simply smirked and writhed in her comfortless drone seat.

"May I be brazen now, Wolfgang? You explain too much, and you always talk sentimental crap. The dead are dead. We're alive. If you forgot about your army of dead men, and climbed in a warm bed with me, I would change your mind about life and death in ten minutes."

"No, you wouldn't change my mind."

"Oh yes, I would. Try the experiment. I can prove it."

"Ten minutes would pass, I agree with you there," said Wolfgang. "But after thirty minutes, we would still face all our same metaphysical, ethical, legal, social, and political difficulties."

Jetta rolled her eyes in disdain. "Fine, then it might take me an hour. I wouldn't mind that, and you'd feel profoundly different, truly, I promise. Because I'm a woman who's more than human, and besides, I like your face. You have such a nice, solid head, Wolfgang. Your head is so stony. Like a marble statue's head."

"You are the marble statue here, my dear. You imagine you will live for two hundred years. But old tortoises and huge pine trees, they're not passionate creatures who can bewilder a man to make some political point. No woman can possess both the splendid moment of passion and the long-term calendar. You are foolish."

"Oh, I know mortal men and their time-bound desires rather better than you do."

"I know what guilt is. I read the classics: the regrets of countless generations."

"You are so impossible! Why are you like this? You should stop all that ugly reading!" Jetta said tenderly. "I know that it sounds immoral, but you need a burst of passion to free you from that mortal connectivism! Your spouse, your children—time will pass. They will grow, they will leave, they will die. I can free you from that bondage. I know how, because I am already free!"

Jetta stretched out her slender arms, touched the cold bulkhead of the drone, and recoiled a bit. "I am cosmic!" she declared, folding her arms. "I broke the chains of my mortality. I can dwell within the fire—because I am the fire. If you and I were lovers, even for one night, you would leave your ghostly world, to enter my cosmic world. I am generous. I can transform you. It would be a kindness."

"That was a wonderful speech," said Wolfgang. "You must have rehearsed that."

"Well, yes, it is rehearsed. Because I have sexual politics, and yes, that must be much considered, because I don't intend to die. A woman who is no longer human cannot act the human wife who offers vows about death parting us. Mortality is simply not for me. Mortal men are fine with me, though. I like clever men, and you are clever. I can please men very well, as long as men don't try to possess me, or tell me what to do, or what to become. Belonging to one man is like breathing through a keyhole."

Wolfgang thought about this sudden confidence. He knew that she was sincere. In her own way, she was as convincing to him as he had been to a group of Tyrolean savages. She was a radiant being from a different plane of the world.

"I don't believe that you need us mortal men," said Wolfgang. "I think you need to understand your own self better. I will never join your Cosmic Council—because they are boring, self-important philistines. However, let me make you a sincere and human counteroffer."

Wolfgang placed his fingertips together. "After hearing you speak your mind to me just now, I believe you have literary talent. This post-anthropology life that you describe is a serious matter. Clearly it's too little known. Other modern women should benefit from your experience. Your personal life is vastly more interesting than any tedious science studies. Express your true self, Jetta. It will take a while for you to be heard, you will have to win your readership—but I know I can help you. And I will."

Jetta considered this. "Wouldn't it be simpler if we were just lovers? With a one-night stand, we'd have a good quick way to stop, and just go our own way, freely."

"No, because I already have a lover. She is stranger and worse than you are. When I first met my Silke, she was a restless, bitter, neurotic girl. She had no idea what to do with her huge talents. I had ideas, though, and now Silke is still a troubled woman—but Silke is tremendous. She is great in ways that science will never measure. She is a world-class artist. So she is all the trouble any man would ever want, and then some."

"So you married a crazy woman? Just because she had talent?"

"No, that's too simple-minded, you don't understand humanity," said Wolfgang. "Actually, I married Silke because of her family. They are lovely people, and grateful that I knew what to do with someone like Silke. Now we have children, and my own family is deeply involved—we're a regular Beau Monde clan. We are families of good breeding! So—although you are pretty, and I admire your charisma—ten of you would never tear me loose. A family is never a science problem."

"Oh, I understand family life," said Jetta, "just not in that smug way that you do. Because everything you just said is entirely hateful to me. All those little burdens that other people are so happy to accept, the duties, the relationships, the kinships, those dirty rags and bones of human obligations, I hate them all. Those little insults are unbearable weights to me, they are restrictions, they are iron fetters, they cut the blood from my feet, they make my hands tremble with rage... You really think I could be a famous writer?"

"Oh yes. If you told the truth about yourself, you would be an important writer from the start. You might become famous someday."

The drone began its sliding descent toward Rome.

"Wolfgang, what does it feel like, to be a famous writer?"

Wolfgang braced himself for the landing. "Why not ask for yourself? Soon we will meet one, here in Rome."

The city of Rome abounded in ruins, for an atomic-terror bomb had flattened half the metropolis. But the Eternal City was no less eternal for adding one layer of crumbling brick and stone to its many other decayed centuries.

The famous Roman writer was awaiting them at the droneport, in a private robot limousine. This prominent world literary figure was over a hundred years old, fat, pale, bearded, and as crumpled as an overstuffed pillow. The author was confined in a medical Japanese wheelchair, which had neatly rolled him inside his tall black medical robot car.

"Oh, Signor Carcano," said Jetta with a false brightness, "I thought you had captured the Winkler for us! But this chair is not the Winkler."

"Your Winkler case has always interested me," said the Roman writer, in a slangy and assertive global English. "I have lived inside my Japanese chair for twenty years now, and I expect to die within it, as so many do. The Japanese are the best in the world with eldercare technology. As a wise people, the Japanese have always preferred old age to vulgar youth. That is why there are so few Japanese in our twenty-second century."

"Signor Carcano knew Akiko Nakamoto intimately," Wolfgang said to Jetta, pretending to explain matters to her. "He wrote about her with strong critical insight, and was highly influential in establishing her European reputation in the arts."

"You two younger people should call me Umberto," said the centenarian Roman, lifting one age-speckled paw from the soft padded arm of his wheelchair. "And, about me and Akiko-chan—well, those sexy rumors are true. But she was from Kyoto. As for me, I will never leave Rome. So it was a sweet adventure, but only a passing one."

"You must be highly ranked in the Ghost Club," Jetta blurted.

Umberto glanced at Wolfgang. "You haven't taught your girlfriend good manners."

"Dr. Kriehn is a scientist. She's from the Cosmic Council," said Wolfgang.

"Oh well, science accounts for any rudeness!" Umberto chuckled. "Those sly old rascals on the Cosmic Council, why, I used to know them so well. Laimer, Brostiva, and Srivastava…are any of my old boys still busy, conspiring against humanity?"

"They might be," said Jetta uneasily. "The Cosmic Council has many senior members I don't know."

"My dear friend Dr. Cipriano, she's dead now sadly, but she was always the Cosmic Council's number-one agent here in Rome," said Umberto. "What a character that woman was. I never once heard Luciana tell a lie. Do you know how hard that is to do in Rome? Dr. Cipriano was a saint! Her naked truth of science was fantastic!"

"I think I have heard her name," said Jetta meekly, "but I don't know what she did as a scientist."

Umberto shrugged within the ductile confines of his cozy wheelchair. "It's always like that. People say that us artists, and you scientists, come from two different cultures. Temporarily, yes, that may be true. In the longer course of history, people never tell us apart. In our posthumous fame, we always become intimate."

Wolfgang felt a need to change the subject. "Sir, why is the Winkler in Rome? You must have a good critical theory."

"Oh well," Umberto demurred slyly, "I haven't been tracking that wheelchair through the wilderness, like you younger writers so enjoy doing. Why, the very concept of some fat old Roman man like me, sitting in my own robot wheelchair, trundling after another, empty wheelchair, that used to belong to my girlfriend... Well, that concept is comical, isn't it? Pure Italian absurdism! So why seek my advice on that topic? I'm an old man from an old city, I'm not like you two people! Why does the world care what I think?"

Wolfgang and Jetta exchanged a swift glance. The wily old author was being coy. Like many retired writers, Umberto Carcano still had ideas in plenty, but he lacked any motive to reveal them.

Jetta tried to coax him. "Sir, you spotted the Winkler in Rome immediately. Your insights must be brilliant, since you are so intimate with the robot's story."

Umberto's jowls wobbled loosely as he shook his bearded head. "Oh, no, there's no plot there, it's pure coincidence. The Winkler happened to be spotted in Rome by a disciple of mine. That boy is not Beau Monde like us, he's no cultured intellectual. More of a simple family friend."

"Is it true that the Winkler is speaking aloud here to people in Rome?" said Wolfgang. "It's exchanging dialogue with human beings?"

"Well, it speaks to us Romans, yes! But there's nothing to a robot that speaks!" Umberto protested. "My own wheelchair can speak any human language, on any topic, for as long as you please. And it listens well, too."

Umberto lowered his voice. "In Japan, they always had certain wonderful robot techniques. Their eldercare robots, like this one that embraces me now, were the world's finest. Why? Because the Japanese are so social. Their robots were carefully programmed to serve the medical needs of millions of aging Japanese."

The Roman writer knew that he had seized their attention, so he slyly continued his narrative. "The Japanese created colossal databases of every known ailment, pang, and discomfort of the oldest population in the world. My dear friend, Akiko Nakamoto, became the great adept of all that data. She understood social medicine, so she perceived what this vast software monument to a nation's death was doing to her—as a woman, as an artist. By reinventing her wheelchair, Akiko embraced and extended her own death. It is Akiko's rolling gravestone that has finally arrived here, among us again, here in Rome."

The Roman writer leaned back triumphantly. "And why here, why in Rome? you may ask me. Well, I, Umberto Carcano, I don't like to flatter myself. But I was somewhat famous once, and Akiko Nakamoto, who rather liked my little stories and parables, came here to Rome to meet me. We hit it off, so, here in Rome, I showed that little Japanese girl a good time." Carcano chuckled wetly. "A pretty woman can forget any number of admiring men, but forgetting Rome, that is another matter."

"Umberto is the champion of the Winkler 'collective unconscious' theory," said Wolfgang to Jetta. "That theory says that the Winkler is a kind of summary, a condensed software pastiche, of all the desires of the ill and the dying. The Winkler roams the world freely because, for dying people in a medical confinement, that was their great unconscious aspiration."

"The sufferings of millions of dying people generated the Winkler's software," Umberto told her. "Many people come here to Rome because they suffer. Despite all the suffering we Romans ourselves have endured, Rome is still the city of this world's redemption."

Leering with conviction, the Roman writer leaned forward confidentially. "Have you ever heard of 'prosopopoeia'? You have? Well! What do the people of the world worship, here in the city of Rome? They worship God. The Savior. The Ghost that is Holy. The archangels, the angels, and the saints. One and all, those holy idols are the emanations of our human pain. All of them, prosopopoeiac!" He raised one age-knotted finger. "And so is the Winkler!"

Jetta was at a loss. "But sir, why would a robot even care about that word?"

"A Third Order of Being might have its own third order of suffering," said Carcano with dark gravity. "The Winkler suffers for its art—because artists do that. What is 'creativity'? Creativity is our struggle to rearrange the world, as an aspect of our struggle to arrange ourselves. That is what the Winkler does, with those sad little bits of twigs, and straw, and such. It struggles to arrange its cosmos before it, too, must crumble away: forever, like all creatives."

Jetta was stricken. "But that is such a sad and terrible thing to say. Isn't it?"

"Oh, my dear, you are a sweet young woman, misled by your grim old Cosmic Council," said Umberto kindly. "For your heartless science overlords, the whole scheme's just a ridiculous fraud. Time will tell who is cosmic and who is comic, my dear. You should not worry your pretty blonde German head about any sad and terrible things! Leave these matters to my younger colleague here, who has written a few critical essays on the subject that aren't too bad. A girl like you should enjoy a lovely Roman holiday, instead!"

Jetta scowled. "What? Where would a 'girl like me' get a Roman holiday? I'm a science post-doc on a field assignment."

"A woman in a beautiful city should never despair! Life can be sweet for a young woman, when she has pretty gowns, long lunches, boat trips, nightlife, and nice soirees... Roman museums, monuments, the sights and sounds that expand the soul... Much is lost in Rome, because we are so old and so damaged, but much yet remains to us. So, my dear, when we reach our destination, I will simply throw your ungrateful boyfriend right out of this limousine. He has his literary errands here. You should come to see Rome with me."

"This man is not my boyfriend."

"Oh yes, I know that now, I can see that in your faces, but not all of us men who are writers are so cold and ungallant as this sour German fellow is! Let me befriend you, young scientist. Where else is a lonely old man, like me, to find youth? Everyone wants youth. You—I can see that—you want your youth so much that you're not human anymore. So: experience that youth! Become an old man's guest in Rome! I promise that your youthful soul will grow like a blossoming orchid."

"You literary people are diabolical!" Jetta shouted. "You horrible fat old man, are you trying to trifle with me? How dare you! I could break your old bones and eat the bacon off them! I have no use for some decadent old fool trapped in a robot wheelchair! When I'm with a man, God damn it, I want raw ecstasy! I want a frenzy of passion, I want a rapture that's more than mortal flesh can bear! You two wordy idiots, who worship some empty chair—well, I'm a wild demon compared to that thing! I could devour you."

Umberto glanced at Wolfgang, raising his thin brows. "She has literary talent."

"Yes. She certainly does."

"Unfortunate sexual politics, though."

"It's just rather new and different sexual politics," Wolfgang counseled. "Many post-anthropological women are like her. That's a new demographic of readers. They need to find their voice."

"I know a publishing house."

"Shut up!" Jetta screeched. "Stop that, stop patronizing me! Don't you realize that you two are merely human beings, while I am totally different and new? I could run over you like a steam locomotive! There'd be nothing left of you but grease on my rails."

"That is bombast. Now you're overstating your case," said Umberto, slinking back into the deep reactive cushions of his wheelchair. "Sure, you may claim to be more than human, and yet a human woman gave you birth. Birth is beautiful. I love beautiful things. Young women are this world's most beautiful things. So: say no to me, if you please. Say no to all men, go ahead. The world has many women who say yes. Otherwise, there would be no beautiful birth."

Umberto's black limousine pulled up, silent as an eel, outside a rambling Roman structure. This building had once been a twentieth-century office tower of steel, red brick, and glass, but the atomic-terror blast had torn a ragged scoop from it. The ever-enduring Romans had quickly adapted to life in their conditions of atomic ruin. The old building had become a vibrant urban calico of arched cement blocks, carbon nanofiber, robot-mulched plastic conglomerate, and scrounged Travertine marble.

Wolfgang and Jetta escaped the old author's black, ponderous limousine. They stood together on the blast-cracked pavement, amid a scurrying host of absurdly small urban Roman robots.

"Look at this, it's another sad dump in some poor part of town," mourned Jetta. "Every time I put my foot wrong, I'm in a place like this. When will I ever escape from human misery?"

"You refused your chance at the Roman high life," said Wolfgang.

"He praised your writing," Jetta observed. "You should be overjoyed."

They joined arms, and entered the dented metal doors of the Roman social center. The cavernous halls inside were poorly lit and smelled of stale yeast and animal cheese.

The clientele lurking in the miserable Roman dive were mostly poor, mostly young, and mostly foreign. They wore the gaudy, ill-fitting clothes of the poorly educated. Robots circulated, playing cheap music at the tables, for the touch of a thumbprint.

"I'm certainly not dressed for this venue," said Wolfgang, tugging at his fancy Veronese sleeves. "This Roman rabble would kill and eat a Beau Monde gentleman."

"I'm not afraid of the underclass," said Jetta. "I can deal with them, because I'm a post-anthropologist." Jetta folded her pale, long-fingered hand into two tight knots. "My altered bones are strong as iron, while human bones are like glass! If there's any fight, I can shatter them."

Jetta strode boldly into the den. With her unhumanly keen eyes, she quickly spotted their local informant. This Roman fellow was lurking in the shadowed corner of a plaster-cracked wall, under a mounted animal skull.

The young Roman cultural eccentric was scrawny, stoop-shouldered, bearded, and bent. He was feasting on an archaic straw basket heaped with black bread and dense yellow cheese.

"Welcome to Rome," he shouted at Wolfgang in English, over the twittering racket of robotic music.

"Thank you," Wolfgang told him. "Like most Germans, I've always wanted to see Rome."

"So, are you the guy from the Ghost Club? Where is your pilgrim cloak? Where is your spiritual hat?"

"Wolfgang can never speak about the Ghost Club," Jetta interrupted, "and his hat and cloak are in Verona. Where is the goddamned Winkler? Cut the crap and just tell us."

"I don't meet many global Beau Monde agents," said the stranger, scratching his close-cropped head. "Because I'm just a humble Roman cartoonist. I'm a man of street art. I use the tag 'Ponzo.' Ponzo, that is my nom-de-plume. It's my cognomen. My alias. Have you ever heard of me?"

"What does 'cartoonist' mean?" Jetta said to Wolfgang.

Wolfgang poised himself on a wobbling, straw-seated chair, so that he could brace his back against the cracked wall and keep an eye on the profoundly sinister crowd. "'Cartoonist' means Hugo Pratt," Wolfgang said. "It means Moebius. Druillet. Nast. Tezuka."

"Wow!" said Ponzo. "Those great cartoonists are all ghosts now, but no wonder they sent a guy like you to handle this robot."

Jetta leaned in aggressively. "Ponzo, tell us: where is the Winkler hiding?"

Ponzo promptly tilted his close-cropped head toward a nearby niche. "You see that scary-looking, dirty guy, with that drunk hooker, and that undercover cop? Yeah: him. 'The Beast,' we call him. Well, the Beast is sitting in your wheelchair."

Wolfgang stared at the seedy tableau.

"The Beast rode into this club, carried in by that wheelchair," Ponzo related, enjoying their stupefaction. "I myself was sitting here, just eating my cheese—because I really like goat cheese, and it's pretty good in the old club here, so, arrest me, put me on trial for cheese—anyway, I thought the Beast must have stolen Mr. Carcano's wheelchair! Because nobody else in Rome has any chair like that. Umberto is a classy old guy, while that Beast there is a real savage, so I was worried. I called Umberto to make sure things were okay with him. Then things got complicated. That robot creates nothing but trouble!"

"Trouble in what sense exactly?" said Wolfgang.

"Well, that cop is a police spy, and that hooker is Mafia! And now, two secret agents from Art and Science showed up. You two are much more dangerous than simple cops or Mafia, am I right? I never saw two Beau Monde spies traveling together, like you do. So, that wheelchair is from global culture, eh? What a rogue that thing is!"

Jetta spoke up. "The Winkler is indeed more than it seems," she admitted. "It possesses significance."

"Us Romans aren't stupid—everybody in this club knows you don't belong here. So—are you two an item? You can tell me. In Rome, we never gossip about foreign celebrities."

"We are not lovers on a vacation in Rome," said Wolfgang.

"Especially not in Rome," said Jetta.

Ponzo turned at once to Jetta. "That is great news, because you are gorgeous. You have fantastic bone structure. Are all science chicks as hot as you?" Ponzo pulled a big slate from his tattered backpack. "I'll draw your portrait for you! Let me show you what a cartoonist can do!"

In the dank corner of the seedy Roman club, the Winkler suddenly jerked into life and upset the café table. Wine bottles clinked and clattered to the stony floor as the Winkler rolled around in spastic jerks.

The Beast—he was a Roman slum-dweller, in rags, with a knife on his belt—had been thrown out of the erring wheelchair. The Beast's wild hair was so clotted and dirty, and his trousers so torn and decrepit, that he looked half-human, half-goat.

The Beast was confused for one moment, then leapt atop the rolling chair. The Winkler's new master crowed and cackled as the tortured machine rambled along the dirty wall, which was densely hung with skulls and tanned animal skins, and festooned with olive branches.

The Winkler blindly toppled a second table and rotated, counterclockwise, like a broken clock. The savage hopped off, poised on his bare, dirty feet. He dragged the captive wheelchair back behind his toppled table, where his evil companions were laughing at the fun.

The cartoonist's nerves were fraying. He looked eager to leave. "The Beast sneaked into Rome from the wilderness. Rome is big-hearted, so we've got room for migrants, but the Beast can't read, can't write, and lives from begging and theft. Sometimes the robots let him cook his food in the kitchen here. He's awfully good with that knife."

Wolfgang studied the Beast with sidelong, contemplative glances. "Barbarians have their need for bread and circuses."

"I think your ugly Beast is beautiful," said Jetta, tilting her head and plucking at her hair. "He's big, strong, male, and has no manners. I love that in a mortal human being. Why don't you draw his portrait, Wolfgang?"

"Jetta, don't be crass, this is serious! How did the Winkler fall in the dirty hands of that underworld creature?"

"I guess the Winkler approached him," said Jetta. "Your Beast doesn't lack for rude charisma."

"This situation won't end well."

Jetta wrinkled her nose. "The Winkler doesn't deserve to end well. Look what it's done with itself! Your wonder machine is a piece of junk."

Wolfgang confronted Ponzo. "Look here, cartoonist, you are the native Roman among us. How can a robot behave this way in your city?"

"Don't ask me about that!" protested Ponzo, raising both his hands. "I never pretended to be an intellectual! I just draw the fun things that normal people like to look at!" He turned to Jetta. "Such as nude scientists. Do you ever model? You're cute."

"You Roman guys sure have a charm for us tourist girls," said Jetta. She placed one pale hand in another and cracked her knuckles like four bony gunshots. "You, me, and that handsome Beast there—let's all go straight to your place, street artist. We'll all get to know each other better. The two of you boys, both together, might keep me entertained."

"What?"

"You heard me, you little flirt. Put up or shut up. Whenever a girl has needs, you artists are nothing but talk."

"Jetta's not human," Wolfgang offered.

"I can see that." Ponzo hastily shrugged into his backpack and put on his battered hat. "I know when a scene will get ugly. You two are Beau Monde, but there's nothing here for me."

Ponzo left in haste.

"That was witty, the way you got rid of him so fast," Wolfgang told Jetta. "I haven't seen you show your talent for comedy."

Jetta looked sullen. "I wasn't joking."

A house robot arrived and presented Wolfgang with Ponzo's extensive bill.

Wolfgang had no simple way to pay global funds to the local Roman robot. While he was trapped in that financial struggle, the Beast, staggering with drink, abandoned the Winkler. He stumbled out of the club.

The pathetic Winkler rolled after the rascal, as if hoping that the drunken Beast would collapse into its waiting cushions.

Jetta seized a wad of paper napkins. She followed the robot.

When Wolfgang escaped the organized chiseling and fraud within the Roman club, he saw that Jetta had torn small pieces of the tinted paper trash. She had dropped those bits of paper for him, in the darkly slanted Roman streets, like the crumbs of bread in a German folk tale.

Wolfgang followed the scientist's scattered paper trail, although he knew that events were escaping his control. He knew in his sinking heart that tragedy was looming. Jetta, his adversary, had seized the initiative.

The city of Rome was a great world capital. No capital of the world could ever possess true walls. A world capital could only have attempts at city walls, and failures at city walls, and the scars of failed walls built over much older doomed walls.

One of these wrecked Roman walls was a giant ridge of postatomic rubbish. It was a weedy ridge of fried debris, a hell-hill where a failed human civilization had been robotically scraped off, then piled up, to make room for a fresh wave of city-building.

Nobody lived on this atom-tainted rubble; no human being, anyway. However, Roman rubble was a paradise for invading plant life. These silent green children of the Italian soil had invaded every rocky pocket of Roman debris. The weeds came from the guts of birds, from the cheeks of rodents, and borne on the wind. While mankind debated, those wild things grew and grew.

Wolfgang found Jetta alone, on an unsteady slab of broken cement, a jutting cantilever at the top of a wall.

"The Winkler rolled after the Beast," she told him. "It just wouldn't let him be. It was talking to him—in Japanese I think—begging him for something. He climbed this hill of rubble, but the Winkler rolled up the hill. So he grabbed the Winkler and threw it in the rubbish. There it is now."

The hapless robot had been flung into an enormous bramble of wild roses. This colossal mess of junkyard flowers had swarmed from the urban mulch. The rose thicket had strangled all vegetable competitors. It was a vast, dense, wild network of tearing thorns.

Nobody had ever tamed or plucked these wild roses, because they were radioactive. The reeking roses bloomed beyond all control, like some slow-motion vegetable replica of the sinister blast that had brought them into being. Like the thorny splinters of atomic empires, though more slow.

The twenty-second century held many legacies that no one, human or otherwise, would ever disentangle from their tainted roots. The hapless Winkler had tumbled, banging and pitching, into an impossible snarl of thorns.

"What now?" said Jetta. "Whatever can it do, your robot darling?"

Wolfgang stared in horror at the doomed machine. He, among all the people who had followed the Winkler, had just seen the worst occur, and on his own watch. He had failed to protect the Winkler. There it was, tossed aside, wrecked in a ditch by an ignorant criminal.

Wolfgang had never known such shame. "If only I'd been here, I would have thrown myself in the way! I would have died to protect the Winkler."

"Wolfgang, you're not dead. You're perfectly fine."

"How can you not understand this?"

"Don't look so desperate," said Jetta. "I'm a scientist, all right? Let me manage this. The Winkler hit some ferro-concrete and rebar on the way down, but that's just mechanical damage to the chassis. As long as its interior circuitry is still sound, it will function. Someone with a truck and a towline can tear the Winkler out of that thorn thicket."

"A damaged artwork is never the same after a repair."

"The Winkler's just a robot! Even if it's the only robot with a 'Third State of Being,' the only robot that makes precious artworks, it's still a machine. Robots don't live. Robots don't heal. They can only be repaired. Be reasonable."

"It tears my heart out to see the Winkler in this pitiful state," said Wolfgang. "I am its shepherd. Though I know you would prefer to destroy it."

"I have changed my mind," said Jetta.

"Really?"

"That's a prerogative of science. I never thought that some dark-age reactionary would attack the Winkler. He's a Beast! He's a Luddite, with a thick head and no neck! I'm a scientist. I'm Beau Monde. I am an agent of civilization. So, let's haul the Winkler out of there. We'll find some civilized middle ground between Science and Art. It can been done. This is Italy."

Wolfgang gazed down at the Winkler, hopelessly embedded in its awful snarl. "I really don't see how that's possible."

"Look, stop suffering! You're having a fit over a miserable robot. I can invent some way to drag the Winkler out of there, if you'll just let me think. The Winkler's damaged, but we can polish it up. We'll put it in a museum case. All right? It will never come to harm in some glass box in Japan. Everybody will be happy."

"I don't dare to hope, Jetta. I know now that the Winkler and I are both in a kind of hell. I must not part from it. I have to keep it company till the bitter end."

"You are useless."

"Art doesn't need a use."

"Fine. Just wait here with your useless robot, then. I know what to do." Jetta left with a determined stride.

Wolfgang suddenly found himself alone with the Winkler.

It had been some time since the two of them had been alone. Alone, although together. The Winkler, an entity in a world it never made, and Wolfgang, a human being, observing it.

Wolfgang sat down to sketch the melancholy scene in his notebook.

An idyll occurred. No one bothered a man and robot in a radioactive dump. A few seagulls flew overhead. A meter-long serpent hunted rats through a tangle of rusty rebar.

Then the robot moved. The Winkler had been flung to its doom, but a lacerating bed of thorns was merely a human's idea of a doom. The robot had oozed both its arms out. Its uncanny fingers probed at the harsh strands of roses.

The Winkler teased at the tangled ropes of rose stems. In its computational grip, the vines parted as if they had been oiled. The robot tugged, twisted, bent, and kinked, unerringly. The Winkler was parting, arranging, analyzing, and assembling its bed of thorns with a perverse cybernetic glee.

Wolfgang ardently sketched the scene. With his two human hands, he could never do justice to the Winkler's uncanny craft. However, he could bear a true witness to his own human impressions. He knew that he was witnessing a miracle.

To free itself from its thorny bondage, the Winkler was slowly weaving an enormous bird nest. The Winkler was creating a masterpiece fit for a phoenix. The barbed complexity of ten million tangled thorns would shatter human sanity, but human sanity had no agency within the Winkler. Humanity had no stake within the Winkler, no limit to impose.

The robot did not struggle to escape its misery. Quite the opposite: the Winkler was weaving its way ever deeper into the Roman rose thorns. It transformed its torments into elements of composition. The dry and crackling junkyard mess of polluted thorns was becoming a paradise.

Wolfgang was directly witnessing the finest Winkler artwork ever created. It was epic, fantastic, an act of salvation.

With a sudden tipping heave, the Winkler righted itself within its thorn bed. With its four hard wheels poised under its own bulk, the Winkler labored with greater speed, greater ease, greater creative confidence.

Step by step, the Winkler transformed the foul thicket into a triumphal arch.

When Jetta returned, the Winkler was busily weaving a strong green cable of roses to help it climb the wall.

"Hey look, I brought you your criminal!" Jetta announced. Her hair was tousled and her cheeks were flushed. "The Beast is going to help us now!"

Jetta proudly showed Wolfgang the solution she had created: a dirty loop of ruined fiber-optic cable, with a crude grappling hook of reinforcement rods. "See what I just made? This is great, isn't it? The three of us together can snag that robot and haul it out of there!"

Jetta gazed optimistically over the wall, and was stunned by the fantastic apparition of the the Winkler's phoenix nest. "What has it done? What has happened here?" She dropped her hook and cable and put both her hands to her head.

Wolfgang confronted the Beast. He stared into the Beast's bloodshot eyes. The slum-dwelling migrant looked bewildered by the events besetting him. The Beast could not comprehend why his simple, primordial life had taken such a strange turn.

And yet the Beast, despite his nickname, was a man. Unlike the Winkler, a man had life, a man had thought.

Therefore, Wolfgang drew a breath and addressed the Beast, as man to man. "Sir: greetings. I am Wolfgang Stein of Nuremberg. May I ask your own name?"

"Giuseppe," the Beast lied.

"Can you understand global English?"

"The robot talked to me," the Beast complained. "It said bad things. A robot should never speak to me like that. I am a man."

"I agree with that, but what exactly did the Winkler say to you? How did you ever meet the Winkler? What does the Winkler want from you? Why? Please don't think I'm impertinent! I'm an artistic expert, I have excellent reasons to know this."

The Beast bit his underlip. "The robot brought gifts to me," he bragged suddenly. "It gave me three gold coins. From God. To the Pope."

"What?"

The Beast showed three dirty fingers. "Three. Beautiful. Coins. Money from Heaven. The robot is a spy—from Heaven. I am a priest of God. I am holy. I have a soul."

Jetta spoke up. "Wolfgang, it's no use. He's human, but he's a complete barbarian. He's a lot more human than you are, to tell you the truth. He's a man in the complete state of Nature. He's nasty, brutal, short, all of that. He is fantastic. I think I love him."

"How did you get the Beast to come here, back to the scene of his crime?"

"How do you think I did it? I'm a woman, and I'm superhuman! He'll do anything I tell him to do. He's easy."

"Well, get rid of this brutal, lying, conniving savage," said Wolfgang. "The Winkler has survived his assault—and look at this masterpiece it created. I, Wolfgang Stein of Nuremberg, personally saw every moment of its creation. Those artworks it created to date are nothing compared to this. The Winkler has achieved artistic greatness. The Winkler has found its metier. And I was there. I saw everything."

"Dishonorable," the Beast grumbled. "Infamous."

Wolfgang drew Jetta aside. "Why does the Beau Monde endure these awful creatures?"

Jetta took instant offense. "Now what? Do you want me to murder him? Are you complaining about these creatures, these vile, yet virile, two-legged human creatures that grow on the Earth like weeds? Ask yourself about that, humanist. The Cosmic Council never asked for population. Blood and soil, the Earth, humanity—that's all your philosophy. It was never mine."

Wolfgang drew a breath. The crisis was making his head whirl.

The Winkler was spidering, with uncanny skill, up the wall of Roman debris. While they spoke, the Winkler had woven itself a braided noose of strong, living rose stems. It flung that thorny contraption, unerringly, around a small outcropping of concrete rubble.

The Winkler rose, its four wheels whirring stoutly. It screeched and scrabbled straight up the rubble of Rome.

Wolfgang suddenly realized that he would never have any artistic moment more astonishing, more uplifting, than this one. If only he could capture the moment, and display it to the Beau Monde, then he would accomplish great things.

"Doctor, listen to me," he said. "Will you use your slate, and copy this picture I drew, and send it to these addresses?" He began to list the greatest names he knew.

"Oh, that reminds me, I need to document all this," said Jetta, producing her slate. "I can certainly record this phenomenon better than you can, with that pencil."

Jetta busied herself, framing scenes and promptly blasting them into the cloud. "Look, a wheelchair rolling straight up a stone wall! How did that silly robot learn to weave so well? I almost feel proud of the Winkler!"

"Please, Jetta. One simple favor. One sheet of my paper."

Jetta glanced at Wolfgang's sketchbook. "Who needs that? I might get a scientific publication out of this."

Wolfgang sank to one knee. "I am begging you."

"That's more like it," she said. "This 'one simple favor'—for you and your Ghost Club. This is an indiscreet act that is going to hurt me. Isn't it?"

"Yes. Maybe. I don't know. Yes, it is risky to draw the attention of the great and the good. But I will be world famous for that sheet of paper. Please help me. It's my greatest achievement. I will never forget your act of goodwill."

"You mortal men are so sweet when you're all troubled," said Jetta, with a crooked smile. "I know I'm being stupid, but you're so touching that I can't help myself." She photographed the scribbled sheet of paper and shot it into the cloud. "There. That kind act took a few seconds for me. I hope you enjoyed that."

"You are not human," Wolfgang told her, rising from his knee. "But just wait and see how long that brief, yet very good and kindly act, will pursue you. People will know of it when we're both dead."

"Oh, I will live it down somehow. You're just an artist."

"I don't think you will ever live it down. You just touched a living nerve in the Ghost Club."

"You will never scare me with your ghosts," said Jetta. "Never, no matter what. Now, where did my nice little human Beast go? I didn't give him any permission to leave me, and he was here just a minute ago."

The Winkler played out its rope of roses. It rolled briskly down the far side of the rubble. Then Jetta and Wolfgang pursued the Winkler as best they could, groping and scrambling down the shattered wall, arriving scratched and bruised.

The Winkler steadied itself, gathered its computational wits, and accelerated. The fall had badly damaged one of its rear wheels, but it solved that crippling problem through the simple gambit of rolling in reverse.

Jetta wiped her bloodied fingers on her white lab coat. "I don't like to admit this," she told Wolfgang as they pursued the Winkler, "but this goddamned robot is in some category all its own. It never thinks, it never feels—but it never stops its art research, does it? I can see it's getting stronger. It even moves differently now."

Wolfgang caught his breath. His fine suit from Verona was dirtied and ripped. "Yes, the Winkler is different. Existentially different. The central question about the Winkler is 'how different.' I am in the critical school of 'very, very different, and getting more different.'"

"I thank God that woman only made one of the Winklers. What a great, female, Japanese artist."

"She created a genius among robots. A robot Einstein that has discovered its own space and time. The Winkler has an entirely different *umwelt* than any machine or any living being. The Winkler is truly alien."

"That's bad," said Jetta.

"I don't know. Why is it bad? Where is the Winkler's crime? What harm did it ever do to us? There's only one."

Jetta looked at her slate. "I think this new message must be for you."

Wolfgang read it rapidly. "Oh dear. I'm being asked to guard that artwork of roses for the Beau Monde, until someone of rank can come to collect it." He looked up. "This is a moral crisis, Jetta. I can either follow the Winkler—which is my duty—or I can take curatorial custody of the Winkler's greatest work of art, and see that it's properly cared for. That is also my duty."

"You are torn between the artist and the artwork."

"In the art world it is often like that for us, yes."

"How long will these duties take?" said Jetta. "You and your paper-based literary society, you're so slow!" As they spoke, the Winkler was briskly escaping.

"So, shall I run after it?" said Jetta. "Rome is huge. That robot could climb aboard a bus, a trolley, anything. It could vanish."

"One moment. Turn your bright eyes to the sky. Do you see anything lurking up there—drones, airships, anything huge?"

"I don't. Should I?"

"You have tetrachromatic eyes. You might see something that I can't. Perception is political. We can't help it, it's true."

A Japanese goddess flashed into life on the radioactive Roman wall. This heavenly being was radiant and translucent, a supple and shapely creature adorned with long, floating tendrils of simulated silk. She floated in midair at the site of the Winkler's artwork.

"*Buongiorno!*" the goddess called out, beckoning with one elegant hand. "*Dove si trova la corona di rose? Mostrami il capolavoro!*"

Wolfgang and Jetta had to clamber up the broken wall again, in order to properly address this aerial phantom. "Madame, we are not Italians. Please speak global English to us. I am Wolfgang Stein of Nuremberg. I believe we've already met."

"Oh dear, I so love the beautiful Italian language, that is such a disappointment," said the Japanese goddess, switching to a flawless English. "My admiration for the Italian art scene is well known. Rome is my favorite world capital, and the only true Beau Monde city. Look at this splendid Roman artwork, woven from pretty roses! Only in Rome would such a beautiful treasure appear! And, since I'm the first collector to claim it, it's all mine, mine, mine."

Jetta turned to Wolfgang. "What on Earth is happening? What is this huge, glowing monster?"

"She's a Beau Monde art collector. Very powerful, very discerning. And very old."

Jetta stared at the gorgeous phantom, which looked like an animated statue made from soap, smoke, and pearl. "She's a projection. She's two stories high, but she looks more real than you do! How does she do that?"

"What difference does that make? She's Beau Monde. She's global. She exists in the sky. And don't bother to whisper, because she can hear every sound we make." Wolfgang tilted his face to the sky. "So, dear madame: may I offer advice on archiving this Winkler artwork?"

"Dear old Italy," mused the global goddess, "the most wonderful peninsula of Europe. I always thought that Akiko's robot would get to Italy. No one ever understood Akiko as I did. Akiko used to confide everything to me. I was more than her collector. I was her biggest fan. That is true, you know. Ask anyone."

"There is an important procedure for preserving artworks made of natural materials," Wolfgang stated to the Japanese goddess. "This technique is 'aldehyde-stabilized cryopreservation.' First, the artwork is stabilized with glutaraldehyde. Then it is thoroughly marinated with sixty-five percent ethylene glycol. Next, the artwork is tenderly cooled to one hundred and thirty-five degrees below zero. That procedure permanently fixes the authentic, organic colors and all the detailed surface textures. Finally, the art is returned to room temperature as a vitrified glassy solid. The artwork will be guaranteed for centuries."

"That sounds quite lovely! Why, that's perfect!" agreed the goddess. "I'll put that procedure into motion right away. I'll have the nicest robot rose garland ever."

"Madame, I am pleased and proud that you agree with my counsel as a gallerist."

"I do. I must! Everyone, human or not, benefits from the art of my dear friend Akiko. I couldn't be happier up here in my flying saucer," said the art collector. "Your devotion to duty has been exemplary. There is one small matter, though. I must point out that you are not in a proper uniform. The acolytes of Akiko's pilgrim art machine should always be dressed in pure white robes. That way, we can spot you from orbit."

"That is true," Wolfgang admitted. "That was my personal misstep. I regret that."

"To prevent confusion, or any damage to etiquette, I've brought you new white robes from Kyoto. These silk robes will be more fitting to the duties of your office."

"Madame, you have no equal when it comes to the proprieties of the Beau Monde."

A small yet buzzingly efficient cargo drone appeared above Wolfgang's head. The machine dropped a shrink-wrapped packet of silk into his arms. In moments, the air began to fill with other, similar drones. The flying machines were securing a perimeter around the robot's artwork.

"Matters are under control here," Wolfgang loudly announced to Jetta. "We must leave the scene of this artwork now, to further protect the Winkler, which is our duty."

They hurried off the heap of radioactive rubble, out of the blast zone, and into a civilized district of the city where various Roman human beings, slightly tainted by bomb debris but willing to risk it, were carrying on their everyday lives.

Wolfgang stepped into an alley, opened his packet, and hastily changed his costume.

"The Japanese have astonishing good taste," he told Jetta. He casually threw his soiled Veronese suit into a street-side robot dustbin. "Look at these humble pilgrim robes of poverty and celibacy. They were extremely sumptuous, then almost torn to pieces by hard use and suffering. But the rags were stitched and patched together again, and those stitches and patches are even more luxurious that the originals. In aesthetic terms that is called *kintsugi*, or 'healing the wounds with gold.'"

"What the hell are you talking about?" said Jetta, blinking. "Can that monster still overhear us?"

"She is a monster, but she is the Winkler's greatest collector! She gave me a gift of *kintsugi* robes. No other follower of the Winkler has ever received such a gift. This is a signal honor. My world reputation is made."

"Well, you look like a white patchwork clown," said Jetta, crinkling her pale, tetrachromatic eyes. "If you ask me, your flying saucer boddhisatva is bizarre. I'm not human either, so I don't like to be judgmental—but speaking from the point of view of a woman, I'm thinking there's an element of sarcasm in her gift to you."

"You are just jealous," Wolfgang surmised.

"I hate her," said Jetta. "I work for science. I suffer for science. And you work for art. And there we were, together, breathing toxic atomic bomb dust that might kill us both like dogs… The Beau Monde exists in a dark age."

"All ages have a darkness," said Wolfgang. "Yet the age that comes after the human condition: I'm afraid that age will be worse. You new, un-people of the Anthropocene: your tragedy will be bigger than anything mankind has ever suffered. Your mountains are more forbidding, your abysses are deeper. Your lusts are greater, your sorrows are darker." He sighed. "My poor wife Silke, I must never tell her that."

"You may be right, Wolfgang. But we'll do it anyway. What can be worse than what mankind has already done? Whatever happens, we deserve it."

"No—I don't believe that. Because we still have the Winkler. The Third State of Being. Something else, that it entirely different from humanity, or any states that might come after humanity. The Winkler means hope. Maybe that robot is so entirely different from us biological creatures, that our hungers, our sorrows, our limits, our ugliness, our lurking death, can never touch the Winkler. Even that strange woman we confronted just now—she is a goddess, more or less—well, for all her power, I know she understands the Winkler less than I do. She thinks it is a toy, but she's a slave to a toy, she adores it. And we, you and I, we are not slaves. Because we want to know."

"Could that be true? It doesn't sound scientific."

"It isn't scientific, but I feel it. I'm very close to stating it in a way that no one can deny. If I can do that, the world will change."

They hastened together through the afternoon streets of Rome, where the city calmly went about its ageless business. Wolfgang dodged a silent Roman robot taxi, a merrily whizzing device of streamlined edges and one-way windows.

"Maybe we can both learn the truth from the Winkler," Jetta told him. "That's a speculation. Speculations are very often wrong, but why can't we both have some?"

"God help me, I must go home to Nuremberg," said Wolfgang. "I will do well there. I saw the Winkler's greatest work of art, I preserved it, my fame is assured." He bit his lip. "But I still don't understand it! I did my best, but

I'm only human! I know that I was wrong about it from the very first day!"

Jetta looked at him tenderly. "What is hurting you, Wolfgang? What big sorrows are biting you now?"

"I was never the Winkler's shepherd. Its world was never a subset of my world. My human world is the subset of its cybernetic world. The Winkler doesn't live, it doesn't think, but its Third Order of Being is colossal. I am one white knight on its chessboard, but its cosmos is a churning googolplex of chessboard squares. The Winkler is a vast wheeling galaxy, while all humanity is one small, yellow star."

"Wolfgang, sorrows like this will be the death of you. Go home." She looked into his face. "A robot is never a ghost. A robot is made of circuits, software, cables, satellites, databases, protocols, a big stack of frail things. Go home and tend your garden, raise your children. This too will pass. A robot is a gadget. The twenty-third century is waiting. I will be there, I promise. You should be there, too."

"First I must find the Winkler."

"Then I will find it for you. This is Rome! In an eternal city, nothing is legal, but everything is possible." Jetta pulled out her slate.

Her research led them to the riverside. The old Tiber had risen again to break its banks, but the Romans of those districts were used to the misbehaviors of their Anthropocenic river. Every Roman thing that could drown was stacked on bricks and concrete blocks, with many sodden wooden walkways, islands and archipelagos of the screens, stoves, the beds, the lamps, and bottles of an ordinary life.

The Beast had fled into one of these humble and nameless flooded structures. This was a dismal place in Rome where civilized people wouldn't much care to live, but the Beast was uncivilized, and persistent.

The Beast lurked in a vile, ill-smelling, mildewed slum, but no place on the surface of the Earth was foreign to the Winkler. The ever-questing Winkler had cornered the Beast in his squalid little den.

When Wolfgang and Jetta pushed open the sagging door, the Winkler was speaking. It was crooning, singing to the Beast, as it caressed his trembling legs with its horrid little hands.

The Beast gazed up at the two of them, vague hope dawning on his bearded face. "Make it stop."

"We can't talk to the Winkler. We can't reason with it," Wolfgang said to the Beast. "I wish we could."

"We can't even reason with each other," said Jetta. "Believe me, we have tried."

"I hate the robot. It's bad. It's not right. It wants to know me, it wants to touch me!"

The Winkler—it seemed very large in the tiny room, like an oversized car crammed into a grimy garage—made one of its spastic lurches. In a sudden, heartfelt, human response, the Beast stabbed it with his knife.

A kitchen knife was a simple steel tool, not a weapon of any great consequence. But the Beast was strong with shame.

The Beast drove that simple wedge of a knife into the metal chassis of the Winkler, piercing its chassis again and again. He kicked the Winkler till it toppled splashing to the flooded floor.

Wolfgang flung his white-robed body between the Beast and the robot. He was promptly stabbed.

Jetta was not a practiced fighter. Neither was the frantic Beast. But Jetta had unhuman speed and strength. She jumped forward, splashing wildly, and simply drummed the Beast's astonished head with her windmilling fists. She blacked his eyes. She broke his nose. The horrified Beast dropped his weapon. He fled howling out the open door.

Wolfgang's silk robes bloomed red with his own gore as he struggled to rescue the toppled Winkler.

"Leave that robot," Jetta told him. "Lie on that bed, and put your feet up. If you go into shock, you're going to die."

"I'm not hurt."

"Oh yes you are. You're bleeding like a slaughtered pig. Don't become a famous, dead writer-ghost. I won't let that happen to you—not while I'm watching you."

Jetta wrestled him onto the Beast's reeking bed. She wadded his fine silk cloak, and pressed it hard against the long, ragged gash down his rib cage.

The thrill of action faded. Wolfgang realized he was badly wounded. The knife had slashed him from his armpit to his floating rib.

It was amazing how much it hurt to be stabbed.

Wolfgang fetched the broken knife from the dirty flood water. He touched it, he felt it. It was not a complex, mysterious robot, it was just a simple kitchen knife. A tool of the humblest origin, nothing complex or mystical about it, no software, no data, no connectivism. Yet, it sliced living beings to pieces. A kitchen knife could turn a living pig into small chunks on a plate.

"I am human. I am nothing but a pig. I am dying," Wolfgang groaned.

"It just feels that way," Jetta said. "Please, stop explaining everything."

The liquid stuff of life was flowing out of him. His heart labored. He was growing cold. "I want to live. Forget the Winkler. I'm a man, I want to live."

Jetta turned from where she crouched at his bedside. She kicked the perforated Winkler into deep water.

The robot gave one small electric gasp of drowning circuitry. Then it was no more.

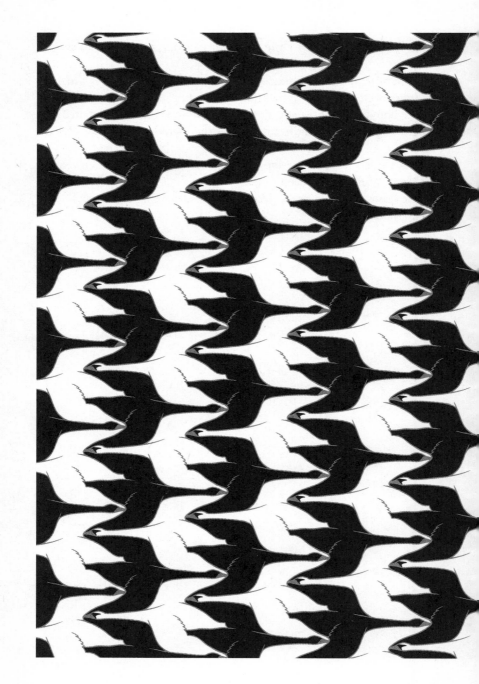

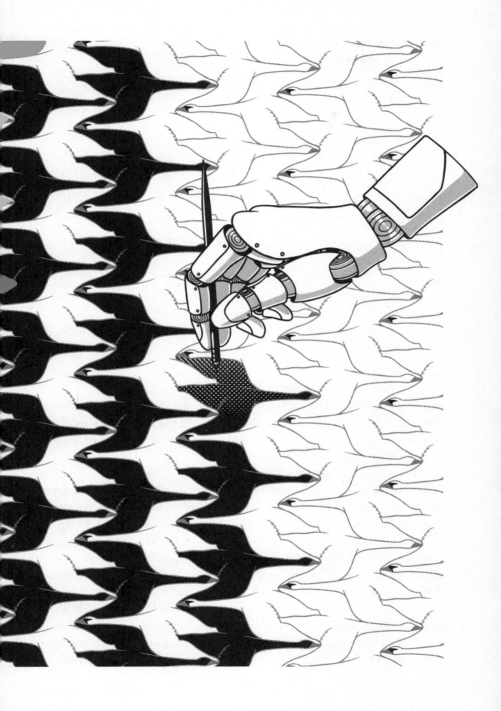

afterword: bruce sterling, erudite dreamer and pirate by

IT'S HARD TO comprehend. Yet sometimes it does happen: The poles are reversed. The pieces on the chessboard change places. The result is particular and surprising: it's called "castling," the only legal move in chess that lets a king leap across two squares.

We authors of Italian *fantascienza*, who since our beginning have tended to gaze overseas, find ourselves, just for once, with a king of the genre on our soil. He examines Italy precisely, he chooses to live there, becoming a sociologist / historian / entomologist of a foreign country—our own.

In these stories he openly declares his love for Italy, and with all his visionary enthusiasm he faces a nation that becomes the construction site for his many dreams. Convincingly, he even chooses an alter ego—"Bruno Argento," the Texan served in Piedmontese sauce.

So the act of castling is complete, and this anthology is its brilliant proof. The chess king settles in a file, in one corner of the chessboard, near where the rook stands, a kind of Italian suburb, a privileged observation point, and a balcony for history, not only recent, and not only Italian.

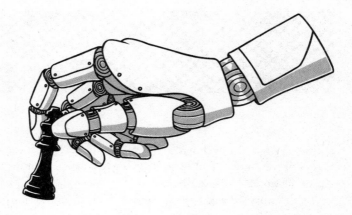

DARIO TONANI

In Bruno Argento's first story, "Esoteric City," his native Turin is portrayed as a black-and-white chessboard. Turin is the only vertex of two magic triangles, with Lyon and Prague on the first, and San Francisco and London on the second. This esoteric Turin is a foundry of magic, both white and black. So much so, that Turin's automotive giant, the FIAT corporation, is hosted in Hell.

"Clearly, modern Italian engineers had been hard at work here in Hell. The casings of Hell's rugged tunnel, which closely resembled the Frejus tunnel drilled through the Alps to France, had been furnished with a tastefully minimal spiral staircase made of glass, blond hardwood, and aircraft aluminum."

This is likely a tribute to the industrial design that Italy has exported all over the world, since design is a theme particularly dear to Sterling / Argento. This Turinese intestine, descending to Hell, has "a delirious surge of spray-bombed gang graffiti, diabolically exulting drugs, violence, and general strikes against the System," while Hell, according to the Turinese

author, "has nothing down here but one huge Italian mess." The dead heroes of the Agnelli family, as FIAT's giant captains of industry, hold up the underworld, like three Atlases.

In the story "Black Swan," Argento's Turin multiplies into a series of alternate universes, where two characters are determined to intertwine their lives, and their business matters, around a Faustian invention destined to forever change the future of computer science. Remember Olivetti, the Italian giant of business machinery? Historically located in Ivrea, a Piedmontese city just fifty kilometers from Turin, Olivetti pioneered computers with transistors rather than valves, computers with magnetic card storage, and a programming language for affordable computers that were truly personal. The digital journalist "Luca" narrating this story is clearly the Bruno / Bruce of cyberpunk novels like *Schismatrix* and *Islands in the Net*.

The story "The Parthenopean Scalpel" has a clear historical setting, in the pre-Risorgimento Italy of the Carbonari rebel conspiracies. Yet it's a weird tale of vaguely Fellinian flavor, with deformed nobles, Siamese twin sisters, political assassins seeking vengeance, and ancient, cynical Transylvanians.

"Pilgrims of the Round World" is a whirlwind of eccentric, crackling encounters, of theatrical and stagey set pieces, set almost entirely within the four walls of an old inn in the Turin of the 1400s. This International-Gothic hotel is managed by two unforgettable Turinese characters: "Agnes" and "Ugo." These dual protagonists are witty, popular, and affable, and in their epoch of grand geographic discovery, they learn of their little-known Round World only through intermediaries. Yet their children have gained prestige, through soul-scarring adventures in distant lands, where opposites face each other down, civilizations, religions, the Moors, the Christians.

The result is a Turinese fresco that lacks any epic heroism, wide-open scenarios, or grandiose battles. It's based on irrefutable common sense, on parental love for children, on back-room diplomacy around the table, and the persuasive magic of their Shroud of Turin, that powerful relic that wrapped Our Lord, taken down from His True Cross.

"Pilgrims of the Round World" is also the only story in the works of Argento that bears a dedication—"For Jasmina Tešanović, fellow traveler in this journey." It's a testimony to the married couple known as the "Globalists of Turin," which is the title of their joint column in the Turinese newspaper "*La Stampa*," written in Italian by Bruce Sterling and Jasmina Tešanović. This dedication is Argento's revelation of the "Globalisti" to the reader, as two citizens of the world, subtle and implacable observers of everything they find beautiful or intriguing, in Turin, or in their worldly pilgrimages, from post to post, in stations scattered around the globe.

Pirate Utopia*, the ultimate Argento story to date, perhaps a kind of scaffold for an Argento novel, is the parable of a Turinese soldier of the Great War, Lorenzo Secondari, set against the uchronian historical background of a period devoured by antic creative impulses—Italian Futurism, Nietzschean Supermen, the angry nostalgia of D'Annunzio, and the fervent political idealism of anarchists, syndicalists, and makers of new constitutions. Set in the city of Fiume / Rijeka, a port that is half-Italian / half-Balkan, it portrays a city as an incubator of ideas and transgressions, a refuge for wandering minorities, a melting pot for impassioned souls. Their utopian goal is to transform a small oasis / enclave into an endlessly boiling kettle of art and culture, a resort town kissed by mild, healthy, and

---

*Published in a separate volume as *Pirate Utopia* (2016, Tachyon Publications).

welcoming weather that becomes a genuine city-state of fierce political-military ambition.

In short, as the story's title declares, it's a city as an authentic "Pirate Utopia," gradually fueled by ever-more bold and extravagant freedoms of daring, sex, ferocity, and heroism. There will be no lack, in this display of erudition, of choreographed meetings between cultures that seem, in most respects, to be placed at the world's antipodes. In the Pirate Utopia appear new versions of the wizard Harry Houdini, and the world-famous science fiction writers Howard Phillips Lovecraft and Robert Ervin Howard.

"Yeah, your little utopia here is just like a pioneer town... Like some lonely place way out in the middle of nowhere, where y'all have only the dreams in your books." This is what Bruno Argento says to his fellow Texan, Robert E. Howard, and then he induces Lovecraft to add:

"Compare that meager, mundane reality to the world you really desire... Do you see the commonality of interests here? Imagine what we might achieve!"

Touché, what a swordsman's jab from Sterling / Argento, who can impale us with stories that surprise, while he also parries and defends. Precisely like the act of castling, in chess.

And what a pirate he is, when to the observant spirit of a wayfarer, he adds the indomitable spirit of a reckless dreamer...

DARIO TONANI

Bruce Sterling, author, journalist, editor, and critic, was born in 1954. Best known for his visionary science fiction novels, he also writes short stories, book reviews, design criticism, opinion columns, and introductions for books ranging from Ernst Jünger to Jules Verne.

Sterling's science fiction novels include *Involution Ocean, Islands in the Net, The Difference Engine* (with William Gibson), *Heavy Weather, Holy Fire, Distraction, Zeitgeist, The Zenith Angle, The Caryatids,* and most recently *Love Is Strange: A Paranormal Romance*. His Shaper/Mechanist series includes the novel *Schismatrix* and the short fiction collections *Crystal Express* (and the omnibus edition *Schismatrix Plus*), *Globalhead,* and *A Good Old-Fashioned Future*. Sterling's nonfiction works include *The Hacker Crackdown: Law and Disorder on the Electronic Frontier, Tomorrow Now: Envisioning the Next Fifty Years, Shaping Things,* and *The Epic Struggle of the Internet of Things*. He was the editor of the seminal cyberpunk anthology *Mirrorshades,* and he has edited two volumes of the MIT Technology Review series *Twelve Tomorrows*.

During 2005, Sterling was the Visionary in Residence at ArtCenter College of Design in Pasadena. In 2008, he was the Guest Curator for the Share Festival of Digital Art and Culture in Torino, Italy, and the Visionary in Residence at the Sandberg Instituut in Amsterdam. Sterling returned to ArtCenter in 2011 as Visionary in Residence to run a special project on augmented reality. He was then the Visionary in Residence at the Center for Science and the Imagination at Arizona State University in 2013, and in 2015 he was the Curator of the Casa Jasmina project at the Torino FabLab.

A renowned expert on science and technology, Sterling has appeared on ABC's *Nightline*, BBC's *The Late Show*, CBC's *Morningside*, on MTV and TechTV, and in *TIME*, *Newsweek*, the *Wall Street Journal*, the *New York Times*, *Fortune*, *Nature*, *I.D.*, *Metropolis*, *Technology Review*, *Der Spiegel*, *La Stampa*, *La Repubblica*, and in many other venues.

Born in Milan, **Dario Tonani** is an Italian fantascienza writer, and the author of the "Mondo 9" series, published by Mondadori, as well as "The White Algorithm," "Infect@," "Toxic@," and other award-winning novels and short stories.

Neal Stephenson is known for his speculative fiction works, which have been variously categorized science fiction, historical fiction, maximalism, cyberpunk, and postcyberpunk. Stephenson explores areas such as mathematics, cryptography, philosophy, currency, and the history of science. He also writes non-fiction articles about technology in publications such as Wired Magazine, and has worked part-time as an advisor for Blue Origin, a company (funded by Jeff Bezos) developing a manned suborbital launch system.

Stephenson is the author of *Reamde*, *Anathem*, and the three-volume historical epic the Baroque Cycle (*Quicksilver*, *The Confusion*, and *The System of the World*), as well as *Cryptonomicon*, *The Diamond Age*, *Snow Crash*, and *Zodiac*. He lives in Seattle, Washington.